You Can Kiss Me If You Want

Marta Westlake

Copyright © Marta Westlake, 2024

No part of this book may be reproduced, distributed, or transmitted in any form or by any means, including photocopying, recording, or other electronic or mechanical methods, without the prior written permission of the author, except in the case of brief quotations used in critical reviews or other non-commercial uses permitted by copyright law.

This book is a work of fiction. All the characters, names, places, and incidents are either a product of the author's imagination or are used fictitiously. Any resemblance to actual persons, living or dead, events or locals is purely coincidental.

ISBN
9798340729491

Dear reader,

Thank you so much for buying this book—it truly means the world to me. I hope you enjoy reading it as much as I enjoyed writing it. I poured my heart and soul into this story, hoping to remind my hopeless romantic readers that true love does exist.

With love, Marta xxx

Chapter One

So this is it. This will be my life now. It's the first week of summer, and Meg, her boyfriend Jack, and I have just rented a flat together in Hampstead. Meg and I will start university in September, and everything seems to be working well. I am going to live and study with my best friend! It's like a dream come true. Lucky, Jack already has a proper adult job at a big company, so he doesn't have to worry about studying. We have a finance guy in the house!

Our flat is a simple, two-storey space just off the main road in a small alley. The ground floor features an open-plan kitchen and living room, while the first floor has two bedrooms and a bathroom. The entire flat is carpeted in bright colours, except for the kitchen and bathroom, which have tiled floors. The furniture is light and minimalistic, which creates a cosy and welcoming atmosphere. It's perfect for us, and I can't wait to decorate it further over time and make it even cosier.

Meg and I are so excited to start at the University of Greenwich this autumn. We'll have to travel there from North London, but I think we can handle that two or three times a week. We have an amazing flat, we got into the same university, so there's no room for complaining. We can do this!

I had a small break before I decided what I want to study, and Meg... she's had a hard time choosing her path in life. She started an art degree in September but quit after two months, then tried architecture in January for three months before quitting again. Meg was struggling to find something she liked, and it affected her a lot. She was feeling sad and lost for months, but when I told her my idea, she loved it and decided to apply with me, so I'm going to make sure she will finish this one. She was initially rejected and very upset, but then they accepted her. And just like that, we're both going to study marketing and advertising.

Tonight, we're heading out to celebrate without Jack, but he might join us after work. Our flat is still full of boxes, but we've got plenty of time to organise everything during the summer before the semester starts.

I rummage through the boxes, looking for something to wear tonight. The evening should be warm, and I want to wear my black-going-out dress, but I don't remember where I put it. Who knew I had so much stuff?

'Damn it.' I mutter under my breath as I open another box, tossing clothes onto the bed.

'Oh my… what are you doing, Maddie?' Meg enters my room with a bottle of Prosecco in her hand, looking around at the mess I've created.

'I am looking for my dress.' I reply with a quick glance her way. 'I thought you knew I'm not a big fan of Prosecco.' I add, grimacing.

'I know, and I know that it makes you tipsy, so we'll drink it before we go out and save money on drinks later!' Meg declares, placing the bottle on the bedside table.

She's right. I don't know why, but for some reason I can get drunk very quickly with Prosecco, so even though I don't really like it, I drink it before we go out. And Meg likes it.

'Let me help you with that mess. You need to arrange your clothes in the wardrobe, you know?' Meg chuckles, crouching down beside me.

We open three more boxes until I find the dress.

'Finally.' I breathe a sigh of relief, and Meg laughs. 'And I'll clean this tomorrow… Or any other day.'

'I'm going to put the bottle in the fridge and I'm going to the bathroom first.' She announces, pointing at me. 'Get ready for girls' night out.' Meg throws her hands in the air, bouncing them before she leaves my room.

I collect some clothes and neatly hang them in the wardrobe, making myself some space on bed for later. I know I'll be too tired and lazy for that when we get back. Since Meg is going to take ages in the bathroom, I have some time to actually clean up here a little bit.

After Meg leaves the bathroom, I take a brisk shower and start getting ready. I go for nude makeup look, and then, I curl and brush my hair, creating soft waves. The square-neck black dress beautifully hugs my body shape, exposing my lower belly a little bit, but it's okay. I still look sexy. I accessorise with a few silver pieces and grab my purse, making sure to pack the essentials for the night.

The black shoes on a platform complement the dress perfectly, so I take them and go downstairs. I know that you should never wear new shoes when you go out, so there is a good chance I'll end up going home barefoot, but it is what it is, right?

'Meg! Come on, move your ass!' I shout, urging my friend to hurry up.

'I'm coming. I'm ready.' Meg replies, rushing downstairs and spinning around to show off her stunning look.

She's rocking a black shirt with a deep cleavage, paired with a matching leather skirt and shoes. We're going to a bar, or multiple bars, in central London, and we're definitely overdressed.

Meg opens the bottle of Prosecco and pours us each a glass.

'By the way, Jack sent me the location of a rooftop bar and it looks boujee.' She moves her eyebrows suggestively, taking a sip from her glass.

When I see the pictures on her phone, the place looks stunning, and we're definitely dressed appropriately for it.

'Okay, let's go there then.' I say with a smile, quickly downing my glass.

We finish the bottle, take some pictures, and head central via tube. The Rooftop, as it's called, is nestled in Trafalgar Square, so we leave the tube at Charing Cross and walk slowly towards the building.

The summer evening in London is buzzing with life, many people going out and spending time with their friends outside, enjoying the weather, long days, and short nights. This vibe gives me so much good energy, and lifts my spirits, or it's the Prosecco circulating in my veins.

Taking the lift to the top floor, we enter a bustling bar. The hostess takes us to the table outside that Jack reserved for us. I am surprised they had any tables available tonight with all these people in here.

'Look at the view.' I smile, gesturing towards the London Eye behind us as we settle into our seats.

I've always loved watching cities at night, especially from rooftops. I love all the twinkling lights against the dark sky and the hustle on the streets below while I sit, enjoying the show in peace.

'Look at the menu.' Meg laughs, handing me the cocktail menu. I quickly scan it, looking for something that catches my eye.

'I'm definitely drinking the Amaretto Sour.' I declare, showing her the menu.

'I want one too, sounds good.' She nods, and we place the order with the waiter.

Once we're alone, we take some quick pictures of each other.

'Maddie, I may have some gossip about *that* girl from college.' Meg says, taking a sip of her drink.

'Please, tell me you mean Amy.' I reply, licking my lips and tasting the sour flavour of my drink.

So the thing is… I hate her so much. I know it's bad to hold grudges, but she deserves it.

So in school, Amy was this spoiled rich girl who thought she was in *Mean Girls*, and created her own circle with other rich girls, showing everyone around how much better they were than others. *So cliche*. I wouldn't care about it at all but… She was the girl who stole my first boyfriend from me after I lost my virginity to him. She slept with him to show me she was better, and then left him anyway.

Leo was my college crush for so long, until one party when we made out and became a couple. I couldn't believe my luck when it happened. Leo was this cute, tall athlete with a boyish charm, brown, curly hair and brown eyes. I have a thing for brown eyes. We were together for two or three months, and I was under so much pressure to lose my virginity because all the girls were having sex, Meg too, and I felt left behind, so I did it with him.

Honestly, I wish I hadn't because it wasn't good at all, and I haven't had sex since, and I'm twenty years old. I became so insecure after that. The thing is I overthink everything. After having sex with Leo, I believed that there was something wrong with me because why didn't I enjoy it? Meg would always tell me how good it feels, but for me, it was uncomfortable and not nice at all. I thought it was because it was my first time, but the second time we had sex it wasn't better. Leo was making all these weird noises which I didn't like. I didn't like the way he would squeeze my boob, which hurt a bit, and I just didn't like the whole thing.

Anyway, when he left me for Amy, I started comparing myself to her and got even more insecure than I was before. Even though she was a bitch, she was pretty, tall, athletic, had perfect brown hair, white teeth, and great clothes. And I was… average? My body was always far from perfect, and I was always insecure about it. I never considered myself ugly, but I never considered myself pretty either.

I was sad when Leo broke up with me, but not heartbroken – I didn't even cry. Instead, I blamed myself for being shit in bed, even though I did nothing, and for not being sexy enough without my clothes on to keep a guy.

'Yes, the rumour says that her father caught her in bed with his friend and took all her credit cards and stuff. Like he cut her off!'

'Ew! That's gross.' I grimace, trying to wrap my head around the scandalous gossip Meg just dropped.

How could she sleep with her father's friend? How could this guy sleep with… I finish my drink, feeling a sudden need for another round.

'Can you imagine that? And apparently, she's not going to the university in New York that she was bragging about all the time.'

'Well, I guess karma is a bitch.' I chuckle, raising my glass to clink with Meg's.

It's actually funny to think that I haven't dated anyone since Leo. It all happened back when I was eighteen, at the end of college. But I'm good at being single and I'm not going to rush into anything just because people do things. I've learned my lesson.

And Meg always says that I'm that kind of girl who needs to find the one, and I believe that too. I just want to fall in love with the right person, and I know everything will be perfect.

After a few more drinks, I feel like I need to use the restroom, so I stand up from my chair, adjusting my dress.

'Pardon me.' I clear my throat, leaning towards Meg. 'I need to go to the ladies' room.' I whisper, and she laughs.

I walk inside, looking for the toilet, but I can't see any sign. Is it hidden or something? Damn it.

I go between the tables to the bar and… Holy Moly! Am I tipsy, or is this bartender the most beautiful man I have ever seen? I stare at him completely mesmerised, forgetting how much I need to pee. He shakes some cocktails, and I watch his muscles tighten with every move.

He's tall, with black hair combed up and a neatly trimmed, short beard. And oh… all the tattoos on his arms. He looks… perfect.

A girl behind the bar says something to him and makes him laugh. And I swear the whole world stopped for a second. Wow, what factory made him?

'Can I help you? Excuse me… ma'am?' I hear a female voice, pulling me out of my trance, but I can't stop staring at the handsome, mysterious bartender.

I shake my head and look at the woman behind the bar. Oops…

'Yes, sorry… Um… I'm looking for a toilet.' I clear my throat, trying to play it cool. She just caught me staring at the guy, God knows for how long.

'Of course.'

I can see her smirk! She'll definitely tell him. Oh no… I mean, I guess I'm not the only one. Come on! Look at him. He's unreal. I bet she has a crush on him too, or something.

'Our toilets are quite hidden. You'll have to go around the bar, and you'll see a long hall on your right. Just keep going straight to the end, turn right, and you'll find the ladies' room at the end.'

'Sure, thank you.'

I take a quick peek at the beautiful bartender as I pass the bar, heading towards the toilet. I'm sure he wasn't here when we arrived. He must have just started his shift or was on a break, or whatever. I would've noticed him when we came in.

I use the toilet and quickly wash my hands. I check how I look in the mirror and fix my hair. My cheeks are rosy from all the alcohol I've had tonight. Do I look tipsy? I hope not. Just in case I meet someone…

As I leave the ladies' room, walking back to the table, my eyes quickly scan the bar, hoping to see the bartender again, but he's not here. Did I just imagine him?

'Meg, I just saw the most handsome man in my life.' I whisper to her as I sit down on my chair.

'Where?' She looks around eagerly.

'Meg stop.' I playfully hit her arm. 'He was behind the bar when I went to the toilet.'

'Well, I guess I'll go to the toilet too. Tell me what he looks like. I want to check him out too.' Meg says, standing up and smoothing her skirt.

'Um… so he's tall with black hair… like combed up. Oh, and he's the one with a lot of tattoos. Trust me, you'll know when you see him.'

'Okay, I'll be back in five minutes.' She winks, heading off to investigate.

'Five minutes?' I squeak as I watch Meg walk away.

I take a sip of my drink and admire the beautiful view. It's gotten much darker, and all the street lamps are lighting up the roads while the London Eye has turned pink.

Meg returns to the table after a while, and I turn towards her.

'Okay, I'm back.' She smirks as she sits down. 'I ordered a bottle of Prosecco from him.'

'What? Why? Are you insane? What do you mean, from him?'

'Like, I asked him to bring it for us.' Meg shrugs casually.

'He's a bartender, not a waiter.' I whisper urgently, feeling a surge of panic. 'Did you look at the right guy, though?'

'I know, he said that too, and that he can't do that, blah blah blah, but…' Meg leans in closer, lowering her voice. 'I told him that my friend thinks he's cute and wants his number, and I think that convinced him.'

'Meg! Why did you do that?' I ask, my voice high-pitched.

'So you'll talk to him, get his number, go on a date or something. He's your type. Of course, you fancy him. Maybe he's Mr. Perfect for you.' She says proudly, wiggling her eyebrows.

'Meg!' I hide my face in my hands.

I can't do that. I'm too shy and would never hit on a guy. Especially not on a guy like him. I always wanted a guy to talk to me first, so at least I would know he likes me.

'I will kill you. I swear Meg. You know I can't do that. I don't know how. He might not even like me. He definitely won't like me. You saw him! He should date a model, not me. He's probably dating a model.' I babble, and Meg laughs. I look at her confused.

'I was just joking. Calm down. I only asked him if anyone could bring us some Prosecco, that's it. Don't panic.' She winks at me. 'A waiter is going to bring it to us. But I still think you should take a chance and talk to him.'

'No, and I hate you.' I shake my head and finish my cocktail with one gulp. 'Wait, why did you order Prosecco? Why not the same cocktails?'

'So you'll get into your brave mood, a bit more… drunk and talk to him. I know you'd never do that if you are not… brave enough, let's say. You're easier to convince to do something after one too many, you know? You're welcome, honey.' She finishes her drink.

'I'm not going to do that even if I'm super drunk. He's sooo out of my league.'

'For fuck's sake, stop it. Where is the bottle?' Annoyed, she looks around for the waiter who appears next to our table at that very moment and pours us our first glass. 'Here, cheers to you. And I want you to finally realise that you are gorgeous, and if you ask him out, I'm sure, he'll agree. Apparently, guys love when girls make the first move. And he looks like a very nice guy. Like he has this good vibe, you know?' She clinks our glass together and takes a sip.

'How long did you spend at that bar to know that?' I chuckle and take a sip too.

I know she hit on Jack, but I would never have enough courage to do that. I'm scared of being rejected. And come on, I'm aware I have no chance with this guy. My self-esteem was always low, and stupid Leo brought it even lower, if possible. I know there's always someone better than me, sexier than me, funnier than me, and I might be just a temporary option for someone until they find someone better. Honestly, I wonder if I will ever meet someone who will put me first. Someone who will truly like me. The *real* me. And I will never question it.

I manage to change the topic with more Prosecco, and I hope Meg will forget about her idea of me hitting on the bartender.

'I need water. We need water.' I mumble, feeling the effects of the alcohol hitting me hard. 'Meg, I think we're drunk.' I slur my words and laugh. Meg grabs the bottle and gives it a shake to see if there's anything left of our sparkling wine. 'I work tomorrow!'

'Who cares. You should quit this job anyway, just don't go. You hate it.' She advises.

'But I need it.' I wave at the waiter and ask for some water. My head is so dizzy, and the world is slowly spinning around.

'And another round of Amaretto Sour, or two.' Meg adds.

'Meg…'

'What? If you don't want to, I'll drink it. But going back to your job. Quit! Your boss is a piece of shit.'

'I can't. It pays well, and I need the money especially now that I'm going to school.' I explain, sipping on my water while Meg quickly types something on her phone, making faces.

'Okay Maddie, listen…' She leans towards me, whispering.

'What?' I do the same.

'Jack is on his way here. Go and talk to that guy, and if anything happens, we'll just leave.' She encourages, gesturing towards the door.

'You're insane. I'm not going to do it.' I laugh.

'Of course, as always.' Meg rolls her eyes. 'You're a coward, you know?'

'Excuse me?' I raise my eyebrows. 'What is that supposed to mean?'

'Well, you never want to take risks. And then you regret it. You see a guy you like and don't even try to talk to him because you're too scared of being rejected. How do you even know if you don't even try? And honestly, who cares? If he doesn't reciprocate, his loss. But what if he does? What if he likes you, huh? It will be a funny story to tell. But if you don't try, you'll regret it for months until another challenge appears, and you run away from the risk again, and regret it again. It's always like that. You're stuck in a fucking circle of avoiding risks and regret. You're too scared to quit your job! There might be a better opportunity around the corner, but no! Miss Maddie doesn't like to get out of her comfort zone. Am I right? Yes, of course I am!' Meg says, answering her own question, leaving me gobsmacked. 'What if something amazing waits for you?' She raises her eyebrows.

'And? I'm not going to do it. If he laughs in my face, I'll die of embarrassment. I don't have to worry about regret.' I shrug.

'Oh my God! Grow up!' Meg rolls her eyes, annoyed.

'What?'

'Yes, grow up. You've heard me. You're too scared of good things. But you know what? Just start living. Go and ask him out, risk it. Don't miss out on anything. Life is about challenging yourself. What if you go out, fall in love, and it turns out to be the best thing you've ever done in life? What if he is the love of your life, and you're wasting your chance? If someone came and told you that this guy is the love of your life but to get him, you have to go and talk to him, would you still sit here and waste your chance? You'll never know the answer if you don't act! Do you want to wake up every day and wonder *what if*? People say it's better to regret that you did something than regret you didn't. And it's true, because if you try, at least you know. You get the answer and don't overthink at night. Deal is done. That's it. Girl, can you take a risk and start living, please? Please! Once in your life, do something!' She says in one breath, grabbing my hand and giving it a gentle squeeze.

'Fine!' I roll my eyes. 'I'll do it.'

'What?' Meg looks at me, flabbergasted. 'Are you for real? Please say you are serious.' She gets excited, shaking her hands in delight.

'I will. And I might be drunk so fuck it. I can't stand any more of your motivational speech. I'll try tonight, and if it doesn't work, you'll never force me out of my comfort zone ever again.' I point my finger at her, and she laughs.

'Deal. I'm so happy. I love you!' Meg shows me her thumbs up, before placing her hands on her cheeks.

'Okay, calm down. I don't even know what to do. I need to think about something… smooth, easy.'

'Just go and say "Hey, you're cute. Do you want to go out with me?" and give him a seductive wink.'

'Of course not.' I make a face, and we both laugh.

'Just go with the flow. Something will come to mind, or maybe he'll say something first. Go.'

'Okay, but I'm scared.' I stand up and fix my dress. 'How do I look?'

'Very sexy! Just go! Good luck!' Meg gives me her encouraging smile.

I take a deep breath and walk inside.

The bar is still lively with people. I notice him behind the bar, talking to the girl who helped me find the toilet. Just great. I'm not going to do this. Not around all these people.

When I turn around to see my friend, Meg is sitting at the table, smiling and showing me thumbs up. My anxiety washes over my body, and I decide to go to the toilet first.

I take a quick pee and wash my hands. My eyes stare at my reflection in the mirror, as I try to convince myself to do it. *You can do this. It will be fine. And if not, at least you did something new in life. You will laugh at it later. Just go and do it. You only live once. You will get your answer. Maybe he will like you. Just take the bloody risk!*

For a short moment, I close my eyes trying to calm down my thoughts. Okay, let's do it. I take three deep breaths and open my eyes. *Just go!*

I grab the door handle and leave the toilet, thinking about all the ways I can hit on this handsome guy. I stop right outside the toilet when I notice *him* at the beginning of the hall, walking in my direction, glued to his phone. My heart beats faster. I feel like I am going to throw up.

I take another step towards him with wobbly legs. He's still staring at his phone, and I feel stress taking over my body. I can't do this… Why is it so hard to hit on a guy? *Stop it. Pull your shit together!* I am a grown woman, and I behave like a teenager. Ridiculous, I need to be confident! Or at least pretend to be.

With my chin up, I walk towards the bartender.

'Hi!' I say, my voice too high and loud.

He stops right in front of me, startled, and looks at me from his phone with his beautiful brown eyes.

'Hi?' He says, confused.

Damn, he's so handsome and smells so good. He literally looks like a man from my dreams. I'm not even joking! Where did he come from? And his brown eyes… I stare at him without saying anything, definitely too long.

'Um.. yes. So…' I chuckle, nervously. I need to say something now. 'Sorry to bother you at work, but I was wondering…' *Just say it!* 'Would you like to go out sometime? With me?'

Not that bad. I said it. Done. Could've been better, but at least I said it.

He gives me a cute smile, and I feel my heart melt. Oh Lord, he's so gorgeous, and I might have a heart attack any second.

'Well… that's very flattering. Thank you.' He says, putting his phone in the back pocket of his trousers. 'But I don't think my girlfriend would like the idea of me going on a date with another girl.' He chuckles and I feel my heart drop the same second.

I force a quick, unbothered smile.

A girlfriend? Of course! The lamest excuse you say when you don't like someone. I knew he wouldn't like me! He's so perfect, and I am so… basic. I knew he was out of my league.

'Yes, sure.' I nod frantically. I need to get out of this situation and save face somehow. 'Good. For her. Lucky girl!' *Why did I say that? Just leave!* 'Anyway, I should go back to my friend. She's waiting for me. Have a nice shift.'

I pass him, quickly walking towards my friend to escape the uncomfortable situation. I can only hear him wishing me a good evening. I want to get out of here as soon as possible. I am embarrassed. To be honest, I was hoping he'd be single and would go out with me. I'm such an idiot.

Meg is smiling at me from the table, excited to hear the news, but when she sees my face and me shaking my head, her face drops. It didn't go well. Of course it didn't. I can't believe I actually went for it, thinking I could get the guy.

'Let's leave. Now.' I announce.

'Why, Maddie? What happened? Did you do it?'

'Yes, I did, and I humiliated myself. He has a girlfriend. Let's pay the bill and leave, please.' I murmur, rushing her.

'Okay, okay. Let's go.'

The waiter comes to us shortly after we give him a sign, and we pay for the bill, leaving a nice tip.

My eyes fall on the bar, and I notice the cute bartender, smiling at me. Oh God… did he already tell the others? Did they laugh hearing about my attempt to hit on him? Will embarrassing myself in front of him be their topic of conversation for the next week, or more? He's definitely going to laugh about it. Maybe even with his girlfriend. He will go home to her and say, *Babe, you won't believe this. Some girl hit on me because she thought she had a chance.* And they will laugh.

I just turn my head, swallow hard, and rush to the exit.

'So… tell me. What did you say? What did he say?' Meg starts asking me, impatient, when we enter the lift. I want to forget about it as soon as possible. It will haunt me every night.

'Let's leave the building first. I feel like I need some fresh air.'

It feels like the lift is taking ages to bring us to the ground floor, I swear. As soon as we leave the building, I inhale the fresh air and close my eyes for a second, trying to gather my thoughts.

'Jack will be here in five minutes, we can take an Uber home.' Meg says, looking at her phone. 'Or should we go somewhere else?'

'I talked to a cute guy and I asked him out.' I say under my breath, chuckling.

'You did.' Meg smiles at me.

'And I got turned down.' I look at her, no expression on my face. I fucked up. That was probably the worst pick-up line in history of hitting on a guy.

'Listen, at least you finally took a risk. I'm proud of you. You did that! The next guy might be the one.' She chuckles, and I roll my eyes at her.

'Maybe. What a night. I just want to go to sleep now, so I'm going to head home. But if you and Jack want more drinks, go and have fun. I'll be fine.'

'I'm a bit tired too. Let's all go home. I want you to tell me everything.' She nudges my arm, encouraging me to spill.

Before Jack arrives, I manage to tell her everything. Meg laughs at my overthinking skills and says that it wasn't that bad, and she believes that if he was single, he would go out with me. But she's my friend. Of course she's trying to console me.

'Hi!' Jack kisses Meg, then hugs me. 'How was your evening, girls?'

'Jack! You won't believe it!' Meg begins.

And of course, the first thing she tells him is how I asked a guy out. I just smile, listening as Meg tells Jack everything, adding in a few corrections to her version of the story.

Meg is a great friend, and I know I can trust her with my secrets because she keeps them. But this isn't a secret or anything serious, so I don't mind her telling Jack. Maybe I would tell him myself one evening over dinner. Jack is my friend too. He's a great guy, and I really like him.

'His loss, Maddie. He has no idea what he's just missed.' Jack winks at me, and I smile. 'Let's call the Uber and go home. You both look like the night is over for you.'

On our way home, Meg falls asleep on Jack's shoulder, and I keep thinking about the bartender. I wonder what his name is. I can't forget about his beautiful eyes and smile. I've never been in such awe of a guy. Anyway, I'm kind of proud of myself for finally taking a risk in life. Even though I got rejected, I feel a bit more confident knowing that I can hit on a guy. And maybe as Meg said, the next one might be the one.

Chapter Two

The alarm wakes me up in the afternoon, reminding me I have to work late tonight. With a groan, I reluctantly reach out for my phone to check the time. I don't feel good at all and have no idea how I'm supposed to work today. Drinking wine with Jack when we got home last night was a terrible, *terrible* idea. If I call in sick, I'll be in trouble, they know I was out yesterday.

Gulping down a glass of water to calm my upset stomach, I already know it won't end well. Shortly after I put down the glass, I feel all of last night's drinks coming back up, so I rush to the bathroom to let yesterday's memories leave my body. Gross. I'm not mixing, or drinking at all ever again.

After I brush my teeth, trying to get rid of the disgusting taste in my mouth, I decide to take a long shower. Last night, I went to lie down for a five-minute nap to stop my head from spinning and… well, I woke up today.

I quietly walk back to my room, careful not to disturb my still-sleeping friends.

This hangover is killing me, but I have to get ready for work. Seated by the window, I steal a few precious moments to gather my strength, inhaling the crisp air before slipping into my uniform, tucking my black shirt into my pencil skirt. A glance at the work schedule makes me feel a little bit better as I'll be working with my work bestie, Chloe. She will save me if anything happens.

With my hair pulled back into a ponytail and a touch of makeup to hide my weary face, I walk downstairs to attempt to eat something. I pop some bread into the toaster and wait for it to crisp up. Thoughts of the bartender from last night creep into my mind again, his charming chocolate eyes and bright smile. I shake my head and retrieve the toast to spread some butter and jam on it. I eat it slowly, just in case my stomach gets upset. So far, it feels okay, so I guess I'm ready to go.

The walk to the tube is brief, and I try to get as much fresh air in my lungs as I can before going down the stairs to catch the train. Thankfully, it's not rush hour, so I manage to secure a seat and close my eyes for a moment.

Upon arriving in Mayfair, I spot Chloe through the restaurant window. Chloe and Caro are the only people keeping me sane at this job, to be honest. Entering the bustling restaurant, I offer my friend behind the front desk a smile. Great, the last thing I need when I'm hungover, almost dying from drink poisoning, is a busy day at work. I head to the staff room to get some water, and prepare myself mentally for this shift.

Exactly at four in the afternoon, I join Chloe at the hostess stand, greeting guests and guiding them to their tables. My role as a hostess at a luxury restaurant isn't overly challenging, it's just some people who try to make it seem like it requires special skills.

By "some people", I mean my managers, one in particular. He always tries to give us extra work, little stupid unnecessary things to do, even though we don't have to do them. He just hates it when we have free time during the day. The place itself is lovely, and they pay well, but it's people who make it... hm, worse than it actually is. Is it a work thing that every manager is a prick? Do they ask you, *how shit you can be to others* when they interview people for this position? Do they say *yeah, when I have a miserable day, I'll make everyone around me suffer, stress them out, and ruin their day* and get hired?

'Maddie, you won't believe what happened today.' Chloe whispers to me, keeping her eyes on the restaurant floor. Yup, she's looking to see if Walter is around.

'What?' I reply, my curiosity piqued.

'I handed in my notice today.' She announces, excited.

'No, you didn't!' I exclaim, my shock adding another layer to my already throbbing headache.

How am I supposed to work here without her? Caro will be my

last hope!

'I did. And sorry for not warning you, but I literally made this decision yesterday, wrote it down, and brought it here.' Chloe explains, nervously biting her lip. 'I'm moving with my boyfriend to Brighton. You can visit any time you want!'

'I know we were talking a lot about it, but I actually didn't expect either of us to leave so soon.' I sigh. 'But congratulations on taking the next step.' I say, managing a genuine smile.

Chloe had been thinking about moving for a long time, but was unsure if she wanted to leave London. I'm actually curious about what convinced her.

'That's not everything.' Chloe continues, her expression growing serious as she places a hand on my arm.

'Please, stop. I don't think I can handle more.' I'm scared to hear the rest, feeling like my stomach is against me too.

'Caro did the same.' Chloe reveals.

'What?' I nearly shout, catching myself just in time.

'Yes, she handed in her notice yesterday evening.'

'No way. Now I have to quit too. There's no way I'll stay here without you two.' I declare, shaking my head in disbelief.

What is going on? I can't stay here without them. I just can't. This place will be unbearable. Will I actually have to change jobs before university? Probably, I've only got two weeks left with the girls. I need to look for something as soon as possible.

To distract myself from getting stressed, I open the reservations book to see how busy it will be today and who's coming.

'I was shocked to hear that from her. It's like we both decided to quit at the same time without even discussing it with each other.' Chloe chuckles, and I give her a puzzled look. 'Maddie, you need to look for something new too. I'm sorry you're hearing it now, but I thought it would be better to tell you in person. Besides, you were out last night, and I didn't want to ruin your mood or anything.'

'It's alright, and I'm too hungover to think about looking for a new job right now.' I grimace at the memory of last night's drinks.

I wasn't in a mood to work at all today, and this news only made my day worse.

'Be careful today, Walter is fuming! He's looking for even the smallest mistake. You know, he's not happy about losing two workers at once. Imagine if you handed in your notice! That would be his last straw, I swear.' She chuckles.

The last thing I need is Walter to come around.

'At this point, if he fires me, it might actually help me.' I laugh.

'I've got your back, girl. If you're feeling bad and need some rest, just let me know.' Chloe gently rubs my shoulder. 'Tell me about your new place.'

After seating our two reservations at their tables, I found a moment to update Chloe about my new place. Walter isn't around, so it's safe to chat a bit. I also can't resist mentioning last night and the handsome bartender. Chloe listens intently, occasionally gasping at some details.

And of course, Walter appears out of nowhere, his face red from anger. I swear, he must have a radar.

'Can you two stop talking?' He hisses at us. 'We do not pay you both to chat at work. Do it on your own time. You're the face of this place, so smile at our guests and be professional. I don't want this restaurant to be associated with gossip. Work!'

With that, he gestures wildly in our direction before storming off.

I exchange looks with Chloe when he walks away and try not to laugh. I mean, this job isn't our life. We won't be here forever, so why stress over some jerk's self-esteem issues? I mean, when I was new, I cared a lot, but Chloe and Caro helped me not to care too much as long as I did my job well. And I do. I don't know why he's so strict about us having a small chat. Are we supposed to stand next to each other all day in silence? Personally, I wouldn't mind if I went to a place and the team was chatting, as long as I was served. I think it actually creates a friendly atmosphere when the team gets along. It's not such a big deal, is it?

'I told you.' Chloe chuckles, shaking her head.

'I see.' I reply with a smile.

Throughout the day, we manage to steal moments to chat whenever Walter isn't around. We want him to leave us alone, so we're being careful. We share tasks, working efficiently to free up time for conversation. Chloe tells me about her plans to move to

Brighton because it's only a couple of hours away by train, allowing her to visit London whenever she wants.

Her boyfriend found them a stunning flat by the sea with a breathtaking view, and Chloe couldn't say no. She quickly shows me pictures on her phone. I can see the excitement on her face when she talks about it. They're getting serious, talking about their future plans, and both of them want the same things: get married, start a family, buy a house. It sounds like the right thing for her, and I'll keep my fingers crossed for them and wait for a wedding invitation. Chloe has a feeling that Ben might propose to her when they move, so we'll see!

As I check the reservations for tonight once more, I notice there are only four left. Not too bad. And thanks to Chloe, I'm feeling much better.

The restaurant quiets down over the next twenty minutes, providing the easy evening I needed. Chloe steps away to the restroom, leaving me alone at the desk for a moment. Glancing around, all I can think about is how urgently I need to find a new job. I can't stay here. Should I hand in my notice now and worry about a job later? I'll start searching for a job when I get home tonight. Or maybe in the morning. I hadn't planned on changing jobs before university, but it seems like I might have to.

Lost in thought, I absentmindedly stare at the reservations when a deep male voice snaps me back to reality. When I look up from the desk, I can't believe my eyes…

'Good evening. I have a reservation for two under Anderson.'

It's the handsome bartender from last night! Holy shit! Our eyes meet, and for a moment, I forget where I am. I actually forget how to speak.

'Good evening…' I stammer, finally pulling myself together. Chloe looks at me confused, coming back to the desk from the toilet. 'Welcome to The Grand Feast, Mr. Anderson.' I say, clearing my throat and forcing a quick smile. I need to stay professional and avoid embarrassing myself, again! I wouldn't survive that. 'Let me take you to your table.' I continue, quickly checking their reservation and leading them to their seats. He came with a girl… his girlfriend. So, he wasn't lying about being taken.

'Your waiter will be with you shortly. Is there anything you need right now?' I ask, stealing a glance at him and then her.

He looks even better today, dressed in black trousers and a black shirt with a few buttons undone. His hair is silky, combed up again. The smell of his strong cologne hits my nostrils, and I slowly inhale it. Great choice. Very masculine and rich. And she… of course, she's stunning. Like a model! With a beautiful face, strong jawline, long black hair, subtle manicure, and a tight red dress that accentuates her perfect body, exposing her slender arms and collarbone. Jesus, they're the most beautiful couple I've ever seen.

'Nothing for now. Thank you.' He smiles, looking at me. She briefly smiles at me too, but then quickly goes back to being very serious.

I politely return the smile and walk away, feeling my heart pounding in my chest. How on earth? How did they end up here? There are thousands of other restaurants in London.

'What happened to you?' Chloe asks, her brow furrowed as she studies me.

I briefly explained to her that he's the bartender I told her about. My eyes already scan the paper, searching for the surname, Anderson. Zack Anderson. I guess I'll have something to do with Meg tonight. She will never believe me when I tell her about it.

Chloe and I land a new "assignment", discreetly observing the stunning couple. He attempts conversation, she snaps a few pictures of food and him, and herself before putting her phone down. He tries to tell her something, giving her a nice smile, and she finally gives him some attention, playing with her hair. He grabs her hand and kisses her knuckles.

Chloe thinks she can guess what the girl is saying by reading her lips, but it's not really working. She's clearly making it up. My eyes are locked on him, watching his moves, expressions, and that gorgeous smile.

'She looks like a freaking model.' Chloe whispers, unable to tear her gaze away.

'I know.' I sigh, nudging her arm. 'Don't stare for too long. I don't want them to catch us.'

'And he... no wonder you hit on him. I would do the same if I was single. He's so fit.' Chloe says, fanning herself with her hand like she's hot.

'And taken, so stop staring at them.' I point out, chuckling softly.

'Isn't it weird? They're on a date and don't talk that much. My boyfriend and I chat all the time, laugh... we're always engaged with each other. And they... I don't know. I shouldn't judge, right?' Chloe looks at me, and I shrug.

'I don't know.' I reply, my eyes move in his direction and our gazes meet. 'Shit.' I mutter, quickly looking away and down at the desk.

'What?' Chloe asks.

'He caught me looking.'

'And what?' Chloe laughs. 'You work here. It's okay to look around and check on our guests. What if they need something? Calm down, girl.'

I gratefully smile at her before we go back to chatting about her new life in Brighton. I need a good distraction from him. Something weirdly strong draws me to him, and I don't understand, or know what.

'I would offer you a job there but it's not going to work for you.' Chloe says with a soft chuckle.

'I think I might try something else here. Maybe a cinema? Or a hotel?' I suggest.

'Okay, but if you want to move to Brighton just let me know.' She jokes.

'I'll remember that. But settle in there first and let me know how the place is before I quit everything and move to the seaside.' I chuckle, and she rolls her eyes jokingly.

'You're horrible, Maddie. I'll miss working with you.' Chloe sticks out her bottom lip.

'Stop before I start crying, and Walter comes to shout at us again for... anything.' I try to maintain a serious tone, but her laughter is infectious.

'Shhh, I think he's at the back.' Chloe clears her throat, and we both quickly focus on our papers.

A few minutes later, Walter appears to inform us that we'll be closing in an hour, reminding us about all the things we already know we have to do. This man is looking for issues, I swear. Sometimes I wonder if it gives people like him some kind of pleasure to be an asshole to others.

We begin to slowly prepare for closing, waiting for our remaining tables to leave. Zack and his girlfriend are the first to leave among the remaining guests. As they approach our desk, he gives me a cryptic smirk before holding the door open for his girlfriend. I try to muster a polite smile, but I'm pretty sure it comes out as a weird facial expression instead.

My heart is pounding in my chest, and I realise I've been holding my breath until they exit the building. Is my heart racing because of yesterday's events, or is it this man's general impact on women?

I watch them cross the street, his hand resting on her back, before turning to Chloe.

'Damn, he's gorgeous.' She says, awestruck. 'The girl is hella lucky. What a catch!'

'I agree with both.' I chuckle.

Finally, when everyone has left, we finish our cleaning and are free to go. I walk to the station with Chloe, chatting about everything and nothing, and luckily, I manage to catch the last tube home.

The ride seems longer than usual, with the tube stopping frequently in tunnels. My mind drifts back to Zack once again. Why is he in my head all the time? Why do I feel captivated by a stranger? I stare at my reflection in the window, wondering how it feels to be next to him. How does it feel to hold his hand, or to be in his arms? How does it feel to kiss him? I shake my head and leave the tube station when I reach my stop.

Walking back to my flat, I catch myself still thinking about him. I wish I could find my answers. I wonder how she feels dating him, waking up next to him, being able to hug him anytime she feels like it. Is he a good boyfriend? Is he loving and affectionate? Does he pay attention to small details? Does he notice things she does when she's nervous? Does he notice things she likes but doesn't talk about them? And why am I thinking about all of that? Am I a psycho?

The lights are on in the kitchen, so I guess my friends are still awake. As I enter the kitchen, I find Meg in her pyjamas, sipping water from a glass.

'Hi.' I greet, smiling as I pour myself some water. 'Why are you awake?'

'Maddie…' Meg laughs, shaking her head, and I make a face.

'Don't tell me more.' I interject, knowing they took advantage of being home alone. 'Listen, I have some news if you have time.' I announce.

'News? I always have time for that. Tell me.' Meg says, sitting on the chair and gesturing for me to join her.

'So guess who came to my work today.'

'Who? Oh my God! Was it someone famous? A singer? An actor? Oh God! Was it Henry Cavill? Theo James? You should have called me if it was him! I need a hint!'

'No. But I wish!' I laugh. 'Well… it was the bartender from yesterday.' I lower my voice as if it's some kind of top secret.

'What?' Meg's eyes widen, and I nod. 'And what? Did he talk to you? Did he change his mind? Did he realise you are the love of his life and searched the whole city for you?'

'No, Meg, stop.' I say, laughing. 'He came for dinner with his girlfriend. She's like a model. They're literally the most perfect couple. And I know his name.'

'Good, straight to the point. Let's look him up.' Meg says, grabbing her phone from the table and opening Instagram. 'So?'

'Zack Anderson.' I say, moving closer to watch my friend type his name, checking every account that appears on the search until she finds him.

'He has a public profile. Bingo!' Meg smiles proudly and scrolls through his pictures. 'Maddie, look at this!' She moves her phone closer to my face, showing a picture of him without a T-shirt at the beach with his friends. 'Damn, the guy is fit.'

'Look, it was like a year ago. Don't accidentally like it, please.' I say, noticing the date under his picture.

We scroll through more pictures, and I find myself constantly biting my lip. He has a few cute photos with his girlfriend, of course, and I don't know why, but it makes my stomach twist. I wish I was her, to be honest. Yeah, I'm a bit jealous.

'She's gorgeous.' I sigh, exchanging looks with Meg, who doesn't say anything.

She goes to his girlfriend's profile, and we scroll through thousands of her pictures with him, or her in sexy poses, smiling at the camera, exposing her perfect body, her with her group of friends, and many more. Looking at the date of their first photo together, it seems like they've been dating for around two months.

'She posts a lot. I wonder what is on her story now.' Meg raises her eyebrows, looking at me.

'Don't do it.' In panic, I try to take the phone away from her, and accidentally, I open the story. 'Shit!'

'Lovely!' Meg smiles and looks at her phone, smug. 'Now we can watch it. You fucked up, babe.'

Well, I guess it's too late now, so at least we can have a look. Also, would she even notice? She has like thousands of followers. Would she even check the viewers and notice some stranger watching her story? Anyway, it's Meg's Instagram, and she doesn't even know her, or me. That could be any random person.

We skipped through pictures of her in front of the mirror last night, her and Zack cuddling on the sofa watching some movie, his eyes focused on the TV like he's not even aware of her taking a picture. And of course, a pic in bed with shirtless Zack smiling at the camera. The newest pictures are from today. One in front of the mirror, with his arm around her and the other one of him in the restaurant. I actually remember when she took it.

We go back to Zack's profile and scroll down through more pictures of him.

'I think that's enough of stalking.' I yawn.

'Maybe. I told Jack I'm going to get some water, and I'm gone for like a half an hour. I bet he's asleep now. Trust me, I got this man tired.' She says, flipping her hair dramatically.

'I don't need details.' I laugh, nudging her arm and getting up from the chair.

'Let's go to sleep, Maddie. I have work in the morning.'

'Well, you decided to do something other than sleeping anyway.'

I look at her seriously, and we both laugh right after our gazes meet.

We split up when Meg entered her room, and I went to mine. When I take a shower, I can't help but wonder how much can happen in two days? I got a crush, hit on him, got rejected, and he showed up at my workplace the next day. The universe is working in mysterious ways and I don't know what it means. Is that some kind of a lesson? Good or bad? Is it a sign not to leave my comfort zone because the consequences will haunt me? Like Zack coming to my work today right after I hit on him the evening before?

I get into my bed, and as soon as I close my eyes, my mind brings back the picture of his deep brown eyes and gorgeous smile. Seriously, I need to stop obsessing over a guy I met only twice.

Chapter Three

Summer goes by too fast, and I spend most of it working, or attending interviews to secure another position. Chloe and Caro already left, and since then, I haven't stopped searching for a new job. I'm desperate to find something new and get out of here as soon as possible, because this place sucks without them. The managers have become even more unbearable, the new staff is incompetent, and I'm simply fed up with this job.

Recently, I had an interview at another restaurant, and it seemed promising. They offered less money, but I genuinely liked the atmosphere, and I'm awaiting a response.

It's already the end of August, our flat is finally clean and organised, and Meg and I are looking forward to starting university next month. We're excited about the idea of meeting new people, forming friendships and hanging out around campus. We've already envisioned how we want our university experience to be, and while it's both exhilarating and nerve-wracking, it marks the beginning of my future. My future career.

Sometimes, I catch myself daydreaming about the charming bartender, or secretly checking his Instagram. I haven't seen him since he came to the restaurant for dinner, so I suppose that's the end of that. But he still lingers in my thoughts.

Meg's laughter, followed by Jack's, reaches my room, prompting me to finally get up and join my friends.

'Hey.' I greet them with a lazy smile.

'Oh, sleeping beauty is up.' Jack jokes, passing me a plate of fresh, warm pancakes. 'You're welcome.'

'Thanks.' I smile, taking a seat at the table.

Gratefully, I drizzle maple syrup over the fluffy delights before digging into them. Jack makes the best pancakes in the world and I absolutely adore him for making them for us on his free mornings.

'Are you ready for your interview today?' Meg inquires, taking a sip of her coffee.

'What interview... Shit! What time is it?' I exclaim, suddenly realising that I have an interview at a small café today.

I absolutely forgot about it. I had applied only two days ago, and the owner quickly responded, scheduling the interview for today. JobToday seems to be working well. Of course, I agreed to the interview immediately. I need a new job as soon as possible. I have to hand in my notice at the restaurant, but to do that, I need a new job lined up. I can't quit without having something waiting for me.

'It's eleven. You have the interview at twelve, and you're still in your pyjamas, Maddie. Are you still going?' Meg asks, shaking her head disapprovingly.

'Oh no, I need to hurry.' I reply, hastily finishing the rest of my pancake and rushing to my room.

Jack's loud laughter echoes behind me as I frantically search through my wardrobe, trying to find something appropriate. It has to be casual because the café isn't fancy, but I also can't show up in leggings and an old T-shirt that I wear around the house. I settle on black trousers, a white top with short sleeves, and a pair of black vans. With a quick glance at the clock, I brush my hair in a rush. I risk being late just to quickly brush my teeth. After all, what's worse than having bad breath?

I scurry downstairs and glance at my friends enjoying their breakfast.

'Wish me luck!'

'You got this!' Meg smiles, and Jack gives me a thumbs up before I leave our flat in a hurry.

On the way to the tube station, I frantically search my phone for the café's address, scanning my conversation with the owner. Suddenly, I stop in the middle of the pavement when I realise it's in Stratford. Why did I think it was in Soho? Maybe they have multiple locations.

I bolt towards the tube, praying I'll make it on time. But deep down, I know there's no chance I'll arrive on time. I hate being late. I'm always on time. Even my resume highlights how punctual I am.

Rubbing my temple, I take a moment to collect myself. It's just an interview at a café, not an interview to be a surgeon at a hospital. It will be fine. Maybe they won't mind if I'm a bit late. I can't help but wonder if the manager of the Jenny Jones restaurant will reply to me soon. I really hope they'll hire me. I think the interview went well, and even the manager said that I'm experienced and seem like the right candidate.

My two weeks notice is already written, just waiting for the exact date of my last day at The Grand Feast. One job offer, and I'm out of there. Or… what if someone better than me showed up and got the job? But it's a big restaurant. They definitely have more than one position, right? As always, I find myself overthinking the situation, and I need to stop.

After transferring from the Northern line to the Central line, where I waited around ten minutes due to a delay, I seriously considered giving up. Why does it seem like the universe is against me today? First, I forgot about my interview, then I missed the train and had to wait for the next one, and now, my final train keeps getting delayed! It might be embarrassing to show up now. But I have to try. I'm desperate.

Finally, I arrive at the café, thirty minutes late. Taking a deep breath, I push open the door and step inside. Instantly, a wave of dread washes over me. This is not what I expected at all. The place looks nothing like the photos. The walls are yellowish, not cream, with a lot of cracks. There are a few dark-wooden tables and chairs with old red cushions, like they should have been replaced years ago, and a small TV playing the news, hanging in the corner by the entrance.

There's a weird smell in the air, definitely not the scent of delicious food, more like damp mixed with burnt, old food. Some grumpy lady behind the counter is making coffee for a customer, and the other, much younger woman is scrolling on her phone on the side, chewing gum with her mouth open, making munching sounds. It annoys me so much, it's one of my pet peeves. Should I leave? I'm already late, and they've probably forgotten about me by now.

But before I can make a decision, the grumpy lady interrupts my thoughts, asking if I need anything while she passes a cup to a customer.

'Hi, my name is Maddie Martin. I have a job interview today.' I announce with what I hope is a friendly smile.

I have a bad feeling about this in my gut. I should have just ordered a coffee and left. Why did I have to mention the interview? Why couldn't I have kept my mouth shut?

'One second.' She replies curtly before turning and disappearing downstairs.

I take this time to look around and notice some pictures of food and landscapes. Then, my eyes scan the menu above the till, which shows they serve both breakfast and lunch here. Interesting, where is the kitchen?

'Maddie!' A male voice calls out, causing me to turn. A tall man in his fifties strides over, extending his hand.

'Hello.' I smile.

'Nice to meet you. I'm Dave. Come with me. We'll do your interview downstairs.' He says, gesturing to follow him, and I go.

As we walk behind the counter to the stairs, I can't help but scrutinise every detail of the place. Downstairs resembles an unfinished basement that needs a major renovation. There's a heavy curtain hanging to the side, and I believe it's being used as a door. What is this place? Am I going to be kidnapped?

The owner sits behind a desk on an ancient-looking, red computer chair, and points at the stool in front of the desk. As I sit on it, it moves to the side, and for a second, I think it will break under me. I smile, hoping to conceal my discomfort. I already feel guilty for being late and don't want to appear rude or fussy just because the place isn't in its best shape. But I can't stop wondering if this place is hygienic enough to serve food or drinks.

'So, Maddie. Your resume is very impressive, and I can see you work for a very good restaurant now. Why do you want to change jobs?' He inquires, raising an eyebrow.

'Well, I think I've progressed as far as I can in my current role and I want to develop new skills that aren't required in my current position.' I begin, realising this answer doesn't sound right here. But it doesn't matter.

Dave nods and moves on.

'So, why do you want to be a waitress here?'

I don't even know what to say. I need money, I need to escape my current job, I need anything before I start university that will be flexible enough. That's it. Brilliant! I don't want to work here, but I'm going to pretend like I do because I don't want to be rude.

'I am going to start university soon, and I noticed you offer flexible hours, which would be incredibly beneficial for me during the term.' I reply with a smile, hoping it sounds convincing.

He nods again.

'Alright, Maddie. Let me show you the place, and we can discuss the pay and schedule.'

'Great!' I respond, maintaining a smile but feeling a surge of panic inside.

Schedule? Does he want to hire me already? Oh God, no.

I rise from the stool and follow him towards a kitchen I hadn't noticed before. And honestly, it doesn't look good at all! Is it even safe to cook here? Where is the chef? And why is the kitchen hidden behind a curtain? It could easily set on fire, and everyone would die in this place!

'So, in this job, you'll basically do everything. If someone orders scrambled eggs and bacon, you come here and make it yourself. That's why we offer that much for this position.' He explains, looking at me, and I just nod along.

Hell no! I thought I would be just a waitress. There's no way I signed up to be a chef too. I don't want to cook for people, especially not here. And I have no clue how much they're offering to pay me.

'Same with coffee and tea upstairs. So, you need to be fast and work well under the pressure.' Dave adds.

'Absolutely.' I mumble, my terror mounting.

I'm not usually picky, but I'm already concerned about the standard of service here. How often do people get food poisoning? I glance at the sink piled with dirty dishes and just want to run away. This is horrible. I must have applied for this job half-asleep. There's no way I was in my right mind. It certainly looked better in the pictures.

He leads me to the staff room, which is a tiny space in the corner behind yet another curtain, and then we return upstairs so he can show me behind the counter.

The grumpy lady watches me the entire time, and I feel judged and uncomfortable. Same with the younger one who checks me up and down. I feel terrible here and want to leave right now, but I plaster on a fake smile and pretend to be interested.

Returning downstairs, Dave wants to discuss the pay and schedule.

'So, tell me Maddie, how much do you expect to earn here?'

'Pardon?' I raise my eyebrows, taken aback by the question. What does he mean?

'Do you have any pay expectations?' He clarifies.

'Not really.' I respond, feeling utterly lost. But deep down, I know there's no way I'm taking this job.

'Alright. I can offer you £14 per hour, and we can work on a schedule that suits you. I am flexible.' He offers.

As he speaks, I can't stop thinking, how is he able to pay someone that much per hour here? I earn £15 per hour at my current job, and let's be honest, the conditions are very different. The restaurant is more… welcoming and cleaner, and I don't do much for that money. That is definitely suspicious.

'So when could you start?'

'Oh, that's a good question.' I chuckle nervously. 'It depends on my notice at the restaurant. I'll need to discuss it with my manager and get back to you, if that's alright.' I force a smile.

'Wonderful. That's absolutely fine. You figure it out with your current job, and we stay in touch. Message me whenever you know when you can start, and I'll put you on the schedule right away!' He takes a piece of paper and writes some numbers. 'I get so many messages about the job that I get lost on this app. But I'll hold a spot for you because I like you.' Dave chuckles, handing me a piece of paper, and I stuff it into my tote bag.

'Of course.' I nod, forcing another smile.

'Thank you so much for coming, Maddie, and hope to see you soon.' He holds out his hand to me, and I shake it.

We walk back upstairs, and I politely say goodbye before leaving. I quickly inhale fresh air into my lungs and walk away as fast as I can. I need to keep looking for another job.

Checking my phone, I realise that forty-five minutes have passed since I entered that place. Forty-five agonising minutes wasted. I shove my phone back into my pocket and head to the tube station. Meg and Jack are out, so I don't feel like going home yet. The Central line arrives, and I hop on, scanning the stops for inspiration. Notting Hill? Why not? It's been a while since I've been there.

The journey is fairly short, and as I emerge from the station, I feel instantly uplifted. It's just gorgeous. I let my feet guide me as I look around at the beautiful and colourful buildings, people happily walking on the sidewalk with their coffee cups, and it feels so different compared to Stratford.

My attention is drawn to a charming coffee shop, Little Heaven. Its white-painted walls and black metal furniture, adorned with green plants in black pots, invite me inside.

I cross the road and enter the coffee shop. It is the loveliest place I've ever seen. It is bright inside with sofas by the walls, pastel green chairs, wooden tables, and big windows that stand from the floor to the ceiling. I look at the display case filled with different types of cakes, pastries, and sandwiches. The wall behind the counter is made of a bright brick and has white hanging shelves with more plants on them. It has such a lovely, cozy and homey vibe that makes me want to grab a seat and stay here for a while.

As I approach the counter, I'm greeted by a warm smile from the cashier, a man perhaps in his sixties or seventies, with hair that has turned completely grey.

'Good afternoon, lovely.'

'Good afternoon.' I smile back at him.

'How can I help you today?'

'Oh.' I quickly scan the menu, realising I paid more attention to the interior than the drinks they offer. 'Can I have an almond latte, please?'

'No problem, my darling. Anything else?' He asks with a twinkle in his eye.

'No, that's everything. Thank you.' I say, tapping my card to the card reader as the price flashes on the screen.

The lovely gentleman turns around to prepare my drink, and I take a moment to admire the charming atmosphere of the coffee shop once more.

'One almond latte.' He announces, placing the drink in front of me.

'Thank you.' I reply, taking my cup and making my way to a cozy corner table.

It feels so nice here, and I just love it. People around are either chatting with their friends, or working on their laptops. The aroma of coffee beans, milk, vanilla, caramel, and sugar fills the place. If only this place was closer to where I live, I'd be here every day.

I take a sip of my latte and scroll through job offers on my phone, making a mental note to be more careful in the future before I decide to apply. Nothing interesting. But I could definitely see myself working here. However, I don't see any posters that they're hiring.

When I finish my latte, I reluctantly leave this amazing place, knowing I'll be back soon, and make my way home.

The streets are bustling with people rushing to catch the tube after work, but I enjoy my slow walk, savouring the last moments of warm summer air. I love summer, and I'm definitely not ready to enter autumn. Summer could last forever for me.

The tube is packed, and I find myself squeezed between sweaty strangers. I already miss the fresh outside air as I feel sweat gather on my forehead. Okay, I don't like this part about living in the city.

As I exit the tube station in Hampstead and get some service, I'm greeted with a message and two missed calls. All from the restaurant! Excitement courses through me as I carefully read the manager's message. *Hallelujah!* They want to hire me! A surge of happiness fills me, and I resist the urge to do a little celebratory dance. I know people will judge me. They'll think I'm some crazy woman. Instead, I stop at Tesco Express to get some wine to celebrate with my friends the end of my shitty job and the beginning of a new one.

I quickly reply that I'll be available to start in two weeks, in accordance with my current job's notice period, and the manager responds right away, inviting me to sign the contract whenever I'm free this week.

I have to stay for two weeks because that's the company requirement at The Grand Feast, and I want them to pay me for my unused holiday credit. I just need to put the date on the notice and give it to the manager tomorrow. I'm so excited! It's finally over. I grab my favourite rosé wine and head to the checkout.

With a bottle of wine in my bag and a big smile on my face, I make my way back to the flat.

Nobody's back yet.

As I rummage through my bag to retrieve the bottle, a piece of paper with a phone number falls out. Without a second thought, I toss it into the bin. I never had any intention of working there, especially now that I've landed a new job.

In just two weeks, I'll be starting as a waitress at an American restaurant. They've promised me a flexible schedule that works well with my university timetable. Sure, I might earn a bit less than I did as a hostess, but at least I have a chance for a new beginning in a place where the managers seem like decent people.

After putting the wine in the fridge, I gather ingredients to cook carbonara. Well, because we only have ingredients for that. We definitely need to go grocery shopping.

Meg comes back while I'm in the middle of cooking and singing my own private concert.

'Hey, Shakira, I could hear you on the street.' Meg teases.

'No way!' I exclaim, covering my mouth in genuine shock and giggle.

'Seriously, Maddie, you're so loud. And why are you so happy? What happened? Spill!' She insists.

'I'm never leaving this house again.' I joke, stirring the eggs into the pasta, mixing quickly. I can picture our neighbours passing by, casting concerned glances at our building, wondering who's making all that noise. 'Let's wait for Jack.'

'Lovely! Jack should be here any minute.' Meg agrees, taking a seat at the table.

I set down plates of steaming carbonara and retrieve the chilled bottle of wine from the fridge, just as Jack walks through the door.

'So… did you get the job at the café?' Meg asks eagerly.

'Hell no!' I grimace. 'I'll tell you about it in a minute. But… The American restaurant wants to hire me!'

'Thank God! Congratulations!' Meg jumps up to give me a hug. 'I love some good news and wine. I'm so happy for you, Maddie. So, what about the café? Tell us about your interview.' She prompts, eyeing the wine as I pour, and Jack gives me his whole attention, both waiting for the story.

'Well, it was awful.' I take a seat and tell my friends the whole story.

Jack laughs at me for going along with the interview and not leaving the moment I saw the place. It's funny to think that I could have saved myself some time by simply not showing up, but in the end, it doesn't matter because I got the job I wanted.

We change the topic from my dreadful interview and talk about Meg and Jack's work day. Meg always knows the drama going on at work, like a dramatic couple breakup in the middle of the bar, or a drunk coworker making a mess, or drunk people dancing and falling off the tables. She tells us about a couple attempting to have sex in a tiny cubicle, and we all laugh. I can't imagine two people in a tiny room where you can barely turn around to pee. People are so gross sometimes.

Jack, on the other hand, works in finance, and the people who work with him seem pretty normal. He never has any stories to tell us, though he occasionally mentions his single friends to me, trying to convince me to go out with them. I will never do it, even though I told Jack, I will one day.

Later that evening, we watch some movies before splitting off into our rooms. Tomorrow is a big day. I finally get to quit the job I hate!

Chapter Four

This week marks the end of our freedom before Meg and I head off to university. The last week we will have free time for ourselves. Soon, it will be filled with either work or university assignments. Which basically means we might not have time for ourselves for the next three years, except summer or holidays.

I'm doing alright at my new job, and so far, it seems to be going well. The people are friendly, the atmosphere is pleasant, and surprisingly, I find joy in serving customers while wearing my cute waitress uniform. It consists of a white shirt, black skirt or trousers, depending on the weather, and an apron where I can carry my notepad and phone. I must admit, I look pretty cute in it. It feels like everything is finally falling into place, and I'm much happier now.

Yesterday, when I got home from work, Jack told Meg and me about a house party his friend is throwing, so we all are going tonight. It's so nice of Jack to take us there, and it's great that his friend doesn't mind it. Jack assured us it wouldn't be the wild party Meg and I had imagined. Yeah, we tend to get carried away with our imaginations, and Jack just laughed at us. But I'm still excited to meet more people and have some fun. These are Jack's friends, after all, of course the party will be great.

Originally, I was scheduled to work tomorrow, but a coworker needed a day off and asked to swap shifts with me. I happily agreed, realising it perfectly aligns with our plans. Now, I have Friday and Saturday off!

With Meg and Jack still at work, I take much longer in the shower, relaxing and enjoying the hot water cascading over me.

Upon returning to my room, I search my wardrobe for the perfect outfit. I choose a casual yet sexy look with black high-waisted trousers paired with a crossover backless halter top. After straightening my hair and applying some light makeup and eyeliner, I admire my reflection in the mirror. I can't deny that I look and feel good. I'm particularly proud of my eyeliner tonight. Usually, I struggle to achieve symmetrical lines and end up wiping it all off, but today it's on point. My self-esteem is definitely better, and I already feel like tonight is going to be great.

I head downstairs, humming along to *Margaret* by Lana Del Rey, and start preparing dinner. Tonight, it's going to be a one-pot chicken and vegetable skillet. Seems like the best food right before a party. Apparently it's healthy– at least that's what the website where I found the recipe said. So of course, I believe it and try to follow the step-by-step instructions.

About twenty minutes later, the front door swings open, and Meg strolls into the kitchen.

'Hey!' I greet her warmly with a smile.

'Oh hey, girl.' Meg replies, looking me up and down before letting out a low whistle. 'Damn Maddie, all the boys will be yours at that party.' She teases, laughing.

'What do you mean?'

'You look hot. Good choice.' She winks at me. 'I'm going to start getting ready now. Oh, and Jack might be a bit late, so we'll have to wait for him.'

'We can't go without him anyway. He knows the address and the people.' I shrug, chuckling.

'Dinner better be ready when I am back!' She jokes as she heads upstairs.

I put on a pop playlist on Spotify and start prepping the chicken. I don't know why, but I hate doing that and usually I would ask someone else to do it for me, but today, I'm forced to do it myself.

Later, I stir in the chicken and vegetables, adding some more seasoning than the recipe suggests. I'm a fan of bold flavours. The aroma wafting from the skillet is already mouthwatering. In the meantime, I set the table and place the wine bottle in the centre.

Jack comes back before Meg gets downstairs, quickly says hi, leaving a shopping bag with beers on the table, and goes to change. I spoon some food to try it before I decide it's ready and tastes great.

Once everyone gathers in the kitchen, ready for the party, we finally dig into the meal.

'Jack, where is the party?' I inquire, taking a sip of my wine.

'We have to go to East London, specifically the Ilford area.'

'What? That is so far!' Meg groans.

'You'll survive, darling.' Jack reassures her, planting a kiss on her cheek. 'We can share an Uber if you don't want to take the tube.'

'Yeah, we can do that.' I agree, pouring us another round of wine.

'And we won't be that late if we leave soon. I mean, it's not like you're going to miss anything.' Jack says, checking his phone. 'It's just a house party, Meg. There won't be any drama. Don't get too excited, you two.' He says, glancing at us knowingly.

Oh, we love drama! We just don't like being involved in it.

We finish our dinner, and while Meg and I tidy up, Jack orders us the Uber. It's a bit of a struggle finding a driver willing to take us to the other side of London on a Friday night, but we finally secure one just as we're about to give up and opt for the tube.

We leave our flat and get into the Uber. I take a seat next to the window, so I can watch the view of London at night. This city never fails to enchant me.

Fortunately, there isn't much traffic on the road, and we arrive at the house before ten in the evening. It's a typical two-storey house made of bright brick, nestled near the street. I mean it looks different from other houses on the street, it looks more luxurious.

Jack leads us inside and begins introducing us to everyone, and Meg and I exchange looks. I swear, I thought I would know at least one person! I don't know how, but I had a feeling.

We grab some cups and quickly down the contents, hoping the alcohol will kick in soon and allow us to loosen up and have a good time. I grimace because whatever was in that cup was absolutely disgusting and strong. Meg wants another drink, so Jack pulls out the beers he brought and hands us each one.

Later, we decide to explore the house, primarily to locate the bathroom, because let's face it, the more we drink, the more we need to pee. Especially me, the friend with a bladder the size of a peanut.

We walk around the massive open-plan kitchen, which seamlessly flows into the living room where people are gathered around a large table, drinking and chatting over loud music. There's a big kitchen island in the middle covered in alcohol bottles and some snacks. A sleek built-in fridge, which looks very cool and I would've never guessed that it's the fridge because it camouflages itself amidst the cabinets, but some random guy opened it seconds ago and that's how I noticed.

I can see the stairs leading upstairs, and I guess the bedrooms are up there. Jack confirms that seconds later. The interior is undeniably modern, with bright walls, tiled floors, and a light carpeted staircase. Small black sofas are arranged in what resembles club booths, so I guess it was moved around for the purpose of the party. Otherwise, it's not very practical for everyday use. There's a massive flat-screen TV hanging on the wall, broadcasting a muted football game, while a few guys watch it fervently, shouting and clutching their hair.

We locate the bathroom near the door to the garden, next to the stairs. Jack opens the garden door for us, and we step outside to explore. My jaw practically hits the floor when I see a swimming pool! There are a few people having fun in the water, splashing each other, boys throwing girls in the water, and playing different games.

Jack leaves us to get some shots, and we stand there, gobsmacked by this place. Jack said it wouldn't be anything crazy... the house itself is freaking crazy! Who lives here? I can't wait to see how the party unfolds.

'We need that in our place.' I nudge Meg's arm, and she nods enthusiastically.

'I would join, but it's quite cold already. How are they doing that?' Meg wonders aloud.

'No, you wouldn't. And maybe it's the alcohol that keeps them warm.' I chuckle.

'The water is actually warm. They have a heater that keeps the water temperature warm enough.' Jack explains as he returns with a tray of shots. 'I made them.' He adds with a smile.

We both try one, and it actually tastes good, so we have two more. It's fruity with a hint of sourness.

'That's my man.' Meg gives him a quick kiss.

'Ew.' I laugh and take another one.

After a while, the combination of wine, shots, and beer starts to kick in, and we start feeling a bit tipsy, ready to mingle with the crowd and engage in small talk. We head back inside to join the others dancing in the living room. Well, it's more like swaying from side to side, but it's still fun.

'I have to go to the bathroom.' I shout into Jack's ear over the music.

'You know where it is, right?'

'I know, thanks.' I pat his arm and rush off to the bathroom, feeling like I might piss myself any second. I definitely held it in for too long.

Relieved after emptying my bladder, I wash my hands, check myself in the mirror, and head back to my friends, only to find Meg and Jack making out. Well, I don't want to interrupt them, so I walk outside.

I take a few sips of the now-warm, flat beer and grimace. People are jumping into the pool fully clothed, and I find myself tempted to join them. Should I?

'I think you should try it.' A voice says from behind me and I turn around.

My beer almost ends up crashing onto the floor when I see the gorgeous bartender, smiling at me. I swallow the beer I was holding in my mouth, trying not to make a face.

'Zack?' I say, surprised by his presence. 'I mean, hi. Hello.' I clear my throat, trying to play it cool. Oh dear God, he looks... amazing.

'So you know my name, huh?' He chuckles, and I feel a blush creeping onto my cheeks.

Shit! I'm over now. *Think, Madison, think! Find some reasonable answer!*

'Um... You know, I saw it on the booking the other day and just remembered. I have a good memory when it comes to names.' I lie, shrugging.

I have an awful memory when it comes to names! But the truth is, I know his name from the booking. This is how I really know it. And it's not like I went home and stalked him and his girlfriend's Instagram with my friend the same night. And then his for the past few months. Not at all!

'Heard you're not working at that restaurant anymore.' He says casually and I turn to look at him sipping on his beer as he watches people playing in the pool.

'How come?' I frown.

'I went back to that restaurant like two weeks ago, you weren't behind the desk, so I asked the manager about you. I had to tell him what you looked like since I didn't know your name. He was quite pissed that I took his time to ask about you. Not the friendliest guy, huh, Madison?' Zack remarks, and I nearly choke on my beer at the sound of my name coming from his lips.

'Did Walter tell you my name?' I look at him aghast, and he nods, smiling. 'I don't think it's appropriate for him to be giving out my name to strangers.'

Walter and the other managers were so mad when I handed in my notice, but at that moment, I couldn't have cared less. It wasn't my problem anymore. All I was thinking about was getting through my final two weeks and leaving that place behind. Forever.

'Well, he didn't want to tell me, but I have my ways.' Zack winks at me, and I can feel my cheeks flushing. He's so charming. Why is it suddenly so warm in here?

'So, did you go back for another date, hoping for my exceptional service and was disappointed when I wasn't there?' I raise my eyebrows, and he burst out laughing. I watch him, confused, but his laugh is so cute, and I swear it's now my favourite sound in the world. 'That's not funny.' I mumble, taking a sip of my beer trying to hide my smile. It tastes gross, but I try to look cool in front of him and try my best not to grimace.

'No, I actually went there alone, looking for a girl that hit on me the other night.' Zack explains, turning his head towards me, and our eyes lock. I feel my legs go numb under his stare.

'Does your girlfriend like it that you chase other girls that hit on you all over the city?' I raise my eyebrows, trying to be serious and manage to make him laugh again. Am I funny? Does he find me funny?

'I mean… I don't think she cares that much since we broke up, and I'm single, so I can pretty much do whatever I want.' Zack gets closer and whispers into my ear. 'Oh… and just to make it clear, I was chasing one girl.'

I pretend that it didn't send shivers down my spine. I try to act unfazed by his warm breath against my skin.

'That's kind of creepy, you know?' I manage to keep my voice steady. Zack shakes his head, laughing, and finishes his drink.

'Do you want to drink something better than that?' He gestures towards my nearly empty bottle with his own empty one.

'Like what?'

'I can make you something. I'm a bartender, you know?' Zack spreads his arms and shrugs.

Oh, isn't he the most gorgeous man on this planet? And the way he looks into my eyes... I don't want to break our intense gaze. I love it.

'Okay. Better be worth it though.' I pretend to be unimpressed, and Zack smirks.

I follow him back to the kitchen, scanning the room for my friends, but I can't spot them anywhere. Zack grabs a shaker from the table, checks if it's clean, and looks at me.

'What flavour do you want?'

'Can you make me something refreshing and… sour?' I pull the chair away from the kitchen island and sit on it to watch him create a cocktail for me. I wonder if this is really happening to me or if I'm dreaming.

Zack carefully selects a bottle of vodka and some green liquor, and without measuring, he pours them into the shaker. He squeezes in a few limes, adds some lemon juice, and shakes it vigorously.

I can't help but admire his muscles and the focused expression on his face as he works. I discreetly glance him up and down. He's wearing a black T-shirt, black jeans, and his hair is perfectly styled and combed up the same way I saw before. I wonder if it takes him long to achieve that look every day.

'Do you live here? You seem pretty comfortable in this kitchen.' I inquire as he grabs two nicer glasses from the kitchen cabinet, pours the drinks, and tops them off with soda water.

'No, my friend lives here, but I'm here quite often. What about you? What brings you here?' Zack asks, taking a sip of his drink, watching me.

'I came with my friends. They are…' I turn around to look for Meg and Jack but I can't spot them in the living room. 'Somewhere.' I finish, waving my hand dismissively.

I have no idea where they've disappeared to. Zack continues to watch me, and I feel a bit flustered under his gaze.

'Try it.' He points at the glass in front of me, so I take a sip. Ohhh… He's good. It's delicious!

'Nice.' I lick my lips, nodding in approval. 'Did you learn this at work?'

'No, I made it up myself. Only you and a few of my friends have had a chance to try it.' Zack explains, leaning in closer to my level.

'Well, I feel flattered then.' I say, my heart racing. 'I didn't see you at the party when I arrived.' I add.

Just like I didn't see him arrive at the bar that night when I first saw him.

'I was working and got here like twenty minutes ago. Then, I noticed you walking outside, so I came to say hi right away.' Zack says, taking a big gulp of the cocktail before putting his glass down. 'Do you want another one and then go back outside?'

I nod eagerly, and Zack quickly prepares us another round. Once again, I enjoy watching his focused, handsome face as he works his magic.

We step outside, and Zack pulls out a pack of cigarettes.
'Do you want one?'
'No, I don't smoke.' I shake my head, watching him light up one and inhale. 'You know it's not very healthy, right?' I blurt out, unsure why, and he laughs.

'I'm aware of that.' Zack nods.

I lean against the wall, my hand between my back and the wall, as I slurp my drink. My head is dizzy as I am getting more groggy. I notice Meg and Jack by the pool, sitting on sun loungers, chatting and giggling.

'Oh! My friends are right there!' I point at them with my finger, and Zack turns around to look.

'I know the guy.' He remarks.

'Jack?' I raise my eyebrows.

'Yeah, he's friends with Luke. We always watch football games here.' He explains.

That's true. Jack always goes somewhere to watch football games with his friends because neither Meg nor I want to watch it. But if I knew Zack was here all the time… Maybe I could've met him much earlier. But I guess that is their kind of men's night.

'It's kinda funny that I've never met you before.' Zack turns his head towards me, finishing his cigarette and smudging it into the ashtray.

We lock eyes in silence for a moment, and I feel some kind of tension building between us. Zack looks like he is about to say something when Meg suddenly appears next to us with Jack.

'Maddie! I was looking for you.' Meg says, her eyes shifting from Zack to me with a knowing smile.

What a liar! She definitely wasn't looking for me, I'm sure of it. She probably noticed me with Zack and wants to know what's going on.

'Oh, I don't think we've ever met before. I'm Meg.' She introduces herself, extending her hand.

'Zack.' They shake hands.

'Hi mate! How are you? Did you watch the game yesterday?' Jack shakes Zack's hand, and they pat each other on the back in some kind of bro hug.

While Jack and Zack exchange some opinions about the game, I down the cocktail Zack prepared for me earlier. Meg shoots me a meaningful look, and I just roll my eyes, which makes her laugh. Jack must have told her about knowing Zack when they spotted us.

'Jack, honey, can you make me a drink?' Meg interrupts,

grabbing Jack's hand and pulling him towards the door, away from Zack and me.

'Sure. I'll see you next time, mate.' Jack waves at Zack as they walk inside.

I clear my throat, and Zack looks back at me, finishing his drink. We're alone again.

'So, do you want to jump in?' Zack puts his glass down and takes off his T-shirt, leaving it on the table along with his phone.

My eyes quickly scan his muscular body and the tattoos adorning his arms and torso. I just can't help it. He's so sexy. This man is just perfect.

When I look up at him, he smirks. Of course, he was watching me gawk at him.

'Come on.' Zack says, grabbing my hand. His hand feels warm and electric against mine, and I'm tempted to never let go.

'I don't think it's a good idea.' I scrunch up my nose. 'And I have nothing to change into.'

'Me neither.' He shrugs, taking a few steps back and jumping into the water, splashing me and the others nearby who start cheering. Zack swims back towards the edge of the pool where I'm standing, pushing his wet hair back. 'The water is really warm.'

'I think I'll stay here. I'm fine.' I smile down at him.

'Come on. Give me your hand.' Zack outstretches his hand, waiting for me to grab it.

'No, because you'll pull me in.'

'I won't. I promise.' Zack chuckles.

'Yes, you will.' I cross my arms, raising my eyebrows. I know he will do that. Everyone does that.

'Okay, just sit down and put your legs in at least.'

'I can do that. But move away.'

Zack takes a few steps back, and I walk back to the table, placing my phone next to his. When I return to the pool, Zack is standing at a safe distance, so I sit down on the wet tiles and dip my feet in the water. Well, my ass is wet now. Great.

'It actually is nice.' I say, moving my feet in the water, wetting the legs of my trousers.

'I told you.' Zack gets closer.

I watch him as he slowly moves my knees apart, making himself some space to stand between my legs. I stare at him, my heart pounding in my chest. He gives me a charming smile before grabbing my hips and quickly pulling me in. A squeak comes out of my mouth in reaction to his sudden and swift move. My hands land on his chest while his hands move up from my hips to circle tightly around my waist.

Our faces are inches apart, our noses touch, and I can feel his warm breath on my lips. My chest moves quickly up and down from all the emotions I feel at the same time. I catch his eyes looking at my lips.

'You can kiss me if you want.' I whisper, my voice shaking as I say that.

Zack smiles before leaning in to softly kiss me. I close my eyes, wrapping my arms around his neck. This doesn't seem real at all, it's like a dream and I don't want to wake up. His tongue makes its way into my mouth, pressing against mine. We make out in the pool, surrounded by people and I couldn't care less. It feels like at this moment it is only us. And the kiss… Oh, he's a great kisser! It's tender and passionate that it makes me feel flushed. I want it to last longer, but the tension between us grows, making it less easy to ignore. I know we have to stop.

Reluctantly, I pull away, meeting Zack's gaze. I bite my lip to suppress the smile threatening to spread across my face. My cheeks flush as I realise we must have attracted some attention, but I'm too nervous to look around. Clearing my throat, I glance down for a moment.

'I'm a bit cold.' I say looking at him, shivering.

'Okay, let's get out then.' Zack lets go of me and exits the water first, then helps me out.

We grab our stuff from the table and walk to the sun lounger.

'Wait here. I'll get you something.'

'Okay.' I wrap my arms around myself, softly rubbing my skin in an attempt to get a little bit warmer. Zack walks inside and quickly returns with a big blanket, he puts it around me as he sits down next to me.

'Better?' He smiles, and I nod.

'Aren't you cold?' I watch him lighting up another cigarette.

'No, I'm fine.' Zack inhales his cigarette and blows out a big cloud shortly after.

'Do you usually smoke that much?' I don't know why I asked, but Zack laughs rather than being offended.

'I don't think I smoke that much.' He looks at me. 'Does it bother you?'

'Not really, I was just curious.' I wrap the blanket tighter around myself. It could easily cover both of us.

'Still cold?'

'I'm better now.' I gratefully smile at him. Zack runs his hand through his wet hair, pushing it back, and takes another puff of his cigarette. 'Can I ask you a question?'

'Go ahead.'

'You know, when you told me that you went back to my job…' I clear my throat. 'Why?'

'I wanted to ask you out.'

'Are you serious?' I laugh, my eyebrows raised up because I can't believe that he actually did that. He came back to my work to ask me out? Like seriously?

'I am being serious. And I thought you would like this idea since you asked me out first.' Zack smirks, putting the end of his cigarette in an ashtray.

'I wish you didn't remember.' I groan, hiding my face in the blanket. 'That was so embarrassing.' I mumble. I feel his hands pulling the blanket away from my face.

'I think it was cute. Just bad timing.' Zack shrugs, a cute smile on his face.

Our eyes meet again, and we don't say anything else. I just think how badly I want to kiss him, to feel his lips on mine again. I slowly lean forward, grateful when he does the same and kisses me, placing his hand on my cheek. This kiss is much shorter, but just as good as the other one, and we both smile at each other when we draw apart. Zack wraps his arm around me, and we sit and talk, his arm holding me close, kissing me from time to time between words.

Meg comes around later to let me know that we're going home

soon. I hadn't even noticed how late it was because I was too distracted by Zack, forgetting about anything else.

Zack walks back inside with me and insists on waiting with us for our Uber in front of the house.

'You should give me your number.' Zack passes me his phone, so I type in my digits and save the contact as Maddie. I start to take off the blanket from around my shoulder, but Zack stops me.
'Keep it. I don't think Luke will mind, and you can give it back to me when we see each other again.' Zack smiles. Well… It sounds like a promise that I'll see him again soon.

'Okay.' I smile.

Our Uber arrives, and Zack kisses my cheek, close to my mouth, before I get in the car. I look outside the window and wave at him. He stands there, smiling and watching us drive away. I turn my head when I can't see him anymore, resting it on the headrest.

'Oh my! Maddie!' Meg clasps her hand over her mouth, excited. 'I saw you two kissing in the pool! And later too. That was hot! I feel so bad for interrupting, but you know… it was time to go home.'

'It's fine.' I laugh, feeling my cheeks burn again.

So they saw us, of course they did.

'I didn't know you liked Zack.' Jack looks at me.

'He is *the* bartender, Jack! The hot bartender she's been thinking about for months.' Meg frantically pats Jack's thigh, thrilled with the situation. 'Oh, and I had no idea they knew each other. I can't believe that! I swear, I would have told you, Maddie.' Meg throws her hands in the air, and Jack rubs the side of his head. 'Anyway, I guess you'll see each other again, right?'

'I guess so…' I smile.

The whole way back, Meg asks me dozens of questions, and Jack just laughs. She doesn't even need an answer, she just needs to release the questions from her mind. Plus she's drunk.

But I can't stop thinking about the kiss, the eye contact, and the tension between us. The way his lips felt on mine. There was definitely something between us, and I wonder if he felt it too.

I keep replaying the kiss in my mind when we arrive home and when I take a shower. I leave the blanket to dry on the chair in my room. When I lie down in my bed and look at it, it reminds me that it actually happened tonight, that it was real.

My phone pings, bringing me back to reality. I reach my hand out from under the quilt and grab my phone. It shows a new message from an unknown number. I unlock my phone and open it. It's him, Zack! He already messaged me. Wow, he's quick.

Let me know when you get home ;) Z.

Home already :)

I reply to him, staring at my phone waiting for an answer. He texts back sooner than I expected. I smile like an idiot at my phone, reading what he sent.

There is a drive-in cinema tonight in North London. Wanna go?

So, he really does want to go out with me. He may actually like me. I save his number in my contacts and reply with a quick message. Luckily, I'm off, so why not? I guess we're going on our first date then.

Sounds fun. Sure :)

I can't stop thinking about the kiss
So, I will pick you up at 6, then. Goodnight xxx

I smile as I read the two messages he sent, one right after the other. I send him a goodnight message along with my address before placing my phone on a bedside table. So, he's been thinking about the kiss too.

It's already bright outside, the clock on my desk says that it's six thirty-six in the morning. I hug the pillow, eyes closed, thinking about Zack, anticipating our first date this evening.

Chapter Five

When I wake up, I'm surprised I don't have an awful hangover, which is a relief since I have a date today! That would definitely ruin everything. I rub my eyes, reaching for my phone on the bedside table to check the time. Oh wow, it's already two in the afternoon. I need to get ready soon.

I get up and walk downstairs, still in my pyjamas, where Meg and Jack are having some lunch, also in their pyjamas.

'Good afternoon, sleeping beauty.' Jack greets me with a friendly smile, munching on his food.

'Hi.' I reply, stretching my body. 'What do you have here?' I sit down at the table beside them and lean over to see what they prepared to eat. 'What are you going to do today?' I ask, putting some scrambled eggs on my plate.

'We just want to stay in and relax for a bit.' Says Jack, taking a sip of his coffee.

'You?' Meg raises her eyebrows at me.

'Um... I'm actually going out around six.'

'With Zack?' She smirks, and I nod. 'Wow, he's taking you on a date already. This guy doesn't waste his time.' Meg and Jack both chuckle, exchanging looks and drinking their hot coffees. 'How sweet. Do you know where you're going?'

'He said something about drive-in cinema.'

'Oh, that is so cute.' Meg pouts playfully. 'You'll have a great time, and definitely kiss a lot. I've heard it's a great place for a date. Jack, we have to go there one day.' She nudges him, and Jack smiles at her affectionately.

'We definitely will, darling.' He says, swallowing his food and giving her a quick kiss.

They're just adorable. A perfect example of a normal relationship where two people truly love each other and enjoy their time together. Every little moment, even just breakfast. They are my relationship goals, and I hope I'll experience this kind of love one day. So pure and real.

'Okay, I'm going to get ready.' I announce later, when my plate is empty, and I clean up after myself.

Back in my room, I sift through my clothes, searching for an appropriate outfit for a first date with a guy I've been crushing on for months.

Nothing seems good enough for tonight. I don't want to overdress, but I don't want it to look like I didn't put any effort into it. Something casual but cute should work, but it feels like I can't create a decent outfit from my own clothes.

I stare at my open wardrobe, hoping something will magically appear. I sigh, rubbing my face. This is my first date with him. Of course, I want to impress him. I want to look good.

'MEG!' I call out to my friend. I desperately need her advice.

'Coming!' I hear Meg's voice from downstairs, followed by her footsteps approaching my room. 'What's up?'

'I don't know what to wear. Help me, please.' I groan, sticking out my bottom lip.

'Of course.' She smiles and shovels through my clothes with a focused face. 'Okay, I think this will look good together.' Meg lays out a pair of black, high-waisted skinny jeans and a blue, off-shoulder flounce-sleeve top on my bed.

'Yeah, that looks good.' I nod, admiring the outfit on my bed and turn to smile at my friend. 'Thanks.' I hug her.

'I'll be downstairs watching some movies with Jack. Call me if you need anything else.' Meg smiles, leaving my room.

Well... It's time to get ready! When I catch my reflection in the mirror, I suddenly feel anxious at the thought of having a date with Zack. The alcohol made everything much easier yesterday. The first and last guy I dated was bloody Leo, who left me traumatised after our very short relationship and shattered my self-esteem. I mean, I had my part in this one too, overthinking everything.

A very hot shower is all I need to relax and clear my mind. After applying countless products on my body and face, I walk back to my room smelling nice and fresh with my wet hair wrapped in a towel.

Sitting in front of the mirror, wearing only my underwear, I struggle with applying nice makeup. Everything looks horrible, so I end up cleaning my face and doing my usual look, feeling nervous about everything already. As I wasted a lot of time applying my makeup, I dry my hair and let my dark-blonde hair fall down my back naturally. I don't have the time or mental strength to experiment with different hairstyles.

When I get dressed, I look at myself in the mirror, and I actually look nice. It seems like a good look for a date, not too much, not too little. I spritz myself with my best perfume and apply some lip gloss.

The blanket from yesterday hangs on my chair. I fold it and take it with me downstairs where Meg and Jack cuddle on the sofa with a fluffy blanket draped over their legs and a movie playing on the TV.

'What do you think?' I walk to the living room and turn around to show my friends how I look.

'You look great! Cute, casual, and kind of sexy.' Meg sends me a warm smile.

'Good choice, Maddie.' Jack smiles too.

'Okay, that's good.' I nod, rubbing my hands on the side of my legs.

When I check my phone, I realise that Zack hasn't messaged me the whole day. Neither have I because I don't even know what to say. But what if he sobered up and changed his mind? I hope we're still going out. Maybe I should have messaged him something? Anything? Even just a "Hi" or "Good afternoon" to see what he says. Did I fuck this up already?

Suddenly, my throat feels dry, so I walk to the kitchen, pour myself a glass of water, and take a big sip. I stare out the window, my mind working fast, overthinking the situation.

'Don't get home too late.' Meg jokes, and I shake my head.

'Fine, mom.' I turn around and wrinkle my nose.

My phone pings, and my heart begins its race when I see that Zack messaged me.

On my way. Should be there in 10 :)

Okay, I am waiting x

I quickly reply to him, smiling. Okay, so it's happening! I slip my phone into my back pocket and take a few more sips of water.

Moments later, there's a knock at the door, and I feel my heart drop because I know it's him.

'Bye Maddie. Have fun!' Meg and Jack wave at me as I walk to the front door, grabbing the blanket.

'Bye.' I smile at them and open the door. Zack stands outside and smiles when he sees me. He's wearing a green flannel shirt with his sleeves rolled up and black jeans. 'Hi.' I say, closing the door behind me.

'Hi. Ready?' He kisses my cheek, and I nod. Zack puts his hand on my lower back as we walk towards his car. 'You look lovely.' Zack says, opening the car door for me, and I take the passenger seat.

'Thank you.' I smile, feeling flustered. I watch Zack walk around his car and sit behind the steering wheel. 'Also, thank you for the blanket.' I lift it up to show him I remembered to return it to him.

'I hope it kept you warm last night.' Zack smiles, taking it from me, throwing it into the backseat of his car.

'So, what movie are we going to watch?' I ask him.

Zack starts the engine and drives away from my flat, slowly joining traffic.

'I think it's either *Mamma Mia* or *Titanic*.'

'Are you joking?' I ask, cheerfully. 'Oh, I love *Mamma Mia*, and I mean it.' I put my hand on my heart. '*Titanic* is a classic but I hope it's *Mamma Mia*. Fun fact, it's my comfort movie.' Words spill out of my mouth, and Zack smiles. 'You know, I watch it whenever I have a bad day, and it always makes me feel better. Even my friend Meg started doing the same, and we watch it together when we both have a bad day. Or when we have nothing to watch.' I keep talking when I should shut up before he thinks I'm crazy. But I feel nervous, and I usually talk a lot when I feel nervous.

'I'll definitely remember that. And I mean it.' Zack smiles, nodding his head.

'Are you mocking me?' I raise my eyebrows.

'Oh, I wouldn't dare.'

'I can see your smirk, you know that, right?' I stare at his beautiful face, trying not to laugh.

Zack chuckles, keeping his eyes on the road, and I take this chance to look at his face. He has light stubble, strong jawline, big brown eyes with incredibly long eyelashes, and straight nose.

'Well…' Zack clears his throat. 'Honestly, I just think that is adorable. That you have a movie that makes you feel better. Actually, I've never seen it.' He turns his head towards me, giving me a short glance before looking back at the road. 'But it's also a little bit funny.' Zack snorts with laughter.

'Well, if they don't play it today, we can watch it together another time.' I offer.

'Deal. Is there any other movie that we should watch?'

'I mean… I have a list.' I mumble, sheepishly.

'A list?' Zack lets out a cute chuckle.

'Yeah. I wanted to make a list of the best one hundred movies I have ever watched.'

'And how many do you have?'

'Around thirty.' I rub my temple, and he sniggers again.

'Okay, maybe I can help you reach the hundred.' Zack offers.

'You are welcome to do that with me.' I reply, smiling.

As I watch the road and all the cars passing us, Zack talks about movies he likes, and I just enjoy the sound of his voice. We definitely have very different tastes. Zack likes a little bit of fantasy, mystery, and of course, he's a big fan of Marvel movies. I prefer musicals, rom-coms, and romance movies.

When we finally arrive to the drive-in cinema, there are a few cars parked already. Zack parks his car in an open spot with a good view and turns off the engine.

'I guess it's *Titanic*.' He announces, pointing at the screen.

'It's alright.' I shrug as we unfasten our seatbelts. 'Can we get some snacks here?' I rub my thighs, looking at him.

'I've prepared for that.' Zack shows me his dazzling smile and leans towards me.

My heart stops for a moment when he gets close to me, reaching into the glove box in front of my knees. The strong smell of his cologne hits my nose, and I slowly inhale it. He smells so good. His hand briefly brushes over my knee as he takes out a pack of popcorn and Maltesers.

'I love Maltesers. Good choice!' I laugh. Zack opens it and offers me some, so I take one and put it in my mouth, letting the chocolate slowly melt on my tongue. 'It's like a piece of sweet heaven in your mouth.' I say, watching him do the same.

'They should use it for their advertisement.' He jokes, licking his lips and I unconsciously bite my bottom lip. 'You know we have something in common. I also love Maltesers.' Zack winks and I chuckle.

Before the movie starts, we talk about different things, trying to learn more about each other. I ask him more about his job and hobbies, I learn that he lives in East London, not that far from his friend Luke, and that he's four years older than me. Zack is twenty-four, and his birthday is in January.

I feel good with him, it feels so natural with him. It might be too soon to say it, but I really like him, a lot. I can see that he's chill, easy going, and lovely. Of course, he's very handsome too, but I like the way he makes me feel around him, even though it's just our first date.

When the movie starts, Zack rests his head on the headrest and tries not to distract me with any more questions. He sometimes mentions things briefly, but then goes back to watching the movie. His hand rests on the armrest near my leg. I can't focus on the movie and keep looking at him from time to time. His face is so calm, focusing on the movie.

I think he feels my eyes on him because he turns his head towards me, and our eyes meet. He caught me. I look away and towards the screen, pretending I'm interested in the movie. I can feel his warm hand on my thigh, bringing my attention back to him. We look at each other in silence, Zack smirking.

'You can kiss me if you want.' He says, glancing at my lips. My heart skips a beat because yes, I do want to kiss him so bad and… didn't he just say the exact same thing I said to him last night?

Zack lifts up his hand and tucks a strand of hair behind my ear, sliding his fingers in my hair. Fuck the movie! I want to make out with him, I want to feel his lips on mine again, I want to feel the electricity between us.

He lunges forward, and I do the same. Our lips finally meet again in a soft kiss. I place my hand on the back of his neck and gently pull him closer to me. With his tongue in my mouth, the kiss becomes more passionate and intense. I feel that same tension building between us. This kiss is definitely hotter than the one last night, and I feel a wave of warmth going through my body. I want more. I want to climb over into his seat and straddle him, to feel him closer to me. But I can't.

Zack kisses so well that I forget about the movie, lost in the moment. And when we draw apart, the movie is nearly finished, showing the last scene of old Rose on a ship.

'Well, that was a good movie.' Zack nods, rustling fingers through his hair.

'Definitely a classic.' I agree.

We look at each other, our faces serious for a brief moment, and start laughing. Zack puts his hand on my cheek and softly rubs it with his thumb.

'I'm glad you enjoyed it.' He smiles, and kisses me again. This time is shorter and more gentle. He pulls away, only stopping the kiss, but our faces are still close, our lips almost touching.

'I did.' I murmur into his mouth, with my hand on his thigh, giving myself some balance as I lean forward to stay closer to him. I can feel his warm breath on my lips, and he briefly keeps eye contact with me before we kiss again.

When I finally sit back in my seat, the movie is over, and I feel like my cheeks are burning. I bring my hand closer to my face and gently bite my thumb. What is this man doing to me?

'Are you hungry?' Zack puts his hand on my knee, softly

rubbing it, and I nod. When I turn my head to look at him, he shows me his gorgeous smile. 'I might know a nice place with pasta.'

'Okay, let's go then.' I smile.

We buckle up, and Zack drives with one hand resting on my thigh, drawing circles with his thumb. He tells me stories of how he got his first tattoo, and after I ask, he tells me about the rest.

His touch sends shivers through my body. I put my hand on the top of his, looking at the tattoos on his fingers and hand. He has quite a few of them, and somehow they all look like they were planned out in detail, not made randomly as Zack says. They match perfectly, each carrying a different story. I mention that I would like to get one too, and he offers to take me to where he goes to get his done.

When we arrive to Calici, a restaurant in Belsize Park, Zack takes my hand as I get out of the car and leads me to the entrance. I give a small smile, looking down at our interlocked hands.

Zack opens the door for me, letting me walk in first, like a gentleman. The restaurant feels very welcoming, with cozy booths lining the bright brick wall and some rounded tables sat by a wall with glass cabinets filled with bottles of wine on display. The whole wall behind the bar is made of small rectangular compartments, each with a bottle of wine in it. We get a table in the corner, by the window, with a view of the impressive wall of wine.

Zack pulls out the chair for me, and I take a seat. He sits in front of me, and we have a look at the menu. I look through all the options and decide to go with something less risky to eat, to avoid getting dirty. The date is going so well, and I don't want to ruin it with my bad eating manners. I can be a bit clumsy when it comes to food. It doesn't happen often, only during important events of my life.

'Do you see anything you like, Maddie?' Zack looks at me over his menu, and his stare intimidates me.

'Yes, I think I'll take the Ravioli.' I point at the menu with my finger.

'Good choice.' Zack says with a smile. 'I'm going to have the

Tagliolini and some Pizzetta All'Aglio for a starter because I want you to try it.' He suggests, his eyes fixed on me.

'Alright.' I smile, nodding in agreement.

The waiter comes to our table when we put our menus down, and Zack places the order. We both agree on water as a drink, Zack drives, and I'm not going to drink alone. Not on our first date.

Shortly after, the waiter comes back with water and the starter. Gosh, I hope my breath won't stink like garlic after this. I take a piece and try it. It definitely tastes better than the frozen one from Sainsbury's I have at home.

'So why did you quit your job?' Zack bites his piece, looking at me.

'Um, honestly? My friends left, and it wasn't the same anymore. I didn't like the vibe, but my new job seems promising.'

'Well, The Grand Feast won't be the same without such a beautiful hostess.' He smiles, sipping his water.

I look down at the table, flustered by his compliment and his eye contact. I bite my bottom lip to stop my goofy smile. Zack grabs my hand, gently caressing it with his thumb, and I look up at him.

'Where are you working now?' He asks.

'At Jenny Jones near Baker Street.'

Our intimate eye contact is broken by the waiter, who brings us our entrees. Zack lets go of my hand, and I miss his touch already. I take my fork, excited to try my ravioli as it looks absolutely delicious. I try to eat slowly and cut it into small pieces to avoid any issues my clumsiness can bring to me.

'Do you want to try some of mine?' Zack puts some pasta on his fork and moves it closer to my face.

'Sure.' I smile and try my best to look chic when I bite the pasta from his fork. 'It's delicious. Now, you need to try mine.' I do the same gesture to him. Zack smiles, trying my dish.

We spend the rest of the evening chatting and laughing before it's time for us to leave before the restaurant closes. Even though I have to work tomorrow, I'd rather risk losing my new job to spend more time with him. He makes me feel so good. Everything comes effortlessly. All the different conversations, jokes, and laughs.

The drive back to my place is short, too short, and I

begrudgingly exit his car when he opens the door for me. Zack holds my hand again, our fingers entwined together as he walks me to the front door.

'I had a great time.' I say, turning to face him. He stands in front of me, still holding my hand.

'Sounds like another date then.' Zack puts his hands on my waist, pulling me closer to him.

'Maybe.' I say before he kisses me goodbye.

'Well… go and get some rest, and I'll see you soon.' He tucks hair behind my ear.

'Text me when you get home.' I smile, and he returns it but doesn't walk away. Zack stays in the same place, holding my hand, looking into my eyes. I place my hands on his shoulders and kiss him, trying to prolong the moment. 'Goodbye, Zack.' I say as we draw apart.

'Bye, Maddie.' He slowly lets go of me and walks back to his car. Zack turns around, opening the driver's door. I wave at him and he waves back, smiling.

Once I can't see his car anymore, I walk inside the flat and lean on the door, closing my eyes. I bite my lip and cover my face with my hands, reminiscing about all the moments of this date. Oh, it was so good! This date was amazing.

As I scurry to my room, Meg leaves the bathroom at the same time, and we bump into each other.

'You're back. How was it? Tell me everything. I was dying to know how it went.' She grins, grabbing my hand in excitement.

'It was… just… so great, Meg.'

'Did he kiss you?' I nod, and she squeaks, excited. 'Which movie did they play?'

'*Titanic*, but well… it's not like we watched a lot of it.' I shrug, tittering.

'Maddie!' Meg hits my shoulder jokingly. 'Who are you?'

'What?' I rub where she hit my arm. 'I had a great date. That's it.'

'You'll have to tell me more details tomorrow, okay? I have to go to work early, but I'd rather stay and listen to everything.' Meg groans. 'I'm glad you had fun. I told you, he could be the one.'

'Okay?' I chuckle, frowning. 'I'll see you tomorrow Meg. Night night.'

'Night Maddie.' Meg replies before we go into our own rooms.

I take a clean pair of pyjamas and go to take a quick shower. I can't stop smiling when I think about Zack. I can't wait to see him again.

When I go back to my room and get myself comfortable under the quilt, I take my phone and see one message from Zack. He sent it when I was in the shower. I type out a quick response, and before I put my phone away, it starts to vibrate, and Zack's name pops up on the screen. I take a deep breath to calm down and answer the phone, trying not to sound too excited.

'Hi, Zack.' I bite my bottom lip.

'Hi, Maddie.' Zack chuckles. 'I'm surprised you're still awake. I thought you'd be asleep by the time I got home. Don't you work early tomorrow?'

'You called me.' I answer with a chuckle. 'You left not long ago, and I just got out of the shower. I was about to go to sleep but you called.'

'That's true. Um, I was just wondering when I can see you again?' His voice sounds so soft through the phone.

He wants to see me again! Perfect, I want to see him before I fully start university to see how things work. I might not have much free time after Monday.

'So, I have Monday evening off after my first day at university.' I mention.

I was supposed to have dinner with Meg, but they changed her schedule at work and she has a late shift right after the first lecture, so we can't celebrate our first day as students. But it means I can see Zack if he's free too.

'Alright. Maybe I can pick you up, and we'll go out for dinner. What do you think?'

'At The Grand Feast?' I joke, and his vibrant laugh fills my ear.

'No, definitely not. Unless you want to go there as a guest. But I want to take you somewhere else.'

'Alright then. I'll see you on Monday, but I seriously need to go to sleep now.' I say, staring at the ceiling, picturing him lying in his bed just like me, smiling at his phone, not wanting to end the call.

'Okay. Goodnight, Maddie.'

'Goodnight, Zack.' I hang up, placing my phone on my chest, unable to stop smiling.

With my eyes closed, I keep thinking about what our relationship would look like if we ever become official, when I would call him my boyfriend, and how much would we progress with time. But at the same time, I don't want to get too excited about things. I should give it time, trust the process, and hope for the best. But my head just works too fast, and I can't stop it.

Chapter Six

Since university officially started, time has been flying by. My days are packed with work, coursework, hanging out with friends, and spending quality time with my boyfriend, Zack. Every minute of my life is occupied, leaving no time for procrastination. Yes, Zack and I are now official, we're a couple.

At the end of September, Zack surprised me with a trip to Brighton. Walking along the beach, the crisp chill in the air prompted Zack to offer me his jacket. It was at that moment he asked me to be his girlfriend, and of course, I agreed. We even went out for Halloween at Luke's place, rocking pirate couple costumes while our friends Meg and Jack nailed it as Mr. and Mrs. Smith. We looked so amazing together, and I was so thrilled to finally have a matching costume with my boyfriend.

In a month, we'll be celebrating New Year's Eve together, and Meg, Jack, and I will be hosting it at our place. I must confess, I'm feeling a mix of excitement and nerves about it all, but so far, everything seems to be going smoothly, and I couldn't be happier in my first proper relationship.

Today, I'm going with Zack to a tattoo studio because he's getting one, and I'm eager to see the design he chose. Afterwards, I'll be spending my first night at his place. He's stayed over at mine a few times, but I've never been to his place before. I need to pack my stuff, preparing for work tomorrow, because Zack offered to drive me there.

I peek at the clock packing my uniform. He'll be here soon. I glance around looking for anything else I might need and toss my hairbrush into the bag.

I'm interrupted by a sudden knock on the door, and before I can even respond, Meg comes in.

'Did you pack your sexy underwear?' Meg asks, moving her eyebrows.

'No, I didn't.' I shake my head, chuckling.

'Oh, come on. You've been together for like what? Two months?' Meg frowns, trying to recall the timeline.

'Almost. It will be two months at the end of this month.' I reply with a casual shrug.

'Yup, you're going to have sex tonight. You're going to his place, Maddie.' She chuckles, taking a seat on the bed, watching me. 'I can't believe you still haven't done it with him.'

'Meg, I just… there's no rush.' I sigh.

I hadn't even thought about it. I didn't consider that Zack might want to have sex with me tonight. It will be just us. Here, there was always Meg and Jack, or one of the two when Zack was staying over. I mean we did touch each other when kissing, and Zack tried to go further, but I panicked and he stopped.

'Are you alright?' Meg's concerned voice breaks the silence.

'What if he doesn't find me attractive?' I finally manage to say after fighting with my own thoughts. 'What if he doesn't like my body? He's so perfect and you remember his ex. Or what if I am bad in bed? It's not like I have a lot of experience. I only did it with Leo, and it wasn't good at all. What if I'm the problem? There must be something wrong with me if I didn't feel good. It's me, definitely.' I make a face at the memory of me being intimate with Leo.

I never agreed to take my top off because I was ashamed of my body and he was okay with it because he just wanted a quick shag, and that was it. Then, I got dumped when Amy opened her legs in front of him.

'He's not Leo!' Meg groans, shaking her head. 'You were a teenager and very unlucky that he was your first. Zack will definitely take care of you. And you can always tell him how you feel.'

'I don't know.' I sigh, looking at my friend. 'He might think I'm weird and leave me. I don't want to ruin everything.'

'You won't. It looks like he really likes you, and he seems like the right guy for you. And I'm sure he'll show you the good things.' Meg moves her eyebrows suggestively, trying to lighten up the mood.

'Stop it.' I can't stop myself from chuckling.

'If you want it, go for it. If not, then don't do it.'

'I mean he's just perfect. He's handsome, sexy, sweet and nice. There's nothing wrong with him.' I say, putting my favourite perfume in my bag and closing it. 'And me… I'm nothing like the girl he was dating, and probably the other ones before. Pretty, with perfect bodies, looking like a model. How can I take off my clothes in front of him? He's not going to like me after that. And I want him to like me.'

'You are overthinking again.' Meg says, giving me a sympathetic look.

'I know.' I admit, sinking down beside her, feeling defeated.

'Are you in love with him already?' She asks after a brief moment of silence. I bite my lip, nodding.

'Is it weird? Is it too fast to be in love with someone?' I glance at my friend, seeking reassurance. 'It will really hurt if he doesn't like me… you know?'

'Of course not. I was in love with Jack after two weeks.' She laughs. 'And I'm sure he will like you. He already does.'

'He's a charming guy. I don't know how I couldn't fall in love with him. And everything seems right when I'm with him.' I confess, feeling a rush of emotion.

'Oh, Maddie. You're so in love!' Meg exclaims, throwing her arms around me and pulling me into a warm hug.

My phone pings on the bedside table, interrupting our moment. I grab it and check the message from Zack.

'Okay, he's gonna be here soon.' I say, typing back a response. 'Do I look good?' I stand up and turn around, so she can check my outfit.

I'm wearing black tights and a white sweater tucked into a short black skirt. I'm going to pair it with my knee-high boots and a trench coat.

'You look great.' Meg smiles, handing me my bag. 'Don't

overthink tonight, okay? Just do whatever feels right. I would say go for it, but it's up to you.' She nudges my ribs playfully, wrinkling her nose, and I let out a soft laugh.

We head downstairs, and just as we do, Zack walks in, chatting with Jack.

'Hi Maddie, look who came to visit.' Jack smiles, gesturing at Zack.

Zack looks handsome in his grey sweater, black jeans and a denim jacket. His hair looks soft and is slightly curly, falling casually on his forehead. I think it's the first time I've seen him without his hair combed up.

'Oh, hi Zack.' Meg smirks.

'Hi girls.' Zack greets us, his eyes locking onto mine.

'Do you want a beer, mate?' Jack offers.

'No, thanks. I just came to pick up Maddie.' Zack replies, nodding towards me. Jack understands and nods in return.

'Next time, Jack.' I pat his shoulder as I pass him, then turn to Zack and welcome him with a kiss before putting on my boots and coat. 'We'll be going. Bye.' I say, glancing back at my friends. Meg winks at me, and I shake my head, smiling.

Zack takes my hand when we walk outside to his car. The autumn air is chilly, and I instantly miss the warmth of summer. I wrap my coat tight around me, feeling a sense of excitement mixed with nervousness about the evening ahead.

'Are you cold, baby?'

'A little bit.' I scrunch up my nose in response.

'I'll put some heating on.' Zack says, opening the car door for me. I quickly hop inside and wait for him to take the seat next to me. He starts the car, presses a few buttons, and warm air immediately fills the car, brushing against my cheeks.

'Thank you.' I smile at him as he drives away.

On our way to the tattoo studio, I tell him about the stress of university life. He softly caresses my thigh to comfort me, and I keep talking about all the assignments and exams that are coming up. The anxious feeling builds in my stomach, and I worry about failing at the beginning of my first year.

Zack parks his car in front of a black-brick building with a

"TATTOO" sign in the window and looks at me.

'You'll be okay, and if you need help, I can help you to study, okay?' He lifts my hand and kisses it.

'Okay.' I nod. All I hope for now is that I don't bore him with all this talk.

We leave the car and step inside the building, where Zack shakes hands with a tall, muscular guy with two full sleeves of tattoos. He shakes my hand too and introduces himself as Andy.

'Shall we start?' Andy gestures towards a chair, and Zack begins to strip off his jacket and sweater, revealing his athletic, strong physique. I leave my coat on the sofa next to Zack's clothes.

Andy has a print ready for Zack's tattoo, so he sprays Zack's chest, cleans his skin, and sticks the paper in place. Curious about the process, I come closer and stand next to Zack. When Andy removes the paper I take a look at two big wings spread across the top of Zack's chest. It's impressive.

'Do you like it?' Zack looks at me.

'Yes.' I smile, feeling his hand on my lower back.

It looks amazing, a perfect addition to the other tattoos he already has on his torso, and I feel more tempted to get one.

The sound of the tattoo machine fills the room as I watch the needle approach Zack's skin. I grimace while Zack lies there, seemingly unfazed. Andy diligently works on the details of the tattoo, wiping the skin and following the lines of the print.

'Does it hurt?' I whisper to Zack after a while, and he chuckles.

'Not that much.'

'Looks quite painful.' I remark, watching Andy working meticulously on the details of Zack's tattoo.

Impressed with Andy's work, I snap a close-up picture, capturing only a small portion of the tattoo and Andy's hand holding the machine, and post it on my Instagram story.

It takes a while to finish the tattoo, and at some point, Andy offers me a chair so I can sit with them and watch. Zack's hand rests on my leg, and he looks relaxed despite his reddening skin. I'm sure it hurts, but he seems determined to play it cool. I make a mental note to ask him later if it really didn't hurt. After all, the needle is constantly hitting his skin at a super-fast pace.

When the tattoo is finally ready, Andy puts some gel on the top of it and sticks something transparent on the top to protect the tattoo. Zack stands up and walks to the mirror with Andy to take a look at his brand new tattoo.

'Do you want one?' They both turn their heads to look at me, and I raise my eyebrows.

'I'm not sure.' I clear my throat. 'I don't even know what I want.'

'I have some small designs if you want to have a look.' Andy offers, passing me a book.

I flip through the pages, intrigued by the options. There are some cute designs that catch my eye, like a small daisy, moon, heart, plane, globe, etc. Zack stands behind me, his warm breath grazing my neck as he looks at the pictures too.

'Oh, I like this one.' I point at a small heart shape.

'Cute.' Zack smiles at me. 'Do you want it?'

'I'm not sure...' I hesitate, staring at the picture.

Do I really want it? I've always considered getting a tattoo, but it's a permanent decision. It's going to be on my skin for the rest of my life. What if I regret it later? Is there any way to remove it?

'Okay.' I finally decide, looking at them. I need to take more risks in life, and as Meg likes to say, it's better to regret doing something than not doing it.

'It will take me like five minutes.' Andy assures me, preparing the chair, exchanging the whole equipment and cleaning the area. 'Where would you like it?'

'Good question.' I consider a spot that will be good for a tattoo and have an idea. 'Here.' I point at the spot next to my ankle on the right leg.

'Alright. I will need you to take off your boots and tights. You can use the bathroom over there.' Andy instructs, pointing at the door.

I rush towards the room, locking myself in. As I remove my shoes and tights, I catch my reflection in the mirror and I stare at myself. It's okay. I can get a tattoo. But what if it hurts? What if I embarrass myself? Is it too late to change my mind? Andy is waiting outside the door for me, he prepared everything. He said it will take five minutes. I can survive five minutes of pain, right?

I take a deep breath and walk back to the main room, holding my stuff.

'Take a seat.' Zack smiles, taking my things from my hands. I nod and sit on the chair as Andy directs.

'Ready?' Andy gives me a friendly smile, and I nod, feeling a flutter of nerves. I'm only scared it will hurt. Andy sprays and cleans my leg before sticking the paper to my skin, just as he did with Zack. 'Is it alright? Do you want to move it lower, higher, more to the side?' Andy removes the paper so I can take a look at the design.

'It looks cute.' I smile. 'And I want it like it is now.'

'Okay. Let's start.' Andy says, turning on the machine.

My heart begins to race at the sound. I glance at Zack, and he smiles reassuringly. As the needle touches my skin, I'm surprised to find that it doesn't hurt. That's so weird. I don't feel it. Not as much as I expected, anyway. I watch Andy carefully inject ink under my skin.

'How is it?' Zack asks softly.

'You were right. It doesn't hurt. It's alright.' I smile, feeling a rush of excitement. I'm getting a tattoo! I can't wait to show it to Meg.

'I told you.' Zack kisses the top of my head.

The pain becomes more noticeable as Andy gets closer to my ankle, but it's bearable. And before I know it, the tattoo is done. I'm surprised when Andy turns off the machine and begins the process of wrapping the tattoo.

'You're all done.' Andy smiles, removing his gloves.

'Thank you.' I give him a friendly smile. 'Well, I'll get dressed.'

I slide off the chair, grab my tights and boots, and head to the bathroom. As I dress, I take a moment to appreciate the cute tattoo Andy gave me.

When I return, Zack and Andy are chatting about something. Zack is already dressed, holding my coat. As I join them, Zack wraps his arm around me, smiling. I catch the end of their conversation and learn that Andy is expecting a baby in spring, so Zack congratulates him.

We shake hands before leaving and walk back to Zack's car.

'So, how do you feel about your tattoo?' Zack asks, facing me with a smile.

'It's cute. I really like it.' I smile back. 'Zack?'

'Yes?'

'Does yours hurt? It looked um… way worse than mine.' I inquire.

'No, it's okay.' Zack shrugs casually.

'It looked painful.'

'I'm okay, darling. You got the same thing, and you know it's not that bad. Don't worry.' Zack chuckles, leaning in to kiss me gently. 'Let's go. Are you hungry?'

'A little bit.' I nod.

On the way to Zack's place, I gaze out at the road while Zack explains how to take care of the tattoo. His hand finds mine, and our fingers intertwine.

I swear, Zack's love language is physical touch. He always holds my hand when we're out, hugs me constantly, kisses me whenever he gets the chance, and plays with my hair or gently caresses my skin.

He showers me with kisses on my hands, cheeks, forehead, neck, and the top of my head. It's all these small gestures that make my heart melt whenever I'm around him. It's silly that I feel absolutely adored by this man, but at the same time, I'm scared that he won't find me attractive without my clothes on.

I steal a glance at his focused expression as he drives, now talking about his work. Zack aspires to become a manager and has already begun his training. Apparently, they think about moving the current one to a different location, and Zack is a perfect candidate to replace him. He radiates excitement as he discusses his prospects, and I can't help but smile, genuinely happy for him.

'We're almost there.' Zack squeezes my hand, and I look outside the window at the view of Canary Wharf in the evening with all the tall buildings with lights on and a dark sky in the background.

As we reach the parking space in the basement of a modern neighbourhood with blocks of flats, I notice Zack parking in a spot marked with the number nineteen, even though there's plenty of space available. There's no way he lives in such a cool place! He even has his own designated parking spot.

Zack rushes to open my door, and I chuckle, pulling my coat tighter around me.

'It's warm up there.' He chuckles, amused by my response to the cold.

'Let's go then.' I scrunch up my nose. Zack places his hand on my back, and we head towards the lift, where he presses the button for the sixth floor. 'Sixth floor?' I raise my eyebrows, intrigued.

'Yeah, I live on the sixth floor, and I have a nice view.' Zack confirms, smiling warmly at me.

The lift ride is short, and I feel a surge of excitement as we reach the sixth floor. Zack leads us down the hallway, which is adorned with modern white tiles with a subtle beige pattern. He stops in front of a dark-brown wooden door and unlocks it. Stepping into the flat, I'm momentarily greeted by darkness until Zack flicks the light switch. Oh, wow.

'Do you live here alone?' I ask, looking at him. Zack helps me out of my coat and hangs it alongside his own on a hook.

The flat has a sleek, white open-plan kitchen with hanging cabinets and dark brown ones below, perfectly complementing the wooden flooring in the living area and the sofa. A fluffy carpet adds warmth to the space.

I glance around the room, noticing the personal touches that make it feel like his own space. Family photos on the walls, a few books sit on the coffee table, and a cozy blanket is draped over the back of the sofa. The glass table stands next to a large window offering a breathtaking view of Canary Wharf. I approach the window to admire the view, and feel Zack's arms wrap around me.

'Yes, I live here alone. Do you want to go on the balcony? The view is much better there.' Zack suggests, opening the door for me.

I step outside and take in the lovely surroundings. He even has a view of the water! I hadn't noticed it before. Despite the cold, I'm drawn to stay outside and soak in the view.

'It's lovely here.' I say, looking back at Zack, feeling a twinge of jealousy that he lives here.

'Thanks.' Zack chuckles. 'This place actually belongs to my parents. I helped them renovate it, and they wanted to keep it for me and my sisters. But since I'm the oldest and moved out first, it's mine.' He explains with a soft laugh.

'Your poor sisters.' I chuckle, shaking my head. I recall Zack mentioning his two younger sisters as we've shared stories about our families.

'They're fine, still living with my parents. Come inside before you catch a cold. You're shivering.' Zack notices.

Zack lets me in first, closing the door behind us. *Shit!* I realise that I didn't take my shoes off and now feel really bad about walking around his beautiful flat with them on. I quickly pull the zip down, take them off, and place them neatly on the shoe shelf next to Zack's.

'Sorry, I should have taken them off first. I just got distracted.' I apologise, glancing at the floor to make sure I didn't leave any marks.

'It's alright, Maddie. Don't worry about it.' Zack reassures me with a warm smile. 'I've prepared some dinner for us.' He adds, leading me to the kitchen.

'What is that?' I ask, curious.

'A firecracker chicken.' Zack replies, turning on the stove to warm up our meal.

'Wow, it looks amazing.' I say, wrapping my hands around his arm, and he kisses the top of my head.

'I have some wine too.' Zack says, reaching for a bottle of wine standing on the kitchen counter.

'I can do that. Where do you keep your glasses?' I ask, taking the bottle and the glasses from the shelf he pointed at. Zack puts the food in small bowls, and I fill our glasses with wine. 'It smells so good.' I smile, watching him sprinkle spring onions on the top of the dish.

We sit at the table and clink our glasses. The food is exquisite, and I think he might be a better cook than me. He'll be the chef in this relationship.

'It's delicious Zack.' I sip on my wine, keeping my eyes on him.

'Thank you.' He says, looking into my eyes, smiling. And there it is. The tension between us is back. Zack keeps intimate eye contact with me while drinking his wine, and I feel my heart beat faster. 'Do you want to watch a movie?'

'Sure.' I nod.

After leaving our plates in the dishwasher, we sit down on the sofa with our wine, and he lets me choose a movie. I play *Love, Rosie*, which seems like a nice, easy movie to watch with your boyfriend on a chill evening.

We cuddle the whole movie, his arm around me, my legs resting on his. Zack's hand traces soothing patterns on my leg, and with each gentle touch, I feel myself relaxing further into his arms. I rest my head on his chest and can feel it vibrate every time he laughs. Oh, his laugh is just my favourite sound. I swear.

When the movie ends, I sit upright giving my body a nice stretch and Zack watches me, smiling.

'I need a shower.' I say.

'Okay. Let me show you the bathroom.'

I follow Zack, bag in my hand, to a beautiful bathroom with white tiles on the floor and brown ones on the wall and the bathtub with a shower. I look at the big mirror facing it and turn my head to face Zack, my eyebrows raised up.

'My dad's idea.' He shrugs.

'I hope it's not a one sided mirror.' I joke, and Zack laughs.

'No, it's not. But I'll think about it. That's a great idea, Maddie.' He gives me a towel and kisses my cheek. 'Call me if you need anything.'

'Okay.' I smile before he leaves the room.

I lock the door and run the shower. As I strip off all my clothes, I can't help but glance at the big mirror and scan my imperfect body. My stomach isn't flat like most of the girls on Instagram, or like his ex. I grab the slight plumpness around my stomach that makes my lower belly more noticeable when I wear tight dresses, which I usually avoid because of that. This always reminds me of my imperfections.

I stare at my big hips and thick thighs and feel my insecurities growing. I feel like I would only like myself if I was perfectly skinny, with slender arms and legs, a flat stomach, and some visible muscles, but I'm not.

I try to push these thoughts away when I finally get under the hot water. It starts to terrify me that if we do anything tonight, he might see me like that, completely vulnerable, with nothing to hide anymore.

As steam clouds the mirror, my reflection disappears, but the image is stuck in my head. I feel a mixture of feelings about spending the night at Zack's for the first time.

I slowly put on my pyjama shorts and a matching top, hang the towel on the door, and leave the bathroom. Zack gets up from the sofa, and puts his phone away when he sees me.

'Cute pyjamas.' He smiles, coming closer.

'Thanks.' I reply with a soft smile.

'Okay, I'll show you to the bedroom, so you can lie down.' Zack opens the door next to the bathroom, and I walk into a room with cream walls and a big white bed beside a massive window. 'Make yourself comfortable. I'll be back soon.' He kisses me and leaves the room.

Shortly after, I can hear the shower turn on. I put my bag to the side and slip under the quilt on the left, closer to the window. It looks so pretty. I take my phone and send Meg a picture of the view. She quickly replies with her usual "What the fuck" message and talks about how cool it is. We exchange a few messages before Zack comes back wearing only his pyjama bottoms and lies down next to me.

'Come here.' He says, opening his arms, so I move closer and snuggle into his warm body.

'How's your tattoo?'

'Good. How's yours?'

'It's fine.' I chuckle, looking up at him.

'You are gorgeous.' Zack says after a while, looking into my eyes and caressing my arm. He moves his head closer and kisses me softly at first, but harder and more passionately later. I place my hand on the side of his neck and let his body slide on top of mine.

The temperature in the room rises, and my breathing gets heavier when he pushes his hips against mine. I catch my breath when Zack moves to my neck, leaving wet kisses on my skin. His hand slowly moves down to my shorts, sliding under the fabric of my underwear. I move my hand into his hair and squeeze the strands between my fingers.

I close my eyes, trying to enjoy his touch, but my mind decides to ruin the moment. I try my hardest to stop the thoughts but I can't. My brain reminds me of my bathroom reflection and that in a few minutes, he might see the same *me* that I saw. The *me* he might be disappointed with. What if he makes a face? What if my flaws will drive him away? I would die right here. The embarrassment I would feel. The pain and heartbreak.

Just like that, my mind wins. The thought of him not finding me attractive ruins the moment, and I grab his hand to stop.

'Is everything alright?' Zack looks at me, concerned.

'I… I just need to go to the bathroom.' I blurt out, and he gets off me and lies down on his back.

I quickly get out of the bed, avoiding his piercing stare, and go to the bathroom. I rest my forehead on the cold wall and close my eyes. *You fucking idiot. If you keep doing that, he will dump you!* Maybe I could join a gym, get sexier, and then, if he waits, we could finally have sex without me panicking about my appearance?

I slowly start banging my head against the wall, trying not to make any sound. The thing is, the night Zack tried to make a move for the first time, I thought we were alone at my place. It was like tonight, we kissed, he started touching me and… I panicked. I was terrified of the thought of Zack seeing me naked and not liking me. When I left to go to the bathroom, I noticed Jack and had an excuse when I came back to the room. But tonight? What am I going to say tonight? We're alone. At his place.

I sigh and look at myself in the mirror. Would he like my saggy arms and un-perky breasts that don't look as nice as in a bra? I was unlucky to be gifted with breasts that are much lower than other girls'. Would he be okay with my imperfections while he is absolutely perfect?

I stay there and stare at myself, for too long. I shake my head and decide to come back to his bedroom and face the situation. Or somehow just have sex with the man I love. That's the thing. I'm absolutely in love with him, and that's why I'm so scared of what he will think about me. I care about what he thinks about me. I want him to like me the way I am. I don't want him to break up with me.

When I finally go back to the room, Zack is lying down, scrolling on his phone, but puts it away when I come into the room. I slowly make my way back to bed, next to him.

'Are you okay?' Zack is lying down on his side, looking at me.

'Yes, I'm fine.' I do the same.

Zack brushes a stray strand of hair away from my face and kisses my forehead. There's a short silence, and I know the moment is ruined.

'So, I'm going to watch a game with my friends on Saturday.' Zack says, lying on his back now.

'Who's playing?' I rest my head on his chest, and he plays with my hair.

'Arsenal vs Chelsea. But I'm free on Friday if you wanna come over. I would like you to come.'

'I think I work until eight.'

'I can pick you up from work.' Zack offers.

'Okay, we can do that.' I look up and kiss him softly. 'I like that idea.'

'Me too.' He gives me a sweet smile.

We stare at each other, and all I hope for is that he doesn't think anything bad about me. That he doesn't consider leaving me because I avoid intimacy.

Zack just lies next to me, softly rubbing my skin with his thumb and kissing me fondly. But he doesn't try to push it further. The moment is gone, and I know I'm the issue. And I need to fix it.

When we draw apart, I rest my head on his chest. We lie there in silence, the only sound being the gentle hum of the city outside.

'Goodnight, Zack.'

'Goodnight, Maddie.' Zack nestles his face in my hair.

I find a sense of peace and safety in his arms and I slowly drift away into sleep.

Chapter Seven

When I wake up in the morning, feeling incredibly hot, I find the reason behind the heat– it's Zack spooning me, his arms wrapped around me tight, holding me close to his chest. I slowly move his arm down so I can push the quilt off too. Zack murmurs something, and I turn to face him, but he is still asleep. His hair falls on his forehead, disheveled, his face calm, his breathing slow and relaxed. I smile slightly and move my hand closer to his face, tracing my fingers around his jaw.

I examine his beautiful face, long eyelashes, a straight nose, perfectly shaped lips, and his bristly stubble. Our noses touch, and I can feel his warm breath on my lips. I place my hand on his cheek, gently caressing his skin with my thumb. Then, Zack turns on his back and rubs his face. I can't help but chuckle as I watch him still half asleep.

'Good morning.' Zack says, his voice husky.

'Good morning.' I reply, lifting my body on my elbow, placing a sweet kiss on his lips.

'Did you sleep well, darling?' He tucks a strand of hair behind my ear, and I nod eagerly before I kiss him again.

But then, the same feeling comes back. The same one I had the first night that I pushed him away. A tinge of guilt runs through my body, reminding me of another ruined moment. I should talk to him before I jeopardise our relationship.

'Zack?' I sigh and lie down on my back beside him. He turns his face towards mine and I do the same, so we can face each other.

'Yes?' Zack smiles as we just look at each other.

He deserves to know that this is just the way my mind works. I just care so much about what he thinks of me that it becomes overwhelming. I want him, I want to have sex with him, but my thoughts ruin it. I want to be intimate and vulnerable with him. I want him to know all of me. I just need to tear down the wall I built to shield myself from another heartbreak.

'Sorry about yesterday.' I mumble, feeling a rush of embarrassment.

'Don't be silly. Nothing happened.' Zack reassures me, drawing me closer and planting a gentle kiss on my forehead.

'No, I am sorry.' I interject, my voice barely above a whisper. 'It's just... This might sound stupid but...' I pause, nervously biting my bottom lip, searching for the right words.

Zack places his hand under his cheek, patiently awaiting for what I am about to say. His eyes emanating adoration and understanding towards me.

'Okay, so... the reason I stopped when we got closer is because... I am afraid you won't find me attractive.' I admit, my words come out in a rush. 'That you won't like my boobs or my stomach when you see me... fully naked. And I'm scared I won't be that good in bed, honestly. I don't want to disappoint you in any way. It might be because it's happened to me before. I want you to like me. Because I like you... a lot.' I finish, my voice faltering with uncertainty.

'Is that it?' Zack chuckles softly, and I nod. 'Oh, Maddie. I like you a lot too. And trust me, you are gorgeous and very attractive. That's why I can't keep my hands to myself when I am around you. I don't understand why you'd fear that I wouldn't like you when I absolutely adore everything about you.'

'I saw your ex Zack. She was much... better.' I mutter.

'She wasn't you, Maddie. You are perfect to me.' Zack says, looking into my eyes. He moves closer and kisses me briefly. 'We don't have to rush into anything. I was actually a little bit worried that maybe I was pushing too much, but this is how you affect me.'

'No, no, no. I wanted it too, but then it all got in my head and...' I sigh. 'It ruined our moment. But I want it.'

'It's alright. We can wait for the right moment. No pressure, darling.' He smiles softly, staring at me. 'And Maddie, I fancy you a lot. Like a lot. Trust me, you are incredibly attractive and I don't want you to feel insecure around me.'

'Oh, stop.' I chuckle, covering my face with my hands.

I feel my cheeks burning. Zack grabs my hands, moves them away from my face, and kisses me hard. His big hand slowly slides down my body and squeezes my butt.

'So sexy.' He mutters in my mouth and I start giggling. He slightly moves his head away from me, smiling. 'I will make you a nice breakfast. You can stay in bed, and I will be in the kitchen if you need anything.'

Zack slowly gets up, and I follow him with my eyes as he walks around the bed, coming back to my side. I raise my eyebrows and chuckle while he places his hands next to my head and leans forward to kiss me again. I wrap my arms around his neck and try to pull him closer, back to bed, but he breaks the kiss, smirking.

When Zack leaves the room, I lie in the same position he left me, staring at the ceiling. I am so infatuated with him. How could I even doubt him? I want to be around him all the time.

I slowly sit up, looking at the amazing view, wishing I could wake up to this view everyday. I reach for my bag and look at my now slightly creased uniform. It should be fine. It's not that bad. I put on my tights, skirt and tuck my white, long-sleeve shirt in.

The smell of pancakes hits my nose, and my stomach rumbles. I brush my hair and put it in a neat ponytail before I spray myself with perfume.

In the kitchen, Zack stands in front of the stove, flipping another fluffy pancake. I smile and walk towards him. I wrap my hands around his waist and press my cheek against his back. Zack glances at me over his shoulder, smiling.

'It smells nice.' I say, caressing his stomach with my fingers.

'Almost ready.' Zack answers and returns his attention to the pancakes. I kiss his back before moving to the side and leaning on the kitchen counter, enjoying watching him cook. 'You look nice.' He glances at me, scanning me up and down.

'Thank you.'

'Take a seat. I'll bring everything to the table.'

'Okay.' I steal a quick kiss and walk to the table.

The table is already set with two plates, one glass of juice for me, maple syrup, Nutella, and some fruits. I take a seat and shortly after, Zack brings a big plate with pancakes and his cup of coffee. He puts it on the table and sits in front of me.

'This looks delicious' I smile.

'Enjoy.' He smiles back and takes some pancakes for himself.

I take some too and chose several different toppings. I try my best to eat without getting dirty before I have to go to work.

'What are your plans for today?' I ask, munching my food.

'I am going to meet my mates and maybe grab a beer. But I work tomorrow, so I won't stay out late.'

'True.' I nod. 'But you can still have a good time.'

'Of course. And I can brag about my girlfriend.' Zack chuckles.

'No, you don't.' I shake my head laughing.

'Of course I do. I tell them about you all the time and how much I like you.' Zack stares at me.

'I thought guys don't talk about their girlfriends. Like, you know, just a quick mention and that's it.'

'My friends and I chat a fair bit about our girlfriends. Not like we're spilling every detail, but we do talk about our relationships.' Zack chuckles, leaning back in his chair. 'But definitely not as much as you girls.'

'Fair enough.' I nod, a smirk playing on my lips.

'Do you tell your friends about us?' Zack's curiosity piques.

'I do, but Meg's the only one who gets a lot more information.' I chew my lip, glancing at him.

'A lot more information?' His eyebrows shoot up. 'What do you mean?'

'Well, let's just say, we share… details.' I clear my throat, feeling a blush creep up.. 'There are things I'd rather not know about Jack.' I chuckle, taking a sip of my juice.

'What'd you tell her about me?' Zack's gaze intensifies and I suddenly feel nervous.

'Um… I say good stuff about you, honestly. And I admitted how I've messed up every intimate moment we've had because she knows me and why I am like that.' I admit, glancing down at my food and fidgeting with my fork.

Zack's silence is unnerving until he bursts into laughter, and I breathe a sigh of relief.

'Did you really tell her about it?' Zack asks, amused.

'I just needed someone to talk to, to get some advice.'

'And what did she tell you?' Zack asks, intrigued.

'She really likes you and thinks you're a good guy for me, so she told me to explain how I feel and why I act that way. She was sure you'd understand and wouldn't dump me because of it.'

'Jesus, I wouldn't dump you because of it, Maddie.' Zack reassures me with a heartfelt smile. 'I like you too much to let something like this ruin my chance with you. I was worried, thinking maybe you were nervous about it all, and I was pushing too hard.' Zack shrugs, his concern melting away my worries.

Zack stands to clear the table, but I stop him, grabbing his hand.

'I got it. You go get ready.' I smile, rising from my chair. 'I will clean it.'

'No, it's fine. I'll do it.'

'Least I can do after you've cooked dinner and breakfast.' I stand in front of him, cupping his face and placing a soft kiss on his lips. 'It's fine.' I smile at him.

Zack hesitates, thinking about it for a while, but then he heads to the bedroom, leaving me to tidy up.

I pick up the plates and bring them back to the kitchen. As I stack the plates, I steal glances at the view of London outside. This part of London feels very different from where I live. I wipe the table with a cloth, then walk towards the bedroom door and knock.

'Come in.' Zack's voice invites me in, so I open the door. He smiles at me when I walk in and close the door behind. 'You don't have to knock, you know that, right?' He chuckles.

'I'll try to remember.' I smile.

Zack is dressed in all black – jeans and a sweater. He pushes his hand through his hair, leaving it a bit messy. The smell of his strong cologne floats around the room as he sprays it on his neck and sweater. I grab my bag, secretly enjoying the scent.

'What time are you going to see your friends?' I ask, watching him type on his phone.

'I think around five or six.' Zack puts his phone in his pocket and walks closer to me.

'You look very nice.' I compliment him and close my eyes when he kisses me. Zack places his hands on my hips and pulls me closer to him. He showers me with kisses, and I can't help but start laughing, tilting my head back. His bristly stubble tickles my neck, making me laugh louder, so I grab his face and slowly push him away. 'Zack, I need to go to work.' I remind him. Zack still holds me tight, a big smile on his face, and I feel like his eyes shine as he looks at me.

'Don't go.' Zack murmurs, his hands gently resting on my hips.

'You're seeing your friends tonight.' I remind him, slowly moving my hands down to his chest, maintaining flirty eye contact.

'I can cancel.' He offers a pleading look in his eyes.

'I'll see you on Friday. It'll only be three days.'

'I can't wait. Oh, and we will watch my movie this time.' Zack smirks.

'Fine. And now, I really have to go before I am late.'

'I will drive you, baby. Come on.' Zack insists, leaning in for a kiss.

We leave the bedroom, and Zack helps me with my coat before we step out into the chilly air. He puts the heating on as soon as he starts the car, and I turn the radio on.

As always, Zack holds my hand while driving, and I enjoy the view outside the window. The warmth of the car and Zack's hand in mine make me wish I could stay with him instead of heading to work.

We arrive at my workplace, and Zack parks his car in front of the building.

'Message me when you get home, okay?' I look at him.

'Okay, and you message me when you get home from work.' Zack requests, brushing his hand against my cheek.

'Okay. Have fun with your friends.' I smile and lean in for a quick kiss before getting out of the car. 'Bye Zack.'

'Good luck, Maddie.' He smiles before I close the door.

When Zack drives away, I walk into work and greet my friendly coworkers before heading to the staff room to put away my things.

The day is incredibly busy, and I run between tables taking

orders and bringing food and drinks. Luckily, time flies by quickly, and I can't even think about anything or speak to anyone because everyone is running around trying to serve each table. There is a table full of obnoxious businessmen, and how lucky of me to serve them, but I try my best to ignore their arrogance and keep on smiling. All I can think about is how bad I want to spit in their food and get my revenge. But I can't do anything. I would lose my job, and I need it.

On my break, I exchange a few messages with Zack and Meg, and their support makes me feel better about the situation. Zack encourages me to drop some soup on their table, and Meg tells me to pee in a cup and then add some drops to their food. Genius but gross! At least it makes me smile and forget about the fact that I have to go back out there in a few minutes.

When my break ends, I take a few deep breaths and put my fake smile on. When this one table leaves, the evening gets much better. The last hour goes before I even notice, and we clean the restaurant. I chat with my colleagues about our day, and I think this is my favourite part of this job. At the end of the day, we share our experiences and just laugh at it while finishing our shifts. When we finally leave the building, I head to the tube station and go straight home.

It's late, and I try to be very quiet when I enter our flat, not wanting to wake up my friends. Jack works a nine to five job, so he needs to get up early Monday to Friday, and Meg always goes to bed early with him when she does morning shifts at the bakery.

Her job is amazing. She was lucky enough to be there when they put the offer out and she took her chance. She quit her old job, so she can't share weird and funny stories with us anymore because the new place is calm and normal.

I take a quick shower, hoping I don't make too much noise and bother my sleeping friends. Dressed in my fresh set of pyjamas, I walk back to my room and wrap myself in my duvet. I send Zack a quick message to let him know I'm home safe before drifting off to sleep.

In the middle of the night, I'm jolted awake by my vibrating phone. I open my eyes, still half asleep, and rub my face. The only light in my room coming from the street lamp outside and my phone. I reach for it, but it stops ringing before I can pick up. The first thing I notice is the time. Three in the morning. Then, I realise I have two missed phone calls from Zack. Panic sets in as I quickly sit upright and unlock my phone. Did something happen to him? Why would he call me that late? My phone rings again, and Zack's name appears before I even dial his number.

'Zack?' I answer quickly, my heart full of worry that something could have happened to him.

'Maddie...' Zack's voice comes through the phone, slightly slurred.

'Oh God... Zack, are you okay?' I press my hand against my chest, my mind racing with worry, and close my eyes.

'Maddie... I am hoooome, darling.' He replies, his words muffled. I feel relief flooding through me at the sound of his voice, knowing he's safe home. I was so nervous.

'Oh, are you drunk Zack?'

'Nooo, I only had a few beers. Only a few.' Zack insists.

'Okay.' I snigger, settling back under my duvet. He's drunk. But he's alright, and that's the most important part. I wonder how he's going to get to work tomorrow. 'Did you have fun with your friends?'

'I miss you.' He totally ignores my question. 'I really miss you. You should have come back to my place. I wish you were here. Eh... I want you next to me.'

'I miss you too. But I'll be over on Friday, remember?'

'Come noooow. No, don't. It's too late for you... you can't travel alone that late. And I am too drunk to drive. But damn, I wish you were here, Maddie.' Zack murmurs, his words trailing off.

'Go to sleep, Zack. It's late for you too. But I am glad you made it home safely.'

'Alright. Have sweet dreams... about me.' Zack chuckles before falling silent.

I wait for him to say anything, but there's nothing. Did he fall asleep?

'Zack?' I whisper, but as an answer, I get his heavy breathing. I smile under my breath. 'Goodnight, Zack.' I keep my voice low and hang up.

Despite the late-night wake-up call, I'm just glad he's home safe.

Chapter Eight

Friday came sooner than anticipated, and my excitement to see Zack tonight knows no bounds. The past three days have been a whirlwind of work, university lectures, and tackling assignments at home. But beside that, I've managed to pull myself together and thanks to Meg's motivational speeches and a dose of inspirational videos, I am finally ready to get intimate with Zack. No more panicking or running away when things heat up between us. I'm ready to embrace this moment with him. I want it and I know he wants it too. Zack's reassurance echoes in my mind, leaving me wondering, what am I waiting for?

In anticipation of tonight, I've even selected a black, lace matching lingerie set. A few days ago, I treated myself to a cute bra with embroidered flowers, perfectly complemented by matching panties. Tonight, they'll finally serve their purpose. Of course, I'll need to freshen up when I arrive at Zack's place. There's no way I'll wear this gorgeous set to work, only to end up smelling like a mixture of food and sweat. Meg insisted I packed my less cutesy, more seductive pyjamas for tonight, so I have my silk navy set in a bag.

Last night, I devoted extra time to my shower routine, ensuring my skin is smooth and smells nice. I'm filled with excitement, ready to fight any negativity trying to ruin our moment tonight. Nothing can ruin this moment, not even my doubts and insecurities. It will be just Zack and I, in our perfect moment.

Work feels unusually quiet today, and time seems to pass painfully slow. Each glance at the clock reveals that only a mere five minutes passed. I still have three agonising hours left before

Zack picks me up. My mind wanders, wondering what he's doing at this very moment. He has the day off, so maybe he's been in bed all day. Then again, Zack is far more active than I am. He's probably at the gym, out for a run, or perhaps even preparing a romantic dinner for us.

As I gaze out the window, rain pelting against the glass, I observe people scurrying to find a place to hide. Recently, the weather has been so bad, and all I want to do is to cocoon myself in bed with Zack, or chat about anything with Meg with a glass of wine or homemade cocktails in front of the TV.

I lose myself in daydreaming these scenarios, imagining a future where university no longer dominates my schedule. A future where I have more leisure time, a stable job, and the freedom to enjoy life's simple pleasures. Well, not that near future since I've only just begun my university journey, but it will be over before I know it. That's what people say. They also say that it's the best time of your life, and I don't know what they've studied because all I get from the university is zero free time, anxiety and never-ending stress.

Later that day, after serving a few more tables, I received a generous tip from an elderly couple celebrating their anniversary. They were so lovely, sharing their love story with me. How he tried so hard to ask her out and she would always reject his offer until one day she said yes, just to make him stop asking and it turned out to be the best date of her life. And they've been together since that day. As I watched them, I couldn't help but envision my future with Zack. Would we continue to go on cute little dates? Would we hold hands across dinner tables, gazing into each other's eyes with the same adoration? Would we laugh together at our memories? Would our future be filled with peace and joy? Will we be happy? And when I picture all these cute scenarios, I feel a warm feeling growing in my heart.

When the clock strikes eight, I make my way back to the staff room to retrieve my bag and get out of here. This is it. The work is done. Now it's time for a better… experience. Something more exciting to do with my boyfriend. Time to finally let down my walls and take the next step in our relationship. I will let Zack see the real me.

Stepping outside, I found the rain has stopped, replaced by a crisp and invigorating breeze. I approach Zack who stands beside his car, a cigarette in one hand and a small bouquet of pink roses in the other.

'Hello sweetheart.' Zack greets me, discarding his cigarette and envelops me in a gentle embrace, lifting me slightly off the ground as he kisses me.

'Hi.' I reply.

'I got these for you.' Zack says, offering the bouquet.

'Aw, thanks.' I say, taking the bouquet and breathing in their sweet scent. 'Any occasion?'

'Do I need one to get my girlfriend flowers?' Zack teases me, raising his eyebrows. 'But I got them from a lovely old lady selling flowers on the street. When I stopped to look at the flowers, she insisted these were perfect for a girlfriend and that you would love them, and, well, she got me.' He chuckles, opening the car door for me.

'That's so sweet, Zack.' I say, planting a kiss on his cheek before settling into the passenger seat.

I've never received flowers from a guy before. Except my dad, but that's different. Zack randomly gives me flowers, saying they remind him of my eyes, something I wore, or just because he thinks I will like them. It makes me feel cherished, knowing there are things reminding him of me.

Zack walks around his car and takes the seat next to me. On the way to his place it begins to rain again, and I am lucky that he picked me up. I am sure that if I had to take the tube the wind would've broken my small umbrella, and I would have arrived at his place drenched.

Zack parks his car and we take the lift up to his flat. I hang my coat beside the door and take off my shoes. I am not going to run around his place with my shoes on like last time. It's so nice and warm here. Zack walks into the kitchen and fills a vase with water for the roses, and I follow him, carefully arranging the flowers.

'Would you like something warm to drink?' Zack's hand brushes against my cheek, but I shake my head.

'No, I'm fine. Thanks.'

'I need to order us some dinner. Do you fancy anything in particular?' Zack asks, his thumb still caressing my cheek.

'Um, maybe some Chinese? Some spring rolls.'

'Only?' Zack chuckles.

'And maybe some sweet and sour chicken.'

'Okay, I will get it then.' He says, giving me a quick kiss before retrieving his phone from his jean pocket.

'I need to take a shower.'

'Sure. Do you need anything?' Zack glances up from his phone.

'No, I think I'm okay.'

'Call me if you need anything.' He winks, and I snigger before disappearing into the bathroom.

Well, I didn't think this through. Eating dinner in my pyjamas seemed fine until I remembered I opted for the sexy set tonight. Changing my mind now would be awkward, and I really need a shower, so I have to go with it.

I jump in the shower and use Zack's shower gel because it turns out I forgot mine. Just great. Looks like I am going to smell like my man tonight. Despite this minor inconvenience, nothing will derail my plans for tonight, not even the lingering scent of masculinity on my skin.

I dress in my chosen underwear and pyjamas, using my phone camera to check my appearance since the mirror is steamed up. Wiping the steam would leave marks all over the mirror, so it wasn't an option. I pick up my stuff and sneak into his bedroom. I can't shake the feeling of self-consciousness, as this outfit reveals more of my body shape and flaws than the pyjamas that Zack has seen me wear.

Taking a deep breath, I join Zack in the kitchen. He smirks as he watches me approach, sipping his water. I know he likes what he sees because I can feel my skin burn under his intense stare.

'Food is on its way.'

'Good.' I reply, grabbing a glass and pretending my outfit choice wasn't intentional. Like it wasn't planned at all.

Zack leans against the countertop beside me, watching me intently. I take another sip, and I feel his arm wrap around my waist. He places a soft kiss on my arm, taking a sniff of his shower gel.

'You smell familiar.'

'I forgot my shower gel.' I purse my lips and he laughs, resting his forehead on my arm. His warm breath on my skin sends shivers down my spine.

'It's alright. You can use my stuff.' He reassures, placing soft kisses on my arm, neck, cheek and finally my lips.

I put the glass down and cup his face to extend the kiss. Zack places both of his hands on my hips pushing me against the kitchen cabinet. His body presses against mine as he kisses me more passionately and oh… fuck the food. I want to do this *now*. I want him to take me to bed.

I move my hands down his chest and slide them under his soft sweater. His skin feels so warm and soft. I slowly move my fingers up, feeling his muscles tighten when I touch his body. I want more, I want us to finally go further but the moment is interrupted by his phone ringing.

'I am going to get it.' Zack murmurs before reluctantly moving away.

I'm left longing for his return, my desire for food replaced by an overwhelming desire for him. I want him back here right now. To continue what we were doing seconds ago. It takes me a moment to pull myself together, while Zack gets the food from a driver and brings it on the table. Running a hand through my hair, I try to calm my racing heart before joining him, eager to resume our evening together.

'What did you do today?' I inquire, taking a bite of my spring roll.

'I had to run a few errands in the city, then I hit the gym downstairs, took a shower, and left to pick you up.' Zack replies with a soft smile. It explains why he smelled so nice and fresh when he picked me up. But the truth is, he always smells nice.

'Busy day, huh?'

'Yeah, but I just couldn't wait for the evening.' Zack says, smiling. I look down, biting my lip to suppress a grin. He's been anticipating tonight as much as I have, I'm sure of it. 'So, how was work?'

'It was pretty boring.' I admit between bites of sweet and sour chicken. 'Hardly anyone showed up because of the weather. It was very quiet.'

'Can't blame them. It's awful out there.' Zack agrees with a shrug.

We chat about his plans to watch the upcoming football game with his friends, while I try some of his duck. He always goes for the more adventurous options, whereas I stick to basics like chicken or noodles. But I am also scared of trying new food and being disappointed if it doesn't taste good.

After dinner, we cuddle on the sofa and Zack puts on the movie he's been wanting to watch with me. Midway through, I stretch out, resting my legs on his lap with my head on a pillow at the end of the sofa. His fingers trail up and down my calves, distracting me from the movie. He continues this for a few minutes.

Eventually, he lies down between my legs, his head on my chest. I run my hand through his hair, enjoying the closeness of our bodies. Zack slides his hands under my back. It feels nice and it doesn't bother me that he makes comments on the movie. He seems so excited to explain everything to me like he's watched it thousands of times, and I guess he did because I caught him quoting the lines.

'Let's go to sleep.' Zack suggests when the movie ends.

'Okay.' I reply, already missing the warmth of his body against mine when he stands up.

I head to his bedroom, Zack following. Before I can get under the covers, he playfully slaps my butt, causing me to gasp. When I turn around to face him, he's just there smirking.

'Sorry, I just had to. You tempted me too much.'

'Of course.' I roll my eyes jokingly.

I get under the quilt and watch Zack undress before joining me. He lies on his back, arms crossed under his head. Should I make the first move, or wait for him? Or maybe I should just tell him to go for it? No, that wouldn't feel right.

'What are you thinking about?' Zack asks, turning to face me.

'Nothing.' I respond, meeting his gaze.

'Okay.' Zack whispers, pushing a strand of hair behind my ear.

I lean in slowly and kiss him. He responds with soft kisses that gradually grow more intense. We resume our interrupted moment from the kitchen, and soon Zack is hovering above me. I run my fingers up his chest and wrap my hands around his neck. I feel the anticipation growing in my body, finally ready for it. Zack gently bites my bottom lip before trailing kisses down my neck. I grasp his hair tightly, feeling his hand move beneath my top, reaching for my breast. His touch feels so good and right. I bite my lip, closing my eyes in pleasure. I smile when his lips meet mine again in a loving kiss.

My chest moves up and down fast as my breathing gets heavier, enjoying Zack's touch. He breaks the kiss and looks me in the eyes. I can feel his hand making its way down to my shorts, and under my panties. Zack maintains intense eye contact, looking for any sign of hesitation in my eyes, but there is none. I want this. It will happen tonight. A quiet moan slips out of my mouth as his confidence grows, his hand venturing between my legs.

'Is it good?' Zack whispers, his breath warm against my skin.

'Yes.' I manage to choke out.

'Good.' He chuckles softly, his focus entirely on ensuring my pleasure.

I feel like my mind is going crazy in reaction to what he is doing to me. I place my hands on his face as we kiss, losing myself in the sensations he evokes. He slowly removes my top, tossing it aside. I watch as he explores my body with his hands, touching every inch of my skin. I don't stop him when he unhooks my bra and throws it next to my top. I feel a bit more confident since the room is dim, but I also prepared myself for this moment.

I don't spot any sight of disgust on his face, or any of the reactions I was worried about. Quite the opposite. His eyes burn with desire and lust as he leans closer, kissing my collarbone. He reaches out to his bedside table, rustling for a while in the drawer until he retrieves a condom. We are both naked now, and I watch him putting it on in the dark. Zack towers over me again, kissing me deeply and I gasp when I finally feel him. I place my hands on his back, pressing my fingers into his skin. My hands wander over his body, reveling in the sensation of his skin beneath my fingertips.

All my worries dissipate because he actually likes me, the *real* me. I can see it in his eyes, and feel it in his touch. His hands are all over me until he grabs my hands, pushing them against the pillow, entwining our fingers. Our eyes meet again and we stare at each other. Our faces close together. Our heavy breathing mixes. I get lost in the moment we've both been waiting for so long.

Afterwards, we lie in bed, not saying anything for a while. Zack places gentle kisses on my lips, still on top of me. I rustle my fingers through his disheveled hair, smiling. He kisses me once again and lies down on his back beside me. I watch him wipe sweat off his forehead with the back of his hand, his chest moving even faster than mine. I place a kiss on his strong torso, and then lips. Zack smiles, sliding his hand through my hair, drawing circles on the back of my head with his fingers.

'How do you feel sweetheart?' Zack asks softly.

'Good.' I reply, mirroring his smile.

'Good.' He chuckles.

'I need to go to the bathroom though.' I add, scrunching up my nose.

'Alright.' Zack laughs, and I sit up, clutching the quilt to my chest.

'Where did you– Where are my clothes?' I look around the bed, and at Zack. He reaches over to the lamp, and turns on the light.

'They're here.' Zack says, bending down from bed and picking up my clothes from the floor.

'Thank you.' I take them from him and dress under the covers. Zack watches me, a wide grin plastered to his face.

'You know we've just had sex? Like I saw you naked?' His teasing tone brings a blush to my cheeks.

'I know.' I reply, meeting his gaze. 'I will be back in a second.' I toddle to the bathroom, his laughter trailing behind me.

I take a quick pee and wash my hands. Taking a moment to collect myself, I smile at my reflection in the mirror. We did it. Finally! And it was incredible.

I wash my face with cold water, trying to get rid of the redness on my cheeks, and fix my hair before I return to Zack's bedroom.

Zack lies down on his back, his arms crossed beneath his head, watching me coming back to bed. He looks relaxed and comfortable.

'Come here.' He smiles warmly, inviting me to join him under the quilt. Nestling beside him, I rest my head on his arm as he wraps the quilt around us, showering my lips with gentle kisses. 'You are so beautiful Maddie.' Zack murmurs, his eyes tracing every feature of my face.

Though he's complimented me many times before, tonight feels different, sending my heart aflutter. I return his affection with a brief kiss, running my fingers through his hair, pushing it away from his forehead. He's so handsome. Zack places his hand on my wrist, rubbing it with his thumb. Well, I definitely feel like the luckiest girl in the world.

'What are you thinking about?' Zack asks with his deep voice.

'Oh, just… things.' I reply, resting my head on his chest.

'Like what?' He kisses the top of my head while playing with my hair.

'How you made me feel tonight.' I admit, clearing my throat.

'And?'

'Well, I had nothing to worry about with you all along. All the things I told you before… They seem so ridiculous and stupid now.' I sigh.

'I didn't lie when I told you how much I like you.'

'I know.' I say.

'You are perfect to me, Maddie.' Zack reassures me and I gaze up at him, his sincerity evident in his eyes.

'Thank you.' I smile.

'And sooo sexy.' Zack adds, playfully squeezing my butt.

'Zack!'

'What?' He laughs.

'You've just ruined such a cute moment.'

'Did I?' Zack leans in, pressing his body against mine, his lips capturing mine in a passionate kiss.

'Mhm.' I mutter, wrapping my hands around his neck as he hovers above me, trailing kisses down my neck.

'Zack, I need to go to sleep.'

'No, you don't.' He bites my skin gently, and I whimper.

'I work tomorrow.' I say, trying to resist the temptation to indulge in another round of intimacy. I really do have to get some rest if I want to function at work tomorrow.

'Do you want to come back to my place after?' Zack suggests, kissing my nose with a charming smile.

'I close.' I remind him.

'I will pick you up.'

'I need fresh clothes.'

'We can stop at your place.' Zack gives me his gorgeous smile and I can't help but giggle at all the answers he has prepared.

'I will think about it.' I reply, resting my head on his chest as he lies beside me.

'Alright.' He whispers, nuzzling into my hair.

We both know I'll end up at his place after work, ready to relive the wonderful moments we shared tonight. And I wouldn't mind if it happened again.

'Goodnight, Zack.'

'Goodnight, Maddie.' Zack murmurs, playing with my hair. I place my hand on the side of his neck and close my eyes.

Despite my insecurities, being with Zack feels like finding a safe space in the chaos of my doubts and fears. I feel good when I am with him. I feel happy next to him. And I guess… this is it.

Chapter Nine

My relationship with Zack is thriving, and I sense it deepening with each passing day. I was worried about us because of our hectic schedules, particularly mine, and that we wouldn't work out. Yet, here we are, nearly seven months strong, and we are doing great.

We spent New Year's Eve together, and I finally had my midnight kiss. Then came Zack's birthday, which he celebrated with his friends during the evening when I was working, and spent the other one with me. I greeted him with a homemade dinner and my first attempt to give him a blowjob. I will never forget Zack's face when I swallowed it, and how I thought I would throw up. Zack's reaction? Pure amusement. He knew it was my first time, and despite my lack of experience, he assured me that I did a great job. I became more confident with more practice and Zack seems to be satisfied every time, so maybe I am not that bad at it.

Zack is literally the sweetest boyfriend on this planet. He tries to help me with my studies whenever he can, and supports me all the time. Also, I think Meg and I got used to studying by now, and I'm doing better, so I feel confident that I won't fail my first year.

Zack suggested we go on a trip during our break at university in April, and after discussing all the details with Meg and Jack, we started planning everything. Honestly, I thought it would never work because of our jobs and different schedules, but it all worked out perfectly! And just like that, we arrived two days ago and are here, to enjoy our week in Naxos.

I'm already in love with Greece. It's so beautiful here, and the small house we rented is so cozy and cute with this amazing view of the island and the water glittering in the sun. Surprisingly, it was cheap too. I just want to stay here forever.

It's our first vacation together, shared with our friends, Meg and Jack, making it feel like a long double date. We came here to have fun together, relax, and make some memories. Meg and I actually had the great idea to spend a few evenings separately, allowing each couple some time alone. Tonight it will be just Zack and I.

Zack is still asleep, spooning me, and I enjoy the feeling of his body pressed against mine. I gently brush his arm with my fingers. Suddenly I sneeze interrupting my reverie, and I wake up Zack.

'Morning, babe.' Zack greets me with a husky laugh as I turn to face him.

'Morning.' I reply, kissing his lips. He tightens his arms around me, and I savour the warmth of his embrace as he pulls me on his chest.

'Do we need to get up any time soon?'

'Not yet. We can stay in bed a little bit longer.'

'Perfect.' Zack smiles, closing his eyes again.

'Are you going back to sleep?' I titter.

'No, I just want to relax a bit longer, with my eyes closed.' He pats my butt, and I shake my head, smiling.

'Okay.' I reply, resting my head on his chest. I move my hand up to his hair and play with them, listening to his calm heartbeat 'Recently you have been so lazy on your days off.' I mumble, making him giggle.

'Said the person who wants to sleep all day on her days off.' Zack says with his teasing tone.

I sit up with my legs around his waist. He opens his eyes, looking at me with a smirk.

'Very funny.' I snort, crossing my arms. Zack puts his hands on my thighs, drawing small circles on my skin with his thumbs.

'Oh, are you mad?'

'Maybe.' I raise my eyebrows.

Zack sits up too, our faces inches away. He attempts to kiss me but I tilt my head to the side, avoiding the kiss. Zack seems amused with the game we are playing and continues.

'No kisses?' Zack tightens his grip on my thighs. I shake my head and keep playing my role. 'Maybe just one?' He suggests, leaning in once more for a kiss, only to find me evading him yet again. 'Alright then. I have my own ways.' He declares mischievously.

With a swift manoeuvre, I find myself on my back, emitting a surprised squeak as Zack seizes my hands, pinning them to the mattress, and begins showering my neck with kisses. I bite my lip, relishing the sensation of his lips trailing over my skin. Damn him!

He knows exactly what to do, exploiting my weakness shamelessly. I try to enjoy it secretly, pretending to be unimpressed, but my body betrays me when a soft moan escapes my lips as his touch ignites a fire within me. His lips continue their journey, trailing from my neck to my collarbone, his hand slipping beneath my top to caress my breast, giving it a gentle squeeze.

Slowly, he moves the kisses up my jawline, cheeks and finally captures my lips in a passionate kiss. This time, I don't avoid it, and let him kiss me. I push my hand into his hair, tangling my fingers around the strands, and place the other one on the back of his neck.

'Jesus, Maddie.' Zack groans against my lips, his hips pressing eagerly against mine as he deepens the kiss. Zack's hand finds my leg, pulling it to rest against his hip as our kisses grow more fervent.

Just when things heat up, there is an unwelcome knock on the door, interrupting our make out and groping session, eliciting an irritated groan from me.

'What?' I bark in frustration. Zack lies down beside me on his back, and I sit up on the bed.

'Are you still in bed?' Meg appears in the doorway, her eyebrows raised in amusement.

'No, we went for a run.' I retort sarcastically, earning a chuckle from Zack.

'Wow, very funny, Maddie.' Meg rolls her eyes, stepping further into the room. 'Jack got us a boat ride that leaves in an hour, so you better get ready. Unless you two have better plans.' Meg adds with a smirk.

'Give us ten minutes. Close the door, please.' I instruct,

gesturing for her to leave before turning back to Zack as Meg exits the room.

'Looks like we have to get ready now.' I say, giving Zack a quick kiss before rising from the bed. 'Come on.' I urge, glancing at him still lying there, his eyes moving up and down my body.

'I need some help.' Zack declares, extending his hand towards me. I reach for it, but before I can assist him, he playfully pulls me back into bed, and I chuckle.

'We need to get ready, Zack.'

'We have ten minutes.' He counters, peppering my lips with a few quick kisses before finally releasing me so we can get ready. I find myself torn between the allure of the boat ride and the temptation to linger in bed with him, indulging in more intimate activities.

I slip into my yellow thigh-split floral dress and a pair of white sneakers, while Zack stands in front of the mirror in his beige shorts and white top, fixing his hair. Standing beside him, I brush my hair and steal glances at him, admiring my man.

As I apply sunscreen on my pale face to avoid getting a sunburn, I catch his admiring smile in the mirror and smile back.

'What?'

'You look beautiful.' Zack murmurs, enveloping me in his embrace from behind and planting a tender kiss on the back of my head. I proceed to do my light makeup, cocooned in his warmth, as he watches me with affection. 'Ready?' He asks, placing his hands on my hips and resting his chin on my arm.

'Yes, but wait.' I reply, grabbing my phone. 'I want to take a picture of us.' I smile as I open the camera.

'Go for it.' Zack holds me close for the picture and nuzzles his face into my hair. I quickly snap a photo of our reflection in the mirror and show him.

'I love it.'

'Yeah, we definitely look good together.' Zack agrees with a smile and I scrunch up my nose, earning a kiss right away.

'Let's go.' I suggest.

Zack takes my hand, intertwining our fingers as we leave the room to join our friends in the kitchen.

'What do you think if we have breakfast by the harbour and then head straight to the boat?' Jack proposes, checking his phone. 'There's a restaurant close by, so maybe we can eat there and then walk like five minutes to the boat.'

'I like that idea.' Meg says, casting a glance at us, to which I respond with a smile and a nod of agreement. Zack chimes in his approval, sealing our decision. 'Okay, let's go then!' Meg exclaims, clapping her hands in excitement.

As Meg and Jack take the lead, Zack and I follow behind, hand in hand. Zack laces our fingers together and I smile, looking at him. I try to capture everything, taking pictures of the views on our way, and candid shots of Zack and my friends. Zack chuckles and playfully sticks out his tongue when he catches me attempting to photograph him once again. He's utterly adorable.

Upon our arrival at the restaurant, we manage to secure a table just before more people arrive. A friendly waiter presents us with menus, and I try to choose something. We all want to try everything, but have to decide only on a few things that we can share.

Zack's arm finds its place on the back of my chair, his fingers tracing patterns along my arm as he chats with Jack about their mutual friends. Meg and I exchange amused glances and silent jokes.

When the waiter brings out the assortment of dishes we ordered, I'm taken aback by the amount of food in front of us. Everything looks so good, and I can't wait to try a little bit of everything. Excitedly, I load up my plate with a variety of food and taste it. Oh, it's even better than it looks.

'I am so full.' I say, placing my hand on my stomach once I've finished my meal. 'But at the same time, I want more. It's so good.'

'I know what you mean.' Meg agrees, dabbing her mouth with a tissue. 'That bread was so fresh and crispy. I need to take some back to London.'

'Good idea.' I nod in agreement. We would love to have some of it for breakfast back home.

'So, are you both going to take bread back with you as a

souvenir?' Zack laughs.

'They are like that, mate.' Jack chimes in, tittering.

'Men.' I roll my eyes at Meg, and she giggles.

'I really liked the keik.' Zack adds, planting a kiss on my cheek. 'We can buy one on our way back, huh?'

'We will get some before our flight back.' I assure him.

'Now that everyone is happy and full, I think we should leave. Our boat leaves in ten minutes.' Jack announces, wiping his hands and settling the bill before ushering us out of the restaurant.

Jack suggested that it would be easier if he paid for everything. He volunteered, and by the end of each day we transfer him the money. I can't help but feel a pang of concern about the trip's expenses, worried it might cost me my whole maintenance loan in the end.

As we approach the harbour, I'm struck by the sight of dozens of boats bobbing gently on the water's surface. We take a smaller and modest one. It's enough for us. And honestly, knowing Jack I was worried he would try to impress us by taking us on a big fancy boat, and that I would have to sell my kidney to pay him back.

Zack holds my hand, helping me board and we settle onto a white cushioned seat on the front deck. Zack wraps his arm around me, and I lean into his embrace, resting my head on his shoulder.

'Do you feel like you're in *Mamma Mia*?' Zack whispers in my ear, making me smile. He remembers. Oh, and it reminds me that I actually never forced him to watch it.

'A little bit. I might just need a bunch of men singing and dancing for me.' I reply, making him laugh. 'But actually, you know what?'

'Huh?'

'This one is more than enough for me.' I whisper, placing a finger over his heart. Zack's smile widens, and he leans in to kiss me.

'Get a room!' Meg's voice interrupts from the other side of the boat, prompting me to playfully flip her off.

Jack brings everyone a glass of champagne, and we raise our glasses in a toast to the wonderful time we're having in Greece.

During the boat ride, I cuddle with Zack as we watch the

breathtaking views and the crystalline waters beneath us. His arms feel like the safest place in this world, providing me a sense of security and comfort. I close my eyes briefly, enjoying the warm wind tousling my hair. In that moment, I wished for nothing more than for time to stand still.

The hour-long journey passed by in what felt like the blink of an eye. As we sail past a lively party boat, pulsating with music and laughter, Meg and I make a pact to reserve it for our next vacation, and the boys protest right away. I'm grateful for Jack's idea, as it granted us an unforgettable experience.

After disembarking, we leave the harbour, heading back to the beach and walking close to the water. I kick off my shoes and tuck my phone safely between my breasts before venturing towards the water. The warmth of the sea lapping at my feet is inviting, tempting me to take a swim. Well, I wish I had a swimsuit. The rest of the group follows me, and does the same.

Out of nowhere, Zack bends down and splashes me with water.

'Zack!' I squeak, watching him break into laughter.

Oh, he wants to play? I kick the water, sending it cascading over him, drenching his T-shirt and shorts. I chuckle and quickly cover my mouth with my hand.

'You think this is funny?' Zack points at his wet clothes as he edges closer to me. I take a few steps back, keeping an eye on him.

'Leave me alone.' I protest, holding my hands out in front of me to maintain some distance, but he grabs them and pulls me closer to him, enveloping me in a tight embrace. He continues to guide me deeper into the water, and I am forced to follow, my heart racing with apprehension. 'Zack no.' I warn, attempting to push him away. I have a bad feeling about where this is headed, and I don't like the idea. Not when I'm fully dressed and my phone is at risk.

'It's just water, Maddie.' Zack teases, his smirk widening.

'But my phone! It can't get wet.' I protest, anxious.

'We'll get you a new one.' He reassures me with a shrug, pretending to dunk me into the water. I let out a scream, worried that he might actually follow through, but he stops short, holding me securely in his arms as he chuckles.

'Zack, please. That's not funny.' I implore, meeting his gaze with pleading eyes.

'I wouldn't do this to you, baby. Don't worry.' Zack assures me, planting a tender kiss on my neck before releasing me safely from his grasp.

'I know.' I reply with a smile.

It's true. Zack would never intentionally do anything to upset me.

I place my hands on his cheeks, gently rubbing them with my thumbs, and Zack responds with a charming smile that never fails to warm my heart. I feel my dress sticking to my legs and I look down to see that it got wet up to half of my thighs.

Taking Zack's hand, we make our way back to the shore, where he picks up our shoes and carries them in one hand, as we stroll along the beach behind Meg and Jack. Once our feet are dry, we stop to put our shoes back on, and continue our walk around the island.

Along the way, we stop at various spots to take some adorable pictures to capture the joyful moments of our trip. Later, I'll look back at these pictures, remembering myself at this beautiful place and the precious time spent here with Zack and our friends.

'How do you still have memory on your phone?' Jack laughs, returning Meg's phone, after another photoshoot of her.

'I have my tricks.' She flips her brown hair, playfully.

'Meg, can you take some photos of us?' I pass Meg my phone and pull Zack to the picture.

'Alright.' Zack smiles, wrapping his arm around me.

'We need one with this beautiful view.' I say, gesturing towards the stunning scenery behind us with all the white houses dotting the hillside, the shimmering water reflecting the sunlight, the crystal blue sky, and the tiny boats floating on the water.

'That's beautiful.' Zack agrees.

We stand looking at each other while Meg takes pictures of us. Zack plants a kiss on my forehead in one shot and my lips in another. Then, he graces me with that adoring smile, the smile he always has when I am focused on doing something and catch him watching me, or when I share something good that happened during the day. It's the smile that says he loves me. Even though he's never said that to me, neither have I.

As Meg hands me back my phone, I scroll through the images she's taken. We do look good together. I show Zack my favourite picture, the one where he kisses my forehead.

'I like this one.' Zack says, sealing his approval with a kiss to my temple.

'You guys are so adorable.' Meg says, smiling warmly at us. 'I'm already hungry. Should we grab a small lunch or something?'

'Yeah, I am hungry too.' Jack adds, patting his stomach in agreement.

This time, we decide to find a random place along the way and end up in a small restaurant by the water. It's very lively and I feel like there won't be any open tables, but Jack really wants to try it after looking at their menu. When we ask for an available table, the waiter leads us outside to a table other people have just left, and he quickly cleans it for us. The table is situated by the edge of water and has this breathtaking view on the island. Once again, we're treated to a delightful Greek cuisine.

'I could stay here forever.' I say, gazing at my friends who seem equally enchanted by the scene.

'Me too.' Meg chimes in, taking a picture of the view.

'Tomorrow we definitely have to go swimming.' I declare, taking a sip of water.

'You didn't seem eager to swim today.' Zack jokes and I glare at him. He chuckles and plants a kiss on my cheek. 'It's true, darling.'

'I was just not ready. But tomorrow I will be.' I reply, smiling as Zack lifts my hand to place a soft kiss on the back of it.

'So, should we go back and get ready for dinner?' Jack suggests, wrapping his arm around Meg.

'Sure.' Meg agrees, checking the time on her phone. 'Are you going to head back as well or are you going to stay around here?' She asks, directing her gaze at us. Zack and I share a glance before responding.

'I think we are going to stay around here.'

'Yeah, we don't have any plans.' I shrug, smiling at my friend.

'But you two enjoy your dinner.'

We all leave the restaurant together, and outside, we say our goodbyes to Meg and Jack, who head back to the hotel to get ready. Zack and I go for a walk, holding hands, walking around charming streets lined with white buildings. There are green plants and trees with pink flowers everywhere. The colourful doors and windows break the white pattern of the walls.

We stop for ice cream and find a spot to sit on a white, concrete-like half wall.

'Why does everything taste better here?' I muse, offering Zack a taste of my fruity-flavoured ice cream.

'Yours is better than mine.' He admits, and lets me try his. Indeed, mine is better.

'Sorry, babe.' I tease. 'But I can share with you.' I offer to share my ice cream with him, which he gladly accepts before stealing a kiss.

'Why are you so adorable, Maddie?' Zack gazes at me, his eyes filled with affection.

'Am I?' I chuckle, feeling warmth spread through me.

'Mhm…' He murmurs, drawing in closer to kiss me. I kiss him back, placing my hand on his cheek.

I am so in love with him. And my love for him grows with each day. It is crazy how quickly I fell for him but… how could I not? He is everything I could ever imagine. Although, there is this one thing that worries me. Neither of us said those three words. I was hoping he would say it first, and also I didn't want to say it too quickly. But we've been together for a long time now, and I just hope he loves me back. Maybe, I need to gather my courage, and be the first one to say it.

Later, we make our way back to the hotel and decide to grab dinner on our way back, because I want to watch the sunset from our balcony. I try not to complain, but my legs hurt so much and I don't know if I can walk anymore. But I keep going.

'How far are we?' I inquire when Zack checks the map on his phone.

'Thirty minutes, walking.' He replies, causing me to halt in surprise.

'What? How far have we walked?'

I had thought we were only ten minutes away at most. The exhaustion hits me like a wave, and I struggle to keep going. I can't feel my legs anymore.

'Are you okay?' Zack looks at me, worried, and I just nod. 'Are you sure?'

'My legs really hurt.' I admit.

'I can see. I will carry you.' Zack offers, smiling.

'No, I'll be fine.'

'Come on, just for a little bit.' Zack insists, crouching down in front of me, and he gives me a chance to jump on his back.

I hesitate at the beginning, but then, wrap my arms around his neck slowly climbing on his back. I wrap my legs around his waist as he slowly gets up keeping his balance. Zack holds my legs and starts walking, and I rest my chin on his shoulder.

'You are the best boyfriend in the world, you know?' I declare, gazing at him and admiring his cute little smile.

'Thank you. Anything for you, babe.' Zack gives my thigh a gentle squeeze.

'Awww.' I plant a kiss on the back of his neck. 'Let me know if you get tired, then I can carry you.' I offer, earning a hearty laugh from Zack.

'Alright, I will.' He agrees, continuing to walk with me glued to his back. As we stroll, I gently rub his chest beneath his top while we talk about our dinner ideas.

We stop at a nearby restaurant and place the takeaway order. Zack collects the food, and we make our way back to the hotel, holding hands again.

Upon reaching our hotel, we take a seat on the balcony to watch the sunset. As the sky blushes with hues of pink and orange, I rise from my chair to lean against the railing. Zack joins me, wrapping his arms around me, and resting his chin on my shoulder. I move my hand back, placing it on his cheek, and he kisses it.

'I love you, Maddie.' Zack says. Finally the three words I've been waiting to hear, and I freeze in astonishment. Did he really say that or did I imagine that? My heart races with excitement and I turn around, but before I can say anything, he repeats himself. 'I love you so much, Maddie.' Zack says with a serious, thoughtful expression, and I can't help but smile.

He did say that! I grab his face, kissing him hard. Zack responds by drawing me closer, his hands resting on my hips.

'I love you, too. Very, very much.' I mutter between kisses.

Zack presses his forehead against mine, and I chuckle. I stare into his beautiful brown eyes, where I find the confirmation of his love for me. I mean I always thought he loved me, but now I know. Zack loves me.

'You have no idea how happy you make me.' He confesses, his smile lighting up his face, and I feel my cheeks get warm. I hide my face in the nook of his neck and he chuckles, holding me tight. Zack kisses the top of my head, softly caressing my back. 'Let's finish dinner.'

'Okay.' I smile and we return to the table.

Zack pulls his chair closer to mine and rests his hand on my back. Throughout the meal, Zack cracks jokes, making me laugh, and I nearly choke on my food.

We stay outside a little longer, wrapped in each other's arms, before finally tidying up and heading back indoors. Zack stands behind me, his hands resting gently on my waist as he softly kisses my neck, while I wash our glasses. Tilting my head to the side, I give him better access, and dry my hands with a kitchen towel, enjoying his lips on my skin. Zack moves his hands to my stomach, then higher to cup my breasts, giving them a gentle squeeze.

'Zack.'

'We're alone.'

He turns me around so that I face him, my back against the kitchen counter. His eyes are filled with desire, and I can feel the sexual tension rising between us. I stare into his eyes as he moves closer, and our lips meet in a fiery kiss. I wrap my hands around his neck as he deepens the kiss and presses his body against mine. Tension crackles in the air, and I know I can't resist him any longer.

'Zack…' I gasp, my words lost in his mouth.

'Hm?' He murmurs, his lips still on mine.

'Bedroom.' I manage to say, before he lifts me effortlessly, his hands gripping my hips, and carries me to our bedroom.

Gently, he sets me down on the bed, his eyes never leaving mine as he hovers over me. Zack leaves kisses along my neck and collarbone, his fingers pulling the straps of my dress down my arms. I reach for the hem of his T-shirt and pull it over his head, our desire for each other intensifies with every passing moment. It's time to finish what we started in the morning. I want him so much.

My hands are all over his body as his hands are on mine. My breath gets heavier as we finally can enjoy ourselves. It's tender, yet intense. It feels so good. The closeness, the passion, and the true love between us. It's just perfect. And I lose it when he moans my name into my ear, his grip on my hands tightening. I know that this is where I belong, in his arms.

I nestle against his chest, listening to the steady rhythm of his heartbeat as he plays with my hair, whispering sweet words and how much he loves me. I look up at the man I love, knowing that I couldn't imagine my life without him by my side.

Chapter Ten

The next morning, I wake up with a smile, wearing Zack's T-shirt. Sunlight floods the room, casting a warm glow, while a gentle breeze stirs the curtains, filling the space with freshness. I rub my eyes, stretching, before turning to find Zack already awake, his gaze fixed on me with an affectionate smile.

'Good morning.' He murmurs in his husky voice.

'Hi.' I reply, propping myself up on my arm to lean in and kiss him briefly. Zack's hand slides under my T-shirt, his fingers tracing patterns along my back.

'How are you feeling?'

'Great.' I grin. Zack meets my gaze, a hint of gratitude dancing in his eyes. 'What?' I chuckle.

'Nothing.' He shakes his head, smiling.

'Tell me.' I insist, gently lifting his chin to meet my eyes.

'It's nothing, Maddie.' He says, his eyes searching mine.

'Zack, tell me.' I urge, brushing his cheek with my fingertips.

'I was just thinking about how lucky I am to have you beside me. Waking up next to the person I love.' He admits, clearing his throat.

'Aww, that's so sweet Zack.' I pout. 'And I can say the same.' I add, smiling, as I plant a short but affectionate kiss on his lips. Zack tightens his grip around me, pulling me onto his chest, and we share a chuckle between kisses. 'I love you.' I murmur against his lips.

'I love you, too.' Zack replies, pushing a strand of hair behind my ear. 'A lot.'

We stay in bed for a while, with me lying on his chest and him softly caressing my shoulder. I nestle my face into the crook of his neck, closing my eyes, and cherishing our moment.

'I think we need to get up.' I mutter into his neck after a while. 'And get ready for the day.' I sigh, sitting beside him.

'What's the plan for today?' Zack asks, his hand under my T-shirt, softly rubbing my back, sending shivers down my spine.

'We are going to the beach, and then I guess we'll have dinner together with Meg and Jack.' I reply, gazing at him as I run my hand through his soft hair. 'Get up, Zack.' I urge him with a smile.

Admiring how cute he looks with his disheveled hair, I feel a pang of desire to stay cuddled up in bed with him all day. But I have to remind myself that we are on a vacation. We're in Greece! We have to enjoy our time here while we have it.

I rise and slip into my white velvet underwire bikini top and matching bottoms, throwing on an oversized white shirt. Holding my matching trousers, I turn to Zack, seeking advice.

'Can I just wear the shirt, or should I put on trousers too?'

'It's hot outside.' Zack replies, buttoning his red shorts with a smirk. 'Go like this, and we can come back for your trousers before dinner or just take them with you in your beach bag.' He suggests drawing closer and pulling me closer to him. 'You look very sexy, Maddie.'

'Oh, stop!' I laugh, tilting my head backwards.

'Well, that's true.' Zack admits, kissing my neck.

'Are you taking a T-shirt with you?' I ask, running my hands up and down his bare chest.

'I can take one for later just in case we won't come back.'

'I can take it for you. And you need some sunscreen.' I say, scrunching up my nose, and making him chuckle. 'I have it in my bag already, so I can put it on you at the beach. I don't want you to get sunburned.'

'I like that idea.' Zack nods, giving me a quick kiss before we leave the room and go to the kitchen. 'Are Meg and Jack coming?'

'I think so.' I shrug.

I don't even know what time they got back yesterday because I was too busy with Zack, and fell asleep afterwards. I check the time on my phone. 'We can wait for them and then go get breakfast.' I suggest, and Zack nods.

Outside, we settle onto two sun loungers, and I scroll through our photos from yesterday, showing Zack my favourite ones, while he rests his hand on my thigh. We choose one picture together and I post it on my story, followed by photos of the views, some with Meg, and a picture of all of us, enjoying our time in Greece.

'Send them to me.' Zack says, turning his airdrop on, and I quickly select all the pictures I took of him and the ones we have together, and send them to him.

Once Meg and Jack join us, we leave the hotel and head to grab breakfast. This time, we try some new dishes at a different restaurant near the beach. I sip on my fresh orange juice, enjoying the warm breeze and Zack's gentle touch on my knee under the table. As we indulge in a selection of bread, pastries, fruits, and yogurts, I wish every morning could be like this.

Satisfied, we head to the beach, where Meg finds a perfect spot with rounded hay umbrellas, sun loungers, and a beach bar. Perfect place for our chill afternoon.

Dropping my beach bag on a sun lounger, I take off my shirt and start searching for the sunscreen in my bag.

'There it is.' I announce, taking out the small tube of sunscreen. Zack watches me carefully, anticipating my request for help. 'Do you want to help with my back?'

'Sure.' He replies with a smirk, and he sits behind me.

Zack seems to enjoy his little task of applying sunscreen, covering more than just my back. He spreads it everywhere he can touch me: my back, stomach, arms, legs, and of course, my chest. I don't protest, allowing him to take care of the job, and then I return the favour.

Zack and I, along with Meg and Jack, take turns going into the water, ensuring someone is always watching our belongings. While my friends play in the water, I lie on my back, trying to catch some sun on my pale skin, with Zack on the adjacent sun lounger.

'Do you want a drink?' Zack asks after a few minutes, and I turn my head to look at him.

'Sure.' I reply, smiling.

'I'll get some for those two as well.' He says, pointing at Jack and Meg, who are making their way towards us, then he heads to the bar.

'Where did he go?' Meg asks, taking a seat on the sun lounger and drying her hair with a towel.

'To get us some drinks.' I reply, watching Zack head to the bar.

The woman behind the bar tries to flirt with him, pushing her breasts towards him. I roll my eyes at the tacky move. Zack patiently waits for our drinks, despite her attempts to gain his attention. I feel anger rising within me as I watch her obvious interest in Zack. So desperate. There's no need to play with her hair so much in front of him.

I clench my jaw because I can see she fancies him. But he's taken! I try to resist the urge to confront her. I don't want to play the jealous girlfriend, or make a scene. But should I? That's *my* boyfriend, and it makes me furious.

Before I can decide, Zack returns with the drinks. I try not to be upset, but the words escape my mouth as he sits beside me.

'Did she try to sell you drinks or her boobs?' I ask, taking a drink from him. Zack bursts out laughing, and my friends join in. I look at them all with a serious expression, trying to understand what's so funny? 'What? I saw it.' I growl.

I feel the urge to march over there and tell her to back off from *my* boyfriend. She can forget about it. And maybe throw that big orange from the bar right in her face.

'Are you jealous, Maddie?' Zack looks at me with a smirk, wrapping his arm around me.

'No.' I roll my eyes, slurping my drink.

'I think you are, babe.' Zack teases, grabbing my chin and turning my head to face him. 'I absolutely didn't pay attention or care what she was doing. I just wanted to get a drink for my girlfriend.' He gently brushes his thumb over my chin. 'And why would I bother when you are the only woman I love and care about?' He says in a lower voice, so only I can hear.

We lock eyes for a moment, and I smile, unable to hold onto my anger.

'I wasn't jealous.' I insist, and Zack chuckles again.

'Yes, you were.' He kisses my lips.

'I only wanted to go and tell her a few things.' I shrug. 'And I could easily fight her if I had to.' I add, flipping my hair, making him laugh even louder.

I don't actually know if I could, since I've never been in a fight. But if it comes to my man? Who knows. Maybe I'd get a sudden rush of adrenaline.

'And I would definitely cheer for my girl.' Zack says, grinning. I shake my head, smiling, and take another sip of my drink.

'Yours are much better.' I admit, licking my lips.

'Because I make special ones for you.' Zack winks.

'That's my man.' I kiss him briefly and then lie back on the sun lounger, resting my legs on Zack's thighs.

Later, after Meg and Jack go back into the water, Zack and I are left alone. We finish our drinks, and I lie back on the sun lounger, setting my glass aside. Zack does the same and gazes at me before settling between my legs, resting his head on my chest. I play with his hair, watching our friends splashing each other in the sea. Zack's hands slide under my back as he nuzzles into my neck, leaving kisses along the sensitive skin. The sensation of his wet lips against my warm skin sends a shiver through me.

'Do you want to go for a swim?' Zack mumbles after a while.

'Yes, they should be back soon.' I smile, looking at him. Zack lifts his head and kisses me fondly.

'Okay, your turn.' Meg appears next to us out of nowhere, breaking our moment.

Zack and I head to the water, holding hands. The water feels so warm, inviting me to get deeper, so I follow, with Zack behind me. I stop when the water reaches my collarbone and turn to face Zack. We spend some time swimming around, diving, and stealing kisses. And this time, I allow Zack to throw me in the water.

It just feels like we're in paradise, surrounded by crystal-clear water, beautiful beaches, and delicious food.

We spend the rest of our afternoon chilling at the beach, taking turns in the water, and sipping cocktails before we decide it's time for dinner.

Zack was right to take our clothes with us, saving us a trip back to the hotel to change. We just get dressed at the beach, once we are dry, and ready to go, we head to a restaurant located between two white buildings, with outdoor tables and lanterns above. It has this nice, cozy vibe with people chatting and laughing around us. After we take our seats, we order a bottle of wine to start the evening.

Throughout the night, we engage in a variety of conversations and laughter, and I feel grateful for being here with the love of my life and my friends. I share my food with Zack and listen to the story he shares with my friends. Zack catches me staring at him, and I give him my affectionate smile, nibbling on his spanakopita. He returns the smile, planting a quick kiss on my lips.

'You two are perfect together. Right Jack?' Meg looks at her boyfriend for confirmation, and he nods.

'Um… thanks.' I chuckle.

'Hey Zack, do you know the story behind why she hit on you that night?' Meg looks at Zack eager to remind him of the night we first met, taking a sip of her wine.

'What story?' Zack looks at me and then at Meg.

'I forced her to do that.' Meg states proudly.

'Oh, really? Maddie never told me about it.' Zack says, intrigued.

'Yeah. You should have seen her when she spotted you behind the bar and ran to the table to tell me about you. My girl was already in love.' Meg laughs, and I shake my head, laughing along.

'I mean–' I begin, but Meg interrupts.

'I had a plan to secretly ask for your number for her because I didn't actually believe she would do it. But she did! I just needed to give her a few more drinks for courage.' She laughs. Zack seems deeply intrigued by the story of the night he rejected me.

'I couldn't believe it either when they told me. Maddie doesn't do this kind of thing, mate.' Jack confirms, shaking his head.

'Yup, and I got rejected, so thanks for the embarrassment.' I chuckle, swirling the wine in my glass and taking a sip.

'I mean… if I was single the night you asked me out, I would have said yes.' Zack says softly, capturing my attention.

'You had no idea how stressful it was for me to do that. But Meg had her way.' I point at my proud friend.

'Well, I think I should thank you then.' Zack raises his glass towards Meg. 'For making her drunk enough to talk to me.'

'You're welcome, Zack.' She clinks her glass with his.

'And Jack, thanks for bringing them to the party that night.'

'No problem, mate.' Jack laughs.

I watch them all laughing, getting along, and having a great time. I feel grateful to have them in my life. Sometimes I wonder what I did to deserve them.

'Cheers to our wonderful trip!' Meg raises her glass again, and we all clink our glasses.

The night goes well and we reminisce about the party and even times when Meg and I were both single. Jack and Zack tell us how they met through Luke, who is Zack's childhood friend and Jack's friend from work.

'Oh, I remember how she met Jack.' I state, putting down my empty glass, feeling a bit dizzy. 'Meg, you remember?'

'Of course I remember.' Meg groans already tipsy. 'I do.'

'So…' I look at Zack. 'Jack and her went to the same gym, and she noticed him one day and then encouraged me to join too and become her workout buddy. The first thing she does when we get there is to show me Jack running on the treadmill, and she tells me that we need a plan to get his attention. Then, I learned that my mission was not to motivate my friend or work out. My mission was to help her get a guy, so I told her to talk to him and she laughed in my face.'

'I did.' Meg chuckles. 'I needed something bolder, you know? To make a good first impression.'

'Yeah, so for the next few weeks, Meg was intensively thinking how to get his attention even though he already smiled at her! And she could just go and talk to him. Or you could come and talk to her.' I say, looking at Jack.

'I mean, I thought she was cute, but you two were always together and I kind of… you know, wanted some privacy with Meg. I was hoping you would go to the toilet or something. But you never did. Or you would just go together.' Jack titters kissing Meg's cheek.

'So guess what, Zack.' I turn to look at my boyfriend.

'Yes, darling?' He smiles.

'One day, we went on the treadmill and ran next to each other. It was the day Jack didn't show up to the gym on time. Meg thought she's lost her chance. Like she was so upset. But then… he walks in. Seconds later, I am on the floor, and why?' I look at Meg, her face red from laughing. 'She pushed the emergency stop button and I fell off the machine!'

'I am so sorry! My intrusive thoughts won.' Meg chuckles, perplexed.

'I twisted my ankle that day and never went back to the gym after. But she got him in the end.' I point at them with my head.

'So you tried to kill my girlfriend to get Jack's attention?' Zack looks at Meg incredulously. 'I don't know what to think now.' He chuckles softly, putting his hand over mine.

'It wasn't planned! Honestly, I didn't think at that moment. I just acted. I am still sorry about that. I didn't want to hurt you.' Meg turns to face me, abashed.

'It's fine. I know.' I smile at her warmly. Meg grabs my hand over the table and gives me a gentle squeeze.

We've been friends forever, since we were little. I can't imagine my life without Meg in it. All the memories we share, the funny stories, support, and love we have for each other. I could never lose it. I forgave her for the accident a long time ago.

'But the scream was iconic, Jack was next to us within seconds.' Meg adds, laughing, and I join her, nodding.

'Yeah, he took us to the hospital, and when I was getting help, these two were flirting all the time. Totally forgetting about my existence and pain.' I chuckle.

'What a wonderful love story.' Jack muses, drinking his wine.

With more wine in our glasses, I feel more and more dizzy. I rest my head on Zack's arm, and he kisses my hair. And as we listen to Jack and Meg trying to prove who is a better driver, knowing it's Jack, I don't say anything. I enjoy the carefree moment we are sharing right now. I place my hand on Zack's leg, hoping this evening could last forever.

Chapter Eleven

The first year with Zack flew by in a blur, and it's surreal to think we've been together for a year, recently marking our one-year anniversary. Unfortunately, we didn't have a chance to celebrate it the way Zack wanted, so instead, we had a lovely dinner at his place. Which I really enjoyed. Zack wanted to take me abroad but because of university and my new job, we couldn't go. Zack told me that he found a lovely place in Italy, and really wanted to take me there. Seeing the disappointment on Zack's face was heart-wrenching, however, I was happy with the way we celebrated because all it mattered to me was that we had a romantic evening together.

Nevertheless, as I managed to get a weekend off at work, we're going to take the train to Paris and celebrate our anniversary, a month later, in the city of love! And yes, once again, I had to look for a new job over the summer because a change in management made the workplace atmosphere unbearable. It seems that every manager is a dickhead, who likes to make other people miserable.

However, I was lucky enough to secure a receptionist position at a hotel at the beginning of summer, giving me the opportunity to adjust before going back to university. I had feared the job hunt would consume my precious summer moments with Zack, but luckily I got this one fairly quick, giving me the opportunity to spend a lot of time with Zack. Most of the days I spent at his place, interspersed with beach visits and some activities I wanted to do with him, like puppy yoga. And I know he loved this one!

Turns out the second year at university is intense from the beginning, and I see Zack even less than last year. I already had two breakdowns since it started. I just need a long break from everything. I wish I could go back to the carefree days of summer, where time with my boyfriend wasn't a luxury. Hence, that's why I can't wait for us to go to Paris and share our free time with each other.

I've never been to Paris before, and I am very excited about our little adventure. I'm also excited to spend a whole weekend with Zack, leaving behind the worries of university assignments. I made sure I completed everything on time, giving me time to focus on Zack and all the things we are going to do.

As we are leaving tomorrow morning, I'm going to spend this night at his place. I had to take my suitcase to work, and of course, I received a lot of questions from Alex, my new work bestie. She's lovely and knows everything that happens around the hotel, so every time I come to work, she has some gossip for me. Alex was the one who told me the latest gossip about Edward. His fiancée cheated on him and they broke up. They were planning a wedding for next summer! Which is crazy. He was very flirty with all of us recently, and I guess that explains a lot. He is looking for a rebound, or a new lover.

Edward is our manager and he's around ten years older than me. He is charming and good looking, drawing the admiration of all the girls at work, excluding me. I know Alex really likes him, so maybe she will have a chance now. I mean, she's six years younger than him, but it's not that bad. So far, Edward is a great manager, trying to make everything work for all of us. He has a friendly attitude and wants to work in a good atmosphere. And thanks to him and Alex, who changed shifts with me, I can go to Paris with Zack. I know she was happy to change with me, so she can be on the late shift with Edward. Maybe she will have some gossip when I am back. Something might happen between these two. Who knows?

Feeling my excitement growing within me throughout the day, I find myself constantly checking the clock, eagerly awaiting the moment I can finally leave work. I check my phone and see a new message from Zack.

How's the day going? Ready for our weekend?

It's alright. I took everything with me to work. And I am so ready for our weekend in Paris!

I smile, sending him another message filled with heart emojis. I actually hope I packed everything. I packed so much because Meg says I have to be ready for anything. And I just think this might give Zack a small heart attack when he picks me up. Luckily, I managed to pack everything into a smaller luggage than the one Meg suggested.

I will pick you up at 8 :)

I grin at my phone, replying with a kiss emoji. Alex comes to the desk after her break, and I notice she spent some extra time on her makeup today. Her face looks flawless.

'Are you excited about Paris?' Alex smiles, and I nod. 'Girl, you are not going to sleep much this weekend.'

'What?' I chuckle.

'Oh, come on. You are going to Paris with your boyfriend. What do you think is going to happen there?' She raises her eyebrows suggestively, and I feel a blush creeping onto my cheeks. 'It's the city of love, isn't it? Trust me. Been there, done that.' Alex raises her hands up.

'Good to know.' I shake my head, laughing.

'Oh, I can send you some spots where you have nice views without big crowds! You know, skip the touristy areas.'

'Yes, please. That will be helpful.'

'So, did you plan anything, or are you just going to go with the flow?' Alex leans on the desk, interested in my plans.

'I know that on Saturday evening, we're going to take the boat along the Seine. We're going to have dinner there too.'

'You better have a cute outfit for this one because it is hella romantic!' She does a chef's kiss, and I chuckle.

'Yeah, my friend made sure I have something special for this one. We chose an outfit together.'

'I will also send you the location for the best macarons!' She puts her pointing finger on her mouth. 'I just don't remember where it was exactly. Anyway, I will look for it and send you all the details.' Alex adds, smiling.

'That will be lovely. Thanks.' I return the smile. 'Oh, before I go, I have to show you this booking.' I say, as Alex comes behind the desk, and I open the message, explaining the issue.

'What? Who do they think we are? Four seasons?' Alex chuckles. 'It is a good hotel, but we are not that luxurious to welcome them with this expensive as fuck champagne. We don't even sell it in the restaurant. Who are these people?'

'I know, I asked Edward, and he said he will handle this one if there are any problems upon their arrival.'

'I think I can handle them too.' She flips her hair, and I laugh.

'I know you can.' I nod, well aware she can handle literally any situation.

Alex is a strong and confident woman and doesn't let anyone play with her. If it was me, I would be freaking out because I don't like to argue with strangers over something I don't even control.

We gossip for another two hours until I finally finish and head to the staff room to get my luggage. When I return to the front desk, Edward is there with Alex, chatting. She bats her fake eyelashes at him, and Edward smiles. He looks at me when I approach them.

'Thanks again for changing with me, Alex.' I smile.

'No problem, girl! You go have fun in Paris.' She winks in my direction.

'So, you are going to Paris, huh?' Edward asks, eyeing my luggage.

'Yes, with my boyfriend.' I nod and so does he. 'I'll see you next week. Bye!' I wave at them both and leave.

Zack waits for me outside with a big smile on his face as I rush towards him.

'What did you put in there? We are going for two days.' He laughs, seeing my luggage.

'Everything I need for two days.' I scrunch up my nose and welcome him with a kiss. He smells so nice and fresh. Looks like someone finished early and had time to take a shower already.

Zack takes the luggage from me and puts it into the back seat while I take my seat in the car, waiting for him to join me.

'How was work today?' Zack asks, driving away from the hotel.

'Um… boring but alright. How was yours?'

'Busy as hell but I got out early.' He chuckles.

'Managers.' I roll my eyes playfully.

Zack got promoted to be a manager in the middle of summer and he's doing amazing. He's able to arrange better workdays for himself or finish early when he needs to.

'You do whatever you want to, don't you?' I tease him, and he shakes his head laughing.

'I had to. I have something important this weekend and need to get ready for it.'

'Oh, really?' I raise my eyebrows as he gives me a quick glance.

'Yes, I'm taking my girlfriend to Paris. Very important.' Zack says, placing his hand on my thigh, and I reciprocate by placing my hand over his.

Zack drives an automatic car, which allows him to do this all the time. And if I am being honest… I love that.

'Lucky girl.' I rub his hand with my thumb and see him smiling. 'Are you going to work out tonight?' I ask out of curiosity.

'No, I don't have time. Why?'

'Just asking.' I shrug.

It's not like I wanted to watch him hitting the punching bag for like an hour or doing any other exercises. He looks so sexy at the gym, and it's become one of my favourite forms of entertainment. The gym is in his building, and I had a chance to go with him a few times over the summer, but I always got distracted by his presence. And now I'm back to not having time, so I can't come anymore.

'Why?' Zack laughs. 'Did you want to watch your man boxing?'

'Maybe.' I scrunch up my nose.

'You should join me one day.' He suggests.

'Me? Boxing?' I laugh. 'Yeah, imagine.'

'You should try. I think you'll like it. It will help you release all the stress from university and work. And I think you will look very sexy.' Zack winks, parking his car.

'Maybe I will try one day.' I look at him and he just smirks. I roll my eyes playfully, leaving the car.

Zack leaves my luggage next to his when we enter his flat.

'You packed already?' I raise my eyebrows.

'Yeah, I am very organised.' He pulls me closer, placing gentle kisses on my lips.

'I'm starting to think you are more organised than me.'

'Nah, nothing can beat you, your calendar and your obsession with putting things back in their place.' Zack chuckles, so I nudge his arm.

I began doing a share calendar including all my work days, university days, days when I have to study and when I am free, and I shared it with Meg and Zack, so I can arrange my free time with them.

'Very funny.'

'Well, it's one of many things I love about you, so.'

'Aw.' I cup his face and kiss his lips. 'I'm a bit hungry.' I manage to say between kisses.

'Mhm.' Zack murmurs, pushing me against the wall and deepening the kiss.

I smile, sliding my hand in his hair, pulling the strands gently, earning a purr from Zack. It's been a while… I can feel his fingers tightening their grip on the fabric of my uniform skirt, and I slowly push him away. He licks his lips, looking at me.

'Do you want pizza or Chinese?'

'Pizza is alright. I'll take a shower.' I reply, picking up my stuff from the floor and heading to his bedroom to get myself one of his T-shirts, but I stop in front of the painting I gave him for our anniversary.

'You put it on the wall?' I turn around to look at Zack smiling and nodding.

'Of course, I did. I told you, I love it.' Zack comes closer, wrapping his strong arms around me from behind, resting his chin on my shoulder.

One day, we visited an art gallery and he really liked a surreal painting of a couple, a painting depicting the unconditional love of two people, expressing affection and their total devotion. So I found an artist with a similar style, sent a picture of us and he painted it for me. The surprised look on Zack's face is stuck in my memory as he tore off the wrapping and saw it. He was gobsmacked. I bite my lip looking at it and turn around to face him.

'It's actually a very special painting for me.' Zack smiles, giving me a loving kiss.

'I love you.' I whisper, cupping his face as our lips meet in a tender kiss.

'I love you too, babe.' Zack replies, planting a short kiss on the tip of my nose. 'Go take a shower, and I will order us some food.'

'I'll be quick.' I promise, turning to head to the bedroom. I grab one of Zack's T-shirts and make my way to the bathroom.

Under the steaming water, I let my mind wander to our upcoming weekend in Paris. A new shower gel catches my eye, and I can't resist giving it a sniff. Damn, this man knows what to use to smell so good. I put the bottle back in its place, leave the shower to dry myself with a towel, and put his T-shirt on. I tie my still wet hair into a loose bun on the top of my head and head back to the kitchen.

Zack stands by the kitchen counter, engrossed in his phone. As I approach, he sets it aside, a smile spreading across his face.

'Nice T-shirt.' Zack chuckles, circling his arms around me. I melt into his embrace, nestling my face in his neck. 'Are you okay?' He asks, concern lacing his words.

'Mhm.' I murmur, closing my eyes and enjoying the comforting sensation of his touch.

'Food will be here any minute.' Zack informs me, planting a soft kiss on my head. 'You look cute with this little bun.' He adds with a grin as I look up at him. Zack checks his phone, still holding me, and straightens up. 'It's here. I'll go get it.'

I take a step back, so he can go and collect our dinner. In the meantime, I take two glasses of water and bring them to the table.

Zack comes back to the flat with two boxes of pizza, and my mouth fills with saliva at the aroma of freshly baked pizza filling the air.

'It smells amazing.' I say, leaning in to see what he got us.

'So we've got Margherita here and Buffalo pizza here.' Zack announces, opening the boxes.

I discovered a new love for Buffalo pizza because it's Zack's favourite, and I had a chance to try it.

'Great choice, babe.' I say, scrunching my nose in delight. Zack takes a seat beside me and we have a slice of each.

'So, our train leaves at seven tomorrow morning from St Pancras.' Zack glances at me, licking his lips.

'Okay, what time should we leave?' I ask, watching his tongue sliding over his lips.

'I was thinking we could take an Uber, so maybe around five?' He suggests and I nod, bringing my attention back to his eyes and earning a cute chuckle from him.

'Okay… so let's get up at four, and then we don't need to rush. And we can double-check if we have everything we need. You know, just to be sure.'

'Of course, darling.' Zack laughs.

'Just to be sure.' I shrug.

'Things aren't going to disappear from your bag overnight, Maddie.' Zack teases, shaking his head in amusement.

'Who knows. Anything is possible, Zack.'

'Alright. Finish your food and we can check everything tonight, so you can sleep well and I promise everything will be okay in the morning. Trust me.' Zack reassures me, placing a soft kiss on my cheek.

'Okay.' I smile, finishing my last slice of pizza.

After our meal, we tidy up together, and ensure we have everything we need for our trip. Zack actually packed himself an extra jumper, which I can already see myself sleeping in.

'Alright, can we go to sleep now?' Zack asks, stretching his arms and stifling a yawn.

'Yes.' I reply with a giggle.

With a playful grin, Zack scoops me up in his arms and carries me to his bed. As he settles me onto my side, I can't help but admire the way the moonlight dances across his features. He places a brief kiss on my lips before removing his clothes and joining me in bed.

'Nice show, Zack.' I tease, biting my lip.

'Oh, did you enjoy it?' Zack smirks, climbing over me, and I nod before he presses his lips against mine.

We share a long and hot kiss before drawing apart. Zack smiles, still on top of me, and I brush my fingers over his cheek.

'I think we should go to sleep.' I whisper.

'We should.' Zack matches my tone and with one final kiss, we snuggle down under the covers.

'Goodnight, darling.' Zack whispers, wrapping his arm around me.

'Goodnight.' I murmur, smiling to myself with my eyes closed. A wave of warmth and love washes over me as I drift off to sleep.

Chapter Twelve

When the alarm wakes us up, we reluctantly get up to get ready. The urge to stay in bed is so strong but I have to fight it, reminding myself where we are travelling today. I feel like I've only slept ten minutes. I'm not really a morning person but I can do it. I can do it for the experience of going to Paris with my boyfriend. The excitement can overcome my tiredness.

I wear my tailored wide-leg trousers and fitted black top with long sleeves that match my boots. I add some accessories and spray myself with perfume casting a gaze at Zack. He looks great in his black trousers and a burgundy turtleneck.

In the bathroom, we brush our teeth together, exchanging smiles in the mirror. I hope we will be like that in the future.

Later, I watch him styling his hair, while I apply some makeup on my face. And when the scent of his cologne hits my nostrils, I close my eyes for a few seconds, enjoying the rich and masculine smell. I love it. Zack places a quick kiss on my temple before we head to the kitchen, so Zack can have his morning coffee. I sit on the countertop sipping my cold orange juice, admiring Zack preparing his drink.

Once our Uber is nearby, Zack helps me with my coat, putting his on after. Autumn this year is quite cold and windy, and I just miss the warm, summer days. After we bring our stuff outside, Zack takes the opportunity to smoke a quick cigarette. I've noticed he smokes less than before. He mentioned a lot of times that he wants to quit, and I am happy to see his progress.

Upon our Uber's arrival, Zack throws away the rest of his cigarette, and we take our seats in the back. Without traffic, the journey takes us around thirty minutes, and I enjoy the calm, quiet of London in the early morning.

As we stroll through the station, to find our Eurostar train, it's already waiting at the platform. We board it and quickly find our seats. Honestly, I thought it would look different from a normal train. Maybe I expected too much, something with a private compartment, or like beds, or big, comfy seats with tables between.

Zack puts our bags above our heads while I take a seat next to the window. When he sits beside me, taking my hand and lacing our fingers, I rest my head on his shoulder.

'You can take a nap if you want.' Zack says, resting his head on mine, softly caressing my hand with his thumb.

'I'll take in some of the views before we get into the tunnel.' I say, looking out the window as the train slowly leaves the station. But then my eyes feel very heavy and I fall asleep. I wanted to stay awake but... my eyes just closed.

'Maddie, we've arrived.' Zack says softly, waking me up.

'What? Already?' I sit up and look outside the window. We've arrived in Paris. The train has stopped at the station and people are disembarking.

'Yes, you fell asleep as soon as the train left London. Hope the view was amazing.' Zack teases me, getting out of his seat and reaching for our stuff. 'Let's go, darling.' He takes my hand and we get off the train at Gare du Nord. I look around when we leave the building, admiring the beautiful city, feeling excitement growing in my body.

'What do you think?'

'It's beautiful.' I smile and peck his lips.

Zack gets us a taxi that takes us straight to the hotel, and he explains to me on the way that there is no chance we will be taking public transport while we're here. I mean, I've heard about the tube here and I'm a bit scared of taking one. So I am alright with a taxi, even though it might cost me a fortune. But how much can we spend on transport in two days?

I look at the views of Paris as we head to the Eiffel Trocadéro Hotel. Upon our arrival, I raise my eyebrows, dumbstruck, as we leave the taxi. I stare at the impressive hotel in front of me. No way…

'Maddie, come on.' Zack's voice brings me back to earth, and I follow him to the reception where we get the key to our room. We take the lift to our floor and I am excited to see where we'll stay for this night. 'Ready?' Zack asks, stopping in front of the door with a big smile on his face.

'I think so.' I chuckle, unaware of what awaits me behind that door.

The moment I enter the room, my jaw drops. He can't be serious. I rush to the window, staring at the breathtaking view.

'Are you serious?' I turn around to see Zack stand a few steps behind me, still smiling. 'A view of the Eiffel Tower? Are you nuts?' I look out the window again, and I can't believe my eyes. I can feel Zack's arms wrapping around me.

'What do you think?' He asks, placing kisses on my neck, and I just stand there still in shock.

'You are crazy.' I shake my head and turn to face him. Zack looks so happy and proud of himself.

'I am, for you. So, I hope you like it.'

'Are you kidding? This is beautiful. I love it.' I put my hands on his cheeks and kiss him hard. 'Thank you.' I mutter into his mouth between the kisses, wrapping my arms around his neck. His hands slowly slide down from my waist to my butt and he squeezes it, kissing me. I chuckle into his mouth and he stops.

'As much as I would love to stay here, I think we need to leave and enjoy the city, hm?'

'Are we coming back before dinner? I would like to change.' I wrinkle my nose.

'We can. Let's go for a walk and come back to get ready for dinner later.'

'Perfect.' I peck his lips and we leave the room, ready to explore the city.

We spend our day walking the streets of Paris, getting delicious pastries, taking a lot of pictures, and enjoying our little trip, checking the places Alex recommended to me in her message. We visit the most popular places too. We go to see the Arc de Triomphe, Palais Garnier, and of course Musée du Louvre, before heading back to our hotel to get ready for dinner. In the end, we did a lot for one day. The most important things are off the list and we can see a little bit more tomorrow, before we have to leave and go back to London.

Since I need more time to get ready than Zack, I take a shower first. Zack follows me with his eyes when I walk around the room, wrapped in the towel. He doesn't waste his chance and slaps my ass before he goes to the bathroom. I shake my head, smiling to myself. The choice of long, tight black dress with long sleeves and front split seems right for the occasion. I finish the look with my knee-length boots. It should look very classy together with my trench coat.

Listening to Arctic Monkeys, I work on my make up for this evening, when Zack leaves the bathroom with a towel wrapped around his hips. I glance at him, getting distracted by him strolling around the room half naked. He goes for tailored black trousers with a well-fitted white shirt that he tucks in. What perfect timing for *I Wanna Be Yours* to play. I wanna be his, a hundred percent. Even more. I am all his. I take a risk and apply red lipstick on my lips.

When I am finally ready, I spray myself with a sweet perfume, watching Zack styling his hair up. He smiles when I stand behind and wrap my hands around him.

'Damn, why do you look so good?' I ask him and he chuckles, turning around to face me. Zack pushes my hair back, placing a soft kiss on my cheek.

'You look stunning, Maddie. But what if I want to kiss you, hm' Zack asks, pointing at my red lipstick.

'I can remove it later.' I say.

Well, Zack knows how kissing and red lipstick work. I wore it once when we went out, got too many drinks and started making out. It was so hard to remove the pink stain off his face, and mine.

'Or we can do this.' I peck his lips and wipe them with my thumb.

'Okay.' Zack smiles.

Zack helps me with my coat and we leave our hotel, our arms linked together, heading for our boat dinner. The atmosphere is so romantic as we slowly stroll through the streets in the evening. Okay, I get it now why all the couples come here.

Zack helps me board the boat like the gentleman he is. Our table is next to the window and a bottle of sparkling champagne is already waiting for us in a bucket filled with ice. We take our seats and the waiter opens the bottle, filling up our glasses.

'To our first year together.' Zack smiles, raising his glass.

'And many more.'

We clink our glasses and taste the bubbly champagne, exchanging bright smiles from opposite sides of the table.

I take a look at the menu and can't decide what to get. Zack suggests that we should get garlic bread and carrot soup as a starter. Then, he goes for a rib-eye steak, and I finally choose roasted salmon steak.

The boat moves slowly and we appreciate the beautiful view of the city at night, with lamps glistening in the dim light. The waiter brings out our starters, and our mains a few minutes after we finish the starters. I snap some pictures of it and then point my phone at Zack. He smiles for the picture, so I take one, and show it to him. He looks so handsome that I actually set it as my wallpaper and he laughs watching me doing that.

'What?' I look at him.

'Nothing, babe.'

'Look how cute it is now.' I put my phone next to my face, smiling. He shakes his head still laughing. 'I will have a very nice glimpse of you every time I check my phone at work. It will definitely boost my mood during the day.'

It's not like the previous wallpaper was not him, but whatever. It just needed an update.

'You're so cute, Maddie.' Zack says looking into my eyes and puts his hand on mine, giving it a gentle rub with his thumb. I put my phone down, giving him my whole attention.

'And you are such a romantic guy, Zack. All of this for our first anniversary? It's just… I am speechless.'

'We deserve it.' He leans towards me, placing a short kiss on my lips.

'You have some lipstick.' I point at his lips and wipe it with my thumb. Maybe I should have gone for the matt one, not glossy which is messier.

I try my salmon and watch Zack putting a small piece of steak on his fork and moving it closer to me.

'Try it.' He encourages me as he knows I have never tried it before. I take a bite, tasting something new, and actually it's quite good. 'And?' Zack raises his eyebrows, waiting for my answer.

'It's better than I thought.' I admit, smiling.

'You see? Do you want some, then?'

'No, I will stay with my salmon tonight. Thank you. You should try this one too.' I do the same gesture to him, so he can taste some of my food.

'Yeah, it's very nice.' He gives me a warm smile.

As we eat our food, we chat about everything that comes to our minds. Zack moves closer to me when we finish, wrapping his arm around me. Shortly after we pass the sparkling Eiffel Tower, I rest my head on Zack's shoulder. It feels so magical to be here with the love of my life. I am happy. I put my hand on his thigh and we stay like that sharing short kisses until the end of the ride.

Zack helps me get off the boat and we go for a short walk, our fingers laced together. We buy some pastry on the way back to the hotel to share it.

When we enter the room, I hang my coat next to Zack's and walk closer to the window to look at the Eiffel Tower. Zack joins me, wrapping his arms around me and pressing his chest against my back. I snap several quick pictures and send them to Meg.

I tilt my head to the side, enjoying Zack's wet kisses on my skin. I place my hands on his, biting my bottom lip as I feel the atmosphere changing. Zack turns me around to face him. He kisses me hard without saying anything, and I return the kiss.

He pulls my dress up and I lift my arms up to help him remove it. It's so tight that it probably removed half of my makeup going over my head, but why would I even bother now. I pull him back into the kiss, slowly unbuttoning his shirt with my trembling fingers and slide it down off his arms. He moves forward, pushing me towards the bed and I fall back onto it when the back of my knees hit the edge of the mattress.

I move higher to lie down on the pillows as Zack climbs over me, kissing my neck, slowly moving down with the kisses. My breath gets shallow with every second and I look down, reaching to his trousers. I unbutton them and he helps me to take them off. Zack quickly takes control over the situation and we make love, kissing, with hands all over each other.

'Are you mine?' Zack pants into my mouth, moving above me, and driving me crazy.

'I am all yours.' I say, trying to catch my breath between kisses.

Suddenly, Zack turns us around and I am now on top. We stare at each other for a moment. The thing is, it might not be my favourite position because I feel exposed and self-conscious, and even though we tried it a few times, it always ended up with us changing again. I am not that confident on top and prefer when he is in control.

'Zack…'

'Maddie…' Zack chuckles. 'Just move.' He whispers and I smile. If he wants that, we can try again.

I place my hands on the pillow, beside his head, and kiss him softly. He gives my hips a gentle squeeze, encouraging me to take control, which I do. We maintain eye contact while I press his hands against the pillow. He smiles at me, breathing heavily, and I enjoy seeing him feeling this good thanks to me. And his moaning reassures me that I make him feel this good.

Afterwards, I let go of his hands, resting my forehead against his, trying to calm down my breathing. Zack kisses my forehead, wrapping his arms around me. His chest is moving fast beneath me and I leave a kiss on his neck while he caresses my back.

'That was great, Maddie.' Zack says after a moment of silence and I look up at him, looking relaxed and satisfied. I move my face closer to leave a gentle kiss on his lips. 'You are so hot.' Zack mutters into my mouth, making my cheeks burn, so I hide my face in his neck which makes him chuckle. 'I love you.'

'I love you, too.' I look at him again.

His hair is messy, so I rustle my hand through the strands. Zack pulls me closer, kissing me again and turning us around, so he can tower over me. I move my hands down his back, smiling through the kiss.

We share another passionate moment tonight. It feels so right with him. He makes me feel good, he makes me feel sexy, and most importantly, he makes me feel loved. He is so affectionate, always making sure I am alright, and satisfied, not only in bed.

We lie down on our backs, beside each other and when I stare at the ceiling, I just start tittering.

'What?' Zack looks at me, smiling.

'I don't know.' I turn my head to face him and he starts giggling too.

'You're absolutely adorable.' Zack says, wrapping his arms around me. 'So what do you think about Paris?' He asks, pushing hair behind my ear.

'It's amazing. Honestly, it could not be better, and the best part of it is that I am here with you.' I trace the shape of his chest tattoos with my finger.

'So, tomorrow I was thinking that we can have breakfast in bed before leaving. I already checked what they have and good news. I can get you more pastries, fresh bread, and homemade jam.' Zack chuckles. 'Then, we can get a closer look at the Eiffel Tower, take some pictures and slowly head back to the station to get on our train back home. I mean we might have some time to see other places in the area your friend recommended but I think the Eiffel Tower will be the most important one.' He says, playing with my hair.

'Mhm, that sounds good. Looks like you organised everything. Very impressive. And even if we miss something, we saw a lot today anyway.' I look up at him. 'Oh, I just need to get some macarons. For my family, Meg and Jack. And Alex, of course.'

'Alright, we will get the fabulous macarons. I might get some for my family too.' Zack says, rubbing his eyes with fingers.

'Okay, so we have big macarons shopping by the end of our trip.' I say and we both laugh. 'Thank you for bringing me here.' I whisper looking into his beautiful brown eyes.

'Of course, darling. This is the first of many places we will visit together.'

'I can't wait for that.' I smile, excited at the thought of us traveling around the world together, exploring new places and new cultures. It all sounds amazing.

'Goodnight, Zack.' I yawn, snuggling my face into the nook of his neck.

'Goodnight, Maddie.' Zack whispers.

We need to gather more strength for tomorrow, so getting enough sleep is essential after our long way here and a busy day.

Our train is leaving in the evening but if we still want to see some places we'll need the energy. Also, we have to carry all of our stuff with us, so that's gonna be fun. But no matter where we are, the thing I like the most is that at the end of the day I can fall asleep and wake up in his arms.

Chapter Thirteen

Zack and I have been together for almost sixteen months now, and everything feels like it's falling perfectly into place. It's as if we were meant for each other. He's all I ever wanted in a man. He's sweet, carrying, respectful, honest, kind, and loving. He has this amazing ability to make me laugh, truly listens to me, cares deeply about our relationship, and shares his thoughts openly with me. I know I can trust him and that he loves me. I'm completely confident in us. We simply make each other happy.

Last week, Zack celebrated his twenty-sixth birthday, and tonight, he's having a party at Luke's house. Meg and Jack were invited, and they are coming with me. The struggle to find a gift for him has been overwhelming. I wanted something special, something that would surprise him. Then one day, while watching a TV show, we saw a Christmas advertisement showcasing gifts for kids. Zack's eyes lit up at the sight of an archaeology set where you can carve a dinosaur from clay.

He shared with me how he got it as a kid for Christmas, and it was his favourite toy, but he lost it when his family was moving. At that moment, I knew exactly what to get him, but now I have to give it to him in front of all his friends and I'm a bit worried that they… well, that they will judge me. He's a grown man and I'm about to give him a kid's toy.

I worry about it, especially when I imagine his friends presenting him with fancy gifts. I mean, his friends are nice, but I do overthink every situation. I know that, but I can't help it. Maybe I should look for something different for the party and save this gift for a private moment between us.

I stare at the carefully wrapped present lying on my bed and have no idea what to do. It's obvious Zack won't tell me if he doesn't like it, just to avoid upsetting me. But I'll be able to tell from his expression if he's disappointed. Over the past year and a few months, I've gotten to know him very well. He's my boyfriend, so naturally, he might pretend to like it. But I can read his face now, he can't hide things from me. I know the look he gets when certain thoughts cross his mind.

Shit. I groan, covering my face with my hands. I need to get ready and I don't even know what to wear. It's a casual house party, so I need to find something that's party-pretty but not too over the top.

As I open my wardrobe and search through my clothes, I realise my cute summer dresses are useless in this January weather. Pushing the hangers from one side to the other, I hope for new clothes to appear. Finally, I grab my white twist-front knitted jumper and my high-waisted jeans from the lower shelf. This might work. After I quickly try it on and check myself in the mirror, I decide to stick with this look. It actually looks nice.

Sitting down in front of my mirror, I begin to apply my usual makeup. Since my hair is straight, I simply brush it and leave it as is. Finishing the look spraying myself with my perfume that Zack said he likes, I feel ready. Glancing at the clock, I realise I don't have time to find a better gift for Zack. Just then, Meg knocks at my door and enters without waiting for my reply.

'We're leaving in ten minutes.' She announces.

'Do we have time to make a quick stop at a shop?'

'Why?' Meg questions, eyebrows raised as she sits down on my bed next to the gift.

'I need a new gift.' I admit, feeling a wave of uncertainty.

'Why? What is wrong with this one?'

'I'm not sure if it's the right gift.'

'From what you've told me, it sounds perfect. It's thoughtful and shows how much attention you pay to him. Besides, we don't have time to stop anywhere.' Meg shrugs.

'Alright.' I sigh, cleaning my makeup products and look at my friend. 'Should I change my outfit?'

'No, you look cute. Come on, let's catch the tube.' Meg urges, getting up and leaving my room.

I follow her downstairs, where Jack is already waiting, wearing his jacket and helping Meg with hers. Another gentleman. I put on my coat and we head out of the flat. My fingers keep tapping the box on the way to the station, catching Meg's attention.

'Maddie, he's going to love it. Trust me.' She says, putting her hand over mine.

'What did you get him?' Jack inquires, nodding towards it.

'It's an archeology set where you can carve a dinosaur.'

'Oh, that's cool.' He admits, giving me a genuine smile. 'Yeah, I remember you mentioning that.'

'You think so?'

'Yes, of course. He'll be thrilled, especially since it's from you.' Jack says with a reassuring shrug.

'Exactly. You always say that it means more if it's from someone special, and you are special to him.' Meg adds, smiling, and I can't help but chuckle.

I do say it. I am a very sentimental person, and it doesn't matter what I get, it will mean a lot to me if someone I love gave it to me. I look down at my box with Zack's name written on it. He will love it. He will…

Upon arrival at our stop, Meg gently taps my shoulder, signalling it's time to exit the train. It's so cold outside and I feel like I lost feeling in my fingers. I can already feel my cheeks flushing and I know that I'll look like Rudolph when we get there. But it actually doesn't matter. I can't wait to see my probably already tipsy boyfriend. Zack had headed to Luke's earlier to help with preparations and messaged me that they've had a few beers already.

My heart beats faster as we approach the door of Luke's house. The music is already on, and we can hear men's laughter. Jack knocks loudly on the door, and within a minute, Luke welcomes us with hugs and a bottle of beer in his hand.

'Who's that?' Zack's voice drifts closer from the kitchen, and he appears in the hall seconds later, beer in hand. He smiles when he notices me, coming closer to welcome me with a kiss. 'Maddie!

My beautiful girlfriend.' He slurs slightly, wrapping his arm around my neck, holding me close to him. Yeah, he's tipsy. 'Hi baby.'

'Hi.' I smile back at him, locking eyes with his deep brown ones.

His stubble has grown more since I saw him three days ago, and his hair looks messier today but very sexy. He looks cozy in his dark green jumper and jeans.

'You look beautiful.' Zack says, checking me up and down.

'Thank you.' I lean in for a quick kiss.

'Happy Birthday, mate.' Jack hugs Zack, and Meg follows, and they both give him their gift.

'Thanks, guys. Let's get you some drinks.' Zack smiles, checking the gift and putting it next to other bags and boxes.

I glance over the different gifts and opened boxes. He received several bottles of liquor with hilarious messages on them, some funny gifts like socks with his friends' faces on them or personalised boarding games. It's clear his friends put thought into their selections, and it warms my heart.

'Come on Maddie, let's get you a drink.' Zack suggests, placing his hand on my back.

'Happy birthday.' I smile, handing him the box.

'What's this?' He smiles, shaking the gift.

'Well... check.' I encourage, watching eagerly as he tears away the wrapping paper. Zack's eyes widen when he sees the gift, and he chuckles, looking at me, gobsmacked.

'I can't believe you got this for me, Maddie. I love it! Thank you.' Zack turns the box around, reading the instructions on the back, and opens it to look inside.

I watch his happy face as he checks the set inside, and I know he truly loves it. It's the look on his face that confirms it. For a moment, he looks like a little boy who just got his favourite toy back.

'It is the same! Where did you find it?'

'I will keep it as my secret.' I tease, scrunching up my nose.

It was not difficult at all. All I needed to do was type it into Google, and multiple shops appeared. I just needed to find the one from the TV. As long as he loves it, that's all that matters.

'Thank you.' Zack grabs my face, planting a loving kiss on my lips.

'Are you joining us?' Luke's voice interrupts from the kitchen.

'Yeah we are.' Zack responds, still holding my face gently. 'Let's get you a drink.' Zack takes my hand, leading me towards the kitchen island where everyone has gathered. 'Do you want a beer or a cocktail?'

'I can have a beer.'

'I can make you a nice drink if you want.' Zack says, reaching for a bottle of Corona.

'I'll be alright with a beer.' I smile, taking the bottle from him.

'To the birthday boy!' Jack raises his bottle, and we all join in, toasting to Zack's special day.

As we head to the living room, Zack settles into a chair, pulling me onto his lap. All he wanted for his birthday was to relax with his friends, enjoy some drinks, and chill. Wrapping my arm around his neck, I exchange a playful wink with Meg as the group deliberates on which game to play first.

'Do or Drink? That would be a good one to start.' James argues with Noah who wants to play Never Have I Ever.

'What do you want to play?' Zack asks, looking at me with a grin.

'Maybe let's play the Do or Drink one?'

'Good choice Maddie!' James shouts, clearly eager for the game to begin.

'Maddie, have you ever played this?' Zack asks, shaking his head and chuckling.

'No, why?'

'You'll see.' Zack says, kissing my arm.

James brings out the box and explains the rules of the game. As he lays out the cards, I can't help but wonder what kind of challenges await us. It can't be that bad, right? What could it be? Eat a very spicy pepper or drink. Or maybe, drink pickle juice or take a shot.

James prepares two decks of cards, black and white, and explains the rules again. Honestly, I never get the rules until the game starts and I just slowly get it in the middle of playing. But I just keep nodding that I understand.

Since it's Zack's birthday, he begins the game by drawing a white card.

'Drink if you are in a relationship.' He laughs, taking a sip of his drink. 'Now you.' Zack smiles at me and I take the white card.

'Draw.' I read and everyone cheers. I have no idea what it means, so I look at Zack.

'You need to get the black card now.' Zack explains, his eyes twinkling mischievously.

'Okay.' I say, reaching for a black card and raising my eyebrows as I read its content. 'Take off one article of clothing every time someone drinks until you're down to your underwear. Stay like this for the rest of the game. Do this, take two shots, or quit playing.'

'I'll bring the shots.' Zack announces quickly, making the group laugh.

'Let her decide, bro.' James interjects. 'This game is supposed to be fun!'

'Shut up, she's not doing that.' Zack retorts, playfully pointing a finger at James.

'I will take shots.' I announce, putting the card down. There is no way I would do that.

I stand up, giving Zack a way to head to the kitchen for shots. He returns with the bottle of vodka and more shot glasses for later. I take two shots and drink orange juice after to kill the burning taste.

As we continue playing and taking more shots, we all get pretty tipsy.

'I go next.' Sophia eagerly picks up the next card. 'Attempt to do the worm or drink twice. Easy.'

Sophia gets on the floor and tries to do the worm, looking more like a fish that got out of the water and desperately throws herself on the floor. I can't help but burst into laughter, hiding my face in Zack's neck. Sophia is like that, always funny, making everyone laugh.

'Pee in the sink. Do this, take two shots or quit playing. Oh, I can do it easily.' James reads, giggling.

'Don't you fucking dare!' Luke interjects, shooting James a warning glare. 'Better take the shots if you want to stay in the game and the *house*.' Luke emphasises on the house, and pours James two shots of vodka which he takes, laughing.

'Spin the bottle and make out with the person it points to. Both of you must do this, take two shots, or quit playing.' Meg reads her card and looks at Jack. 'Too risky.' She takes two shots and kisses Jack who is pleased with her decision.

After a lap dance, embarrassing Instagram posts, shouting dirty things from the card outside the house, rating exes, revealing some Instagram private messages, sending nudes, singing the *Titanic* theme song to a random person in contacts and calling exes, we are drunk.

Zack gently rubs my exposed belly, playing Uno, and loudly argues with Luke because Zack put draw four for him. Zack blocked him in a previous round and poor Luke is the player with the most cards while Zack is about to win.

'You can't do this mate!' Whines Luke.

'Yes, I can.'

'No, you can't put this card on the top of the same one.'

'Yes I can. You did it in the previous round. It's my birthday by the way.' Zack laughs.

The thing is none of us gets the rules, so we just keep playing as it goes, and everyone argues when they get played. And it's much funnier because everyone is drunk. I kiss Zack's cheek who gets his way, and in the end Zack wins and Luke loses.

The next game the boys decide to play is beer pong and we split into teams: girls versus boys. Despite never having played before, I'm eager to compete against my boyfriend. A little friendly competition between us won't hurt anybody.

Sophia and Noah take the first round, and we all watch them on the side. I lean against Zack's chest as he holds me from behind.

'My mom asked when you'll come over for dinner to meet them.' Zack whispers into my ear, and I turn to face him.

I feel awful that I haven't met his family yet. He's asked me a couple of times already, but there was always something in the way. Our schedules never seem to match to make it work. And with each passing day, I feel worse, worrying about what they think of me. What if they think I'm avoiding meeting them on purpose?

'I will. I promise. It's just… I will try to make some time. I promise.' I stutter.

'It's alright, baby.' Zack kisses me softly and smiles.

'I feel bad about it.' I murmur, feeling a pang of guilt in my chest.

'Don't. They know you're very busy, but they are also excited to meet you. Whenever you can. Don't worry about it.' His tender lips meet mine, and I smile. When we draw apart, I lock my eyes with his, feeling the warmth fill my heart. I just love him so much.

After Meg and Jack finish their round, it's time for Zack and me to play against each other. Meg stands next to me, trying to help me through the whole round, but I'm way too drunk to play, and end up losing.

'You did great.' Zack walks around the table to hug me.

'You could've let her win, Zack.' Meg nudges his arm.

'It's my birthday!' Zack chuckles. 'I'll teach her another time.' Zack says, leaving a soft kiss on my temple, and I smile. His eyes are hazy, indicating he's very drunk, which means I need to sober up because I'll probably have to take care of him later.

'How are you feeling?' I caress his cheek.

'I am gooood. Very good.' He blurts, moving his face closer to mine.

'I can see.' I laugh. Zack stares at my lips, so I whisper. 'You can kiss me if you want.'

Zack kisses me greedily, wrapping his arm around my neck as I return his drunken kiss. And for this short moment, I feel like it's just us in the room.

'I love you.' Zack mouths before his friends steal him for a smoke.

I go to the kitchen to make myself a drink and chat with Meg.

'Did he like the gift?'

'I think he did. He seemed truly happy when he opened the box. He even said it was the same one he had as a kid.'

'I told you he would like it.' Meg raises her glass and we clink them together.

For the rest of the night, Zack drinks even more because his friends constantly want to take shots with him. He's wasted, and I wonder how he is still awake.

Later that night, we're back on the chair, me sitting on Zack's lap, playing with his hair while his friends play us a little concert. Turns out, Noah is great with the guitar, even though he's intoxicated, James actually has a very nice voice, and Florence surprises everyone rhythmically shaking a tambourine. I had my chance with the instrument but failed very badly.

It feels so carefree to sit here like this, enjoying the music, but I need to sneak out to the kitchen with Meg to light up the candles on the cake for Zack. We got him a simple, Marvel-inspired cake with "Happy Birthday Zack" written on the top.

When we slowly return to the living room, the band begins to play *Happy Birthday*. I try to control my breath, making sure I don't blow out the candles by accident. Zack turns to face us, rising from the chair while we all sing for him, and I stop right in front of him.

'Make a wish.' I smile at Zack.

Zack maintains intense eye contact with me, thinks about his wish for a few seconds and blows out all the candles. Everyone starts to cheer and clap. Zack plants a kiss on my cheek before I put the cake down.

'Don't be shy, mate, kiss her properly.' Luke jokes, and seconds later I'm in Zack's strong embrace with his lips on mine, and this small scene entertains all the guests. I chuckle when we draw apart and pass the knife from Meg to Zack so he can cut the cake.

A few drinks later, people start leaving, and I look at Zack, sitting on the sofa with his hands on his head. At that moment, I know he's regretting all his drinking decisions tonight. I join him on the sofa, rubbing his back.

'Are you okay?'

'Mhm…' Zack mumbles.

He's not okay. He's wasted, and it's time to take him home.

'We are going to go. Are you going to be okay?' Meg places her hand on my arm while I order Uber to Zack's place.

'Of course.' I assure my friend.

'We can help you get him to bed and then go home.' Meg offers, pointing at Zack with her head.

'No, it will be okay.' I say looking at Zack. I can handle him. I think…

'Okay, we are going then. Good luck. Text me when you arrive, okay?'

'I will.' I smile. Meg and Jack hug me and say bye to Zack before leaving.

'Zack, our Uber will be here in two minutes. Let's go outside.' I say after a while.

'Mhm…' He mutters.

I help him get up, holding his arm and then wrapping it around my neck. I actually struggle to get him to the car, but Luke, who is also wasted, somehow manages to help me.

The ride to Zack's place is short, but Zack falls asleep on my arm, so I have to struggle to get him out of the car when we arrive. This pisses off the asshole driver who was complaining to me about drunk passengers the whole ride.

When we finally reach Zack's flat, I walk him to bed, and he limply falls onto it, murmuring something under his breath. I carefully take off his clothes and cover him with a quilt. Seconds later, he's deep asleep.

After a quick shower and removing my makeup, I walk back to bed wearing his comfy jumper and send a quick message to Meg. Zack sleeps in the same position I left him, so I lie down next to him, resting my head on his arm. My fingers trace the contours of his jaw, feeling the stubble beneath them, trailing down to his neck and strong chest.

His full lips are slightly parted as he calmly breathes through them in his sleep, and I can't resist the temptation to kiss him, so I place a short but gentle kiss on his lips. As I settle back onto my side, I can't help but wonder what tomorrow holds for us, hoping that Zack will wake up feeling alright.

Chapter Fourteen

Eighteen months have flown by since I first started dating Zack, and with each passing day, he continues to prove to me he's the best boyfriend in the world. I've never been happier. It's hard to think how my life was before I met him.

Balancing university and work still consumes much of my time, but somehow, I've managed to find a way that allows me to fulfil my responsibilities while also cherishing moments with Zack, and my friends. I always try to find some time for Zack. From time to time, he picks me up from university, and we go to his place to have some time alone. Even though I don't see him everyday, we try to spend as much time together as we can. And on days when I have a lot to do, he comes to my place and either offers to help with my assignments, or he watches football games with Jack while I work alongside Meg.

Of course, I also find time for girls dates with my best friend. We need our time to gossip and talk about our boyfriends, and life in general. And through it all, Zack remains understanding and supportive.

The calendar works miracles for all of us. Of course, things happen, but we always find a solution. Like, if he suddenly needs to cover someone's shift at work, I would just do my coursework and arrange some free time for him the other day.

Tonight, Zack picks me up from work and we are going to his place. Also, this weekend Alex is doing a Vegas themed birthday party and I take Zack with me. With Meg's wonderful help, and her amazing eye for clothes, I bought a very sexy dress, which I hope my boyfriend will like when he sees me wearing it.

I glance at the clock. Excitement bubbles within me knowing that in just a couple of hours, I'll be wrapped in his arms after five long days apart. We've talked on video but it's not the same. Zack's had a lot on his plate this week, and I had to reschedule my calendar to make some time for us.

As I sit at the desk, thoughts of the upcoming evening play in my mind, and then Edward appears out of nowhere. He's been a source of tension between Zack and me since the infamous staff Christmas party. That night, we all got pretty drunk, and when Zack came to pick me up, he wasn't pleased with Edward's behaviour.

Edward had been overly flirtatious, jokingly holding me and reluctant to let go of me. I've explained to Zack countless times that Edward is like that with all of us at work, not just me, and it doesn't mean anything. He's just naturally friendly and had too many drinks that evening.

Zack is the only man I love and care about, and I would never do anything to jeopardise our relationship. He is the love of my life. However, Zack's jealousy towards Edward persists, and I understand it, having experienced similar feelings myself. To be fair, I wouldn't appreciate it if some girl at Zack's workplace was overly friendly with him either. It's a two-way street. There are a lot of girls at his work who hit on him, just like I did. Despite this, I trust Zack, knowing he loves me and would never intentionally hurt me.

I try to maintain a friendly relationship with Edward since he's my manager, but I'm quick to shut down anything that crosses the line into flirtation from his side. I've had a serious conversation with him about it, making it clear that I have zero interest in anything beyond a professional relationship. My strongest argument? Reminding him that I have a boyfriend. Thankfully, he respected my boundaries and even apologised for making me uncomfortable.

'Maddie, can I ask you a question?' Edward asks, and I know what he wants, and there is no way. Tonight, I have plans with my man. Plans that I won't compromise for anything or anyone else.

'Sure, what's up?' I respond.

'I might need you to stay a little bit longer tonight. Like until ten or eleven, maybe.' Edward says, his hands tucked into his pockets.

Ha, I knew it! But I'm out of here at seven, and that's it. Tonight is reserved for Zack, and I won't let anything derail our precious time together.

'Sorry, Edward, but not today. My boyfriend is picking me up, and we already have plans.' I assert gently, sensing his disappointment.

'Eh, it's fine.' He sighs, nodding grimly.

I can't help but feel a twinge of sympathy for Edward. They need to hire someone new, because myself, Alex or anyone else can't do a two-people job. At the moment, I have university and need to focus on my education. I can't be here full-time.

'Maybe call Alex? Have you found someone new?' I inquire politely, and he shakes his head.

'Nobody. And yeah, I might call her.'

'You will find someone soon, surely. Don't worry. Anyway, I've heard you are coming to Alex's party on Saturday.' I interject, attempting to shift the conversation away from the workplace issues.

Edward is actually the cool kind of manager, which is something rare and that's why I want to maintain a good relationship with him at work. We all get along very well here and I like it. The friendly atmosphere here is great, and everyone is so helpful when another person needs some help or a shift change.

'We'll see. I'm not sure yet.' He responds wearily, rubbing his eyes with his fingers.

'I think you should come. It'll be a good distraction from work, a chance to de-stress.' I suggest.

'Anyway, enjoy the evening with your boyfriend.' Edward says, patting the desk with his hand before he walks away. This poor man seems constantly stressed.

As my shift comes to an end, Edward comes to switch with me, so I can go home. Alex is coming to help him, probably ready to continue her crush mission.

'Good luck.' I smile at him, friendly.

'Thanks. I'll see you on Friday, Maddie.'

'Bye.' I wave, leaving the building.

Outside, Zack waits for me by his car, a bouquet of red roses in hand. My heart leaps at the sight of him, and I hurry towards him with a grin plastered on my face.

'Hello, darling.' Zack greets me with a smile that mirrors my own, and I nearly throw myself into his arms in excitement. I missed him so much.

'Hi.' I murmur, wrapping my arms around his neck and planting a loving kiss on his lips. His arms encircle me, pulling me close, and I enjoy the warmth of his embrace.

'I missed you.' He murmurs against my lips as we finally part. 'And… I got this for you.' He presents me with the bouquet of roses.

'Aw, they're beautiful! Thank you.' I exclaim, taking the flowers and giving them a quick sniff.

'I hope you're hungry. I made us dinner.'

'I'm starving! What did you make?' I inquire eagerly as Zack opens the car door for me.

'I made pasta with shrimp.' Zack winks, knowing all too well how much I like this dish. I never know how to prepare shrimp, so Zack makes it for me because his culinary skills are much better than mine.

'Oh, I can't wait.' I reply, about to take my seat when Edward's voice interrupts us.

'Maddie!' He calls from the top of the hotel stairs. Zack clenches his jaw, his mood changing within a second.

'What does he want?' Zack's tone sharpens.

'I don't know. I'll go and ask.' I say, clearing my throat as I place the flowers on my seat. Glancing at Zack, who rolls his eyes, I make my way towards Edward.

'What's up?' I inquire, stealing a quick glance at Zack over my shoulder. He watches us from where I left him with the expression I can't read.

'I forgot to ask you. We have this big event on Saturday and I was wondering if you know someone who would like to work that day. Just for this event. It's very important. Or I can offer them a position at the hotel since we're hiring. If they would like it.'

Edward explains.

'I might ask some people, maybe they will agree. Oh, maybe my friend. She actually needs some extra money for a holiday with her boyfriend.' I chuckle.

'That would be so helpful.' Edward responds with a grateful smile, resting his hand on my arm.

'I will let you know what she says. I need to go.' I say, stepping back slightly to distance myself from his touch.

'Thank you, Maddie. I can always count on you.'

'It's alright. Bye.' I offer a slight smile before making my way back to Zack. I can already sense his tension brewing. 'Let's go.' I say, but Zack remains silent, his gaze fixed on Edward.

Zack doesn't say anything, so I take my seat. He closes my door and walks around the car, his eyes still locked on the hotel entrance as he starts the engine and pulls away.

'So, how's work?'

'I don't want to talk about work, Maddie.' Zack replies curtly.

'Alright, then.' I say, diverting my attention to the bouquet of roses on my lap, tracing my finger along the edges of their petals.

'Does he always try to touch you?' Zack's question slices through the silence, and I feel a sinking feeling in my chest.

Here we go again. He's angry. We had this conversation after the Christmas party and I didn't like it at all. We didn't argue, but it wasn't a pleasant conversation.

'Zack, don't start please.' I sigh.

I don't want to have the same conversation again. How many times do I have to tell him that it doesn't mean anything? He just touched my arm. It was just a reflex because he was relieved I'm trying to help him. It didn't mean anything.

'Fine.' Zack snaps, his focus returning to the road.

The tension in the car is palpable, and I can feel my own mood changing. Great, just great. Is our date already ruined? I don't even know how to explain to him anymore that he's the only man in my life that I love and care about, he should trust me.

The rest of the journey passes in heavy silence, and I don't even attempt to turn on the radio. It saddens me that this issue continues to affect our relationship. This is the only issue we have, and I try to figure out how to bring an end to it. I wonder if Zack has trust issues or if I've ever given him a reason to doubt me. I had been looking forward to our evening together, but my romantic mood is long gone, and now I just want to go to bed.

Upon arriving at his flat, I arrange the roses in a vase while Zack warms up our food. Still not speaking, I struggle to find the right words. I wonder what's going through his mind. Quietly, I approach him from behind, resting my hands on his back and wrapping my arms around his waist, pressing my cheek against his back as I close my eyes, trying to gather my thoughts.

'Zack?' I murmur softly.

'Hm?'

'I don't want you to be jealous. You have nothing to worry about. I promise. I love you, and there's no one else for me but you. You should trust me more.' I say, exhaling deeply. Zack turns to face me, leaning against the countertop. 'Do you trust me?' I ask, searching his eyes for an answer.

'I do. I don't trust this bastard, though.' Zack replies with a shrug, rubbing his face with his hands. 'I'm sorry, Maddie.' He adds, his hand cupping my cheek gently as I lean into his touch, relishing in the comfort of his presence. A hint of guilt in his gaze as he looks at me.

'Well, he's just my manager, okay? He knows not to cross the line with me. It's just work.' I assert, meeting Zack's eyes with sincerity. 'Nobody can compare to you.' I smile sheepishly, hoping to lighten the mood. 'So handsome and so sexy.' I add, moving closer to him and planting a soft kiss on his lips. Zack's hands find their place on my hips, pulling me as close to his body as he can. 'Nobody could ever take your place in my life.' I say, leaving short kisses along his jawline. Zack bites his bottom lip, enjoying the change of mood. 'You have no idea what you do to me. Since the day I met you. I can't stop thinking about you. You're always on my mind.' I whisper, my lips grazing his ear.

'I'm crazy about you too, Maddie.' Zack confesses, resting his forehead against mine. 'I'm sorry. I just lost it when I saw him touching you.' He sighs, closing his eyes.

'I don't want us to argue.' I say softly, my hand caressing his cheek.

'Me neither. I want to have a nice evening with you. I missed you so much over these past few days. I want to focus on only you tonight.' Zack says, cupping my face before leaning in to kiss me.

'Let's eat. I'm very hungry.' I murmur, and Zack chuckles in agreement.

As we enjoy our meal, we catch up on each other's lives over the past five days. Zack listens attentively as I share updates about university, while he opens up about the chaos at work since the addition of a new manager. Zack has to work with him, sharing shifts and responsibilities, and it seems to not be working well.

'So, now I have to clean all the mess left by the previous manager and deal with the new one on the top of that. If I had known what waited for me, I would never have agreed to take this position.' Zack vents, taking a sip of his beer.

'They should have told you.' I sympathise, placing my hand on top of his and rubbing it gently with my thumb. 'Anyway, you're a great manager, even though you have to deal with this bullshit.' I reassure him with a smile, and he returns it.

'Let's not talk about it anymore. Do you want to watch something?' Zack suggests, changing the subject.

'Sure!' I agree, eager to shift our focus to something more enjoyable.

After we finish cleaning the dishes, we settle in the living room, Zack wrapping his arm around me and leaving a kiss on the top of my head. I turn the TV on to see what's there to watch, but I can't find anything interesting, so I give the clicker back to Zack. I rest my head on his arm while Zack decides to just play *Friends* on Netflix. We cuddle together while Zack plays with my hair, a gesture I adore.

'I missed you.' Zack whispers, kissing my temple.

'How much?' I tease, playfully moving away from him.

'A lot.' He responds with a grin, so I repeat my move.

A smirk creeps up on Zack's face as he plays along. We continue to do that until my back hits the cushion, and Zack towers over me. He kisses me softly and I slide my hand into his hair.

'I missed you too.' I murmur against his lips.

Our kisses grow greedier with every passing second. Zack's hand slides under my uniform shirt, sending a shiver down my spine. With a gentle tug on his hair, I earn a silent groan from him. As his kisses trail down to my neck, I tilt my head back, offering him more access. I eagerly grab the bottom of his grey jumper and pull it over his head, running my hands down his muscular chest. He's incredibly sexy, and I just can't stop myself from touching him. Zack responds by swiftly getting rid of my shirt, tossing it carelessly to the floor.

The anticipation hangs in the air, fuelled by the longing we've both felt during our time apart. With no time to waste, we surrender to our desires, needing to feel as close to each other as possible. I feel so… desperate. And I can sense that Zack feels the same way.

He's all over me, his hands exploring every inch of my body, his lips seeking mine with a fervour. We take our time to enjoy ourselves, letting all the tension melt away as we lose ourselves in the pleasure of being together once again.

Turns out, the sofa wasn't the best place to have sex, as my head kept banging against its side. So, we ended up on the fluffy carpet, moving the action to the bedroom later.

As we both lie on our sides, our gazes locked, I bring my hand to his face, gently tracing my fingers around his features as if trying to memorise every detail. Zack watches me with an admiring smile, his thumb caressing my cheek tenderly.

'Gosh, you're so beautiful.' Zack cups my chin, his thumb brushing lightly over my lips. I can see his eyes locked on my lips.

'Just kiss me.' I chuckle, igniting a spark in his eyes.

Without hesitation, Zack leans in, kissing me with a passion that leaves me wanting more. His lips are tender against mine, and I reciprocate eagerly, gently biting his bottom lip as my hand finds its place on the back of his neck, earning a low groan from Zack.

'Zack?' I whisper as we part, our faces still inches apart.

'Yes, Maddie?' He responds, matching my tone.

'You need a new sofa.'

'Really? Why?' Zack asks, a mischievous smirk playing on his lips.

'I mean, this one isn't bad, but maybe you could get a slightly bigger one?' I suggest, trying to keep a straight face.

'Why's that?' Zack teases, clearly aware of what I'm getting at.

'Because…' I clear my throat. 'Just to have more room for cuddling.' I admit, unable to suppress a giggle.

'I'll think about it. Although the floor didn't seem that bad, huh?'

'Well… the carpet is quite soft.' I chuckle, shaking my head. 'Anyway, tomorrow we are going to Little Heaven, remember?'

'Of course I do. What's better than getting some coffee at our favourite spot?' Zack says, turning to lie on his back, his eyes already closed.

I watch him for a moment, playing with his hair before I realise he's fallen asleep. I press a soft kiss to his cheek and snuggle into his neck.

I've been taking Meg, Jack, and Zack to Little Heaven whenever I get the chance. It's become our go-to spot, and I love the warm welcome we always receive from Mr. and Mrs. Brown. They run the coffee shop together, and I've become their favourite regular customer, often receiving homemade cookies from Mrs. Brown.

Sometimes, I come here alone and we chat about our days. They seem genuinely interested in what I have to say. I know they have two sons and one daughter. The older son is a lawyer, the younger son is doing his placement at the hospital after graduating medicine, and their daughter studies history and wants to become a teacher.

Their coffee shop became my favourite place, ever since I walked in there the day of my horrible interview.

Chapter Fifteen

Saturday has finally arrived, and tonight Zack and I are heading to Alex's party. Meg was eager to assist me in getting ready before rushing off to help at the hotel event. They actually pay well, and when I mentioned the opportunity to her, she went for it. It's great for her, especially since she's saving up for a vacation with Jack and could use some extra cash.

I watch her carefully applying products to my face, trying hard not to burst into laughter at her focused expression. I wouldn't dare to spoil the look she's enthusiastically crafting.

'You look stunning, Maddie.' Meg beams proudly.

She's so good with eyeliner, and the foxy eyes she creates on me look much better than the ones I have tried myself. Usually, I stick to basic makeup because, frankly, anything beyond that is beyond me.

'Oh my God, Meg.' I exclaim, still in awe as I gaze at my own reflection. My face looks different from my everyday self. And the lip gloss is on point! I need to buy myself one after the payday. I look… beautiful.

'Wait, let me fix this.' Meg interrupts my thoughts, brushing my hair once more to achieve that subtle wave before securing it with a spritz of hairspray. 'That should stay for a night. Quickly, put on your dress. I want to see the whole look before I head out.'

'Okay.'

Back in my room, I carefully slip on black tights, determined not to snag them. I then shimmy into my strapless, feather-adorned mini black dress, slipping on Meg's black platform high heels. We wear the same shoe size, which allows us to swap shoes. Is there anything better than sharing shoes with your best friend?

Since Meg is a tad shorter, she always wears tall shoes. But me with these platforms… I wonder if I'll be taller than Zack. He's quite tall, but so are these shoes. I add some silver jewellery we picked out earlier and head back to Meg's room to present my final look.

'Yes, Maddie! You look like a million dollars. Wow.' Meg exclaims, clapping her hands and scrutinising me from head to toe as I slowly turn around. 'Damn, you're tall.' She adds with a laugh, gazing up at me.

'I feel like the gloves might be a bit much.'

'No, no, no. Everything is perfect together. I wish I could see Zack's reaction when he sees you like this.' Meg teases, moving her eyebrows suggestively. I chuckle, shaking my head. 'He might not let you out to the party. If you know what I mean.'

'I do.' I reply, rolling my eyes playfully.

'Just make sure you keep it in your room and remember, we all share the sofa. Just saying.'

'Meghan!' My jaw drops in disbelief.

Alright, I might have mentioned the sofa situation at Zack's place to her, but the audacity to throw it in my face like this? Unbelievable.

'Anyway, I think we'll head to his place after the party since we're both off tomorrow.' I interject, clearing my throat.

'Well…you two have fun then.' Meg teases, nudging my arm with hers.

'I swear Meg if you don't shut up…' I laugh, threatening her as we head downstairs together.

Before she leaves, she snaps a quick selfie with me to post on her story.

'Good luck tonight.' I call after her from the doorway, waving as she walks away, waving back and returning the smile.

Alone in the flat, with Jack out with his friends and Meg at work, I settle onto the sofa with a glass of juice, flicking on the TV to kill the time until Zack arrives. It's almost eight, and he should be here any minute.

A few minutes later, there's a knock at the door, so I put the glass down and hurry to let him in. Zack stands before me, looking absolutely breathtaking in a black shirt with a few buttons undone and black trousers. I let him in, and as he opens his mouth to speak, he pauses, his gaze fixated on me for a few seconds. He stands there, biting his bottom lip, desire burning in his eyes.

'Wow, Maddie. You look... wow.' Zack finally manages to choke out, grabbing my hand and slowly turning me around. I can't help but giggle.

'Speak for yourself.' I say, placing my hands on his chest and leaning in for a brief kiss.

'You're so tall.' Zack chuckles, his big hands resting on my hips as he pulls me closer. We're practically the same height now. I feel his hands move from my hips to my butt. 'What do you say if we skip the party, hm?' He suggests, planting kisses on my neck, and I tilt my head to the side, closing my eyes. I love when he does that.

'Very tempting offer, but it's Alex's birthday, so we have to go. It would be rude not to show up.' I manage to say, lightly pushing him away. He knows neck kisses are my weakness, so I have to resist.

'Alright, darling.' Zack relents, kissing my lips.

'Now you have my lip gloss on your face.' I chuckle, wiping it off his mouth with my thumb.

'Let's go.' He says, helping me with my coat before we head out. The evening air is still chill, and I'd definitely freeze without a coat.

'Are you driving?' I frown as we approach his car and Zack retrieves the keys from his pocket.

'I'm not going to drink. I don't feel like it tonight.' He explains, opening the door for me. 'But you can. I'll take care of you.' Zack adds with a smirk.

During the ride to the party, Zack showers me with compliments, his hand squeezing my leg constantly. Oh, he definitely likes the look. And I enjoy the feeling of being wanted, desired.

When we arrive, the party has already started, and we enter holding hands. I brought Alex a bottle of her favourite champagne, because that's what she wanted, along with a small bag filled with pink-themed goodies. Zack contributed.

'Hi! You're finally here!' Alex greets us.

'Happy birthday!' I exclaim, hugging her tightly and presenting her with the gift.

'Happy birthday Alex.' Zack adds, kissing her cheek.

Alex takes us to the kitchen, where she and I take a shot before she rushes off to welcome other guests. I pour myself a drink into a plastic cup and glance at Zack, feeling a pang of guilt that he's not drinking. Maybe I should have convinced him to leave the car and drink.

'This party looks cool.' Zack admits, smiling at me as I nod. It's got a Las Vegas theme, and her house is massive. Her parents must be freaking rich.

'They're playing poker over there. We should join.' I suggest grabbing his hand and pulling him towards the table to watch.

Zack wraps his arms around me from behind, and I rest my hand on his. I've never played poker before, but I'd like to learn someday. Maybe Zack can teach me.

'You should try.' I tell him.

'Maybe.' He replies, observing the players before eventually joining in on the next round.

I watch my man, drinking in the meantime. His poker face is incredibly sexy, and he's actually quite good. I mean, I knew he was good because I saw him playing with his friends. Unfortunately, he doesn't win.

'You were still the best.' I assure him with a smile, giving him a kiss.

'How many drinks have you had already?' Zack chuckles.

'Like three. And two more shots with Alex.' I confess, wrinkling my nose.

The party keeps going on, and I find myself drinking more, feeling the effects quickly. I attempt to dance with Zack, who watches me with a smile, pulling me closer for a kiss. It's then that I spot Edward in the corner, talking to Alex, when Zack turns me around.

'Um, Zack.' I clear my throat, facing him. 'Edward is here.' I inform him and notice the instant change in his expression.

'What is your manager doing here?' Zack's tone sharpens.

'He's good friends with Alex.' I explain with a shrug. Zack rolls his eyes.

'I hope he stays away from you, though. I need to smoke.' Zack adds before taking my hand, and leading me outside. I observe him as he lights up a cigarette.

'I thought you were quitting.' I say as he lets out a big cloud of smoke from his mouth.

'I am.' He says. The evening breeze makes me shiver and Zack notices that. 'You're cold. I'll bring your coat from the car before you catch a cold.' He says, leaving a kiss on my lips before heading off.

Leaning against the cool wall, I rub my arms in an attempt to warm up, feeling the dizziness of the alcohol creeping in.

'Maddie! Hi.' Edward's voice breaks through my thoughts, coming out of nowhere. He's clearly had a few too many. I can see it in his eyes. 'My hero!' He smiles drunkenly.

'Hi.' I offer a friendly smile.

'You saved my life tonight with your friend. They called me and said she's brilliant. Thank you so much.' Edward exclaims, suddenly pulling me into a hug.

I stiffen, swiftly pulling away before Zack catches sight of us and misinterprets the situation.

'You're welcome.' I reply, clearing my throat. Edward sighs, his breath smelling like alcohol, his gaze lingering on me intensely.

'Listen, Maddie...' Edward's voice trails off as he draws closer, attempting to touch my face but gets pushed away immediately. Edward staggers, catching balance and saving himself from falling.

'Stay the hell away from my girlfriend.' Zack growls, standing protectively between Edward and me, my coat in his hand. *Shit.* Panic floods through me, and I grasp Zack's arm, trying to intervene.

'What the fuck, man?' Edward frowns, moving closer to Zack.

I step between them, desperately trying to get Zack's attention, but his focus remains fixed on Edward. Placing my hands on Zack's chest, I feel his heart racing beneath my touch.

'Zack, stop.' I urge.

'Try to touch her ever again, and I swear…' Zack's threat hangs in the air, but Edward interrupts with a scoff.

'What? You gonna hit me? Are you threatening me?' Edward's laughter only fuels Zack's rage. He takes a step forward, but I block him with my body. I can't let them cause a scene and ruin Alex's party.

'Zack!' I raise my voice, finally capturing his attention. I've never seen him this angry before.

'We are leaving.' Zack declares, grabbing my hand and pulling me towards the car.

As we walk away, I can hear Edward saying *See you on Tuesday* in the background, while I try to catch up with Zack's fast steps.

'Zack, wait… I didn't even get to say goodbye to Alex.' I protest softly.

Zack opens the car door for me, his gaze still fixed on the house. I take the coat from him, slipping it on as I look in the same direction, spotting Edward walking back inside. I actually forgot that I was cold because of all of that.

'Zack?'

'Get in the car.' He hisses, his attention still fixed on the house.

I settle into the seat and wait for him to sit next to me. Unsure of what might happen, I watch him walk around the car, fearing that he might go back inside to confront Edward, and I will have to run to stop that. Thankfully, he slides into the seat beside me, and we drive off.

We remain in a tense silence until I decide to speak. I'm both intoxicated and upset by Zack's behaviour tonight. What was he thinking? He can't just push people around or drag me out of a party without saying bye to my friend.

'What do you think you're doing?' I turn to him, frustration evident in my voice. 'You can't behave like that, Zack. You could've ruined Alex's birthday party. You–'

'Me?' Zack cuts me off, his hands tightening on the steering wheel. 'I wasn't the one cozying up to my manager.' He accuses.

'I didn't hug him…' I protest. It's true. Edward hugged me, and I was caught off guard by his actions. I didn't expect this at all. 'I moved–'

'I saw everything, Maddie.' Zack interrupts, shaking his head.

'I moved away.' I defend myself.

'You told me he doesn't flirt with you anymore, so what was that?' Zack glances at me briefly. 'He's always trying to touch you, Maddie! Always putting his hands on you!' Zack's voice rises as he gets angrier. Zack's never been like this before, and I get he's mad, but I don't like it.

'That's not true! He was just grateful for my help tonight and hugged me like a friend. He was just drunk, so I think–' I attempt to explain, but Zack interrupts me again.

'Does he do that at work?' Zack demands.

'No!' I deny immediately.

'Don't lie to me, Maddie! I saw it the other day when I picked you up from that fucking job!' Zack's shouting now.

'I'm not lying!' I yell back.

Zack takes a sharp turn, pulling into a parking lot and bringing the car to a stop.

'Do you like him?' Zack's eyes look into mine, his anger blazing.

'What?' I frown. What is he trying to say?

'Do you like him? Do you like his attention? Do you like that some older guy flirts with you and tries to touch you all the time?' His words cut deep, and I'm taken aback. 'Do you–'

'You're crossing the line now, Zack.' I warn him, hurt and frustration bubbling within me. I understand he's mad but how dare he speak to me like that! How dare he insinuate such things?

'Why are you so fucking naive, Maddie?' Zack raises his voice again, and I shudder.

'Excuse me?' I raise my voice at him too. My heart hurts from the words he's saying.

'Can you open your eyes and see that this guy wants to fuck you!' Zack yells at me, clenching his fingers tight on the steering wheel.

His chest moves fast up and down. Tears prick my eyes, and his words pierce my heart. Why does he speak to me like that?

'Can't you realise how fucking toxic your jealousy is?' I yell back at him. I feel the tears trying to escape my eyes, my voice breaking, but I continue. 'Look how you are talking to me right now, Zack! To your girlfriend! I don't accept it nor deserve it!' I look at him, and he remains silent. 'What's next? Will you forbid me from having male friends because you're jealous? For fucks sake Zack! I don't control other people! I can't control what they do! But you know what? I can control myself! Is that really how little you think of me? We've been together for so long, and is that what you think of me after all that time? Do you even trust me Zack?' I choke out, but Zack remains silent.

His silence speaks volumes, slowly killing me. So it means he doesn't. And it hurts like hell, fuelling my anger.

'Fuck it then! Fuck all of this, Zack.' I trail off. 'Drop me off at the station. I'm going home.' I say, my voice breaking, and I turn away from him, staring out the window.

As Zack begins to drive, I fix my gaze on the road ahead, silently observing as we pass all the tube stations on the way, but still heading towards my place. I can feel warm tears trickle down my cheeks, so I quickly wipe them away with the back of my hand.

The silence is a fucking torture to me. My heart aches with every beat, the weight of Zack's words heavy on my chest. The way to my place seems to take forever, but relief washes over me when I finally recognise my neighbourhood. After a tense drive, Zack pulls up in front of my flat.

'Maddie…' Zack begins quietly, but I don't wait to hear more.

I leave his car as soon as I can, shutting the door behind me. Zack's words have hurt me deeply tonight. I actually don't want to see him or be around him right now. I just want to be alone.

With my trembling legs, I rush to my front door, dropping my keys on the doormat as I struggle to unlock it.

'Fuck!' I mutter under my breath.

Tears are streaming down my face now, blurring my vision. The lights from his car still light up the door. I quickly pick up my keys, desperate to escape inside just in case Zack decides to go after me. I close the door right behind me, not looking in Zack's direction, and lean against them. I cover my mouth with my hand as the uncontrolled sob leaves my mouth.

When the lights fade away after a few minutes, I know he's left.

I leave Meg's shoes and my coat at the door before heading towards the stairs, to my room.

'Maddie? Is that you?' Meg's voice echoes from the top of the stairs as she flicks on the lights. I flinch at the sudden brightness. 'Are you crying? Maddie, what happened?' Meg rushes down the stairs, and grabs my arms, but I can only shrug, unable to speak. There's a massive lump in my throat blocking my ability to speak. 'For God's sake, Maddie, what's going on? Did someone hurt you? Where's Zack?' When Meg mentions his name, I cover my mouth with my hand again and shut my eyes tightly, crying. 'Maddie, you're scaring me right now, what is going on?'

'I broke up with Zack...' I finally choke out, my voice shaky. Hot tears continue to stream down my face.

'What?' Meg's eyes widen in shock. 'What... But... Why?' She asks, and I just shake my head trying to catch my breath. Meg pulls me closer, wrapping her arms around me and comforting me.

'It's over...' I sob.

'Let's put you to bed. You can tell me everything, okay? Come on. You look exhausted.' Meg says with concern, wiping the tears from my cheeks. 'Let's go.' She places her hand on my back as we head to my room.

Meg leaves me in my room for a second and returns with a glass of water. The pain in my chest feels unbearable.

'Here, drink some water.' Meg says, passing me the glass.

I take a sip, but it makes me sick right away, so I rush to the bathroom. Meg follows, holding my hair as I empty my stomach of what seems like all the drinks I've had tonight. She rubs my back gently, waiting patiently for me to finish.

Once I'm done, I brush my teeth and wash my face with cold water. Meg removes what remains of my makeup with wet wipes, not saying anything. We return to my room in silence, bumping into Jack in the hallway.

'What is going on?' He asks, standing in the door frame, yawning.

'Go back to sleep Jack. I'll be back in a few minutes.' Meg says, kissing his cheek.

'Alright, darling. Night Maddie.' Jack retreats back to his room as Meg and I continue to mine.

Meg doesn't pressure me to speak. She simply sits on my bed, waiting for me to change into my pyjamas. As I climb onto my bed, still sobbing, she lies down beside me.

'So… Do you want to tell me what happened?' Meg asks gently.

There's a brief silence again, while I take some deep breaths, trying to calm down. I try to explain the situation through my tears, but my voice keeps breaking. Honestly, I don't know if she understands anything from my mumbling.

'And when I said *fuck that*, he didn't say anything. He was just… silent.' I sniff.

Meg seems to take a few seconds to put her thoughts together before she speaks.

'Maddie, listen… First of all, yes, Zack crossed the line and should never speak to you like that, especially when you're drunk. Secondly, it was a big argument, but maybe it doesn't mean it's over. And thirdly, I can't believe he said all those things to you. What the hell? I would never expect it from him. And I think he should be the one to apologise.' Meg frowns in exasperation.

'Me neither.' I clear my throat.

'I know he doesn't like Edward, but it doesn't justify his behaviour. You can have male friends, and he just hugged you. Zack needs to stop being jealous and trust you. You love him, and I know you would never do anything stupid. Because for what? To hurt someone you dearly care about? To lose the love of your life? That's ridiculous.' Meg sighs.

'I don't fancy Edwards at all… He's just my manager, a work friend. Nothing more.' I choke out. My throat burns when I speak.

'I know.'

'I don't want to lose him Meg…' I confess, my voice breaking again as a new wave of tears hits me. I'm terrified that this might be the end for us.

'You won't. It was just an argument. You two will work this out. But not when you are drunk. Sober up, and maybe he will call in the morning and you can talk.' Meg reassures, kissing my head.

'I love him. But he hurt me. His words hurt so much…'

'I know, Maddie. Everything will be okay. Now, have some rest, and we can talk more later, okay? For sure there is some solution to this.' Meg comforts.

'I hope so.' I whisper.

Exhausted from crying and overwhelmed with emotions, I drift off to sleep, grateful for Meg's comforting presence by my side.

Chapter Sixteen

Days pass by since our argument, neither of us have reached out. Zack hasn't contacted me. I haven't called or messaged him either and well… I think it proves that we broke up that night. A faint hope lingers in my heart that Zack will be the one to call first. The fear of humiliation holds me back, stopping me from making the first move. After all, it was Zack who crossed the line. He was the one who said too much. Meg thinks we should talk things through, emphasising that communication is the key. But she also said that Zack should be the one to apologise first and I agree.

Did I truly do something so wrong to deserve such hurtful words? Zack hurt me deeply with what he's said. But I would lie if I said I didn't miss him, that I didn't think about him every night, or that I didn't check my phone every five minutes just in case I missed his call. Though I put on a brave face each morning, pretending that everything is alright, I cry every night to my pillow. My mind tells me to move on from him but my heart still has a hope for us.

Today, I'm scheduled to work with Edward for the first time since the party, and I just hope everything will be alright. I feel the need to apologise to him for Zack's behaviour and have a small chat to remind him of my boundaries.

During the tube ride, I think about everything. About the conversation I am going to have with Edward, about Zack not contacting me at all, worrying that I might have been single for the past three days… but was it really a breakup? He didn't confirm it. But does he have to? And I actually didn't say anything like *we're over, we're done,* or *I break up with you.* Should I call him and at least get confirmation, or something? I might need closure, so I can move on.

Stepping off the tube, I make my way to the hotel for my morning shift. I check if we have any bookings for today, and there are quite a few people arriving. Maybe a busy day will distract me from my thoughts.

Hours stretch endlessly as I check my phone obsessively, hoping for a sign from Zack. I have nine more hours left of my twelve hour shift. I decided to do doubles here because it gives me more days off for myself, and for all the things I have to do. And to have more time to see Zack but well… It feels like a cruel joke now.

The memory of the party haunts me throughout the day, and I keep thinking about Zack. I feel like I'm about to lose my mind. Was there anything I could've done to prevent all this shit? It's so weird not to speak to him for that long. Definitely too long. I sigh, staring blankly at the computer screen.

The day passes by painfully slow, each minute stretching like an eternity, and I just can't stand it anymore. I want to get out! On my way to the staff room, I see Edward in the hall, scrolling on his phone.

'Hi.' I greet him, unsure of his mood after the party.

'Hi, Maddie. How are you?' Edward responds, flashing a smile.

'I'm fine, thanks.' I reply, clearing my throat. 'Listen, I'm so sorry about Saturday.'

'It's alright Maddie. I'm not mad at you.' He shrugs. 'How's your boyfriend?'

'Um…' Why is he asking?

'I guess he got quite mad when he saw us.' Edward continues casually.

'Us? What do you mean?' I furrow my brows. 'He just… doesn't like… um…' Well… *you*, but I can't say that.

'Me? Yeah, I noticed.' Edward chuckles. Oh, I guess he got the answer himself. 'But I couldn't care less, Maddie. Don't worry. He's just a kid. But I get it. I would be jealous too if I had a girlfriend like you and there was an older guy around her, someone more mature. I guess he might feel threatened.' His words hang in the air, leaving me stunned. What is he talking about?

'What?' I stutter, trying to process all the information.

'I think you should be with someone more… mature, I would say. I don't think this kid is right for you. You are too good for–'

'No, wait. Stop.' I interject, feeling overwhelmed. I cover my face with my hands, giving myself time to think.

'Maddie…' Edward reaches for my hands, moving them away from my face and I recoil in response to his touch, as if I got burned.

'What are you doing? Don't… Just don't touch me.' I blurt out, taking a few steps back. 'Listen, I've told you before that I don't appreciate you flirting with me. I'm not interested, and I have a boyfriend.' I hope I still have. 'I don't want you to touch me in any way other than shaking my hand. You're my manager, and that's it. I appreciated our friendly relationship at work, and I'd like it to remain that way, but… Jesus I don't like you that way. I love Zack!' I manage to say in one breath, my heart racing in my chest.

Was Zack right, then? Will I have to change my job again? Did I do anything? I was just friendly… like all the girls, and even less than them. I was just being nice. That's it. Did he get mixed signals from me?

'Please, let's keep it professional. I don't want any issues and I need my break.' I stammer before hurrying to the staff room.

When the door closes behind me, I reach for my phone, intending to call Meg but then I think it's better to talk to her privately when I get home. Walls have ears. Someone can hear me, and the last thing I need now are rumours.

As I sit in the corner, eating my food, I keep staring at my phone. I miss Zack so much. Despite the hurt, I hope we're not over. I feel the urge to call him and apologise. I just want him to hug me, to feel his strong arms around me.

The last five minutes of my break I spend outside, trying to get some fresh air, wishing I could go home already, and talk to my best friend. Meg always knows what to say, and how to console me.

I return to work for the remaining four hours, and luckily, everyone is nice today. I swear, one wrong word from a customer and I'd have a mental breakdown right here. There are too many thoughts swirling in my head, too many emotions, and I just need a break. A break from life. Or a hug. But the one Zack gives me. The one where I feel safe, happy, and forget about the whole world and all the problems.

While I was on my break, Edward went home, and he will be on a holiday for the next two weeks, so I don't need to worry about any awkward situations for now.

Relief washes over me when Alex comes for her night shift. Our shifts overlap, giving us a couple of hours to chat. After the party, I apologised to her over the phone because I felt terrible about leaving without saying goodbye. She was aware of the situation, so I apologised about it too. Alex was understanding, asking me how I felt. She doesn't seem upset about me leaving early, or about the situation, which is good.

'Maddie?' Alex looks around hesitantly. 'So, I tried to make my move on Edward at my party, but when he came back from outside, after the thing…' She clears her throat, indicating the messy situation between Zack, Edward, and I. 'He seemed so pissed, you know?' She looks at me, and I simply nod, unsure of what to say. 'Maddie?'

'Yes?' I finally respond, meeting her gaze.

'I think he likes you.' Alex says, playing with her fingers.

'I… Um, Alex…' This is bad. What is going on in my life now?

'I got this feeling today, too.'

'What?' Alex looks up from her fingers, confused, so I explain to her the conversation I had with Edward earlier. She likes him, and I feel like I owe her explanation. 'I'm sorry.' I sigh.

'Why? It's not your fault.' Alex assures me.

'But you like him.' I point out.

'Yes, but it's not like you were hitting on him behind my back or anything.' She shrugs. 'Maybe he's still not over his ex.'

'Maybe. But why me? I have a boyfriend.'

'Maybe that's the thing. Oh my God! Maybe that's the *thing*!' Alex exclaims, her eyes widening as if she's just solved a mystery. 'You know his fiancée cheated on him, right? So maybe he wanted to see how it feels to break up someone else's relationship.'

'That's fucked up. For sure it's not the real thing.' I chuckle nervously.

'Who knows. He was normal before and then started acting weird when he found out. That would actually make sense. Because why else would he be after you if you are taken? I mean, don't be offended, you're gorgeous but there are rules. You don't hit on people who are taken.'

'Who knows, Alex. Honestly, this is the least of my worries right now.' I admit.

'Ah, you'll be okay. Just call him. Make the first move. You have nothing to lose. What's the worst that can happen?'

'Him telling me we are over?' I clear my throat when I feel the lump in my throat coming back.

'I mean, at least you will know, right?' Alex offers, rubbing my arm for comfort. 'But I don't think so. You two will be fine.'

'We'll see.' I sigh, quickly changing the conversation away from Zack and me.

I don't feel like talking about us right now. I might go for a short walk after work to think about everything, without anyone else's input in the situation. I appreciate everyone's advice, but this is something between Zack and I, and it's up to us to resolve it.

We spend the rest of my shift chatting about some random stuff and I'm happy that Alex isn't upset about Edward. I was worried she might blame me.

Later, I take my bag from the staff room and put my coat on before returning to the desk.

'I'll see you in a few days.' I smile at Alex.

'Good luck with your presentation tomorrow.' She gives me a thumbs up.

'Thanks, good luck with your shift. Bye.' I wave as I leave the building.

It's getting dark outside, like it's about to rain, and maybe I shouldn't go for a walk today. I stop at the bottom of the stairs when I spot Zack leaning against his car, smoking a cigarette.

My stomach twists when he notices me, dropping the cigarette. Despite missing him, I don't feel happy to see him right now. I feel the same pain in my chest I felt the day we argued. It actually hurts me to see him. No, I don't want to talk to him right now.

Wrapping my coat tighter around me, I walk past him, feeling tears well up in my eyes.

'Maddie!' Zack calls out, grabbing my arm and turning me around to face him. 'Wait, please. I want to talk. I'm sorry.' Zack's voice trails off as he mumbles, his expression reflecting sadness and exhaustion.

'I don't want to talk to you.' I assert, freeing my arm from his grip and taking a step back.

'Please, give me five minutes.' Zack pleads, locking eyes with me.

'I think you said all you had to say the other night.' I reply, looking away and he places his hand on my cheek, turning my face back to meet his gaze.

'No. Please, let me apologise for that.' Zack says, attempting to take my hand, but I cross my arms, avoiding his touch.

'Go on. I don't have much time.' I reply, staring at my feet.

'Okay, so…' Zack clears his throat, gathering his thoughts. 'I want to apologise for the way I spoke to you. You were right, I crossed the line. You didn't deserve that, and I should not have said those things out of anger. I didn't want to hurt you, but I did. I want you to know that I do trust you. I really do. And I don't know why I said what I said. That's not how I truly feel about you. Even if I was angry, I should have not brought it on you. I also want to apologise for my behaviour at the party. I should have handled the situation much better. I got so jealous seeing him so close to you…' Zack pauses, visibly struggling with his words.

'I just lost it. It wasn't the right way to react, and I should have considered how it would affect you. And I know it's not an excuse, but I'm sorry for not coming earlier to apologise, but I was caught up with work. You might know from your calendar.' He adds with a nervous chuckle. I know that he was busy, and yes I saw it in my calendar.

'I thought it would be better to talk in person rather than through a text or phone call, so I waited. You deserve a proper apology, in person. I couldn't sleep for the past few nights. I just kept replaying our argument in my head, and I was so mad at myself for reacting the way I reacted, and treating someone I love like that.

I'm so sorry, Maddie. I should have followed you when I dropped you off at your place. I should have stayed with you that night. And I wanted to see you because… I miss you so much. I fucked up badly, but I hope we can work this through. I am truly sorry, Maddie. I will never let this happen again. I'm sorry.'

As Zack moves closer, his hands finding their way to my cheeks, I don't pull away this time. We lock our eyes, without saying anything.

'I missed you too.' I whisper after a short silence, and Zack smiles warmly.

He wraps his arms around me, snuggling his face into my neck. I close my eyes, returning the embrace. This is the hug I needed so much. I missed his smell. I missed his touch. I missed his beautiful eyes. I missed his smile. I missed him close to me. I missed everything about him.

But I have to tell him about Edward. He deserves to know and I am not going to hide it from him. Especially when he was right about the situation. I just hope we can sit down and discuss it calmly, without yelling at each other. I don't want to argue with him anymore. But when should I bring it up?

We stand in the middle of the sidewalk, holding each other until Zack breaks the hug and kisses me gently, his hands cupping my cheeks.

'I'm so sorry, darling.' Zack whispers, resting his forehead against mine.

'It's alright. We're alright now. You don't have to apologise anymore. And I'm sorry, too. For everything. For putting you in this situation, for starting the argument, for not calling.' I sigh. 'But let's promise each other. No more arguing, no more yelling. From now on, we'll always sit down and talk about anything that bothers us, okay?'

'I promise.' Zack smiles, planting another tender kiss on my lips. 'Never again. It was a torture not seeing or talking to you.'

'I was worried we broke up.' I admit quietly, meeting his gaze.

'No chance, Maddie. It was just an argument, and I hurt you, but no. That wasn't a breakup. These three days without you were like a nightmare, and I can't imagine my life without you by my side.'

Zack declares, his eyes filled with sincerity. I smile, pulling his face closer to mine for another affectionate kiss.

I can say the same. It was awful without him.

'I need to go back home and get ready for my presentation tomorrow.' I say reluctantly when we part.

'I know. I'll drop you off.' Zack offers, taking my hand and intertwining our fingers as we walk back to his car.

'You can stay for the night.' I suggest when we're both settled in the car.

'I can.' Zack smiles, driving away from the hotel.

Zack holds my hand the whole ride to my place, and it feels the same as it was. As if nothing happened. We'll be good, I know it.

Zack parks his car on the street, and we walk to my flat together. The kitchen light is on, so either Meg or Jack, or perhaps both, are already home. As I open the door, the aroma of chicken parmesan greets us, and my stomach grumbles in response. We hang up our coats and make our way to the kitchen together.

'Hi.' I smile at my friends, enjoying their late dinner, and wrap my arm around Zack.

'Hi Meg. Hi Jack.' Zack greets them, his hand resting on my back.

'Hey.' They both reply, and Meg stares at us.

'So you two… are good?' She asks, and I nod, smiling.

'Are you hungry? Come, join us.' Jack invites us to the table, waving his hand.

'Actually yeah, I'm very hungry.' I say, grabbing two plates for Zack and me as we take our seats.

'Well, I'm happy for you then.' Meg gives me a warm smile. 'Do you want some wine?' She stands up and brings two more glasses, pouring the red liquid into them.

'Thanks.' I reply, taking a sip.

'I know you two have missed each other and might have some plans to catch up tonight but…' Meg clears her throat, and I kick her under the table, giving her a warning stare. 'Zack, make sure she is ready for tomorrow. We have an important presentation.' Meg points at Zack, her expression serious.

'I know, and I'll make sure she's ready.' Zack chuckles.

We enjoy our dinner in a friendly atmosphere, chatting and laughing. I can't help but wonder how it would be if all four of us lived together. It will probably never happen, but I think it would be fun. Meg and I are best friends, and Zack and Jack get along very well. We could have breakfasts and dinners together, movie nights, invite friends over. I think it would be the best household I could've ever imagined.

After dinner, I help Meg with the dishes before we split off to our own rooms. Zack lies down on my bed and picks up the sheets of paper from my pillow, raising his eyebrows.

'That's for tomorrow.' I inform him, taking fresh pyjamas from my wardrobe.

'That's a lot.'

'I know. I am going to take a shower, and I need to memorise it.' I say, leaving the room and heading to the bathroom.

The shower is quick because I want to go back to bed for two reasons: Zack is here, and I want to cuddle, and I need to read my speech a few times, making sure I remember every word before I go to sleep.

Clean and fresh, I return to my room to find Zack in the same position he was before, reading my speech.

'The bathroom is free if you need to use it.' I inform him, getting under the covers and looking at him.

'Alright, I'll be back in five minutes.' Zack quickly kisses my lips and heads to the bathroom.

I take my notes and start reading them. However, I feel like I don't remember any of the words even though I've been practicing this speech for the past few days. What if I don't go? Will they fail me, or will I be able to present another time? Or maybe it will be worse if I am the only one speaking. I better focus.

Zack returns, and I get distracted right away. I watch him leave his clothes on my chair and slowly come to lie down next to me, wearing only his boxers. He smiles and opens his arms, inviting me to move closer. I snuggle into his embrace and rest my head on his arm.

'Zack?'

'Yes, darling?' He asks, playing with my hair.

'I need to talk to you about something.' I look up at him, feeling the need to tell him about Edward. Maybe then, I'll be able to fully focus.

'What's going on?' Zack stops playing with my hair and rests his hand on my arm, his gaze focused on mine.

'So, I had a chat with Edward today.' I begin, noticing Zack's jaw clenching at the mention of Edward, but he remains silent, waiting for me to continue. 'So um, I think you were right. He said a few things like that you're *not right for me* and that I *should be with a more mature guy*. And it was so weird. And he tried to touch me but I moved away.' I say, letting out everything in one breath.

'Fucking bastard.' Zack growls, rubbing his face in frustration.

I sit upright, watching him closely. Is he going to get angry? Yell at me? Will we argue again?

'Zack…' I reach out, placing my hand on his wrist. 'I told him that I don't want him to flirt with me or try to touch me in any way. I want us to remain professional at work. And that I don't want any issues. I told him that I love you. I said that I don't like him this way, you know? And that I would appreciate it if nothing changed at work.' I stutter. Zack remains silent, his gaze fixed on the ceiling. 'I want you to know that my decision is to stay at this job because I like it, and I don't want to quit, but if Edward makes things harder for me, I think I will have to. Anyway, I wanted to tell you because I don't want to hide things from you, and you should know.' I sigh.

I can see the anger brewing on his face. Suddenly, Zack sits upright, looking directly at me.

'Maddie,' Zack takes a deep breath. 'I hate this guy so much. He's your fucking manager.' He says, his tone filled with frustration as he takes my hand and squeezes it gently. 'I know you like this job, but he needs to know his place. This is inappropriate and it makes me so mad. At him, not you.'

'I know.' I mumble.

'Thank you for telling me. I appreciate it.' Zack kisses my cheek. 'If he's acting like that, report the bastard somewhere.'

'But I don't want issues…'

'He creates them, not you.'

'He's on a holiday now. I'll see how things are when he's back.' I clear my throat.

'Just do what you think is right for you, okay? And I'll be here for you.' Zack reassures me, kissing my lips gently.

'Okay.' I smile.

'Let's focus on your speech for now. How's it going?' Zack points at my notes.

'I feel like I don't remember anything.' I admit, lying down and sighing.

'Keep reading. I'm sure you know every word. It's just stress.' Zack says, lying down beside me and wrapping his arm around me. 'You can read it out loud for me.'

'Okay.' I clear my throat and start reading all the words I wrote on the paper.

Later, I sit on his torso, speaking to Zack while he follows the words on the paper and rubs my thigh.

'Okay, maybe you should have some rest. It's quite late now and you are definitely prepared.' Zack suggests with a smile. 'You did amazing.'

'Thank you.' I reply, lowering my body to kiss him briefly before lying down beside him. Zack wraps his arms around me, pulling me closer to him.

'Goodnight sweetheart.' Zack kisses my head.

'Goodnight baby.' I smile and snuggle my face into his neck, slowly falling asleep in his embrace.

Chapter Seventeen

The past month has revolved mostly around university for me, as Zack has been busy with work and assisting his dad in refurbishing the art gallery. His schedule didn't leave much room for free time, so I tried to catch up on everything I'd fallen behind on, aiming to have more time for us once he's less busy. While we managed to meet a few times, our nightly calls and frequent texts just weren't the same as being together in person. Zack felt guilty about not having much time for me, but I reassured him endlessly that I understood and wasn't bothered by it. I believe some father-son time was good for him.

Being preoccupied with coursework helped me to clear some dates on my calendar, so I am going with Zack to the new exhibition at his family's art gallery, where I'll meet them for the first time. After nineteen months of dating, it's about time they met me. To say I'm nervous would be an understatement. I am dying of anxiety, fearing that I'll say or do something stupid, and they won't like me.

'Meg, I feel so sick when I think about it.' I confess to my friend, who's lying beside me.

'Just stop it!' She groans in response. 'They're his family, for crying out loud. Look at how well they raised Zack. Of course they'll be nice and like you. You're just overthinking things again.'

'But what if they don't?'

'But what if they do? Why are you so negative?'

'But… I mean, they must know how long we've been together, and imagine, I've never made time to meet them before. How terrible does that make me?' I lament, burying my face into the pillow with a groan.

'You study and work. Of course, you don't have that much time. It's not that bad. Some people don't introduce their families to each other until the wedding day, or never. Imagine that!'

'I could never.' I respond, glancing at Meg. She's engrossed in texting Jack, who went grocery shopping for us.

'Exactly. So it's not that bad. Try to find something positive in this situation. At least he wants to introduce you to them. He could always keep you as a secret.' Meg jokes. 'And this poor man was in a way worse situation when he met your parents.'

'Oh, don't even remind me.' I groan.

Weeks ago, my parents decided to surprise me here. Funny how they showed up the morning after the one evening I had with my boyfriend after a long time apart. If not Meg, they would have found us making out, naked in my bed. It wouldn't have been the best first impression, I guess.

But Meg kept them downstairs, offering coffee and tea, giving me time to prepare as she spoke louder than usual to my parents. Thanks to her, we had some time to quickly get dressed before heading down. Well, maybe just me.

Poor Zack had to meet them topless because I grabbed his T-shirt in a rush. I was the first one to welcome my parents, and Zack joined us shortly after, sheepishly, wearing only his trousers. I felt so bad about it because it was my fault, of course, and I know he wanted to impress my parents and show them how good he is for me.

Anyway, he handled it very well. Zack is very charming, so my mom instantly liked him, and my dad tried to pretend to be strict, but it didn't last long. He quickly got along with Zack.

'You'll be fine. He handled it without being prepared to meet them, and you? At least you know you are going to meet his family.'

'It's Zack. He's perfect, cute and charismatic. There is no way someone would not like him.'

'I mean, if it was me, and my father met Jack like that, trust me, Jack would have to run for his life. Being charming wouldn't help him at all. It was so obvious what you two did the night before.

And that damn fresh hickey on your neck. Such bad timing for Zack to give you one.' Meg laughs. 'But maybe your parents didn't notice.' She shrugs.

'Stop it. My mom was giving me looks the whole day, even when Zack left for work.' I chuckle. 'She knew! I felt so awkward, even though I'm an adult!'

'What time is he coming to pick you up?'

'I think five, so I can meet his family before the event. I don't even know what to wear. I need to ask Zack if there is a dress code. I should have thought about it before.' I sigh.

'Okay. Take a shower first, and then we'll find something. I am sure there is something in your wardrobe, something not black, that you can wear.'

'Black is chic and elegant.' I defend, getting up from my bed.

'It is, and you wear a lot of it. Colours look nice on you too.'

'I will be back in... I might actually take a bath.' I say, stretching and heading to the bathroom.

I gaze at myself in the mirror while water fills the bathtub. Will they like me? Or will they pretend to like me and tell Zack to dump me behind my back? It's important to me that his family likes me. I love him, and the last thing I need is the cliche romance movie drama where the family doesn't accept the girl and drives the couple apart.

I sink into the bathtub and use the relaxing salt, hoping it will actually work, leaving me super relaxed and ready to go. Resting my head on the side of the bathtub, I close my eyes, trying to breathe slowly and rhythmically.

My phone pings, so I dry my hands and reach for it from the shelf. It's Zack.

My family is already excited to meet you! :)

My stomach twists from the nerves, and I feel like throwing up. This relaxing bath salt is definitely not working. I type back to him and receive a quick response.

Can't wait to meet them, too. But I am a bit nervous.

They will love you as much as I do! Don't overthink babe xxx

Putting my phone back on the shelf, I try to relax again. I overthink every situation. Even Zack knows it already. I've already considered a few things that could happen. Like, what if I enter the gallery, trip over, and fall on my face in front of everyone? Or what if my dress rips on something, and everyone sees my ass? Or what if I touch some art because I mistake it for something else and ruin this important event for Zack's dad? What if I say something inappropriate or dumb because I'm too nervous? What if I break something? There are so many things that could go wrong.

I leave the bathtub when the skin on my fingers looks like raisins and walk back to my room wrapped in a towel. Meg looks at me with raised eyebrows. I just shake my head and type a quick message to Zack.

Any dress code? I don't know what to wear :(

I open my drawer and choose a pair of underwear. I squeeze into my panties under the towel without exposing myself to my friend, then I carefully put on my bra without flashing my boobs at Meg. I pick up my phone to see a message and a pic from Zack. Damn, he looks so hot in a crispy white shirt and black tailored trousers.

Nothing too crazy but definitely not jeans. You always look great sweetheart <3

Okay, I will try something. What time are you coming?

I will finish helping my dad and might come earlier x

I am waiting then. Love you!

He messages back, and I put my phone away. Zack looks very handsome and elegant, and I think I should match him or something. I look at my friend, still lying in my bed.

'Meg, we need to find a good outfit. Zack's wearing a white shirt!'

'Okay, let me see.' She responds, getting off my bed and standing next to me, so I show her the picture of Zack.

We both stare at my open wardrobe, and Meg starts to rummage through my clothes.

'What about this red top with a skirt?'

'Too much cleavage. Good for a date with him but not to meet his parents, I guess.'

'Yeah, you might be right.' Meg agrees, shuffling through the clothes. I don't even have that many, but I know she desperately tries to find something not black.

'Damn Maddie. Maybe this dress?' She suggests, showing me a black, long-sleeve dress with cleavage. 'It looks classy and sexy and... just try it on, so we can see if it shows too much boob.'

'Okay.' I agree, taking the dress and putting it on. 'It's a bit tight.'

'No, you look great. It accentuates your waist, the cleavage is not that deep, and it has the perfect length. Not too short and still exposes your legs. I think you should wear this one.' Meg advises, as I watch myself in the mirror. Yeah, my muffin top is definitely accentuated.

'Okay, so this one.' I confirm, sitting down in front of the mirror and looking at my makeup products.

'Do you need my help or do you want to do it yourself?'

'I think I'll do it myself. I don't want to go as *too much,* you know?'

'Fine, go on. I am here just in case.' Meg says, sitting back on my bed, scrolling on her phone, as I proceed with applying different products on my face.

I can see Meg checking on me from time to time in the mirror. I brush my hair and decide not to do anything with them.

'And?' I inquire.

'You look gorgeous.' Meg smiles. I take a bottle of my good perfume and spray it on me. 'Ready to meet your boyfriend's family, lovely?'

'Stop.' I chuckle nervously.

There is a knock on the front door a moment later, making my heart race because I know it's him.

'That must be Zack. And we lost your boyfriend I am afraid. Where is he?'

'Nah, he's getting more stuff. And I will get it.' Meg says, jumping off my bed and rushing out of my bedroom to open the door.

I can hear their hushed voices and both of them giggling. I check myself in the mirror again before Zack enters my room, with Meg behind him. I turn around to face them both. Zack gives me his dazzling smile that always makes my heart skip a beat, checking me up and down.

'You look stunning, Maddie.' Zack compliments, coming closer and welcoming me with a kiss. I smile at him.

'Okay, you two have fun and let me know how it was.' Meg smiles at me. 'Good luck Zack, she could panic any second. She's a walking bundle of nerves.'

'I won't.' I mumble, and Meg laughs before leaving my room.

'Don't worry, darling. Everything will be alright. You're just meeting my family.' Zack says, shrugging and pushing a strand of hair behind my ear.

'First impressions are very important, Zack.'

'Tell me about it. What did your parents think about me, hm?' Zack chuckles and I purse my lips.

'I had no idea they would come. Anyway, they asked me about you over the phone yesterday.' I say, placing my hands on his chest.

'Really?' His eyes shine in excitement.

'They said that you seem like a lovely guy and stuff. Mostly my mom. I think you're accepted.' I say, cupping his face and kissing him. Zack places his big hands on my waist, pulling me closer.

'I haven't met your brother though.' Zack mentions, circling his arms around me. 'Is he going to interrogate me?'

'I bet he doesn't care at all if his sister has someone. He only cares about his job and girlfriend.' I shrug casually.

'You never know with cops.' Zack chuckles.

'Not him.' I reply, staring into his deep, brown eyes. 'But is there anything I need to know before I meet your family? Are there things I should not mention? Or like… what do I do?' I ask, feeling a bit nervous. I've never met my boyfriend's family. Well, Zack is the first serious boyfriend I've had.

'No, they are very easy-going. I told you not to worry or overthink it. It will be fine.' He reassures, kissing me again. 'Let's go.'

'Okay.' I nod.

When we are downstairs, we shout a quick bye to poor Meg studying in the living room, and leave to go to Zack's car.

'So, you have two younger sisters.' I remark, looking at him as he drives. 'Tiffany and Francesca. Francesca is the older one.'

'That's right.' Zack smiles, his warm hand rubbing my leg to comfort me.

'And your parents are Lauren and David.'

'Correct. And your parents are Rebecca and Paul.' Zack tries to lighten my mood. 'And you are Madison Martin. My girlfriend. My love. My future. My everything.' He says, and I just laugh, shaking my head. I put my hand on the top of his, feeling much better with him next to me. I missed him so much.

When we arrive at the small gallery, Zack drives to the back of the building and parks. My heart pounds in my chest as I step out of the car, and I feel my legs tremble.

When we walk inside through the glass door, there are only a few people inside for now, and Zack explains to me that for the moment, only his family, workers, the artist, and artist's friends are here. Later other people who were invited should arrive. It's a private event where they present the work to some big names before they open it to the public, hoping to get some sales.

'Is my face red?' I ask Zack before we join anyone. I feel like it got red from the nerves.

'No, you look beautiful.' Zack reassures me, placing a gentle kiss on my forehead. 'Ready?' He asks, squeezing my hand. I nod, lacing our fingers as we walk towards a group of people and a few faces turn our way.

I can recognise his family. His dad is as tall as Zack and has the same hair. His mom is much shorter and very beautiful. And his sisters, very similar to each other with much lighter hair than Zack's. Francesca is taller than Tiffany. They all look beautiful and are dressed very elegantly.

We come closer to them. Zack lets go of my hand and places his hand on my lower back instead.

'Mom, dad, Francesca, and Tiffany, this is Maddie. Maddie, meet my family.' Zack smiles at me and returns his gaze to his family.

'It's nice to meet you all.' I say, wanting to shake hands with his dad, but he pulls me into a friendly hug instead.

'Maddie! It's so nice to finally meet you.' His dad beams.

'Zack talks about you all the time. Oh, and you are even more beautiful than he told us.' His mom says, kissing my cheek, and the girls do the same. I look at Zack and he chuckles nervously, scratching his temple.

'You're going to university, right? Marketing and advertising?' His mom asks.

'That's correct.' I confirm, smiling.

'Very interesting. I must say, I was impressed when Zack told us. Clever girl.' His dad nods approvingly.

'Thank you.' I keep smiling at them.

'My girls want to go into fashion. Francesca studies fashion design. She wants to be a big designer! And Tiffany wants to be a stylist. They might open a family business.' His dad says, proudly wrapping his arms around his daughters.

'Zack mentioned that to me. I think that's great, very creative choice of career.' I nod, feeling Zack's arm wrap around me again.

'Let me show you what we have here today before it starts. And you are always welcome to visit Maddie. Whenever you want.' His dad offers warmly, leading us around the gallery to check out the new exhibition.

As we walk, I feel the stress slowly leaving my body. His family is genuinely lovely, showering me with questions about university and future plans.

Tiffany is a bit shy, but she opens up about her dreams of dressing celebrities in the future, doing big events, and red carpets.

Francesca shows me the stunning fashion designs she created for her university project, and they all look incredible. Each piece presents a minimalistic aesthetic with an element of surprise and unconventional cuts. Meg would love to wear some of her pieces. I wouldn't mind wearing them myself.

And Zack's mom? She is so lovely and sweet. She showers me with questions about my hobbies, and how I manage everything with university and work. She even asks if I make sure to have some time for myself, which is absolutely heart-warming. And when she asks if Zack treats me well, I can't help but beam as I happily confirm.

Zack was right. I had nothing to worry about. I mean, I didn't expect them to be mean or rude, or anything like that. I think it is pretty normal to feel anxious before meeting the family of the person you love. I was just worried that I would do something wrong. But it looks like everything is going well.

Zack doesn't leave my side for a second, ensuring I feel comfortable and don't get overwhelmed with all the new faces arriving and greeting us. But I feel good. He's here and as always everything seems much easier. I can see where he inherited all his good values. His parents have done a great job raising him.

As the evening progresses, I even have a chance to meet the artist. However, I have no idea what he's talking about when he explains to me the concept of his project. It's all a bit too philosophical for me. Too deep, I guess. I wish I could understand but I still think his work is amazing. I might need a simpler explanation. Perhaps I will ask Zack later when we are alone. For now, I just nod and smile, enjoying sips of champagne from my glass. I had a wonderful time and am grateful to have finally met Zack's family.

Chapter Eighteen

Today, Meg and I have our own little date. No boys. It's girls night only! The anticipation of spending quality time with my bestie and sharing some gossip washes over me like a wave. We are going to make some pizza, bake cookies, paint, do face masks, and watch movies. We're done with our second year at university and today is our well-deserved break, a day to unwind and let go of all our worries. Zack works tonight, and Jack is visiting his family for a weekend, but will be back late tonight.

Since I have zero responsibilities, I decide to take my time and stay in bed as long as I want to. Stretching out lazily in bed, I reach for my phone to check the time, wondering if Zack is getting ready to work now. I decide to give him a call.

'Hello, darling.' Zack's soft voice greets me after just two rings.

'Hi.' I reply, sinking back into the pillows with a smile. 'What are you doing?'

'I'm getting ready for work. You?'

'I'm still in bed.'

'Jesus, Maddie it's almost twelve.' Zack chuckles.

'I have a day off, okay? And I am getting up soon to go get some groceries and buy other stuff for today.' I defend myself with a laugh.

'Ah, yes. Your date with Meg.'

'Exactly. Are you coming tomorrow? We'll have some good stuff left over after today.'

'What are you two up to?' Zack's laughter fills the line.

'We are going to make pizza and bake cookies.' I explain, pulling my phone away from my ear to press the camera button. I want to see him. Seconds later, Zack's smiling face pops up on my screen.

'Still in your pyjamas, huh?' Zack says, adjusting his phone against something stable, so it doesn't fall, and I watch him as he gets dressed. 'And yeah, I'll come then. Never turning down homemade food from my girl.'

'You look handsome.' I compliment him, unable to resist biting my lip.

'Thanks, babe.' He replies with a wink. I swing my legs off of the bed, holding my phone as I head to my wardrobe. 'Oh, look who got up.' Zack teases.

'Shut up.' I retort, laughing. 'You always stay in bed late with me.'

'Yeah, because it's with *you.*' Zack emphasises. I look at him and see a big smile on his face. He's just... Uh, I want to hug him so bad right now. 'Anyway, gorgeous, I've got to get going.' Zack says after a while, ready to go.

'I know.' I sigh. 'Well, have a nice day at work.'

'And you have fun with Meg. Tell her I said hi.'

'I will.'

'Bye Maddie. I'll see you tomorrow. Love you.' Zack blows a kiss through the phone.

'Love you too.' I reply with a smile before I hang up and put my phone away.

It's time to get dressed. I decide to wear comfy black leggings and a black jumper Zack left here a few days ago. I sniff it and it still smells like him. Good as hell.

I head downstairs to pour myself some juice from the fridge, and Meg joins me a few moments later.

'Maddie!' She exclaims, her excitement palpable.

'What's up with you?' I ask, raising an eyebrow.

'Nothing. Just excited to spend the day with my best friend.'

'Come on. I know you.' I prod gently, knowing her too well to buy into the innocent act.

'Well...' She bites her lip. 'I got the internship! I start on Monday!' Meg squeaks.

'No way!' My jaw drops in astonishment. Meg had been

worrying whether she'd secure it or not. It's an internship in one of the better marketing companies in London. 'Congratulations!' I exclaim, pulling her into a tight hug.

I am so proud of her because I know how much this opportunity means to her. Meg is incredibly ambitious. I should do one as well, but I am too lazy now, and decided to do a short one later in summer. Honestly, I don't want to sacrifice more time with my boyfriend for an internship but I have to do it.

'We're definitely drinking for that.' I declare, pointing at her.

'Yeah, we're getting some good wine, or champagne tonight.' Meg beams.

'And definitely not the cheapest one. It deserves a proper bottle.' I add with a serious expression, earning a laugh from Meg.

As we leave our flat, the good mood accompanies us to the shop. It's a bit chilly today, but I don't mind since we are going to stay at home. We grab everything on our list for the evening, along with some extra crafty supplies.

Spending a little extra time in the alcohol section, we try to decide over which rum would be perfect for homemade mojitos, we then head back to the fruit section for the remaining ingredients before heading to the checkout. The cashier shoots us a curious glance as he scans two bottles of rum and a bottle of champagne. I exchange looks with Meg, trying not to laugh. It's definitely going to be a good evening for us.

We stroll back home with our grocery bags, chatting and laughing.

'Okay, should we just take quick showers and stay in our pyjamas for the rest of the day?' Meg suggests.

'Yes! Let's do that!' I clap my hands excitedly. Spending the whole day in pyjamas sounds like absolute bliss.

'Okay, I'll go first!' Meg declares, leaving the grocery bags on the table and heading to the bathroom.

In the meantime, I take charge, unpacking the groceries and putting the alcohol in the fridge to chill. As Meg takes ages in the bathroom, I put our snacks in small bowls and arrange them nicely in the living room and light some candles.

'Your turn.' Meg announces, returning with wet hair. 'It looks nice.' She compliments, looking around the living room as I finish with the candles.

'Alright, I'll be quicker. Definitely.' I chuckle, heading into the bathroom for my turn.

My shower is brief, and as I stand there with droplets of water cascading down my skin, a mischievous idea crosses my mind, so I grab my phone. Should I send Zack a nude? I'm sure he would love it.

As I open the camera, trying to take a sexy pic of myself, a wave of caution washes over me. What if he opens it around someone? What if his boss sees my boobs? Or what if some other female coworker sees my stomach and laughs? What if I send it to the wrong number? No. I don't think it's a good idea anymore. Too much to risk. With a sigh, I push the idea aside and slip into my pyjamas before joining Meg in the kitchen.

'Ta da!' Meg presents two glasses of freshly made cocktails as I enter. The kitchen smells like limes and mint, and I love it.

'Let me try it.' I say, taking a sip. 'Oh… it's so good.' I murmur, enjoying the refreshing taste.

'What do we do first?' Meg asks, slurping her cocktail.

'Let's cook before we get tipsy and burn the house down.' I laugh, and Meg nods in agreement.

We dive into our cooking spree, shaping pizza dough into heart shapes and topping them with savoury ingredients. Meg puts some music on, and soon we're having our private concert in the kitchen, singing and dancing to ABBA, our cocktails in hand.

Feeling particularly playful, I record Meg singing into a wooden spoon, pointing the camera at myself later, with Meg dancing in the background.

'Show me.' Meg requests, resting her chin on my arm as we watch the video, both of us laughing. 'Post it and tag me please. We're so funny.' She chuckles, taking another sip of her drink.

'Okay.' I grin, adding it to my Instagram story and tagging her. 'Now, let's finish the pizza.'

'And we need more drinks.' Meg adds, showing me her empty glass, so I quickly down mine.

We sprinkle some cheese on top of our pizzas, before putting both of them in the oven and setting a timer. Meg prepares us another round of mojitos before we move to making cookies. I read the recipe, passing Meg all the ingredients, and she mixes them all. I quickly chop the chocolate, so we can sprinkle it on the top of the cookies.

When the pizza is ready, we replace it with the cookies in the oven.

'Smells amazing.' I sigh, closing my eyes for a few seconds, inhaling the delicious scent.

'Let's have some.' Meg suggests, slicing a few pieces. We both grab a slice and take a bite, savouring the flavours.

'So good!' I exclaim with a mouthful of pizza, and Meg nods in agreement, munching her slice.

We either did a great job and it's that good, or it's the mojitos enhancing our taste buds. I lick my fingers and wipe them with a kitchen towel, before I grab my phone, finding a couple of messages from Zack.

Why are you so adorable in that video?
Glad to see you two having fun x

'Oh, I love him so much.' I murmur under my breath, but Meg overhears anyway.

'What?' She leans in to read the messages. 'That's cute.'

'I know.' I reply, biting my lip.

'Cookies are ready!' Meg announces, perhaps too loud, as she opens the oven. Once again, the delicious and sweet aroma fills the kitchen.

'Oh, I need one right now.' I laugh. The batch of chocolate chip cookies calls out my name, telling me to eat them. But they're definitely too hot, so I finish my drink instead.

With another round of refreshing cocktails, we clean all the dirty dishes, move the remaining pizza onto a large plate, and put it in the fridge.

With the plate of cookies in hand, I head to the living room while Meg pops some popcorn in the microwave. She joins me on the sofa, and I eagerly grab a handful of popcorn as soon as she settles beside me.

'Did you try the cookie?'

'Not yet.' I admit, reaching for one and splitting it in half to share with Meg. We munch on the soft and sweet treat. Zack and Jack will be pleased tomorrow with all the food we've made.

'Okay, so I think we should put on the face masks and paint.' Meg suggests, grabbing two sachets from the table, and we proceed to apply the creamy white mask to each other's faces.

'This feels nice.' I comment, enjoying the cool sensation on my skin as we both take a seat on the floor. Meg opens our paint set, while I distribute various brushes between us.

'This is so exciting. I feel like a child!' Meg giggles with excitement.

'I know! And you might be tipsy. Your cheeks are pink.' I tease, noticing a slight flush on her face, before picking up a brush.

'Shut up.' Meg laughs, grabbing a brush and eagerly starting to paint.

As I stare at my blank canvas, I realise I have no idea what to paint.

'Meg, I don't know what to do.'

'Anything! Don't even think about it, just start doing it. That's what I do.' Meg shrugs.

I dip my brush into a vibrant blue paint and begin creating lines on the canvas, adding splashes of pink and orange as inspiration strikes.

I end up painting some kind of sunset. The more I drink, the better it works. And suddenly, I'm transported back to that beautiful sunset in Greece when Zack confessed his love to me. And now I know exactly what I'm painting. At least, I try. In the meantime, we mix up another round of drinks.

'This is so relaxing.' I remark, glancing over at Meg. Her tongue sticks out in concentration, her face focused. I can't help but chuckle and quickly snap a picture of her.

'What are you doing?' She asks, looking up at me.

'Sending it to Jack.' I reply, hitting send before she can protest. The message lands in our group chat, and Meg checks her phone. Within seconds, she bursts into laughter.

'Jack already liked it.'

'Ew! Gross!' I screw up my face when he sends a dirty message about her tongue. He quickly deletes it, sending another one saying "sorry" and that it was meant to be privately for Meg. Too late, mate.

'Oh, like you're so innocent?' Meg raises an eyebrow, taking a big sip of her cocktail.

'I mean…' I clear my throat.

'Maddie.' She laughs, shaking her head. 'You're definitely not. Not with Zack.' Meg teases.

'Anyway, how's your painting?' I quickly change the subject, glancing at her canvas presenting a beautiful garden. 'Wow! This is great.'

'Show me yours.' Meg gestures, and I show her mine. 'And you said you didn't know what to paint.' She chuckles.

We set our canvases aside to let the paint dry and head to the bathroom to rinse off the face masks.

Afterwards, we return to the kitchen for another round of cocktails, preparing some extra snacks to bring back to the living room. We slump onto the sofa, the evening stretching out before us in a relaxing mood.

'Cheers to us, Maddie.' Meg raises her glass, and we clink them together.

'To us.' I echo, taking a sip.

'Let's talk about real stuff now.' Meg says, turning to face me. 'You and Zack, how serious are you? I mean, you've been together for like a year and a half, nearly two… so?'

'We're definitely very serious. He has all the good qualities, you know?' I say, a smile spreading across my face as I talk about Zack. 'He's such a gentleman, he opens the car door for me, brings me flowers without any occasion, always asks how I feel, tells me that I'm beautiful and how much he loves me.' I scrunch up my nose at all the sweet memories running through my head. 'There are so many things I love about him. And honestly… he's definitely the one.' I admit, my voice softer as I bite my bottom lip. 'He's so perfect, inside and out. And the way he looks at me. His eyes tell me everything, Meg. He doesn't have to tell me that he loves me all the time. I see it all in his eyes. And his actions.'

'You are so in love.' Meg chuckles. 'And now you're finally having sex with him, after all your ridiculous issues with yourself.'

'Oh yeah and it's great. He makes me feel so confident and sexy when I am with him.'

'Well, I hope he goes down on you often, huh?' Meg watches me closely as she sips her drink.

'Um, yeah.' I titter sheepishly.

'And you? Do you go down on him? Did you use my tips?' Meg smirks mischievously, and I nod in confirmation.

'Yes, and thanks. But he also tells me how he likes it, so let's say we communicate.' I reply, feeling a slight blush creeping onto my cheeks, unsure if it's from the alcohol or the conversation with Meg.

'Look at you! What incredible progress. I feel proud of you.' Meg chuckles, shaking her hand. 'That's it for you then. You have a great man who loves you, great sex, which is important in a relationship, and you are so happy with him. I've never seen you like this before. I'm glad you met him.'

'Me too. Thanks to you!' I pout slightly, and we warmly embrace each other. 'Thanks for pushing me that night to hit on him.'

'You're welcome. I told you he might be the one!' Meg laughs as we part from the hug. 'Look at us, both happy with the right men.'

'What about you two? All good?' I inquire.

'It's all perfect!' Meg beams. 'And I feel like he's thinking about proposing.'

'What?' I squeak, my jaw dropping in astonishment, and Meg nods affirmatively.

'Yes. He looks at my hands and checks my rings sometimes when I wear them. He's never done that before!'

'How do you feel about it?'

'This is exciting! Of course I want to marry him. He's the one for me, for sure.' Meg chuckles, looking at me. 'But, we've talked about not taking the next step while I'm at university. So if he proposes, my whole focus would be on getting married instead of studying. I can't fail my last year.'

'True. I get that. But Meg… that would be amazing. You two getting married. I can't wait for that day.'

'Well…' Meg giggles. 'It will come one day for sure. But not as long as I am a student. So, I hope he remembers. But it's so exciting! If he really wants to marry me! Ahhh, I can't wait for that day! For our future life together.' She says, her hands on her cheeks. 'You see? Just thinking about it makes me thrilled. Imagine if it happened. I would definitely forget that I even attend university.'

'I wouldn't let you.' I smile.

'You'll be my maid of honour when I get married.' Meg extends her pinky finger to me, and I intertwine mine around hers in a pinky promise.

'I would be honoured.' I smile.

'Okay, we need more drinks!' Meg exclaims, grabbing our empty glasses and scurrying to the kitchen. I glance at my phone and decide to reply to Zack's earlier messages, feeling the dizziness setting in.

> I might be a bit drunk… Meg's mojitos are quite strong.
> I wish you were here. I miss you already.
> Love you so much xxx

I'm definitely drunk. The next drink will put me to sleep. I gaze at my phone, wishing Zack was in my bed, waiting for me to come after drinking with Meg, so I could sleep in his arms.

'Drinks are ready.' Meg announces, returning to the living room, no longer walking straight, and I chuckle.

'That's the last one.' I declare, taking a glass from her.

'Why?'

'Meg, we're drunk.' I look her in the eyes as she sits next to me.

'Maybe, but who cares.' She shrugs, making me titter.

'Jack's gonna love it when he's back.'

'I'll be gone before he's back.' Meg laughs.

'Yup.' I scrunch up my nose and take a sip of my drink.

We spend the rest of the evening chatting about our dream

future, what we want to do, about Jack and Zack, and about silly things that make us laugh so hard that we cry.

We even share our Pinterest ideas about weddings which is crazy since none of us is even engaged yet. I mean, Meg might be close to that. I can't help but picture myself marrying Zack one day and building a life together. There is nobody else in this world for me. It's only him.

Meg excuses herself to the bathroom, leaving me alone. Suddenly, an overwhelming urge to hear Zack's voice washes over me. I grab my phone and dial his number.

'Hi. You alright, darling?' Zack answers immediately.

'Hiiiii. Yes. I am… fine. I just wanted to hear your voice.' I babble, feeling a bit lightheaded.

'Are you drunk?' Zack chuckles, knowingly.

'I might be. Her drinks are so strong, Zack. And Meg is a strong player. Trust me.' I say, tilting my head back against the sofa, feeling the room spin. 'Yup, I am drunk.'

'You know I am working, right?'

'I know. I'm sorry. I shouldn't have called you.' I sigh. 'I just wish you were here, you know?'

'It's alright but maybe you should go and lie down?'

'Maybe I will. Will you be there?'

'Where?' Zack asks.

'In my bed?' I giggle.

'Not at the moment.' He chuckles. 'I need to go back to work, sweetheart.'

'I wish you were next to me.' I murmur, rubbing my eyes, tired.

'I know. Me too.'

'Come then.' I say softly.

'I have to finish work.' Zack's laughter sounds from the phone. 'I really need to go. I love you.'

'I love you too!' I murmur to the phone before he hangs up.

'I love you too!' Meg mimics me, returning from the bathroom and sitting beside me.

'I love you too, Meg.' I smile and look at my friend. 'I am wasted and I think it's enough for us tonight. I am so tired and drunk.' I say, resting my head on her arm.

'Me too.'

'Let's go to bed then.' I suggest, as she rests her head on mine.

We both struggle to maintain our balance as we walk up the stairs, laughing at each other's stumbling. After saying our goodnights, we split into our bedrooms.

My body limply flops onto bed, and I remain like that with one of my legs on the bed and the other one dangling above the floor, my arms spread open. My eyes feel so heavy, and I can't keep them open any longer.

I sense someone lifting my body and tucking me in under the quilt. I struggle to open my eyes. It's dark and I can't see much anyway. As I try to sit up slowly, a strong hand stops me.

'Go back to sleep, Maddie.'

'Zack?' I whisper.

'Yes, it's me.' The familiar voice replies. The mattress sinks as Zack settles beside me, wrapping his arms around me.

'You came…' I smile, snuggling my face into his neck. He actually came after my messages and drunk call.

'You wanted it. Have some sleep, darling.' Zack murmurs, planting a kiss on the top of my head, his fingers gently tracing patterns on my arm.

I try to express my love for him, but only unintelligible words escape my lips before I drift back into sleep. Perhaps I'm only dreaming, and he's not truly here. But at that moment, it doesn't matter. I feel safe and loved.

Chapter Nineteen

When I wake up the next morning, a wave of sickness crashes over me. I am aware that the moment I get up, I'll have to run for my life to the bathroom. As I slowly roll to the other side of the bed, I bump into something warm and soft. Reluctantly, I open my eyes, only to find Zack's sleepy face next to mine. I move my face slightly away, praying to the universe to help me survive what is coming.

Zack is here. He came because I wanted it. A fleeting smile dances across my lips as I reach out to caress his adorable face, but I feel yesterday's mojitos coming up.

'Oh no…' I whimper, sitting upright. My chest heaves as I attempt to stop what is coming with deep breaths. Placing a hand on my stomach, I squeeze my eyes shut. Did we really have that much last night? For sure we didn't.

'Maddie, are you okay?' Zack's morning voice sounds in my ears. I open my eyes and look at my beautiful man as he rubs his eyes and yawns, tired.

'No, I feel sick.' I confess. His gaze locks with mine, and he shifts onto his elbows, his expression filled with worry.

'Do you want water or something?'

'No, I have to… I just need to go to the bathroom.' I manage to say, slowly getting out of the bed. And then it hits me. It's coming. 'Just stay here.' I say quickly, rushing out of my bedroom straight to the bathroom. The last thing I want is for Zack to see me throwing up.

There is a silent knock at the door just as I close it behind me. I know it's Zack, but before I can say anything, I throw up… ugly and loud. Shit, I had hoped for a quiet one, something easier to cover up. A bit more graceful than this.

I can feel Zack's hands grabbing my hair and holding it. Great, now he will definitely be disgusted with me. I'm disgusted with myself, after all. Zack doesn't say anything. He simply stays there, holding my hair back and rubbing my back in soothing circles.

As I rise from the bathroom floor, I swiftly flush the toilet. I reach for my toothbrush, scrubbing away the vile aftertaste in my mouth. I don't want to kill my boyfriend with my bad breath.

'Do you feel better?' Zack's concerned voice breaks the silence, drawing my attention.

'A little bit.' I clear my throat. Turning to face him, I find Zack leaning against the wall next to me. He looks exhausted. 'What time is it?'

'It's nearly five in the morning.'

'What?' My eyebrows shoot up in disbelief. I was sure it was afternoon by now.

Zack nods wearily, rubbing his face.

'I'll get you some tea. Go back to bed.' Zack offers, already turning to leave, but I grab his arm, stopping him.

'It's fine. Don't worry about it. You're tired–' I begin, but he interrupts me.

'No, I will bring it to you. Go lie down.' He insists, pressing a tender kiss to my forehead before slipping out of the bathroom.

I sigh, splashing my face with cold water before making my way back to the bedroom.

Crawling back into bed, I pull the quilt snugly around me, stealing a glance at the clock. 5:23 in the morning. Wow, it really is early. What time did he get here? Poor Zack was working late last night, and now he is dealing with his still-drunk girlfriend. Oh, my head is still dizzy.

'Hot tea, darling.' Zack returns, a steaming mug in hand, placing it on my bedside table as I sit up.

'Thank you.' I murmur gratefully, watching him settle into bed beside me. 'What time did you get here?' I inquire, blowing on the steam rising from the mug.

'I think it was past two. I called to see if you were awake, but you didn't pick up, so I used the key you gave me.' Zack explains, folding his arms behind his head as he gazes at me.

'Sorry.' I mumble, taking a small sip of the hot tea.

'Why?' Zack chuckles softly.

'For calling, dragging you here, and falling asleep before you even came. Oh, and for waking you up so early.' I confess, feeling guilty for disrupting his sleep.

'Maddie.' Zack shakes his head. 'It's fine. You could call me in the middle of the night and say that you want to cuddle, and I would be on my way. I always want to be next to you, and seeing you after a long and stressful shift makes my day better. Even when you're drunk. By the way, you looked so funny on your bed when I came. I should've taken a picture of you.' He adds, laughter bubbling in his voice.

'Stop it.' I chuckle, taking another sip of the tea.

'Let's get some sleep.' Zack suggests.

'Okay.' I smile, nodding in agreement.

'Hope you feel better.' He whispers.

'I do now.'

And it's all because he is here. Next to me. He truly does make everything better.

As I slowly sip on my tea, I glance at Zack, noticing his eyes are closed. Setting the empty mug aside, I slide back under the quilt, resting my head on his chest trying not to wake him up. His arm circles around me.

'Zack?'

'Yes?' He murmurs with his deep voice.

'Thank you.' I whisper, pressing a tender kiss to his cheek, and Zack smiles with his eyes still closed. I rest my head on his chest again, slowly falling asleep in his warm and strong arms. I feel incredibly lucky and grateful that he is my boyfriend.

When I open my eyes, it's already bright outside. I can hear birds chirping as the sun tries to get into my room through the curtains. My stomach feels a little bit better, and I hope that I won't throw up anymore today.

Stretching lazily, I reach for my phone to check the time. Eleven thirty. Not that bad, I suppose. I slowly sit up, trying not to wake up Zack, and carefully slip out of bed. I make my way to the window and open it, letting fresh air in the room.

Today, Meg and I had plans to clean the whole flat, but I don't feel like I want to do it anymore. All I want is to stay in bed all day with Zack.

As I open my wardrobe, I retrieve my leggings and a plain, black T-shirt. It's simple, but comfort is key for a day at home. My face looks pale and my hair falls flat around my shoulders. A few quick strokes of the hairbrush and a spritz of perfume on my neck is enough.

I slowly walk back to the bed, my knee sinking into the mattress as I lean over Zack. He looks adorable and peaceful in his sleep. I can't resist the urge to kiss him, so I gently press my lips against his. The simple touch of affection wakes him up, and he welcomes me with a sleepy smile on his lips.

'Morning, gorgeous.'

'Morning.' I smile as Zack wraps his arms around me, pulling me on his chest.

'How do you feel?' Zack asks, brushing a strand of hair behind my ear.

'Better. Did you sleep well?'

'Can't complain. Someone was keeping me warm.' He chuckles, running his fingers up and down my back.

'I'll make some breakfast.' I offer, preparing to get up.

'Stay here.' Zack insists, turning us around and blocking me with his body. 'Five more minutes.' His voice is muffled against my neck as he snuggles closer. 'You smell nice.'

'Thanks.' That's why I used perfume on my stay-at-home day.

Since I don't have to rush anywhere, I decide to stay in bed with Zack. I run my fingers through his hair, wishing we could be lazy and cuddle for the rest of the day. Unless, my friend forces me to clean, but I don't think she'll be in a mood for that either.

'Do you have any plans today, or do you want to stay here with us?' I ask, moving my fingers up and down his back.

'Are you going to clean?' Zack asks, his gaze meeting mine.

'Yup. At least, that's the plan.' I admit, looking down at him still snuggled into me.

'I will stay. Someone has to make sure you do all the work instead of binge-watching TV shows.' Zack teases.

'We don't do that!' I protest.

'No?' Zack teases, raising his eyebrows. 'Didn't you two spend, like, five hours watching *Married At First Sight* last time?'

'Um… only because it was a very interesting season.' I defend with a playful roll of my eyes.

'Of course, baby.' Zack murmurs, his voice rich with affection as he shifts his body, towering over me.

I find myself lost in his beautiful brown eyes, feeling my heart skip a beat in response. He moves closer, planting a soft kiss on my lips, and I wrap my arms around his neck as we kiss passionately. I try to pull him closer, but Zack resists, so I throw my leg around his hips, putting more effort in bringing his body closer to mine.

'Maddie.' He chuckles into my mouth, breaking the kiss. 'You need to do your things.'

'This is more fun.' I say, attempting to sound seductive as I gaze into his eyes. With a playful smirk, I slowly slide my hand down to his boxers, but he stops me by grabbing my wrist.

'I have an idea.' Zack says, grabbing both of my hands and pressing them against the pillow above my head. That's hot.

'Yes?' I smile, attempting to seduce him.

'You do what you have to do today and then we'll go to mine.' Zack leans in, planting a short but affectionate kiss on my lips.

'Or…' I start, trying to free my hands, but Zack tightens his grip.

'No, Maddie. I'll make sure you don't procrastinate, and then…' Zack's voice trails off as he leans in closer, his warm breath caressing my ear. 'I will do all the things you like.' His words send a shiver down my spine as he gently nibbles on my earlobe, pressing his hips against mine, and I groan in anticipation.

'Okay.' I manage to choke out, my desire growing.

'Great. Get up, now.' Zack says, releasing my hands and rising from the bed. I watch him dress, still lying in the same position he left me. 'Maddie, you need to move.' Zack teases, a smirk playing on his lips.

I grimace, reluctantly leaving my bed. Zack approaches me swiftly, cupping my face in his hands and kissing me. His lips are so soft and tender, and I want him to kiss me forever.

'Gosh, even hungover, you are beautiful.' He murmurs, drawing apart, still holding my face.

'Stop being so cheesy.' I chuckle, feeling a blush creep into my cheeks.

'That's true, darling.' Zack says, his lips brushing against my cheek.

'Let's have some breakfast.' I suggest, moving away from his embrace. Just as I turn to leave the room, his big hand grabs my ass, giving it a squeeze. I squeak in surprise, turning to see his smug expression.

'So sexy.' Zack says, moving his eyebrows, and I chuckle.

We head to the kitchen, where I try to make us omelettes while Zack stands behind me, his arms wrapped around my waist, his chin resting on my arm. I love when he holds me like this, when his chest is pressed against my back, when his hands rub my stomach, and when he kisses my neck. I can't help but smile to myself, pouring the mixture on the frying pan. I make some extra ones for my friends too and set out plates on the table.

Zack sips his morning coffee, his attention fixed on his phone. I steal glances at him as he scrolls through messages. How come this man is in my life? Seriously. He's absolutely perfect, and his presence brings me the joy I never knew I was missing.

Zack glances up from his phone, catching me staring at him. He sets his phone aside with a smirk on his face.

'Sorry, work.' Zack says, giving me his whole attention.

'It's alright.' I assure him with a smile.

'Hi guys.' Meg yawns, entering the kitchen and taking a seat at the table. 'What are you doing here, Zack?'

'I came last night.' Zack replies casually, helping himself to an omelette.

'Nice.' Meg nods in acknowledgment, taking an omelette.

'I need to leave soon and just pop into work. There's an urgent meeting I have to attend.' Zack announces, turning his gaze to me.

'Alright.' I respond. I glance at Meg, who looks truly exhausted.

I guess she's had a rough night. 'Am I going to see you tonight?' I inquire, redirecting my attention back to Zack.

'Maddie darling, you have the key to my place. Come whenever you want, and I'll be there after.' Zack assures me, giving me his cute smile, and I return it.

'Okay.' I lean in to plant a kiss on his cheek.

'I need to go. I'll let you know when it's done, and I can come to pick you up and we'll go to my place.' Zack promises with a wink, and my stomach twists with excitement at the memory of his promise earlier. He rises from his seat, finishing the last bite of his omelette. 'Good luck with your chores.' He adds, gesturing towards Meg with a playful chuckle, shaking his head. Oh, he knows we'll do nothing.

'Yeah, I think we have some things to do.' I reply, wrinkling my nose. There's no way any of us will be able to do anything. All I truly want is to crawl back into bed, preferably with Zack by my side, but he has to go.

'I'll see you later.' Zack says, leaning in to kiss my lips.

'Can you stay?' I blurt out, instinctively grabbing his hand.

'Maddie...' Zack begins.

'Call in sick.' I plead.

'I wish I could but they say it's important. It shouldn't be long. I hope.' Zack responds, his hands gently cupping my cheeks.

'Okay.' I nod as he kisses me softly once more.

'Ew, you two. Get a room!' Meg's voice interrupts our moment.

'I'm going. Bye Meg.' Zack chuckles, and I walk him to the door, stealing one last kiss before he goes.

As I return to the kitchen, I find Meg sitting with her head resting on the table. I already miss the warmth of Zack's body next to mine. I sigh, moving closer to my friend.

'Are you alright?' I ask, rubbing her back gently.

'Mhm.' Meg murmurs, straightening her body and continuing her breakfast.

'I love him so much.' I confess after a moment of silence.

'I know.' Meg smiles feebly. 'And he loves you too. I can't believe he actually came yesterday right after work just because you drunk texted him.'

'And he took care of me in the morning when I got sick.' I add, feeling grateful for his kindness.

'He's the one, Maddie. He truly is.'

'I know.' I chuckle, meeting her gaze. 'He really is.'

'By the way, I feel like shit. I don't know if I can do anything.' Meg sighs, changing the subject.

'Me neither.' I agree. 'Let's have a small break and see if we feel better later.'

'Okay. Good idea.'

'Where is Jack?' I ask.

'I don't even know what time he came back yesterday, but he left early to work. And he left me a cute note on the pillow.'

'What note?' I raise my eyebrows, taking a sip of my juice.

'He said he loves me and he didn't wake me up because I looked cute asleep. And he will try to be back early tonight, so we can have some time together. And trust me, drunk me was everything else but not cute, for sure.' She laughs.

'Definitely.' I laugh, avoiding a punch Meg aims at my arm.

'I need some painkillers. I feel like my head is about to explode.' Meg announces, getting up to search through our shelves. 'Paracetamol? Eh, it should be fine, right?'

'I think so.' I shrug.

'Do you want one?' Meg offers.

'No, I think I will be fine. I had great help in the morning.' I reply, remembering Zack's comforting presence.

'Lucky you.' Meg says before throwing two pills into her mouth and washing them down with a glass of water. 'I think I need to lie down. Wanna watch a movie?'

'Sure!' I reply with a smile.

We settle down on the sofa, draping our fluffy blanket over our legs. *Life as We Know It* is all we need to survive the day. And what is better to watch with your hungover bestie than a rom-com?

'Only this one. We should do something today.' I say, snuggling deeper into the blanket.

'We will.' Meg assures me, turning her attention to the TV. 'I promise.'

'Alright.' I smile, looking at the screen.

I feel a wave of determination to accomplish something today. The anticipation to see Zack later excites me throughout the day. He will ask for sure, and if I did nothing, he will make fun of Meg and I watching TV. And I will not let it happen this time.

Chapter Twenty

January this year feels incredibly cold, and I can't help but feel a bit jealous of Zack, who went to Tenerife with his friends for his birthday trip. Scrolling through his Instagram stories, I saw a few pictures of them wearing beach shorts, no tops on, or drinking some beers at the beach bar with palm trees in the background. It all looked incredible.

Zack turned twenty-seven just a couple of days ago, and his mates gifted him a ticket to Tenerife along with tickets to a football game. And honestly, that was a brilliant idea. I should have thought of something like that myself. Anyway, Luke was very kind and checked to see if I had any plans with Zack before they finalised everything. I couldn't take this chance from Zack. I had been planning a surprise dinner at his place, but I can do that when he's back. I couldn't say no to this trip. I was so excited for him to go, and I even dropped him off at the airport.

Zack entrusted me with looking after his car while he's away, so I made sure it's safely parked and untouched right outside my flat. He also wants me to pick him up when he's back.

This month marks two years and five months since we started dating, so I wanted to leave him a little something to remind him of how special he is to me.

I inserted a small love note in his bag before he left. Though, I don't know if he read it because he didn't say anything over the phone. It's not like he called or messaged much anyway. I wanted him to have fun there, and not be disturbed by his phone, so I didn't bother him with phone calls, or a lot of messages either. I trust Zack, and I don't need him to report to me his every move.

When he returns, we'll sit on his sofa, and he'll tell me all the stories from his four-day escapade.

Although I'm not the best writer, I poured my heart into that note. Expressing my feelings on paper turned out to be more challenging than I thought. Goodness, I hope he liked it. If he even found it. Maybe it got lost? Maybe someone else found it, lying somewhere Zack had accidentally dropped it, and read it. The thought makes me blush with embarrassment. I still tend to get shy and insecure about things. I haven't even let Meg take a look at it. It's meant exclusively for Zack. Deep in my heart, despite all the thoughts in my head, I know he'll love it.

As I roll over to the other side of the bed, reaching out for my phone, I check to see if I've received any new messages from Zack, but there are none. He's having fun. It's fine. I need to go to work before I pick him up in the evening.

Lately, Edward has been acting a little strange around all of us, and I happen to be working with him today. Unsure of how to approach the situation, I mentally prepare myself for whatever may come. I don't know what happened. We were fine after the conversation we had months ago, we both maintained professional behaviour at work, and there was no drama. I was genuinely happy about that, and I hope it will stay like that. But something's changed with him recently. Maybe I should try to talk to him.

Slowly dragging my body out of bed, I slip into my uniform. My face looks slightly puffy from last night's tears. Well, it was just a mental breakdown, nothing more. I can't wait to be done with university, as this dissertation might just be the end of me before I even graduate. My goal was to finish a chapter yesterday, but I spent most of my time crying, unable to write. I needed to hear Zack's comforting voice or a hug from him, but he's away. Just four more months of this stress, and I'll be free. All I want to do afterwards is spend all my free time with Zack.

I apply a bit of makeup to conceal the redness on my face, knowing I'll have to touch it up after my shift before I head to the airport. I want to look nice when Zack sees me. After I manage to cover all the redness, I let my hair fall down my back, giving it a quick brush before tossing the brush into my bag. Of course, I'll be staying at Zack's tonight. Even though Zack is in Tenerife now, I know he misses me as much as I miss him. I'm sure he's looking forward to this evening too.

Meg and Jack have left already, so I quickly make myself some toast and spread Nutella on it. The balloon I asked Meg to buy for me yesterday is slowly floating around the kitchen. I watch it as I munch my sweet toast, smiling. I grab the ribbon attached to the blue balloon that reads "Welcome Home" and head out of the house.

Driving in London isn't my favourite thing, but I have to do it since I have Zack's car, and I'll be picking him up later. I settle into the driver's seat and start the engine. The pink car air freshener with the words "Beep Beep Bitch" dangles from the rearview mirror, filling the car with the sweet scent of strawberries. I bought it the day Zack left me his car, and I know he'll love it. He might tease me about it at first, but deep down, I know he'll secretly enjoy it.

The road to work is smooth, without any traffic, and I arrive even earlier than I expected, giving me time to catch up with Alex and get some work updates.

'Hi, how was the night?' I smile as I enter the building.

'Hi Maddie, haven't seen you in ages! Who cares about work. Tell me everything about you. How are things with Mr. Perfect? Oh, is that his car you parked over there? Did he give it to you? Tell me everything!'

'Slow down.' I chuckle.

Yes, it's been a while since we've seen each other, as she's been on a long holiday, travelling the world, and I still can't figure out how she got the time off. I quickly update her on my life recently.

'Everything is great with Mr. Perfect. He's in Tenerife with his friends, and I'm picking him up from the airport tonight, which is why I have his car.'

'Still happily in love. How are you? How's university going?'

'I am good, thanks. And yes, we are happily in love. Actually, it gets better every day. And university... honestly, this workload is slowly and painfully killing me. I can't wait for it to be over. But, anything about you? Anything new in the *L* world?' I raise my eyebrows as she stiffens. 'Alex?'

'There is a thing…' She lowers her voice cautiously. 'It's been happening for a while now. But nobody knows, and nobody can know about it.'

'What? What is going on?' I lower my voice too, puzzled by her secretive tone.

'Can I trust you?' Alex asks, her eyes searching mine.

'Of course you can.' I assure her.

'Okay, so I've been seeing Edward for a while now.' She whispers.

'What?' My reaction is faster and louder than expected, and I quickly cover my mouth with my hand.

'Shhh…' Alex waves her hand, signalling for me to quiet down. 'Yes. But it's a secret. Actually, it's nothing serious. Nothing like you and Zack. It's more like friends with benefits, but we hang out with each other a lot.'

'Oh, are you okay with it?'

'I guess so.' Alex shrugs. 'I don't complain, and it's actually fun. I kind of like it this way too. No pressure, you know? Just as long as nobody knows.'

'That's good. I'll keep it to myself.' I smile at her. 'I need to get ready. See you in a bit'.

Walking to the staff room, I feel a bit bewildered by this information, but I always saw it coming. As long as Alex is happy, I am happy for her. I mean, she's always had this massive crush on him. Maybe they will actually be together at some point? Maybe that is why Edward got a bit weird recently? Like he didn't want anyone to be suspicious or something.

Later, I join my friend behind the desk and begin my ten-hour shift. A few more months, and I hope to start working my nine-to-five job in some big marketing company in London. I'll miss my days at this hotel and the shifts I had with my friends, but I see myself wearing smart outfits, working a proper adult job, and having enough money for my lifestyle.

I'll hang out with Zack and my friends on the weekends, or go on small two-day trips, because I will have a regular work schedule. I'll be able to plan every weekend for the whole year, because I'll always be off on the weekends. Not like now. It must be nice to have a routine. And finally, I will have all the free time for Zack. I will be able to make all these plans because I will have a nice, stable corporate job. It all will be better.

I catch myself checking the clock every five or ten minutes. Zack will be boarding his plane in a few hours and landing at Heathrow after eight in the evening. This balloon needs to survive its stay in the car and the ride to the airport.

'Earth to Maddie, hello?' Alex waves her hand in front of my face, calling my name, and I blink quickly, giving her my attention.

'What?' I look at her.

'You zoned out. Edward is here.' Alex informs me.

'Oh alright.' I nod understandingly.

Edward comes to the desk five minutes later, looking grave.

'Hello, Alex, Maddie.' He greets us.

'Hi.' We answer simultaneously.

Glancing at both of them, I try to find some kind of connection between them or a spark. But they both pretend like they don't care that the other is here. That sucks. If they like each other, why would they hide it? I mean, there must be something forcing them to hide it, right? Is there a written rule that you can't date your coworker?

'Maddie, when do you graduate?' Edward looks at me, pushing his hands into the pockets of his trousers.

'By the end of May.'

'Okay, I'll have to discuss your position here with you closer to May then. I understand you will be here full-time, right?'

'Uh… yeah, sure.' I nod.

It will depend on when I find my dream corporate job. But he doesn't need to know my plans, not yet. Only my closest friends know. Now, I can't even tell Alex because she's sleeping with Edward. She may accidentally tell him. These things happen to her, I've noticed.

'Okay, great then. Alex, come with me for a second.' He gestures at her, and she follows him. That's interesting, some action. Maybe he took her for a snogging session at work.

Using the opportunity of being alone, I quickly check my phone to see if Zack messaged me anything, and there is one message. Since nobody is in the lobby, I click on the notification and open the message saying that he just woke up, is hungover, misses me, and that we will see each other in the evening. I smile, typing him a quick reply, and put my phone back.

A few hours later, I get an update that Zack is already at the airport, waiting for his flight, and he even sent me a picture of all the boys, sitting on the floor, wearing sunglasses. I know that all of them regret drinking too much last night. Well, I'm glad they had fun.

When my shift is over, I quickly change into my jeans and white V-neck jumper, fixing my hair and makeup. I check the time and grab my black coat before leaving the hotel and jumping into Zack's car.

It's time to pick up my man! The balloon is where I left it and it looks alright. Some air might have left it, but it's still holding up. Excitement fills my veins, slowly taking control of my body. Okay, it's time to go. I set the GPS, which shows the drive should be quick and easy. I reverse carefully and join the other cars on the road. The radio plays a selection of my favourite songs, and I have a little concert, singing to myself. It relaxes me while driving.

I arrive fairly quickly, grab a ticket at the gate, and park the car in the closest free spot, making a mental note of where I parked. Pressing the key and hearing the car beep, I know I can go. Holding the balloon tightly, I walk straight to the arrivals. He should be landing any minute now. Checking my phone, my heart beats faster with anticipation. I can't wait to see Zack again. I've missed him.

A lot of people come through the door, but I can't see Zack or his friends. My feet pace the floor anxiously, my eyes scanning every face until I finally spot him. He's here, wearing black jeans, a yellow hoodie, and black jacket. His face looks tired, but a radiant smile spreads across it when he notices me. Zack laughs, his eyes twinkling as he spots the balloon in my hand.

He rushes towards me, his travel bag swinging from his arm, and when he's finally in front of me, he flings his arms around me, pulling me close. Our lips meet in a loving kiss, and I wrap my arm around his waist.

For a moment, the rest of the world fades away. It's just us, holding and kissing each other in the middle of the airport. Zack holds me tight against his chest, his strong arms enveloping me as if he hasn't seen me in ages. It's a hug that I've missed dearly, one that I've needed so badly. He's back, and at this moment, time seems to stand still.

Suddenly, we feel a soft push, and we reluctantly move away from each other, noticing his friends. Luke playfully nudges Zack with his elbow to get his attention. As I glance at each of them, I can tell that they're exhausted, and it's a little bit funny. Poor boys.

'Do you need a lift?' Zack looks at his friends.

'Nah mate, we'll get an Uber.'

'You sure? We can drop you off.'

'Don't worry, we already arranged a ride, and it'll be here in ten minutes. The driver will drop us off at our places, so it's all good. We'll see you soon anyway, mate.' Luke pats Zack's shoulder. 'See you, Maddie.' He gives me a friendly hug, and I wave at the rest of the boys as they slowly make their way towards the exit, waving back at me.

'Bye.' I smile, bringing my attention back to Zack.

'That's cute.' Zack says, pointing at the balloon.

'Welcome home.' I smile warmly.

'I missed you.' He leaves a soft kiss on my lips and pushes a strand of hair behind my ear.

'I missed you too. Let's get you home.' I say, taking his hand and entwining our fingers. Zack takes the balloon from me as we walk to the parking lot, looking for his car.

I end up being the driver because there's a high chance that alcohol is still present in Zack's blood, and he's too tired to drive anyway. I wonder if he even slept last night. But I might know the answer to that.

'What is that?' Zack grabs the air freshener and reads it.

'I bought it.' I clear my throat and buckle up.

'Beep Beep Bitch?' He laughs loudly, looking at me. 'And it smells like…'

'Strawberries.' I say, giving him my innocent smile.

'You know, it's a guy car. It should smell like a man. Like masculinity.' Zack teases me.

'It's a *I have a girlfriend* car now. And it smells like you have a girlfriend too.' I raise my eyebrows, and he gives me another hearty laugh that I love, tilting his head backwards.

'I love you so much, Maddie.' Zack shakes his head, still laughing, and I just smile softly.

As I drive us home, I'm very careful to show Zack that I'm a good driver and that his car was safe with me while he was away, even though I didn't drive it. He said I could, but I just didn't want to.

On our way, Zack tells me about Tenerife and the game they went to on their first day there. I know the team they were cheering for won, so they went to a pub to get some beers. And then they ended up swimming drunk in the hotel pool in the middle of the night. Zack looks so happy talking about it, and his upbeat mood passes onto me. I knew this trip would be good for him.

I breathe a sigh of relief when we finally arrive, and I park Zack's car in his parking spot. We take the lift to his flat, and he opens the door for us.

'We have to go to Tenerife together, Maddie.' Zack says, hanging his jacket, and I hang mine next to his.

'Maybe we can go when I graduate?' I suggest.

'We should. You'll love it.' Zack comes closer, brushing the back of his hand against my cheek. 'It was fun, but I'm happy to be back. I couldn't wait to see you. I was thinking about you every minute of the day.' Zack confesses, his gaze fixed on me.

'Me too.' I admit, resting my hands on his chest. 'Are you hungry?'

'I am starving and I need a shower. Should we order something?'

'I will get us something and you can go take a shower.'

'Or we can shower together?' Zack suggests with a mischievous grin as he pulls me closer.

'Zack.' I laugh, feeling his lips against my skin.

'Come on...'

'Fine.' I surrender. He got me with neck kisses. 'But it will be a quick shower. We order food now, and then we have to be out before it arrives.'

'Deal. I'll get us our usual.' Zack says, taking out his phone and quickly placing the order from the same restaurant. 'Done, we have thirty minutes now.' Zack announces, taking my hand and leading me towards the bathroom.

Once inside, he pushes me against the wall, kissing me fervently. I moan softly into his mouth, reaching for the hem of his hoodie, but he stops me. I look at him confused when he moves away.

'I need to tell you something first.'

'What?' I ask, watching him closely.

'So, in Tenerife, the boys and I got very drunk the first night.' Zack begins with a serious expression, and I feel a knot form in my stomach. Why does he look serious? What happened? I don't like where this is going. 'And I did something.'

'Zack…'

'Maddie.' He clears his throat and my mind races with possibilities. No, he wouldn't do anything to hurt me.

'What did you do?' I take a step back, my voice barely above a whisper, my heart pounding in my chest. Zack frowns. 'Just say it.' I try to keep my voice calm.

Instead of speaking, Zack simply removes his hoodie and T-shirt. Why is he taking off his clothes when we're about to argue?

'Maddie.' Zack laughs, further confusing and frustrating me. I stare into his eyes, waiting for an explanation. 'Darling, I tattooed your name on my chest when I was drunk.' He finally admits, pointing at his chest.

My eyes follow his finger, and there it is. Oh shit! My name, tattooed on his skin, *forever*. My eyes widen and my jaw sags in shock. I come closer to look at it.

'What did you think I did?' Zack asks.

'Nothing.' I mumble, staring at the tattoo.

'Maddie.' He says softly, and I sigh, straightening up and meeting his gaze. I clear my throat.

'You made it sound bad.' I mumble, feeling a mix of relief and embarrassment.

'I would never do *that*. I love you.' Zack chuckles, pulling me into his warm embrace. 'Never.'

'Don't laugh. You scared me for a moment. I was worried. I–'

Before I can finish, Zack grabs my face and kisses me. I close my eyes, returning the kiss and relaxing in his arms. It's the way he affects me. He can calm me down so easily. Even just with a kiss.

'I just wanted to be a bit dramatic, build some tension, but not to scare you.' Zack says as we draw apart. 'Do you like it?'

'You're crazy. This is forever.' I gently run my fingers over the tattoo.

'I know. I'm pretty much aware of it.' Zack chuckles. 'But so are we.' He says, gently touching my cheek with his fingers.

'We are.' I look into his beautiful, shiny, brown eyes.

'Do you like it?' He repeats the question.

'I do.' I smile.

I let him undress me before we get in the shower. Zack enjoys helping me to clean my body, and I have to stop him from being too handsy. We don't have time for this. However, we end up having a passionate and hot snogging session, which takes more time than cleaning each other.

Wrapped in a towel, I leave the bathroom with Zack politely following me to his bedroom. I rummage through his clothes and find his AC/DC T-shirt, which is going to be my pyjamas tonight.

When I turn around, Zack is leaning on the wall watching me, a towel loosely hanging around his hips.

'Did you find what you're looking for?' He asks.

'Yup.' I wave the T-shirt at him. Zack slowly approaches me and gives me a short kiss.

'This can fall on the floor so easily.' He says, grabbing my towel. I chuckle and pull the T-shirt over my head before he pulls down my towel. Zack shakes his head, smirking, and slides into his boxers and pyjama trousers.

We head back to the kitchen just as the food arrives. Zack brings the boxes to the table while I pour us some juice.

'Very romantic.' I say, grabbing some spring rolls, and Zack chuckles.

We enjoy our food, and I can't stop staring at his tattoo. I can't believe he did it. My name is tattooed on his chest. A drunken tattoo, but still. I smirk because I know he couldn't wait to show it to me. He actually seems proud of his drunken act.

'What?' Zack looks at me.

'It's a nice tattoo.' I reply.

'I knew you would like it.' He admits proudly.

'I do.'

'Me too. I actually really like it. You should see my face when I woke up in the morning and saw it in the mirror. I said to the guys, *damn Maddie will think I am insane, but she's gonna love it.*'

'And you were right. You are insane. But I think it's cute.' I chuckle, and we both smile at each other. I am happy he is back.

Chapter Twenty-One

I wake up to Zack spooning me, his warm breath against my neck, sending tingles down my spine. I know he's awake because I feel his finger tracing gentle circles on my stomach beneath my T-shirt.

With a slow turn, I shift to face him. Zack watches me with a soft smile on his lips.

'Good morning, darling.' He greets me, his voice filled with warmth.

'Morning, handsome.' I reply, leaning in to plant a tender kiss on his lips.

Waking up and falling asleep beside Zack is one of life's greatest joys. Well, being next to him in general. All the time.

As I run my fingers along his jawline, I catch his gaze, his eyes shining with affection. His hair, silky and slightly disheveled, invites my touch, and I can't help but run my fingers through it.

His big hand trails over my stomach, then upwards, reaching my chin where he captures it gently between his thumb and forefinger and kisses me. It's so delicate and loving that sparks seem to ignite between us. I place my hand on his chest, right where the tattoo is.

Zack pauses the kiss, his gaze softening as he looks down at my hand. I trace the ink of his tattoo with my finger, but he stops me, intertwining our fingers together.

'I wish you were here all the time.' Zack whispers, his eyes locked with mine.

'Me too.'

'Move in with me.' Zack drops a bombshell.

'Zack…' I being, struggling to find the right words.

I'm staggered, caught off guard by the suddenness of his offer. I mean, it's wonderful and I'd love to live with him. Be with him all the time. Living with Zack is something I've imagined, dreamed about even, but never really considered it happening in the near future. Never gave myself a deadline or a time frame for it to happen. Not yet. I mean we've never actually talked about it and this is something we need to discuss properly.

But this would be our reality. This would be our every day. Us together all the time. It's a massive step forward in our relationship. It excites me, but I know we need to approach this with caution, ensuring we're both ready for this commitment.

'I would love to.'

'Why do I feel like there is a *but*?' Zack asks.

'Because there is. First of all, I have a tenancy agreement.' I admit with a chuckle.

'Until when?'

'September. But, then...' I lean in to plant a quick kiss on his lips. 'We can live together. But let's have a proper conversation before jumping in.'

'Alright.' Zack agrees, his gaze softening. 'Do you like my place? Or do you prefer something else?'

'Your place is amazing, but do you think there's enough room for both of us?'

'Of course there is. I'll make more space here for you. We can rearrange things too.' Zack reassures me.

'Okay, but I have a lot of things. Even though it might not seem like it. Trust me. I was surprised too when I had to move in when I started university, and now, I probably have even more.' I admit with a chuckle.

'Well, we can start here, and then maybe we will look for something else? Something bigger where all our stuff can fit in.'

'Okay. Let's discuss it in the summer, alright? Sit down and talk everything through.'

'Alright.' Zack nods, a smile spreading across his face as he pulls me in for another kiss.

I thrust my hands through his hair, slightly pulling it as Zack presses his body on mine, pushing me to lie on my back. He is towering over me. The heat between us intensifies, and I feel the anticipation growing in my stomach. But then, my stomach decides to make itself known, rumbling loudly.

'Are you hungry?' Zack asks, breaking the kiss with a laugh.

'I'm fine. Ignore that.' I insist, trying to pull him back in for another kiss, but my stomach protests again.

'You are hungry, baby.' Zack insists, getting off the bed. I feel the warmth of his body leave, and I reach for the quilt to cover myself. 'I'll make us some breakfast.'

'I'm not hungry. Come back here.' I protest weakly, reaching out for him.

'Your stomach says something else.' Zack teases as he stretches his muscular body.

What a view in the morning. I could get used to seeing this every day when we move in together. I definitely wouldn't complain about it.

'You can stay in bed, and I'll bring it to you. How does that sound?' He walks around the bed and leans in to kiss my lips.

'Sounds amazing.' I murmur into his lips, placing my hands on his cheeks.

'Okay, I will be back in a few minutes.' Zack promises before leaving the bedroom.

I move to his side of the bed, resting my head on his pillow. It smells like him. With my eyes closed, I snuggle my face into it. But then I realise, he's here, so why am I lying in his bed while he's in the kitchen making breakfast? I could be hugging him instead of a pillow.

I jump out of bed right away and toddle to the kitchen. The smell of pancakes greets me as I enter. Zack is humming some songs under his breath, completely absorbed in his cooking.

As I come closer, I circle my arms around his waist from behind, feeling instantly much better as I press myself against him. His muscles tighten under my touch, and I can't help but smile.

'So you got up, hm?'

'I was bored there without you.' I admit, moving to the side and leaning on the countertop. 'Can I help you with anything?'

'No, I've got everything.' Zack assures me, leaving a soft kiss on my forehead.

'I'll set the table at least.' I decide, taking two plates from the cabinet and placing them on the table along with the maple syrup. I also prepare a coffee for Zack, knowing he'll want one once he's done with the pancakes.

With his coffee machine, it's not too difficult to make one. I set a coffee for Zack and pour myself a refreshing glass of orange juice, placing them on the table as Zack brings over a stack of fresh, fluffy pancakes, and we both take our seats.

'Enjoy.' Zack says with a warm smile, and I eagerly help myself to the pancakes, drizzling maple syrup over the top before passing the bottle to Zack. 'So, when I arrived in Tenerife, I found something very interesting in my bag.' He starts, his gaze fixed on me, and I suddenly stop chewing my pancake.

The love letter. So he must have found it and read it. He remembers about it. I slowly swallow food I was holding in my mouth for too long.

'What?' I pretend that I don't know what he's talking about as I continue eating my pancake.

'Maddie. You know exactly what I'm talking about.' Zack chuckles softly. 'I still have it if you don't remember. I can get it.'

'No, no, no. It's fine. I actually remember it.' I respond, clearing my throat.

'Nobody ever wrote me a love letter, you know? That was the sweetest and loveliest thing I've ever received.' Zack reflects, reaching for my hand and giving it a gentle squeeze. 'Can you believe I heard your voice in my head reading that?' He adds with a chuckle.

'Maybe that inspired your tattoo.' I tease.

'Maybe.' Zack agrees, and I can't help but smile to myself. He liked it. He liked my love letter that I was so worried about.

After breakfast, we tidy up and return to Zack's bedroom. He rummages through his bag with determination, and I can't help but wonder what he's searching for until I notice the paper in his hand.

'Ha! Got it.' Zack exclaims, turning to me with a wide grin.

'My letter.' I murmur, stepping closer as my eyes scan over my own handwriting.

We both stare at it, silently reading it. I know he's reading it because I can see Zack gently tracing his thumb over the paper, following the lines of my writing.

Zack,
Every day I wake up feeling incredibly lucky that you are a part of my life. I never knew how effortless it could be to fall in love with someone. I never expected to fall in love so hard for someone until I met you. You make everything seem so much easier, you give me comfort, and always support me. You never fail to make me smile, you always make my heart skip a beat when I am around you, you give me shivers when you touch me. Surprisingly, you've never given me butterflies, and now I know why. They say that you have butterflies when you are anxious and things are not right. But it's never happened with you and it will never happen because you are the right person. You are right for me. You are the one for me. I know it. I feel safe with you, I feel loved, I feel happy, I feel secure, I feel calm when I am with you. I can't imagine my life without you by my side. I love the way your eyes shine when you look at me, I love your laugh, I love your gorgeous smile, I love your pure heart, I love the way you touch my body, I love how you always hold my hand, I love how you play with my hair when I fall asleep, I love how you make me feel when I am with you, I love that you give me your time, I love that you listen to me and pay attention to small things, I love that I can be completely myself around you, I love that I don't have to pretend to be anyone else around you, I love that you love me for being me, I love that you trust me, I love that you share your troubles and happiness with me, I love that you let me know the real you, I love absolutely everything about you. I love YOU.

Yours forever,
Maddie

'I need to put it in a safe place.' Zack says, walking over to his bedside table and placing my letter in the top drawer.

'Next to your bed? Very safe.' I tease, laughing at the thought.

'Yes, it will be right next to me. Just for now. I will find a better place for it later. Maybe I'll frame it.'

'You are so sweet.' I say, touching his cheek gently before giving him a short kiss.

'So, I've got something for us to do today.' Zack announces, his hands resting on my hips.

'Oh, what is that?' I ask, intrigued by his sudden enthusiasm.

'You'll love it. Trust me.' He assures me, planting a gentle kiss on my forehead before heading to his wardrobe to get dressed.

I retrieve my beige leggings and cream woollen jumper from my bag and start getting dressed. Sitting on the bed to pull on warm socks I watch Zack as he changes into black sweatpants and a white T-shirt. When he turns around, I notice the slight raise of his eyebrows as he looks at me.

'Are you that cold? I can set the heating higher.' Zack offers.

'No, I'm very warm and comfy.' I assure him with a smile.

'Okay. Let's have a date then.' Zack suggests, taking my hand and leading me to the living room. 'Wait here, I need to bring something.' He adds before disappearing back into his bedroom.

What did he prepare for us? I wonder what he's up to as I gaze out the window at the beautiful view. It will never stop fascinating me, day or night. Always pretty.

'I have everything.' Zack returns, placing a big box on the floor in front of the sofa, and I eagerly join him to see what he's brought.

'What is that?' I ask, curious.

'So, I got two mugs, two plates, and two bowls.' Zack explains, taking them out of the box and placing them on the table. 'I thought that we could paint them, and they'll be our special dishes. We can use them whenever we eat together.'

'Oh my God, I love it. This is so cute, Zack.' I exclaim, perking up at the idea of having our own dishes.

It will feel special to use them because they'll always remind us of this day. I can't wait for the moments in our future house when we'll invite friends over, and they'll ask about them, and we'll share this story.

Zack takes out paints and brushes, and I move from the sofa to the floor, because this is where we will paint. Actually it's very smart because knowing me, I'll accidentally spill some paint on his nice sofa. Zack puts on some music, and sits beside me.

I stare at my mug, contemplating what to paint on it. Zack is already skilfully moving his brush over his mug. Alright, I need to start with something simple, just like when Meg and I did some painting together.

The first thing that comes to my mind, and I paint it, is our initials in a heart in the middle of the mug. Then, I try to add small flowers in different colours all around.

Out of nowhere, Zack kisses my cheek, and I look at him.

'Looks cute.' He smiles, pointing at my mug.

'Is that us?' I ask with a chuckle, looking at his mug and pointing at the stick couple he painted on his.

'Yes, you here and me here.' Zack confirms with a grin.

'Wow, we look good.'

'Are you making fun of my picture of us?' Zack questions, a playful spark in his eyes.

'No, I wouldn't dare.' I respond, attempting to keep a straight face, but I break quickly under his intense stare, and start laughing. Zack places his hand on the back of my neck, pulling me closer to him for a kiss, but our lips don't meet.

'That's rude, you know?' He mutters, his lips brushing against mine as he speaks, but he still doesn't kiss me.

'Is it?' I play along, feeling the anticipation building.

'Mhm.' Zack murmurs, biting my bottom lip teasingly before finally giving in and kissing me.

Our lips meet gently, tongues intertwining, and I lose myself in the sensation. It feels so good. The electricity between us sends shivers down my spine and I don't want to stop it. Zack's hand rustles through my hair, and my body instantly reacts to his touch, making my heart beat faster. As the heat grows between us, I know it's the moment to break the kiss. We have things to do.

'Let's go back to painting.' I suggest with a smile.

'Of course, princess.' Zack says casually, but the word *princess* fills my heart with love and happiness.

I watch Zack as he paints his mug, completely absorbed in what he's doing. He's so focused, biting his bottom lip from time to time, paying attention to every detail of his picture. His big eyes follow every movement of the brush in his hand. I need to stop staring at him. Bringing my attention back to my mug, I focus on adding more flowers until my mug is covered with them.

When we finish, we place our mugs next to each other, both of us smiling with satisfaction. Zack's eyes shine as he looks at me, and I can tell we're both enjoying this time together. I know we both feel the same now. Happy.

Zack passes me a plate, showing me that he's written my name on his. I do the same, writing his name in the middle, and we proceed to decorate each other's plates.

Sitting back to back, we paint in silence, so the final reveal will become a surprise. I try my best to paint a nice dinosaur on his. I glance around Zack's living room and spot the dinosaur figurine I gave him for his birthday, standing proudly next to the TV.

I still remember watching Zack, working on this gift the day after his birthday party. We were sitting in the same place where we are now, and Zack was working on getting his dinosaur. He was so happy, and very hungover, and told me the story from his childhood again. And I listened, even though I knew the story already, but he was so excited to talk about it once again that I didn't want to interrupt him. I just wanted to listen to him. Then later that day, the dinosaur found his place next to the TV and hasn't moved since.

I add two more dinosaurs on my plate, so he has friends, or a family. Zack can choose whatever he prefers. Then, I surround the plate with green leaves as food for little green lads.

Finishing my plate, I feel excited to share my artwork with Zack, but he needs a few more minutes. I examine my painting to see if I should add or fix something, but I think it's perfect as it is now.

'I am ready.' Zack announces.

'Me too.' I say and we turn around, still keeping our plates hidden from each other.

'You go first.' He suggests.

'Okay.' I turn my plate to reveal my painting. Zack chuckles, leaning in to examine the picture closely.

'This is so cool! Great job, Maddie.' Zack compliments, his eyes scanning every detail. 'So, I've got a family of dinosaurs.' He adds with a joyful smile, kissing my cheek.

'Can I see mine?' I ask eagerly.

'Ta da!' Zack presents his painting, and I can't help but smile.

Once again, he's found a way to show me that he listens and cares about the things I like. He painted all of that on my plate. There is a small palm tree, a sun, a little wave, a plane, I guess a dog and a cat because I said I want to have animals in the future, a camera, flowers, a loaf of bread, a jam jar, a pack of Maltesers I guess, a little radio, a few stick people for friends and family, and of course a little heart with Z in it.

'That is so adorable, Zack.' I exclaim, pecking his lips. Zack looks proud of himself, as he should be. He did a wonderful job, and I absolutely love it! 'I have an idea for the last one.'

'What is that?' Zack asks, intrigued, watching me as we put our plates next to the mugs, letting them dry.

'Give me your hand.' I request.

Zack obliges, placing his hand in mine as I paint his thumb with blue and press it against the surface of the bowl. Then, I paint mine pink and repeat the process. Zack watches me with curiosity, and his face lights up with a bright smile when he realises what I'm doing. I press our fingerprints together, creating a heart shape.

'This is genius. I think we should make the whole bowl like this. I mean both of them.' Zack suggests excitedly.

'Okay.' I agree, smiling back at him. 'It might take a while though.'

'We have time.' Zack replies, looking into my eyes with a big smile on his face.

With that, we continue refreshing the paint on our thumbs and leave our fingerprints on the dish.

Now that Zack understands my idea, the process goes much faster. We leave our fingerprints, swapping bowls and finishing the other one. I watch Zack trying his best to leave a perfect fingerprint for the heart shape.

At this moment, I realise that this is just the beginning of the things we'll do together in the future. We decorate our dishes now, but as we'll be going through this life together, we'll decorate our future flat together, then a house, a garden. Whatever we have, we'll do it together. And the thought fills me with warmth and excitement, knowing that we have a lifetime of adventures ahead of us.

Chapter Twenty-Two

Thirty-two months ago, Zack and I officially became a couple. I have less than a month left of university, and it feels so surreal to think about how graduation and the beginning of my proper adult life are just around the corner. Soon, I'll be looking for jobs and moving in with my long-term boyfriend. Although we haven't had the official conversation yet, the anticipation of sharing our everyday lives together fills me with joy, and I'd love to do this now, but I have to remain patient.

With my busy schedule focused on completing all my assignments on time, Zack is coming to my place, taking care of dinner, allowing me to focus on my coursework. Since Meg and Jack are going to see Jack's friends at a party, I have the flat for Zack and me only.

As I sit in my lecture, my mind drifts to thoughts of Zack and our future together. This era of my life is coming to an end. There's a pang of nostalgia creeping in, reminding me that I may actually miss these university days.

Attempting to write some notes, I feel like my brain isn't working, overloaded with all this information, or maybe nothing seems to be important enough. One of those for sure. Meg shoots me a puzzled glance, and I simply shrug in response. I don't understand much either. Why do we still have lectures if university is almost over? I'd much rather be at home, finishing assignments and getting ready for our final presentation. It feels like a waste of time to sit through lectures all day, especially when we're so close to the finish line. But then again, there's a part of me that'll miss being here, learning new stuff with my best friend by my side.

I'm just relieved we've already handed in our dissertation. That thing was a nightmare! I swear, it made me cry every time I had to start working on it. Poor Zack had to put up with a lot of my breakdowns, but he was always there for me. Meg and I went through hell trying to finish it, trying to motivate each other and making sure we both finished. We pulled so many all-nighters just to get it done. *Insane*!

It's crazy to think about how we even got into this university in the first place. We had no clue what we were doing most of the time, but at least we had each other, right? We can survive university. I mean, we're almost done with it.

I feel like this lecture will never end, and my stomach starts to rumble. I always get so hungry here, even though I had my breakfast before we left the flat! I purse my lips, and Meg shoots me a knowing glance, trying not to laugh, so I kick her leg under the table. I'm a bit embarrassed that someone could hear it, so I play it off by pretending it wasn't me and doodling something on my paper. Just a few more weeks, and we'll be free!

Surprisingly, our teacher finishes the lecture early and lets us go.

'I need some food.' I whisper to Meg as I pull her outside the classroom, and she chuckles.

'Yeah, I could hear it. Everyone probably could. Maybe Greg finished his lecture early because he was worried you would die of starvation?' She laughs, and I playfully hit her arm. 'There's a Tesco next to the station. Let's go.'

We leave the building and head to the shop around the corner, so I can grab a pastry before catching the tube home. As I nibble on my pastry, we head back to the tube, squeezing between the rush hour crowd.

It's so packed that I can't eat anymore. My fingers tighten around my bag, making sure it's secure. We could have stayed in some cafe until it calmed down, but we need to get home. Meg has a party to get ready for, and I need to tidy my room before Zack comes over. Plus, I'd rather be home earlier. Surely, we can survive a packed tube ride.

When we exit the tube, I finally finish my pain au chocolate as we walk home. Meg rushes to her room to get ready, and I head to the kitchen to check for leftovers from yesterday's Mexican food, because I'm still hungry. Sadly, Jack ate everything. *Typical*! Is this what living with a man is always like? Great, it was the same with my dad and my brother.

With a pack of cookies, I head to my room. Sitting with my laptop resting on my lap, I stare at the screen, unable to focus on anything. My eyes keep darting from my laptop to my phone until I finally give up and decide to message Zack.

How's work?

I wonder what he's doing. And I guess he's not very busy since he replies right away.

It's dead, so I hope to get out early ;) Do you need anything? I can grab some stuff on my way.

Maltesers?

I actually fancy some, and I know he likes them too. It brings back the memories from our first date.

Sometimes, I can't believe we have been together for over two years! And in September, we'll have our third anniversary. Where did the time go? Well, it also reminds me that I need to think about something big for our anniversary. I should surprise him. Maybe with a trip? Maybe I could work the whole summer and save some money for that? Some place he's always wanted to go?

Definitely gonna get some. Anything else, baby?

No, it should be fine. I will do some work now and hope to see you soon.

I'll be there ASAP! Love you xxx

Love you too!

I can't help but smile as I read through our messages, feeling incredibly fortunate to have Zack in my life. He's more than I could have ever dreamed of in a partner. Zack is literally perfect. I never thought I would meet someone like him. Here I am, in a happy relationship with the man of my dreams. Soon to become even more serious, as we may be moving in together in a few months.

Meg distracts me from my thoughts, coming to my room to show me her outfit options, and I point at the red dress. When she leaves, I try to clean the mess I made in my room over the past few days.

When I hear Meg leaving the bathroom, I grab my stuff and go take a shower. I want to be all fresh and smell nice when Zack comes. I put on my navy, satin shorts and matching buttoned shirt and tie my hair in a loose bun on the top of my head.

Back in my room, I use my vanilla mist before sitting back on my bed in front of my laptop. I need to focus on finishing my workbooks. My goal is to do as much as I can before Zack comes. But I feel like the more I do, the more unfinished things appear. But here I am, clean, fresh and motivated to finish it.

A few moments later, Meg comes to my room to show me her look. And here comes another distraction.

'Wow, you look absolutely stunning.' I smile at her as she gives me a slow spin.

Meg always looks great, no matter what she wears. She's the kind of girl who doesn't even need to try.

'Thanks, Maddie. What are you doing?' Meg asks, sitting next to me, and I show her the screen. 'Shit, I need to make sure I've done this one. I had no idea we had this assignment.'

'I just did it. Honestly, I forgot about this, but it was on the website.' I sigh, rolling my eyes. 'There are still so many things to do, and I am so done with all this bullshit.'

'I know, and I feel so tired. I don't even want to go to this party, but I promised Jack. I don't even like this Ryan guy. I kinda feel like he doesn't like me either. He bothers me so much, and he always makes these stupid comments about Jack and me.' Meg sighs. 'Anyway, I'll try to get out early, have some decent sleep, and do some of my work from early morning. I'd rather be studying than be in the same room with this guy.'

'You'll be alright. It's just a party.' I give her my comforting smile. 'Where is Jack?'

'He'll be here soon. But he's only going to change, and we'll have to go.' Meg stands up and flips her hair. 'I am going to leave you alone with this and go to see if my man is back. Good luck, Maddie.'

'Have fun!' I manage to say before she leaves my room. When I check the time, it's already a few minutes after seven. Where is Zack?

Later, I can hear my friends leaving the flat. With my laptop in hand, I go downstairs to sit in the living room, and wait for my boyfriend to come.

My worry intensifies once it's past eight, and he's not here yet. I thought he would leave early. I check my phone and nothing, no messages, no missed calls. What is going on? Is he alright? I close my laptop and walk to the window.

A feeling of relief washes through my body when I see car lights on the street and Zack leaves his car seconds after. I rush to the door when he walks towards my flat with grocery shopping bags, and I open the door for him.

'Hi.' I smile, noticing roses in his hand.

'Hello, darling.' Zack walks in and kisses me fondly. I throw my hands around his neck and stand on my toes, extending the kiss for a little bit longer. 'I got you something.' He smiles when we draw apart and presents me with flowers.

'Aw, thank you.' I take the bouquet from him, giving it a quick sniff. 'What is it for?' I ask, raising my eyebrows.

'I just saw them and thought of you.' Zack says casually with a shrug, and I chuckle. Isn't it cute that he thought about me when he saw these flowers? And got them for me?

Together, we walk to the kitchen where Zack leaves the shopping bags on the table.

'That is very sweet, Zack.' I take a vase and fill it up with water, so I can put my flowers in it.

'I am very proud of you for studying so hard.' Zack admits,

circling his arms around me from behind and leaving a gentle kiss on my neck. I turn my head to look at him and receive a wet and tender kiss on my lips. 'I'm going to make you a delicious dinner. How are things going?' He asks, moving away from me to unpack the groceries, and my body instantly misses the warmth and closeness of his. I watch him as he removes things from the bag and places everything on the table.

'I think it's not bad. But I still have so many things to do and zero motivation. I get distracted all the time.' I say, my eyes scanning all the taco ingredients he bought for tonight. Oh, I am already hungry.

'You need a break, sweetheart.' Zack looks at me, concerned.

'I don't think I can have one. The assignments are due soon. Trust me, I want this to be over, so I'd rather work my ass off now instead of doing it during the summer. Or what's worse, repeating the year!' I reply, heaving a dramatic sigh and placing my hand on my forehead, earning a hearty laugh from Zack.

'I'm sure, you won't fail. You've worked too hard for it.' Zack reassures, giving me a soft smile. 'Go and do what you need to do. Maybe I can help you with something after dinner.'

'Well, I appreciate it, but I don't think it's possible.' I say, moving closer to him. Our eyes meet, and I add. 'But thank you for coming.' I pull his T-shirt and kiss him shortly before I return to the sofa and all my assignments.

From time to time, I steal glances at Zack from behind my laptop. He looks incredibly sexy in the kitchen, focused on cooking, his eyes fixed on preparing the meat. I smile to myself and go back to my tasks. Finally, I feel like I can concentrate on what I'm doing and feel a rush of motivation.

When Zack's arms wrap around me, my focus shifts entirely to him. He places a gentle kiss on my neck, prompting me to turn and face him.

'Dinner is ready, Maddie.' Zack announces with a warm smile.

'It smells delicious.' I admit, putting my laptop on the side and rising from the sofa.

'Come on.' Zack smiles, and I follow him to the kitchen.

Everything is neatly organised on the table, so we can grab a taco shell and fill it with anything we want. As we seat next to each other, I put a mix of different fillings in my taco shell.

'I made guacamole myself.' Zack says, proudly, passing me the bowl.

'Oh, I need to try it then.' I eagerly put some on my taco and have a bite. 'Mmm, this is so good.' I admit after swallowing the food and licking my fingers.

Zack chuckles softly, making himself one while I make satisfied noises, happy with my food. For a moment, I can relax and forget about all the things I have to do. For a moment, I can just put it on the side.

As we chat about our day, Zack confesses that he's been thinking about quitting his job, aiming to become a manager elsewhere. However, he hasn't found the right opportunity yet. He is constantly looking and applying to new places. Rushing such decisions isn't necessary until he discovers a better fit. I get that, being a manager at a fancy place can be quite stressful.

Over the past few months, things have become messy, and Zack has finally reached his limit. I can't blame him. He doesn't get along with the new managers, who complicate things unnecessarily, while Zack tries to make everything easier for everyone. They want to bring their own rules and change the place.

Even the staff has started complaining to Zack. Essentially, the new people are assholes and ruined the nice atmosphere that was once there. But I hope he finds a new position soon. I know he really likes this place, but it's not the same anymore, and he's aware that the good people who work there will start leaving soon. They've already expressed their intentions to him. Poor Zack, constantly trying to make things better for the team, but it's him against the new management.

Later, after tidying up and leaving leftovers for my friends, we head upstairs to my room. I settle into bed with my laptop, waiting for Zack to finish his shower. However, I feel like I can't write anything anymore, my motivation evaporating, but I try to push myself to do something.

When Zack joins me in bed and snuggles under the duvet next to me, I decide that this is enough for today, setting my laptop aside.

'All done?' He asks, crossing his arms behind his head.

'Not quite, but I've had enough for today. I can't even think properly anymore.' I admit, moving closer and resting my head on his chest, craving the comfort of his strong embrace. 'I feel like my head is about to explode.'

'I hope not.' Zack chuckles, planting a kiss on the top of my head. Looking up at him, I shift my body closer, bringing my face closer to his, so I can kiss him.

'I am so tired.' I mumble, burying my face into his neck.

'Get some sleep, baby.' He suggests softly.

'No, I want to stay awake. With you.' I yawn, fighting against the heaviness in my eyelids.

'Maddie, I'll be here when you wake up. In fact, I'll always be here whenever you need me. Have some rest.' Zack reassures me, gently playing with my hair.

Reluctantly, I close my eyes, slowly drifting off to sleep. However, the sudden noise of the front door slamming startles me awake. Zack sits up, mirroring my confusion.

'Fuck you, Jack!' Meg's drunken voice echoes from downstairs, but there's no response from Jack. Concerned, I climb out of bed.

'Where are you going?' Zack frowns, nonplussed.

'I am going to see what is going on.' I whisper, my mind racing with worry.

Are they arguing? Why is Jack silent? Why has everything suddenly gone quiet? I look at the door as I hear Meg sobbing in the hall, and getting into her room.

'I'll be back.' I give Zack a quick glance before I open the door.

As I reach Meg's room, her cries intensify. Shit, what is going on? I knock softly and enter when there's no response. She's curled up on her bed, tears streaming down her face.

'Meg?' I whisper sheepishly, entering her room slowly. My eyes quickly scan the room to see if Jack is there and maybe I shouldn't come at all, but he's not there. I rush to Meg, and sit on the edge of her bed. 'Meg, what happened? Why are you crying? Where is Jack?' Questions fall out of my mouth. She doesn't reply and starts crying even more. 'Meg…' I lean towards her, gently pushing hair from her face.

She looks at me with her wet, red and puffy eyes, trying to catch a breath, and my heart sinks at the sight of her distress.

'We broke up.' Meg whispers, and I'm left staggered. No, this can't be happening.

'What?' I gasp, dumbstruck.

They couldn't. They were the perfect couple, an example for me. They never argued, and yet they broke up just like that? How does that even happen?

I lie down beside Meg, wrapping her in a tight embrace, trying to offer some comfort. I try to think about all the things that might have gone wrong, while Meg sobs in my arms.

'I'm here if you need me, okay?' I whisper gently, stroking her hair. 'Do you want to talk about it?' I ask warily, but she shakes her head.

My heart aches as I watch her suffer. Did something go wrong at the party? What led to their breakup? Did they get a little bit too drunk and argue about something stupid, drunkenly breaking up and will get back together in the morning when they sober up? Maybe Meg just thinks they broke up. But then, why isn't Jack here? I hope they can resolve whatever happened.

I sit with her in silence, letting her cry and trying not to make her feel worse. She'll talk to me when she's ready, and I'll be here to listen. Pressuring her won't help, especially since she's drunk. It's best for her to sober up and gather her thoughts before we talk.

I stay by her side until she drifts into sleep. Careful not to disturb her as I cover her with a quilt, ensuring she's warm, I get out of her bed. Casting one last glance at her, I quietly slip out of the room and return to mine.

As I open the door, I notice Zack has fallen asleep with his phone in hand. Quietly, I make my way to the bed, gently moving the quilt aside to join him. Retrieving the phone from his hand, I see he was watching football videos. Can't blame him, I'd fall asleep too. I turn off his phone and place it on the bedside table.

Zack mumbles something in his sleep and shifts to his side. Taking the opportunity, I snuggle closer to him, and he instinctively wraps his arm around me and I close my eyes.

The image of heartbroken Meg is stuck in my mind, and I can't stop thinking about her, alone in her bed with no sign of Jack. Will he be back soon? Will they wake up together and reconcile? Or perhaps the situation between them is worse than I realise. I need to know the full story before I can help my friend.

Zack sleeps with his mouth slightly open, breathing slowly. I gaze at his relaxed face, unable to imagine us in a similar situation. Memories of past arguments flicker through my mind, and I hope this will never happen to us. I hope we'll be happy forever. I hope that if any challenges arise, we'll face them together. We did argue before but we went through it together. We worked on our issue and solved it.

Tomorrow was meant to be our day off together, but if Meg's situation doesn't improve, I might have to change our plans. Spending the day with Zack is something I've been looking forward to, but I didn't expect my friends to break up. If the situation doesn't get better, I'm sure Zack will understand that I need to be next to my friend.

As I lie in bed, in the arms of the man I love, I feel torn between my love and my best friend.

Chapter Twenty-Three

When I wake up the next day, I instinctively reach out to hug Zack, but my arms meet empty space. Confused, I prop myself up on my elbows and scan the room. Zack's side of the bed is empty, and his clothes are nowhere in sight. That's weird. Did he leave unexpectedly? Did he get a call from work? Did something happen? My mind races with questions as I slowly rise, thinking I might still be dreaming. A pinch to my skin doesn't wake me up, so it's definitely not a dream.

As I make my way downstairs, I stop at the bathroom door, checking if it's locked, but it's not. He's not there either. He's not downstairs in the living room or the kitchen. Peering out the window, I spot his car parked outside. But where could he be?

I pour myself a glass of water, taking small sips as I reach for my phone, hoping for a message, or something. But once again, there's nothing. Calling him should've been my first move. Should I be worried? What's happening?

I open my recent phone calls and just as I'm about to dial Zack's number, the door opens, and Zack walks in, a bakery bag in hand. The aroma of freshly baked goods fills the air.

'Are you looking for me?' Zack asks with a grin, crossing the room to greet me with a soft kiss.

'I thought you'd left, but your car was still here.' I confess.

'Why would I?' Zack frowns, puzzled by my concern, and I shrug in response. 'I woke up early and thought I'd get something nice for you for breakfast. And for Meg.' He explains, a hint of pride in his voice.

'What did you get?' I inquire, curious.

'Fresh bread, still warm, and some pastries.' Zack replies, a smug grin playing on his lips.

'You went to get me some fresh bread for breakfast?' I pout playfully, touched by his thoughtfulness.

He nods, his eyes gleaming with affection. Cupping his face in my hands, I leave a tender kiss on his lips. Zack's hands find their place on my hips, drawing me closer to him.

Isn't he lovely? He went to the bakery because he knows I like fresh and crispy bread. I am too lazy to do it, even though the bakery is around the corner. I could easily do it myself nearly everyday, but I just don't want to leave the comfort of my bed in the morning.

'Okay, let's eat some.' I say, smiling at him affectionately.

I take some jam and butter and set them on the table while Zack begins slicing the bread. Joining him, I eagerly prepare a few slices with jam for us to taste. As I take the first bite, I instantly get obsessed with the delicious taste.

'Oh, this is so good. So crispy.' I say, savouring each mouthful with closed eyes. Zack's hearty laughter fills the room, so I open my eyes and meet his gaze.

'Yes, it's very good, darling. You need so little to be happy.' Zack admits with a chuckle.

I just want to spend today with him, but thoughts of Meg cloud my mind. The memory of my friend sobbing in her bed weighs heavily on me. I should check on her, see how she feels. With a heavy sigh, I put my bread down on the plate.

'What's wrong?' Zack inquires, noticing the change in my mood.

'It's Meg.' I confess, licking the remnants of jam from the corners of my mouth. 'I don't think she's okay, Zack. I think she and Jack broke up last night.' I lower my voice, wary that Meg might be awake and can hear me. I hope she's still asleep, getting the rest she needs.

'Damn, really? That's not good.' Zack says sympathetically.

'I know. She looked absolutely devastated. It broke my heart to see her like that. I stayed with her until she fell asleep, and she was crying the whole time.' I explain.

'So...' Zack begins, clearing his throat. 'I guess you want to spend the day with her, huh?' Zack asks, placing his hand on my thigh. I meet his gaze, feeling a pang of guilt in my chest, but I nod.

'But I also want to spend this day with you. We hardly get any time together because of my deadlines and work, and–'

'Hey, it's okay. You can message me later, and if Meg feels better, I can come over, like last night. You can stay with your friend, it's fine.' Zack assures me, squeezing my thigh gently. 'We'll have plenty of time together once you're done with university.' He reassures, leaning in to place a gentle kiss on my cheek.

'Come here.' I put my hands on his cheeks, drawing him close, and I kiss his lips. 'I love you so much.' I whisper, gazing into his warm brown eyes.

'I love you too.' Zack replies, his smile filling me with warmth and peace. He truly is the best. I kiss him again before I take my hands off his face, so we can finish our breakfast.

Later, we settle on the sofa, enjoying each other's company as we cuddle. His gentle fingers trace soothing patterns on my back as I lie against his chest, my eyes closed, listening to the calm rhythm of his heartbeat, playing with his hair.

'Do you know what happened between them?' Zack asks softly.

'I have no idea. She didn't want to talk last night.' I sigh.

'They'll figure it out.' Zack reassures me, his words offering a glimmer of hope.

'I hope so.' I murmur, lifting my head to meet his gaze.

We spend a few more quiet moments on the sofa before Zack decides to leave, allowing Meg and me some time alone. Perhaps she'll be ready to talk today, but I won't rush her. I'll wait.

Zack will go to see his friends, maybe get some beers, and come back in the evening. I want him to come, so we can spend the evening together at least, watching a movie, or something.

When Zack leaves, I head to the kitchen to prepare some pastries and hot tea for Meg. Balancing the tray and mug carefully, I make my way upstairs to her room. I struggle a little to open the door and when I finally manage to get in, almost dropping the plate on the floor, I'm met with the sight of Meg lying on her bed, her eyes red and swollen from crying.

'Morning.' I greet softly, trying to smile as I come closer. 'How are you feeling?'

'I'm not hungry, Maddie.' She replies, rolling onto her back to stare at the ceiling.

'But I brought something nice for you. Actually, Zack got it, but I'm bringing it to you.' I offer, sitting down beside her and placing the tray on her bedside table.

'Thanks, but I really don't feel like eating right now.' Meg murmurs, pulling the quilt over her head.

'Alright.' I sigh. 'Do you… want to talk or something?' I ask warily, clearing my throat as Meg peeks out from under the covers.

'I don't know.' She whispers, her voice barely audible as she struggles to hold back tears.

'Well, I'm here to listen whenever you feel ready. And if you don't want to say anything, that's fine too. I'll stay here with you, okay? I just want to make sure you're going to be alright. It hurts me to see you like this, Meg.' I reassure her, reaching out to squeeze her hand gently.

'I know.' Meg sniffs, her voice breaking with emotion. Damn, I wasn't supposed to push her. 'I'm glad you are here right now. Just give me a few minutes.' She adds, gripping my hand tightly.

I scoot up higher on the bed, sliding my legs under the quilt as Meg gathers her thoughts. I know she is about to speak and I prepare myself for what she's about to share.

'You know this fucking party. Uh, I wish I'd never gone. I wish I'd told Jack to stay home.' Meg says, her eyes glistening with tears. 'So Ryan, of course, was a dickhead from the moment I walked in. He was like *oh Jack is still with you* and stuff. Like there are so many girls in this world, and he's stuck with me.' She rolls her eyes, recalling his words.

Ryan is this idiot in Jack's friend group who has some issue with Meg. And no one knows exactly what it is. All of Jack's friends like Meg, but Ryan. Jack used to be close with him, but since he's rude to Meg, he distanced himself from him. Maybe that's why the problem got even worse. Jack mentioned that Ryan changed after his breakup with his girlfriend a year ago. She really broke Ryan's heart. He's become bitter, treats girls poorly and is unable to commit.

'He thought it was funny, but how can that be funny? Like you're a piece of shit, and everyone knows it. Even his friends are fed up with him. But they also know that Ryan needs them, otherwise, he'll hit rock bottom. I talked with Jack about it, and that I don't like this when Ryan acts like that. Jack said that all the boys told Ryan to get a grip and be careful with how he treats others. They thought he'd change, that he'd think about the way he behaves, but nope.

Imagine, they've been friends since childhood, so they care about him. They still hope he'll get his shit together. I know Jack is in a tough spot because he feels bad for how his friend treats me. He apologises all the time, and I didn't want to be the one to make him choose between his girlfriend and his friend. That's not fair, you know? Friends support each other in tough times. Like we do. Jack is so sweet and always cares about others, and I just couldn't. I promised myself that I would ignore Ryan for Jack's sake, hoping Ryan would change.'

Meg takes a deep breath after pouring out her words.

'So, of course the guy is drunk as fuck when we arrive, probably on drugs too. Who knows? He was acting really strange at the party. I could see Jack was worried and talked to the other guys about it, but I minded my own business. I ignored Ryan the whole time. I had a few drinks, as did Jack. So, Ryan got even drunker, and at one point, all the guys decided to talk about it again. I wanted to give them some space and went to the kitchen to get some water because I was getting tipsy and needed to sober up a bit.

And lucky me! Fucking Ryan stumbles into the kitchen and starts saying all sorts of vile things to me, like *You know what Meghan? You'd be much hotter if you shut up,* or *how can you have such a hot body but an annoying personality?* And imagine, we're alone in the kitchen and I want to leave, but he stops me by grabbing my arm. You know, he's quite a big guy. Fucking gym rat. Then, he has the audacity to say he'd fuck me right there in the kitchen. So I slapped him as hard as I could.'

'What?' I choke out, my shock turning to anger. 'I can't believe it! That's disgusting.' I fume. What an asshole! I want to hit him too!

'Wait…' Meg's voice trembles. 'He said that he likes it, pushed me against the wall, and pressed his body against mine. I could barely breathe. I swear I got a bruise from the impact when my body hit that wall.'

Meg pauses, needing a moment to collect herself, taking a deep breath.

'And I try to free myself, but he's too strong.' Meg closes her eyes, and I listen in disbelief. What the hell? 'The same moment Jack comes in, Ryan tries to kiss me! And Jack sees us. Everyone else comes in too. Of course, Jack is furious, ready to fight, and the rest of the boys react quickly to prevent the worst. For a second, I feel relieved that they helped me, but then… Jack was so mad, Maddie. Mad is not even enough to describe the way he looked. He didn't want to listen to me. He didn't even want to look at me. But I did nothing wrong.' Meg starts crying, covering her face with trembling hands.

'Oh shit.' I gasp, clasping my hand over my mouth. I am absolutely dumbfounded. I can't find the right words to say. But then Meg continues.

'I wanted to explain, but Jack was shouting about how I could do this to him. That he loves me so much and how could he be so blind and never noticed anything. I felt like I was talking to a wall. None of my words were reaching him. Like he didn't hear a single word I said. He was in some kind of trance, shouting at me but more to himself, assuming that there was always something between Ryan and I. I never saw him this angry.'

Meg stops to wipe the tears from her cheeks and blow her nose.

'He leaves, and I run after him. I try to get his attention, but he ignores me. I beg him to listen to me, and then… He looks at me and says something like *This is bullshit. I saw everything. You should leave right now.* He gets his phone out and orders me an Uber. I desperately try to explain everything to him, but he doesn't believe me. Like he already created this scenario and believes it.

When I cry in front of him, he's just there, absent, and doesn't even look at me. He says that we are over. When the Uber arrives, he says that I betrayed him and broke his heart.' Meg breaks into tears again, and I hug her tight.

This is too crazy. Their relationship ended in one night. Just like that. It's over. This thought actually terrifies me. One wrong thing and everything can be over.

'He didn't believe me, Maddie.' Meg mumbles, and I gently caress her back.

Why didn't Jack listen? Why didn't he believe her? Now that I know the full story and knowing how stubborn Jack is… I'm worried that this is over for real. I mean, this situation is so messed up, but I have to have hope. For her. For them. They were so in love. I know they are made for each other. This can't be the end of their story. I thought they'd get married, have a family, and grow old together. They should talk, clarify everything, but as much as I want to see something positive here, I don't think there is anything good.

'Meg.' I say softly, clearing my throat. 'Maybe he sobered up by now and will talk to you.'

'No, he won't.' She responds with a shake of her head, her eyes filled with pain. It kills me that there's nothing I can do. 'I've never seen him like that. So angry, so heartbroken. He couldn't even look at me. I was crying and trying to stop him, but he left me. He just walked away from me. Fuck!'

I try my best not to cry myself. I need to stay strong for her. I hold onto the hope that Jack will return and they'll have a chance to talk. I know how much he loves her. Actually, where is Jack? But I can't ask. I don't know if Meg even knows. Jack lives here, all his stuff is here. Where could he have gone? He'll have to come back at some point.

After what feels like an eternity, Meg finally stops crying, and we sit in silence on her bed. I gently rub her arm, thinking about all the ways I can help her through this, but have no idea. No ideas of how to soothe my friend's pain come to my mind. How do you help someone with a broken heart? How do you ease the pain of losing someone who meant everything?

My phone buzzes, breaking the silence. I quickly check it and see a message from Zack.

How's Meg?

Not good at all. She told me everything. It's really bad :(

'Is that Zack?' Meg asks, sniffing as she wipes her cheeks.
'Um, yes.' I answer, meeting her gaze with a sympathetic look.
'At least you two are happy. Sorry for ruining your date today.' Meg says, lying down and hugging her pillow.
'No Meg, you didn't ruin anything. He's actually asking about you–' I reassure her, nudging her arm gently.
'Go and spend the day with your boyfriend, Maddie. I'll be fine. I'll just stay here.' Meg interrupts me. 'I don't want to get between you two.'
'He's okay with it Meg, so stop talking bullshit. And he'll come later when you feel better. Anyway, Zack wants me to stay with you until you feel better. You both are very important to me, and today you needed me, so I am here for you. It's alright.'
'He's such a lovely guy.' Meg looks at me. 'I'm happy that you two met, you know? He's good for you. Keep him.'
'I know, and I will. And we're together thanks to you, remember?' I smile, trying to lighten the mood. 'Come here.'
I wrap my arms around her, giving her a gentle squeeze. She's so fragile now, and I don't want to mention how happy I am while she's just had her heart broken. It's the last thing she needs to hear.
Meg and I spend the whole day in her bed, and she finally manages to eat some food, and even stops crying at some point. It seems like she's just run out of the tears, or maybe she's gotten dehydrated.
There's no sign of Jack, but I don't want to risk mentioning his name. Maybe I should message him later, but who knows if he would even reply or answer his phone. He'll know I know everything and might think I'm trying to get them back together. Or that I'm calling to call him a dick and shout at him. Yeah, he'll probably ignore me.

I send a quick message to Zack to see if he'll come later. I want to see him, even if it's just for a little bit. I need his comforting presence, and his strong arms around me. I need to feel safe and happy with him beside me. I want to have him next to me. I need him.

Later, I leave Meg so she can take a shower and rest before she goes to work tomorrow. I'm worried about how she'll manage. I think she should call in sick and take some time off for herself. I even suggested that to her. But knowing Meg, she'll pretend to be strong, put a mask on, and run the show. She won't let other people see her pain. Only people she trusts can see her like that. No one else.

I head downstairs to find the pack of Maltesers Zack brought. It's still sitting on the kitchen countertop, so I grab it and make my way back upstairs to Meg's room. She's already tucked into bed, in her comfy pyjama set, looking at her phone. My heart sinks at the thought that she might be checking for any messages from Jack.

'Hi, I have something for you.' I say, offering her the red pack with a soft smile.

'Thanks, Maddie.' Meg replies, placing it to the side and meeting my gaze with sad eyes. 'Is Zack here?'

'Not yet.' I respond, clearing my throat. 'But he'll be here soon. If you need me, just let me know, okay?' I search her face for any signs of another breakdown, but she just nods. She looks exhausted, so getting some rest would do her good.

'I'll be fine. Don't worry. I'm going to sleep. Say hi for me.' She says softly.

'I will.' I reply, giving her a brief glance before closing the door and heading back downstairs to get some water.

A few minutes later, Zack arrives, opening the door with the key I gave him. I welcome him with a hug and a long, loving kiss. He wraps his arm around me, and I snuggle my face into his neck, inhaling his strong and masculine scent. I needed that today, and every other day.

'Are you okay, baby?' Zack asks, gently caressing my back.

'Mhm. I'm okay now.' I assure, looking up at him with a smile. It's true. I always feel so much better when he's around. Life was good too before I met him, but he made it even better. He makes me so much happier.

'Do you want to lie down?' He asks, lifting my chin with his fingers, his smile warm and adoring.

It's the smile he always gives me that makes my heart beat faster. His eyes are full of love, love for me. I nod in response, and we make our way to my room.

I excuse myself for a moment to take a shower and return, ready for bed. Zack takes his turn in the bathroom, while I get comfy in bed. He comes back with a towel in his hand, looking very sexy, wearing only his boxers. Damn, he's gorgeous with wet hair. I pat the pillow next to me to show him I'm waiting. Zack chuckles and quickly joins me under the duvet, his warm arms pulling me close for a snuggle.

'So, how was your day?' He asks as I lie with my head resting on his chest.

Zack plays with my hair while I tell him about Meg and Jack. He doesn't interrupt and attentively listens until I finish.

'So what now?' Zack inquires.

'I don't know. I mean, I guess either they'll somehow reconcile, though I doubt it's possible at this point, or he'll move out. Then, Meg and I will have to figure out our living situation because we can't afford the place on our own. We need a third person. But at the same time, we can't break the contract, which sucks. It's all messed up now.' I explain, sighing in frustration.

We have to stay in the flat until September or until we find replacement tenants, so we won't have to pay a hefty fee for moving out early. But I really like this place.

'Maddie.' Zack says, drawing my attention with his voice. He pauses for a moment before continuing. 'You know you can move in with me anytime you want.'

Of course I know that. I would love to do it, but I can't do that to my best friend. At least not right now.

I feel terrible for poor Meg. She's lost Jack, and I couldn't bear to add to her loneliness by leaving her alone. I can't imagine Meg searching for a new place by herself, living alone after all the time we've spent together.

I always knew we'd eventually stop living together, but I thought it would be because we both found our life partners, not because she broke up with the love of her life, and we *have* to move out. The thought of Meg going from being surrounded by people who love and care about her to having nobody around absolutely breaks my heart. I wouldn't want to be in her shoes. I can't do this to her. She would never do this to me.

Zack notices my long silence and clears his throat.

'I mean, no pressure. I know how much you care about Meg, but we've talked before about living together anyway. I hope you haven't changed your mind.' He adds, chuckling nervously.

'No, I haven't. I just feel bad for Meg. You know, I thought she'd be living in a new place with Jack, and we'd be living together, and everyone would be happy.' I explain, feeling a lump form in my throat.

'I know, darling. You want everyone to be happy. But sometimes things don't go as planned.' Zack says, meeting my gaze. 'You can't control everything. Things happen, and I'm sure Meg will be alright. I really want to live with you. I want to come from work and know you're there. I want to see you every day, not just a few days a week. I want you next to me when I wake up and when I go to sleep. I want you to be my future.'

'I want that too.' I say, leaning in to give him a long kiss.

For a moment, excitement rushes through my body at the thought of us living together. Zack and I all the time. The first big step towards our future together. But then reality hits me again. Meg has never abandoned me when I needed her, and I've lived with her and Jack for years. I can't leave her broken hearted like this.

'I'll see how things go and talk with Meg about what she's going to do.' It would be much easier if she was still with Jack, if nothing had changed. But then, a great idea crosses my mind. 'What if you move in here? With us?' I suggest, placing my hand on his cheek and giving him a hopeful smile.

I hold my breath, waiting for his response, hoping he will confirm that this is a great idea. Zack bites his bottom lip, thinking about it.

'I don't know…'

'Oh.' Why did I expect him to say *yes, let's do this* right away.

'Maddie, I like my place and I like the idea of just the two of us living together. Of having privacy with you. I know Meg is your best friend, but you know that both of you will not live together for the rest of your life, right?'

'Yeah, but I imagined it all going differently.' I sigh and lie down on my back, staring at the ceiling.

For fuck's sake, why does it have to get so complicated? I want to live with my boyfriend, but I know I will feel like I somehow betrayed Meg if I did.

'Hey…' Zack shifts his body and looks down at me, concern in his eyes. 'Are you upset?'

'No. I feel torn.' I confess, meeting his gaze. 'Zack, I want to live with you. I want us to have our own place where we can build our future together.'

'But?' Zack inquires gently.

'I feel bad for my best friend. I can't imagine being in her position right now. It sucks. If it was me, I'd wish she was by my side. And I know she would never leave me. We always support each other, no matter what. How could I build a happy life with you if at the back of my head, all I could think about is how I left my friend at her lowest? It's such shit timing.' I groan, covering my face with my hands.

'It will be okay.' Zack moves my hands away from my face and kisses my lips gently. 'We can talk about it another time, hm? See how things will go. But I still want it.'

'Okay, I promise. And I want it too.'

'You know I want to marry you one day, and if it means taking Meg with us, I will do it.' Zack chuckles, and I am gobsmacked.

He wants to marry me! Holy shit! I mean, I was dreaming about it, but him saying this out loud makes me realise it can all become true one day. Like, we don't talk about things like that, but I guess him wanting to live with me means that a wedding is somewhere down the line in our future.

'Are you proposing?' I joke, a flutter of excitement in my chest.

'Well, if you say yes, we can consider it as a pre-proposal

proposal.' Zack pushes my hair behind my ear.

My heart begins to race at the thought of him going down on one knee and asking me to be his wife. It actually means that he's thought about our future as much as I do! Maybe not as much as me, but I guess he is more realistic about it. He is the reasonable one.

'Yes.' I say softly, pulling him in for a kiss. His soft lips press against mine, his chest against mine as he lowers his body.

All I can think about now is that Zack is going to be my husband one day. That we'll be married! *Happily* married. Husband and wife. I will be Mrs. Anderson.

And just like that, all my worries are gone. Because he's all I want. I want my future with him. I want to live with him, get married, get pets, kids, whatever we both want, whatever life brings to us.

I know that if I was in Meg's shoes, I would want her to be happy and would never stop her from moving on with her life. I would be there to support her. I would figure out my life slowly but would never stop her happiness because of my misery. I know I'll have to sit down and talk to her when things calm down. I have to stop putting myself in other people's situations. I know Meg will support me, because she always makes sure I am happy. She wants me to be happy and I want the same for her. She's a big part of my life and we'll find a perfect solution together. Maybe she can live with her parents again for a while.

I can finally feel all the tension leaving my body. Zack looks at me with his beautiful brown eyes and smiles. And I know everything will be alright.

'I love you.'

'I love you too.'

Chapter Twenty-Four

The first week after the breakup, Meg spent most of her days in her room, depressed, only leaving if she had to. It was evident from the sound of her crying at night that she was going through a heartbreak.

One day, Jack showed up to collect some of his belongings while Meg was out, but he didn't want to speak to me either. When Zack and I returned home, Jack was about to leave, and I attempted to speak to him, but he told me to stay out of it and that it's none of my business.

His dismissive attitude made me so angry. How could he be so callous? He was the one who had shattered Meg's heart into a million pieces! Of course it's *my* business if my friend is crying because of him every night, walking around the flat with sadness in her eyes and zero will to do anything. As I was ready to start arguing, Zack stepped in to calm me down, and stop whatever was coming. After all, Jack was hurting as well. Yet, my loyalty lies with Meg, my dear friend. It breaks my heart to see them both like that. But what can I do?

I did everything I could to support Meg through all this time until one day she came downstairs, declaring she was fine. Fine? How could she be fine seven days after their breakup? I mean, she looked fresh, relaxed… and just different. No signs of crying, nothing. She was just glowing as per her usual.

Of course, I was happy to see her like that, but deep down I suspected that she might be in her denial era, or that something was coming and she'd be back to being depressed in her room within a few days. How much could she change overnight? I feel suspicious about this sudden change, to be honest. I even suspected that Meg and Jack got back together and kept it as a secret. Just to give themselves time to work things out, without anyone telling them what to do. I would be so happy if they walked through the door, holding hands, announcing that they got back together.

Meg strongly focused on her coursework as she had a lot to catch up on and the deadline is in two weeks. She actually managed to finish everything, and I couldn't be happier that my friend will graduate with me in the end. For a second there, I was truly worried that she was about to mess this up and I wanted to slap her. But she did it!

She also started applying for jobs and has some interviews already. She has fully focused on herself since the breakup. She put herself first. Damn, I should do the same and start applying for jobs, but I'm too focused on discussing my future with Zack. I still have to talk with Meg, and I think she's good enough to have this conversation. And I can mention that Zack "proposed" to me.

I secretly started working on my proper Pinterest board with all the wedding ideas. I've had this board for years, but now things are getting serious, so it's not a teenage dream anymore. This will actually happen! I don't know when, but it will.

Today is my day off, which I'm going to spend with Zack. He's working, but he'll come here right after he's done. I sit in the kitchen, enjoying my usual breakfast, which is bread and jam, and I can't stop wondering what my life with Zack will look like. Will we find a perfect place to live for now and be able to save up money to buy our first house? I want us to have a house. Will we get a dog? Or a cat? Or both? Will we have kids?

We talked about it, and it turns out that neither of us want them now. But what if he wants kids in the future? The thing is, I don't know if I want to be a mother at all. I'm not ready yet, but maybe I will change my mind in a few years. Who knows.

I am nearly twenty-three. I am too young for this right now, to even think about it. But I don't want this to be an issue in the future. For now, we want to focus on ourselves and our careers first. But if anything happens, then we will deal with it together. If we are going into a very serious stage of our relationship, we will have to talk about it again, I think.

I gaze down at my breakfast, contemplating how I might surprise my boyfriend with something better. As a future wife, I feel a pang of responsibility to improve my breakfast game beyond the usual cereal or bread with jam.

I envision myself preparing fancy meals early in the morning that Zack and I will share before he heads off to work. I picture us eating together, Zack with his coffee and me with my tea or juice. I imagine us leaving our house together, maybe Zack dropping me off, or perhaps I'll have my own car, or continue taking the tube. I smile to myself, lost in the sweet anticipation of our shared mornings when Meg comes downstairs.

There is definitely something on her mind. She looks distracted. Could it be Jack? Is she hiding something? Or what if she's met someone new already? *Oh my God!* This thought didn't even cross my mind! Is she seeing someone else? Is that why she's been so secretive? Because why would she hide Jack from me? There must be someone new! I mean, whatever makes her happy.

'Morning.' I greet her, unable to hide my curiosity about her plans. She's dressed in bright jeans and a white crop top.

'Hi.' Meg replies with a smile.

'Where are you going? You look nice.' Meg has her flawless makeup on and her hair falls straight down on her back. She's definitely going to see someone.

'For a walk. I need to think about something.' Meg explains vaguely.

'About what? Tell me.' I press, unable to contain my curiosity.

'I'll tell you later.' She winks, leaving me intrigued.

Am I right? Is there someone? That would be crazy considering that the rest of Jack's stuff is still here.

'Alright then.' I shrug, deciding not to push her further. Instead, I decide to share some news of my own. 'I want to tell you something too. I was waiting for you to feel a bit better though.'

'Oh my God, spill!' Meg exclaims eagerly, taking a seat in front of me, and helping herself to some cereal.

'So, Zack wants me to move in with him. Like for real, it's not just talk anymore. We thought about it seriously, slowly planning things, and–'

'That's fantastic, Maddie! I'm so happy for you.' Meg interjects, her smile bright and genuine.

'I know, but I've been thinking about you. How we've been living together for years, and it's sad to think that it's coming to an end.' I admit, feeling a pang of sadness at the thought of leaving our shared home behind.

'Oh, trust me Maddie, I'll be okay. And hey, we always knew this day would come.' Meg reassures me, waving off my concerns with a nonchalant gesture.

I raise my eyebrows watching her. Something is *definitely* going on. But I'll wait for her to tell me. No pressure. Even though I am dying inside to know.

'Um, and he kind of proposed to me.' I add, unable to contain my excitement.

'Shut up! No way! What? When? How?' Meg's reaction is immediate and I nod.

'Well, we were just talking, and he mentioned that he wants to marry me one day. And then I joked about whether he was proposing, and he said that if I said yes, it would be like a pre-proposal proposal. So, I said yes.' I explain, giggling at the memory of our conversation. 'And yeah, we've been discussing our future plans together. Things are getting *serious*.' I add with a soft chuckle.

'Look at you, Maddie. Ah, I always knew he'd be the one. Remember that night? When I told you he might be the one? I'm so happy that I forced you to hit on him.' She chuckles, reminiscing about the moment that set our love story in motion. 'Can you believe that? If someone told you that morning that this would happen, you would have laughed in their face. And here we are today. You're almost married, Maddie!'

'Well, we'll always be grateful for that, Meg. Zack and I.' I say, a surge of gratitude washing over me. 'In fact, Zack even mentioned that we could talk to you about moving somewhere together if you don't want to live alone.'

We actually talked about it on one of the nights Zack heard Meg crying. Zack suggested that we might stay here until she feels better. Like, he would move into my place! I think he realised why I didn't want to leave her alone. Being lonely sucks. But being lonely during tough times is even harder.

'He even offered to move in here with us until we find something better, and you can move with us if you would want to.'

'No, stop it! You two should have your own space, and I might have some plans. So don't worry about me.' Meg interjects, her tone firm but with a hint of mystery that leaves me intrigued.

'What's going on?' I can't help but press, desperate for answers.

'I'm working on something, but I'll tell you later, Maddie. I'll be back.'

Meg excuses herself from the kitchen, leaving me alone with my thoughts. Something is going on for sure. I just can't suss it out.

After tidying up and sending a quick message to Zack to check in on his day, I settle onto the sofa and pull the fluffy blanket over my legs.

My phone buzzes and Zack's name appears on the screen. I quickly grab it and answer.

'Hi.' I greet him with a smile evident in my voice.

'Hello, darling.' His sweet voice sounds in my ear.

'I guess you're not that busy, huh?' I tease.

'I'm in the office, and it looks like it will be a quiet day, so I might get out early.' Zack replies with a soft chuckle.

'How early?' I bite my finger, thinking about how much extra time I might have with him tonight.

'I hope around five. Should I grab us dinner on the way?'

'Maybe. Or we can order when you're here.'

'Nah, I will get us something. Do you think Meg will want something, too?'

'I don't know, she's acting weird, Zack.' I admit, struggling to put into words the complexity of Meg's recent change.

'What do you mean?' He chuckles.

'Weirdly happy? Excited? Hiding something?' I'm not even sure how to explain it, but there's something in the air.

'Isn't it good?'

'I mean, there's something going on. She'll tell me later, but I don't know what I need to prepare myself for.'

'Okay, I'll get something for her, too. If she wants, she can eat with us. Is she going to her parents' tonight?'

'Yeah, she's going later in the evening.' I confirm, biting my bottom lip at the thought of what we'll do tonight.

Since Meg will be studying at her parents' house tonight, Zack and I will have the place for ourselves. It's been a while since we last had intercourse. I've been too busy making sure Meg was alright, and Zack was working all the time. Gosh, I miss his touch. His lips on my skin. His body on mine. His...

'Well then...' Zack's suggestive tone sends a shiver down my spine, and I playfully roll my eyes at his teasing.

'Shut up, Zack.' I chuckle softly.

'I didn't say anything!' Zack protests, his laughter contagious even through the phone. 'Anyway, I think you should study as much as you can before I get there. You won't have much time for that later.'

'Oh, really? I think you can help me with a few things.' I say, playing with the hem of the blanket.

'I definitely do.' Zack responds, his voice thick with promise.

'Not like that!' I giggle, knowing exactly where his mind is wandering. I know exactly what he wants to help me with, and it's nothing related to my coursework.

'Babe, I should go and do some work, but I'll be with you as soon as I'm done, okay? I love you.'

'Okay. I love you too.' I say before hanging up.

Thankful for the regular laser hair removal sessions Meg had urged me to do, I don't need to worry about shaving. Always ready. The best thing I've ever done, and since I'll be busy tonight, Zack is right and I should do some coursework.

I switch off the TV and head back to my room, determined to finish as much as I can. I can't believe university will be over soon! It will soon be nothing but a memory, a chapter in my life story waiting to be told.

I type like crazy on my laptop, attempting to focus on my remaining tasks, but the sound of Meg returning from her walk interrupts my concentration. No, I need to study. She'll come and tell me herself.

I try my best to fight the urge to go to her room but with each passing second, my curiosity grows, until I can no longer resist the urge to seek answers. Sod it! I leave my laptop on the side and make my way to her room, determined to uncover the truth.

With a quick knock at the door, I enter Meg's room. She's sitting on her bed with a laptop resting on her lap.

'Hi.' I greet her, taking a seat beside her on the bed 'What is going on?'

'Maddie.' Meg begins with a smile. 'So, I have this crazy idea. I mean, it's a great opportunity, but...'

'What is that?' I peer over at the screen of her laptop, my eyebrows furrowing in confusion at the information displayed there. An internship in Sydney? What does this mean?

'Yeah, I want to move to Australia. Not forever. Just for a year, to do this internship and then come back. I mean, they offer this internship in the same company but in different countries. Like they have an office in London and many other places. It's with a worldwide marketing and advertising company. But this one is in Sydney! I've always wanted to go there, and this internship will open so many doors for me. Like, I could get a job in this company later. I could have a career. I could come back to London and already have a job.'

I listen to her excitement in utter shock, thinking that my friend might be thousands of miles away from me soon. I don't even know what to say. Is it even safe? Is it a scam? I can't believe that I won't be able to see her everyday if she actually goes there. I was worried about leaving her alone here and now she wants to move to the other side of the world? I mean yes, she did mention a few times that she would love to visit Australia or travel, work, and live there for a while but...

'Maddie?' Meg's concerned voice pulls me back to the present moment.

'Yes?' I respond, trying to gather my thoughts amidst the chaos in my mind.

'So, I was thinking about you too. I wanted you to apply with me, but of course, you have Zack here, so this is not the right thing for you to do. Your life is here. But they also offer an internship in

London. It could be a great opportunity for you too.' She shrugs and shows me the details of the offer.

They recruit people for different departments at their company across various cities like Sydney, New York, London, Barcelona, Tokyo, Toronto, and Rome. Honestly, it sounds like I could do this too. Something that I would love to do. And all the city opportunities! Absolutely crazy. However, I can only apply for London. Which is great too because I can be here with Zack, working on my future career. I can apply for it. But why can't Meg do it in London too?

'Why not another city?' I blurt out.

'I feel like I need to go somewhere far away for a while, have a fresh start, you know? Where no one knows me. Try something new.' Meg clears her throat and I know what she means. It's all because of Jack. So, they're not back together. 'Life's short. I want to see the world, take every opportunity this life offers me. And this one appeared out of nowhere. It feels like fate.' Meg explains.

'But, what about Europe?'

'No. I want to go to Sydney. As I said before, I've always wanted to go anyway, and I am going to do it, Maddie.' Meg asserts firmly. 'I am going to apply now. I thought about everything. I talked with my family and asked them their opinion. I wanted to talk to you too. I feel like it's a sign from the universe to do it. It feels like the perfect time. Our flat contract ends in September, you're moving in with Zack, I'm single, it's like everything has aligned for this.'

As Meg speaks with conviction, I can't help but admire her courage and determination. I know deep down that I have to support her in this decision. It's her dream.

'But... it's so far.' I sigh, the weight of Meg's decision settling heavily on my shoulders. 'I mean, I want you to be happy, and if it's really something you want to do, then I'm going to fully support you. But damn, I'm going to miss you so much.' My voice breaks as I get emotional thinking how much our lives might change soon. I want her to be happy, but I don't want to lose my friend.

'Oh don't cry! They might not accept me.' Meg reassures me,

her chuckle easing some of the tension in the room. 'But I'm still going to try. So, do you want to apply too?'

'I mean, I can try for the London one.'

'Yes! Let's do it!' Meg exclaims, clapping her hands.

Honestly, I don't know why, but I have a bad feeling about this. It feels like this will bring something bad into our lives and I don't know what.

Meg and I sit together in her room, filling out our applications and selecting our desired cities. Meg helps me with the application because she's almost finished hers. She chooses Sydney, New York, and Toronto. Literally everything far from here. I selected London, Sydney, and New York since they require you to choose three. It would be fun to go there, but I only consider London.

I'm just curious to see if I would even have a chance in these two big cities. I don't even feel like they'd consider me at all because I barely did one short internship during university while Meg completed two long ones! My lazy ass is going to pay for it now.

After a couple of hours of typing and crafting cover letters, our applications are completed. It was chaotic, but the deadline is at midnight, so let's see what happens. Our fate is now in the hands of fate itself.

'Ready?' Meg asks, her eyes sparkling with excitement, and I nod. We press send at the same time and look at each other in silence. 'Oh my God.' Meg puts her hand over her mouth.

'It's done.' I mumble.

'I am so excited!' Meg exclaims, her laughter filling the room. 'If I get it, I'll be in Sydney this summer! Oh my God!' Her joy is infectious. I haven't seen her this happy since the breakup. But does it mean she will leave in summer? That's so soon!

'Well, I hope it works out for you.' I reply, my smile faltering slightly as the reality of her potential departure sinks in.

'What's wrong, Maddie?'

'I mean… I just… I'm a bit worried, you know? A whole year without you? What if you forget me? What if you decide to stay there?' I confess, unable to suppress my fears any longer.

'Are you joking?' Meg laughs, pulling me into a tight embrace.

'Never! I'll come back. London is my home. I just want to try something new. And no one could ever replace you.' Her words offer some comfort, and I force myself to push aside my anxieties for the time being. 'Anyway, let's not think about it until I get an answer. And I hope you get the one in London.' Meg continues, attempting to lighten the mood.

'Me too.' I reply with a weak smile, though a part of me wishes Meg had applied for London as well. As I glance at the time on her laptop, I realise how late it is.

'Shit! Zack might be here soon.'

'Go get ready then. I need to catch the train soon anyway.' Meg says, rising from the bed.

'Zack is going to bring some food for all of us, so we can have dinner before you go. And I'll use the bathroom first.' I smile before leaving her room.

After a quick shower, I head back to my bedroom. I put on my white T-shirt dress and wrap a black belt around my waist. I quickly check my phone to see if I got any new message from Zack, but there's nothing. Okay, I still have some time, so I apply a touch of makeup. And just as I apply some lip balm, I get a message from Zack.

Be there in 5 ;)

I quickly spritz myself with the perfume he likes, and check myself in the mirror. Nice. Satisfied with my appearance, I run a brush through my straight hair and head downstairs to await Zack's arrival. He shows up later, and I wait by the door, ready to greet him with a kiss.

'Hi.' I say, offering him a smile as he enters.

'Hello, beautiful.' Zack replies, his eyes lingering on me with a playful smirk, and we make our way to the kitchen, where Zack sets the food on the table. 'You look very pretty, Maddie.' He says, turning to me with a warm smile.

I can't help but blush at his compliment, as his hands find their way to my hips, drawing me closer for another kiss. I rest my hands on his chest. His big hands move down to my butt and squeeze it.

'Oops, am I interrupting something?' Meg chuckles, appearing in the doorway.

'Hi, Meg.' Zack greets her with a smile, opening some boxes. Meg winks at me discreetly as she approaches.

'What did you bring Zack?'

'Some Mexican food.' Zack replies with a chuckle. 'There's a new restaurant near my work, so I thought I'd bring some for you.'

'Oh, it smells good.' I comment, watching eagerly as he reveals an assortment of nachos, tacos, enchiladas, quesadillas, empanadas, and tostadas.

'Are you feeding an army, Zack?' Meg jokes, causing Zack to laugh.

'I got desserts too.' Zack announces, opening a box to reveal sweet tres leches.

'Oh, I love this one!' I exclaim, biting my lip as I glance at Zack.

'I know.' He murmurs, leaving a soft kiss on my temple.

'Alright, let's have some. This delicious food is waiting for us.' Meg declares, bringing plates to the table so we can try everything.

I sit next to Zack, while Meg takes a seat opposite us. We have a little chat, enjoying the mouth-watering food, before Meg has to go and catch the train. She tidies up after herself and turns to face us.

'It was very good, Zack. Good choice.' She smiles gratefully. 'Thanks, and I'll see you two tomorrow.'

'Bye!' I call out as she leaves, leaving Zack and I alone.

'She seems good.' Zack admits casually, his attention turning back to me.

'She is, I think.' I reply, my mind preoccupied with the internship application we just submitted. Should I tell him now, or wait for the response? The excitement bubbles within me as I think about the possibility of landing the London internship and surprising him later. 'Anyway, let's talk about us.' I suggest, placing my hand over his.

'I love that.' Zack responds, his gaze warm as he turns in his chair to face me. 'So, do you know what you want to do?' He asks, placing his hands on my legs and caressing them with his thumbs. I take a sip of my water, nodding in response. 'And?'

'I want to move in with you first. Then, if we need to, we can look for something bigger once I get a job and have a bigger budget.' I say, feeling a rush of anticipation at the thought.

'Really?' Zack's face lights up with a broad smile.

'Yes.' I confirm, leaning in for a kiss. He does the same and our lips meet in a sweet kiss.

Zack kisses me softly but passionately. I slowly get off my chair, taking a step forward, and stand between his legs. Zack moves his big hands to the back of my thighs, finding way under my dress, lazily moving up, until he can grab my butt. His touch sends shivers down my spine.

'Does this mean I am going to have you with me every day?' He murmurs between kisses he leaves on my neck.

'Mhm.' I reply, biting my lip as I feel my body responding to his touch when Zack slides his hand between my legs.

'Good.' Zack whispers, a smug grin spreading across his face. I let a moan out of my mouth, while his fingers dance across my skin. 'Kiss me.' Zack orders, pushing his fingers harder and I obey eagerly, losing myself in the moment of our passion.

I wrap my hands around his neck and kiss him hard. He drives me crazy. We're breaking the house rule right now. As Zack's fingers work their magic, I find myself unable to control myself.

'Oh, God. Zack…' I gasp, resting my forehead on his.

My hands squeeze the fabric of his T-shirt as I finally feel the pleasure washing over my body. I close my eyes for a second while Zack places gentle kisses on my neck.

'Let's go to your bedroom.' He whispers. I open my eyes and look at Zack, licking his fingers.

With a swift movement, he slides his arm under my knees, effortlessly lifting me and carrying me to my bedroom.

I watch him with anticipation as he removes his T-shirt and jeans. Damn, he's so hot. He climbs onto the bed, his lips crashing into mine in a passionate kiss that leaves me breathless. As he removes my dress, tossing it aside, his hands roam over my body, tracing every curve with gentle caresses.

'You're so sexy.' Zack murmurs, his touch sending electric

sparks through my skin.

I made sure to wear my black lace underwear, and I can see the desire in Zack's eyes as he admires me. I smile and pull his face closer to mine for a kiss. As I slide my hand down his strong chest, he grabs it before I reach his boxers, placing both of my hands above my head.

I can feel his warm body pressing against mine, so I eagerly press my hips against his, urging him for more action. With a sexy smirk, Zack removes my bra and panties, his lips trailing kisses along my heated skin. I tangle my fingers in his silky hair, enjoying the closeness of our bodies. His warm skin rubbing against mine. I can finally feel him. Oh, it feels incredible. I missed it so much.

Our heavy breathing mixes and I let out a soft moan in his ear, his name escaping my lips. I know he loves it. I move my hands to his face and our gazes meet. He looks so good on top of me. The eye contact he keeps feels so intimate, and I just can't hold it anymore.

Zack bites my bottom lip teasingly, lying on top of me. The next round is mine. With a newfound confidence, I shift our positions, now taking control as I hover over him, our hands intertwined as we share sweet kisses.

Later that night, I lie down on his chest, his heartbeat soothing me as he plays with my hair.

'How do you feel?' Zack asks softly, his voice filled with tenderness.

'Very good. Thank you.' I reply, looking up at him with a smile.

'I can't wait to live with you.' Zack confesses, his eyes reflecting his genuine affection.

'Me too.' I murmur, tracing my fingers along his jawline, scanning every part of his beautiful face, and Zack watches me with a cute smile glued to his face.

I swear, I fall in love with him more and more every day. Zack waits for the moment our eyes meet again and kisses me. I feel a sense of hope blossoming within me. Perhaps this internship will mark the beginning of our future together, a future filled with love, laughter, and endless possibilities.

Chapter Twenty-Five

Within a week of submitting the application, Meg received a positive response. They accepted her in all the cities she chose, and, of course, she chose Sydney. It meant only one thing, she's going. I received mine a day after hers, but unfortunately, I wasn't offered the internship in any of the cities I selected. I won't lie, I was pretty upset about getting rejected. I tried not to get my hopes up too much, but at the same time I couldn't help but imagine how amazing it would be to land this internship in London.

    Nonetheless, I'm genuinely happy for Meg. But it stings to know that my friend will soon leave for Sydney, and I won't see her for a year! The thought alone makes me want to cry. She's already sorting out all the paperwork so she can leave in July.

    We still need to figure out what to do about our lease. Since we're all moving out, ending our lease earlier could be a major issue unless we find someone to take over the place. I mean, who wouldn't want to live here? I also need to have a serious talk with Zack about living together soon. We have to discuss all the details and get everything organised.

    I'm thrilled to be moving in with my boyfriend, but it's bittersweet knowing that my friend won't be around. She won't be here to share moments, drop by Zack's flat for a chat and some gossip, or go to our favourite coffee shop together. I want nothing more than for her to be happy, so I'll keep smiling and supporting her. But honestly? I wish she had decided to stay in London.

    I'll be counting down the days until her return. At least she'll be here for my birthday next week. I initially wanted to throw a big house party, but given all the changes, I think I'd rather spend the day with just Zack and Meg. Just the three of us.

I head to Meg's room and gently knock on her door, a wave of sadness washing over me as I realise these are the last times I'll be coming to her room, the last moments we'll share in this flat.

'Come in!' Meg's voice calls out, breaking my thoughts.

'Hi.' I smile as I step into her room. 'What are you up to?'

'I need to fill out all the information for the visa and stuff.' She replies, her eyes fixed on her laptop screen. I take a seat beside her and glance at the form.

'How's it going?' I ask, trying to keep my voice steady.

'Almost done!' Meg responds with a bright smile.

'I can't believe you're actually going. I'll miss you so much.' I say, a lump forming in my throat.

'I know! It's crazy.' Meg responds, giving me a quick glance before returning her focus to typing. 'I wish you were going with me, honestly. It would be so fun. You have no idea how much I'll miss you. But I trust Zack, and I know he'll take good care of you.'

'But I got rejected.' I confess, fiddling with the fabric of my dress.

'That sucks. Their loss, Maddie. I'm sure you'll find something here, and you'll be great at it.' Meg assures me, her words offering a small comfort.

'Well, I hope you'll do great in Sydney and come back here ready to take over London.' I say, trying to sound optimistic despite the ache in my chest.

'I'm going for an internship, not applying to be the next president, Maddie.' Meg laughs, but her laughter quickly fades. 'Gosh, I'll miss you so much. I want to FaceTime you every day, but this fucking time difference!'

'Hey, we'll figure out something.' I reassure her, placing my hand on her arm and giving it a gentle rub. 'I can stay up late, and we can have a call or something. It'll work out.'

'Don't get married without me, okay?' Meg suddenly says, her tone half-joking, half-serious.

'What? I'm not even engaged yet.' I laugh.

'You kinda are, I mean, he asked you, right? Now, it's just a matter of time until he puts a ring on your hand.' Meg says with a knowing smile, and I can't help but blush at the thought.

'Yeah, but we were just joking.' I say, biting my lip. 'Anyway, I would never do it without you. I need my maid of honour.'

'If he proposes when I am away, you *have* to call me, even in the middle of the night. I will pick up the phone anytime. But honestly, I wish I was here when it happened.'

'Me too.' I chuckle softly. 'And I promise to call you right away.'

'Thanks.'

'So, do you know where you are going to live? How does everything look?' I nudge her arm.

'No, they will send me all the details when everything gets approved and I get my visa.' Meg responds, putting her laptop aside. 'I feel stressed, Maddie. Maybe I should stay? I don't know if I can actually do it when I think about it now.'

'You know I would love it if you stayed, but this is something you really wanted. I know it's scary but you'll be fine.'

'But I'm going alone. Honestly, I didn't expect to be accepted, and I was hoping that if I do, you will get in too, and we would go together. Like if they accepted you in Sydney. I mean, Zack could go too, since he's looking for a job anyway. Like, he could try something there. Maybe you two can go with me?' Meg suddenly grabs my hand excitedly. 'You both can find some nice jobs there. You have nothing to lose, right?'

'Meg, I don't think it's possible.' I chuckle lightly. 'I don't have that many savings to risk going there without having any job secured, and I don't know about Zack. I don't know if he would be interested in moving to Australia.'

'Eh, it's fine. I just thought it would be a great idea.'

'You'll be fine.' I assure her, giving her a warm smile. 'You will smash it and tell me everything when you're back. We will go to our coffee shop, get a latte and catch up on everything. A year will pass by quickly, and I'm sure you'll have wonderful stories to share with me when you are back.'

'Girl, you'll be updated every day.' Meg laughs. 'I need daily calls.'

'I hope so!' I chuckle, shaking my head. 'Just go there and show them what Meg can do. Live your life.'

'I love you, Maddie.' She says, wrapping her arms around me in a tight hug.

A knock at the front door interrupts us.

'Are you expecting anyone?' I ask, and she shakes her head. 'Alright, I'll get it.'

'Did you forget your man is coming?' Meg jokes, and I playfully flip her off.

'He's working, and he has a key, so he doesn't have to knock. I will check to see who it is.'

As I leave Meg's room, I head downstairs to open the door. Shock washes over me when I see Jack standing there with a massive bouquet of flowers. I can't believe my eyes! My jaw drops on the floor. What is he doing here? Did he come to apologise? Of course he did. He has flowers! Shit! What an awful timing since she's leaving for Sydney. Or maybe she will stay…

'Jack?' I whisper, dumbstruck.

'Hi. Is Meg home?' Jack asks nervously, peering over my shoulder.

'Yes, let me get her.' I reply, stepping aside to let him in before I run upstairs. Bursting into her room, I find Meg sitting on her bed, looking puzzled.

'Are you okay?' She frowns, looking at me.

'Meg…' I pause, grabbing her hand and pulling her to stand up. 'Come downstairs. Quickly.' I add, out of breath.

'What is going on?' Meg asks as I pull her hand harder, urging her to follow.

'Just come. Please.' I say, leading her downstairs.

I can feel Meg hesitating on the stairs, so I glance at her, but her eyes are fixed on Jack. I purse my lips, my gaze shifting between Meg and Jack. I have no idea what is about to happen, but obviously, I hope for the best.

'What are you doing here?' Meg asks, her voice stern.

'Hi Meg, can we talk?' Jack asks, his voice tinged with nervousness.

'I will leave you two alone, okay?' I give Meg a quick look to see if she wants me to stay, but her eyes are still on Jack. There is some emotion in her eyes that I can't read… Is she happy to see him, or is she angry?

As I walk down the stairs, I pat Jack's arm before leaving the flat. I hope they will reconcile. I hope they will finally talk, and explain whatever happened that awful night. He came with flowers, so it means he wants to apologise. Of course, he missed her and still loves her. Otherwise, he wouldn't come at all.

I smile to myself as I walk, but then suddenly stop when a thought crosses my mind. How will he react when she drops the Sydney news on him? Will she stay for him? Or will she tell him to go away? Will Jack let her go? Will he wait for her here, in London? Will he go with her? Maybe I should have stayed in my room and eavesdropped? I just hope that they can sit and talk about everything. They will be fine, I know it. They will figure it out.

Glancing down at my phone, I decide to send Zack a quick message to check in on how he's doing at work, but he doesn't reply. Well, he must be busy.

With a fruity smoothie from a nearby shop, I take a stroll in Hampstead Heath. Making my way to the top of the hill, I settle into my favourite seat with a breathtaking view of London. The warmth of the day surrounds me, and with all my assignments finished and submitted, I'm technically university-free, allowing me to simply sit and relax.

Luckily, the bench is free, which is a relief since I'm wearing a white, romantic dress and sitting on the grass would be a nightmare to keep it clean.

Sipping on my smoothie, I find myself lost in my thoughts about my life and how much it has changed. If someone had told me three years ago that I would graduate, move in with my absolutely perfect boyfriend, and have my friend leave for Australia, I would have never believed it.

Life has been crazy busy these past few years, but I feel blessed to be surrounded by people I love. I've even managed to maintain my relationship, which seemed impossible at the beginning. I know Zack loves me. I see it in his eyes, the way he looks at me, the way he holds my hand, and in his actions.

A smile plays on my lips as I think about him, his beautiful smile and eyes, the sound of his laugh that melts my heart, the way he holds me close to him, and when he plays with my hair as we drift off to sleep, or when…

My thoughts are interrupted by a message notification on my phone. I quickly check to see if it's from Meg or Zack. It's Zack.

Sorry, darling. We're very busy today. See you tonight?

Of course! Can we go to yours, though? I think Meg and Jack might reconcile.

Oh wow, Jack came? Sure. I can pick you up after work.

Yup, and no, it's fine, I can get the tube. See you in the evening.

Sure. See you later, sweetheart.

I put my phone back and enjoy the warmth of the sun on my skin. Maybe, I will get a tan on my face.

As I soak in the tranquility of nature surrounding me, a fantastic idea suddenly pops into my head, so I quickly get up to head back to the flat.

Despite my eagerness, I hesitate halfway there, wondering if Meg and Jack need more time to talk. Glancing at the time on my phone, I realise it's been two hours, so I guess I can sneak into the house without interrupting anything. I just need to grab some stuff, and then I'll be on my way. Slowly, I resume my walk, thinking about a surprise for my man.

I stop outside the door, trying to listen for any noise, but it's silent. With a slow turn of the key, I cautiously enter the flat. My eyes scan the room, and I spot Meg and Jack on the sofa.

'Oh, sorry, guys. Don't worry about me. I'm going to leave soon. Just needed to grab something, and I'll be out in five minutes. I promise.'

'Maddie, stop. It's fine.' Meg chuckles, resting her hand on Jack's thigh.

'Are you two okay?'

'Yes, I think. I mean, we talked and explained things, but we need to talk more if we want this to work. There are things to discuss.' Jack nods along with Meg's explanation. 'But I think we are heading in the right direction.'

'Definitely.' Jack lifts Meg's hand and places a kiss on it.

'Aw, guys! So, you're back together, right?' I exclaim, placing my hands on my cheeks. 'Anyway, like I said, I'm leaving in five minutes, so you can keep talking. I'm going to stay at Zack's tonight, so um…' I clear my throat suggestively. 'You have time for everything.' I wink at them, and Meg rolls her eyes with a cheerful smile. 'It's good to see you, Jack.' I smile before heading towards my room.

I grab my bag and pack some essentials. Well, I definitely won't need any pyjamas, as I'm planning to steal one of Zack's T-shirts. I retrieve the key to his flat from my drawer and slip it into my bag, a smile spreading across my face as I recall the day he gave it to me.

Once I have everything I need, I head downstairs again, waving goodbye to my friends who are in the middle of conversation. Meg is already giggling, and Jack keeps his eyes filled with love for her. Yup, they are going to have an interesting night for sure.

With a smile on my face, I enter the tube station to get to Zack's place in East London. Throughout the ride, I can't stop thinking about my two friends getting back together. I'm so excited for them. I hope the Sydney situation will not ruin it. Oh, did she even tell him? What is she going to do now? I will need answers.

Lost in my thoughts, I almost miss my stop. I walk straight to Tesco for some groceries for the evening. I want to make him some lasagna, and I should have enough time if I get to his flat now. We will need some wine for it too. On my way to the till, the flower stand catches my attention, and I stare at the lovely selection of different bouquets. I grab one with pink roses. Why not? He always gets me flowers, so I can give him a bouquet too. I go to the till to pay and leave the shop with everything I need for my lovely evening with Zack.

I start cooking as soon as I reach his place and unpack

everything. Zack's flat is amazing, and I can't wait to live here with him. I can picture us cooking dinners together, listening to our favourite songs, watching movies on the sofa and cuddling, or watching the sunset from his balcony. I can't wait for all of that. I can't wait for everything that is waiting for us.

As I play myself some music, I follow the recipe I've tested on my brother multiple times, knowing Zack loves it too. I sing some ABBA lyrics as I layer the lasagna in the baking tray. Turning around to grab a glass of water from the kitchen cabinet, I almost have a heart attack. Zack is leaning on the wall, watching me with a smile. I place my hand on my pounding heart and close my eyes for a moment.

'You scared me.' I say, opening my eyes.

'Didn't want to interrupt the show.' Zack chuckles, getting closer to me. 'I was quite enjoying it.'

'When did you get here?' I ask, wrapping my hands around his neck.

'Like five minutes ago.' Zack answers, kissing me softly.

'I didn't hear you.'

'I know. But I like what I see.'

'Dinner is not ready yet.' I tell him, gesturing towards the unfinished lasagna, and walk back to my dish to finish the layers. Zack stands behind me, wrapping his strong arms around my waist while I sprinkle cheese on top.

'Lasagna?' He kisses my neck, sending shivers down my body.

Reluctantly, I have to break our closeness to put lasagna in the oven. When I turn around to look at Zack, he's leaning on the kitchen countertop, watching me. With the lasagna in the oven, I steal a moment to admire the bouquet of flowers I picked up earlier.

'I got you some flowers.' I say, gesturing towards the bouquet.

'For me?' Zack's eyes light up with surprise. I nod, feeling a rush of affection for this man who never fails to make me smile.

'They just need some water.'

'I can't believe I got some flowers. Thank you.' Zack chuckles, searching his cupboards until he finds a vase, fills it with water, and puts the flowers in. I watch him smiling at the bouquet. He turns to face me, our eyes meet, and I feel the atmosphere changing around us. 'Thank you.'

Before I can say anything else, Zack pulls me into a passionate kiss, his lips leaving me breathless. I rest my hands on his chest, gently pulling back after a short while.

'Dinner will be ready in around half an hour.'

'I need a shower. Wanna join?' Zack grins mischievously, his eyes sparkling with excitement.

'You can go, and I'll stay here just in case it burns.' I chuckle, feeling the temptation tug at me.

'Are you sure?' He asks, raising an eyebrow.

'I'm sure. Go.' I say, squeezing his cheeks playfully and giving him a quick kiss.

Zack slowly heads towards the bathroom, his gaze constantly flickering back to see if I'll follow. I suppress a laugh as he tries to tempt me by taking off his top and dramatically tossing it onto the sofa. But I resist, knowing I can't risk burning our dinner. We can't have a take away again.

While Zack showers, I check on our food and set the table. When he returns, all fresh and with wet hair, wearing his pyjama bottoms, I can't help but smile.

'Smells good, darling.' Zack says, kissing my cheek.

'Ten more minutes.' I reach for the bottle of wine, pour it into glasses, and pass him one. 'For us.' I raise my glass. Zack smiles, clinking his glass against mine. As he wraps his arm around me, I rest my head on his chest, sipping my wine. 'It feels so good.' I murmur as he kisses the top of my head. 'Feels right.' I look up, meeting his happy gaze.

'I know.' Zack whispers, leaning in to kiss me, and I close my eyes, returning the kiss. 'I love you so much.' He adds, brushing hair behind my ear.

'I love you too.' I say, wrapping my arms around him and snuggling my face into his neck.

Our moment is interrupted by the oven's beep. I check if dinner is ready, and it looks perfect. The cheese has melted on top, filling the air with a mouthwatering aroma.

'Dinner's ready, honey.' I announce.

'Let me help you.' Zack offers, chuckling as he removes the hot dish from the oven.

I cut it into pieces and try to plate the lasagna, but it's too hot, and everything falls apart.

'Well.' I sigh, looking at Zack.

'Delicious. I'm so hungry.' He says unbothered, taking the plates from me and setting them on the table, and I follow him with wine.

We spend the evening chatting about us, our future, reminiscing about the past, discussing how far we've come as a couple, and how much is still ahead of us. As we laugh and share stories, I realise how deeply in love I am with this man. Nothing can scare me with him by my side. I feel ready to face anything life throws at us, holding his hand every step of the way.

Chapter Twenty-Six

Nearly thirty-three wonderful months with Zack in my life, and soon we'll be living together. Soon, all our plans will turn into our reality, and I couldn't be more thrilled. However, there's one thing nagging at me, and it's the fact that Meg is still leaving for Australia.

Despite being back with Jack, her determination to go remains unwavering. I was concerned that their reunion would be short-lived, but Jack surprised me. He's willing to wait for her, even if it means a year apart! His heartfelt speech to her melted my heart.

Meg shared all the details, of course. Jack apologised for not listening and for doubting her that night. He returned with a determination to win her back. He realised how much she means to him and that he can't imagine his life without her. He simply couldn't bear to be without her and would rather wait a year than risk losing her again. He'll let her go, make her dreams come true, and he'll be waiting for her return, here in London. Isn't that cute?

He loves her so much. I always knew it. He's even planning visits to Australia, constantly searching for flights and dates. And it gives me hope that she'll come back. Although it still stings, I want her to pursue what's best for her. Do whatever makes her happy. I'll be here, waiting with Jack. Also, having Zack next to me all the time will help me deal with the longing.

But, today is my birthday, and I refuse to let anything upset me. I want to celebrate with my friends and boyfriend. Originally, it was supposed to be just the three of us, but with Jack's return, he'll be joining. It feels like old times.

Even Zack surprised me coming last night, ensuring he'd be

here when I woke up. So, when the clock hit midnight, I got a little birthday gift from him. Very satisfying.

When I wake up in the morning, Zack is peacefully sleeping on his back, his arm wrapped around my waist. I watch his chest rise and fall with each breath before leaning in to place a gentle kiss on his lips. Zack wakes up, murmuring something under his breath.

'Good morning.' I chuckle.

'Good morning, princess.' Zack replies, stretching his body, the muscles in his arms flexing as he moves. 'Happy birthday.' His strong arms pull me close, and he gifts me with a loving kiss.

'Thank you.' I smile, feeling warmth spread through me at his affection.

'Any wishes?' He asks.

'I might have a few.' I say, biting my lip, my fingers tracing down his stomach.

'That's for later.' Zack chuckles, stopping my hand and intertwining our fingers. 'Anything in particular you want to do today?'

'I just want to spend the day with you, Meg, and Jack. I don't really mind what we do.'

'Alright. Let's get you some breakfast first.' Zack suggests.

'Okay.'

I happily climb out of bed and reach for the birthday outfit I picked out the day before.

Today is for my friends, and on the weekend, we're all going to my parents' house for a BBQ. As I slip into a pair of tight jeans with ripped knees and a white rhinestone fringe crop top, I catch Zack watching me in the mirror with a smirk plastered to his face.

'Aren't you getting ready?' I ask, raising my eyebrows as I apply some foundation to my face.

'I was enjoying the view.' He replies, walking over to me and placing a short kiss on my arm.

Zack goes for an all-black outfit: jeans, a T-shirt, and a leather jacket. He stands next to me, deftly styling his hair up. He does it so effortlessly. As I slowly brush my hair, I catch his warm smile in the reflection.

'You look beautiful.' He says sincerely, making my heart flutter.

'Thank you.' I say, scrunching up my nose.

When we're both ready, he takes my hand and leads me downstairs. White and pink balloons are scattered across the floor, some floating near the ceiling with shiny serpentine attached to them. The air is filled with the sweet scent of pastries and fresh pancakes. Meg stands in the kitchen next to Jack, holding a white, rounded cake adorned with the words "Happy Birthday Maddie" and a few candles.

'Happy Birthday!' They all shout as Zack and I enter the kitchen.

'Oh my gosh, guys.' I gasp, clasping my hand over my mouth.

This gesture is so sweet and thoughtful. They must have put in a lot of effort to surprise me like this. A warm feeling envelops my heart as I take in all the friendly faces. I feel truly special right now. They did this all for me.

'Come on! Make a wish!' Meg urges me to blow out the candles.

I close my eyes, trying to think of what I want, but I realise I already have everything I could wish for. My friends, my lovely boyfriend, my family. I just wish for this happiness to last forever, for us to always be together, happy and carefree. That's it, that's my wish. I'm happy with my life right now and I want it to stay like that.

I take a deep breath and blow out all the candles at once.

'Done.' I say with a smile, meeting each of their gazes.

'You cut the first piece.' Meg says, passing me a knife.

'Cake for breakfast? I love it.' I chuckle, cutting a piece for each of us.

We gather around the table, where they've laid out an array of sweet treats, fruits, and champagne. What a delightful start to the day.

Zack grabs the bottle and pops it open.

'Let's raise a toast to the birthday girl.' He says, pouring the bubbly liquid into our glasses.

We raise our glasses and clink them together before taking a sip. Pure happiness rushes through me as I gaze at their smiling faces. I'm happy, truly happy right now.

'So we'll take you to some place today.' Zack says, looking at me.

'Where?' I ask, raising my eyebrows.

'It's a surprise.' Jack chimes in.

'Oh you will like it!' Meg adds with a smile.

'Do I need to change for this or–'

'No, this is perfect. You'll be fine.' Meg interrupts with a wink.

'Alright, I trust you.' I say, pointing my fork, loaded with cake, in her direction, and she laughs. 'So, when did you prepare all of this?' I ask curiously, taking a bite of cake.

'Well, last night. Zack came to help after… you fell asleep.' Meg says, clearing her throat suggestively. I feel my cheeks flush at the thought that they might know what Zack and I were up to before he came downstairs. 'And then he just needed to make sure you stayed in bed long enough for us to get everything ready.'

'He was still asleep when I woke up.' I chuckle, stealing a glance at the handsome face of the man I love.

'Zack!' Meg gives him a playful look.

'What? She always stays in bed until I wake up anyway.' Zack says with a wink in my direction.

It's true. Unless I need to use the toilet or something, but I prefer to stay wrapped in his arms.

'Thank you guys.' I say, giving them all my most grateful smile.

We enjoy our breakfast, chatting about our days, and I try not to dwell on Meg's upcoming departure. By afternoon, I'm slightly tipsy. Drinking for breakfast was quite the idea. But the mood is good. Soon, we're off to the surprise, and I can't help but wonder where they're taking me.

Zack wanted to drive, but since he's had some drinks, we're going to take the tube, and I don't mind it at all. He should be able to celebrate with us without worrying about driving. Besides, it's my birthday, and I wouldn't let him drive even if he insisted.

We slowly walk to the station, Zack's hand firmly holding mine, with Meg and Jack leading the way. I sneak a glance at Zack and find him already looking at me with a smile.

'We need to go to Canary Wharf.' Jack informs us, checking the tube map.

We change trains along the way, but we reach Canary Wharf without any major issues. Jack leads us to a place called Fair Game, and as we step inside, I'm already impressed. They were right. The place is buzzing with activity, filled with various games like skeeball, shoot the clown, basketball arcade, space race, and my favourite, an air hockey table. We'll definitely be spending most of our time right there.

Zack grabs my hand, and we all head to the bar to grab some drinks first. My eyes roam around, taking in the lively atmosphere, observing couples and groups of friends having a blast. This is going to be a great day, especially after a few drinks. I smile at my friends as we raise our lagers for a toast.

After finishing our pints, we dive into playing different games to find our favourites. When we come across alley hoop, we all compete against each other. Surprisingly, Meg wins against all of us. Zack, being the wonderful boyfriend he is, lets me claim third place, just after Jack, making himself lose the game. As a consolation prize, I give him a sweet but swift kiss, knowing there's more to come later. Judging by the look on his face when I pull away, he's thinking the same thing.

'Oh! Let's try this one!' Meg exclaims, pulling Jack towards a horse racing game. We join them, although I don't quite get the game, but we still give it a try. It turns out we're not fans.

Finally, we make our way to the air hockey table, a few more drinks later, and I'm feeling rather competitive. I crush Meg and Jack in that game, and then it's Zack's turn to face me.

'Let's bet.' He says, looking smug.

'Fine. If I win, we'll have a romance movie marathon, and you can't complain.' I smile defiantly.

'If I win, you'll strip down for me and give me a lap dance.' Zack declares with a mischievous smirk, and I hear my friend gasp.

'Oh, this will be exciting to watch, Jack.' Meg chimes in, sounding far too amused by our bet.

'Deal.' I agree, grabbing my hand-held disc, determined to defeat my boyfriend. Oh, he thinks he's so clever with this bet? We'll see. It's my birthday, after all.

When the game starts, I expect Zack to go easy on me since it's my special day, but he's surprisingly eager to win. Nevertheless, I refuse to let him.

Despite my efforts, Zack scores three seconds before the time ends, winning by just one point. I stare at him with my mouth wide open as he walks around the table, clearly proud of himself. He puts his hands on my waist and pulls me closer.

'I'm sorry, baby. I had to win this one.' Zack chuckles, kissing my forehead.

'It's my birthday.' I whimper, feeling a bit disappointed. His arms tighten around me, and I look up at him.

'I'm sorry.' Zack says, flashing me his charming smile before leaning in to kiss me. The kiss is long and tender, and well, I can forgive him for that. He's too adorable to be mad at him.

We spend at least three hours getting tipsy, and playing all the other games. I laugh in Zack's arms as I watch Meg giving her all to beat Jack in the basketball game, playfully blocking him with her arm. I rest my head on Zack's chest, and he kisses the top of my head. I try to savour this moment, storing it in my memory because who knows when we'll get to do this again.

Later, we leave the place and head back to our flat. Jack orders us some pizza while Meg and I prepare our special mojitos, and Zack... Zack watches us, nibbling on a piece of my birthday cake. It seems like he really enjoys it. I smile as I watch him, and our eyes meet when he looks at me from his plate.

'Open your mouth.' He says, moving his finger, with a piece of cake on it, closer to my mouth. I'm busy cutting limes, but I lick the cake off his finger.

'Save it for tonight, guys.' Meg says, looking at us with a smirk. I feel my cheeks flush, and Zack chuckles.

We bring everything to the living room and gather around the table.

'Since we're waiting for the food, should we do the presents?' Jack suggests, giving Meg a knowing look as he brings a medium-sized box to the table. 'Happy Birthday, Maddie.' He says with a smile, passing me the gift. I raise my eyebrows, curious.

'Open it.' Meg can't contain her excitement.

'Okay.' I smile and remove the top of the box.

Inside, there are many things, so I pick up the first one and unwrap it. It's a book. I flip through the pages, admiring the pictures and short stories about us. It's a book about our friendship. It begins with Meg and I through the years, and then Jack and Zack join the story.

There's a candle that I remember sniffing in a shop some time ago, and Jack proudly explains that it was his idea, recalling that I liked it. There are various pink-coloured items, like skincare products, which I know Meg chose, along with a framed collage of pictures from our vacation in Greece, and more.

But the last gift brings tears to my eyes. At the bottom of the box, there's a framed picture of a map with two little hearts pinned to Sydney and London, connected by a pink string. It breaks me because Meg will leave soon, and I'll miss her so much. I didn't want to dwell on it, but she surprised me with this gift.

Zack wraps his arm around me, peering at the gift.

'I knew she would cry, Jack!' Meg says to Jack, resting her hand on my thigh.

'I'm fine…' I manage to blurt out in a high-pitched voice. Zack kisses my temple, trying to comfort me. 'I'll miss you so much.'

'I'll miss you too.' Meg says, her eyes growing moist as she moves closer for a hug.

We sit like that, holding each other for a while, until Zack decides to lighten the mood.

'Okay, time for my gift. I promise, this one is fun.' He says, walking to the corner of the room and retrieving a box from behind the curtain. So this is where they hid them?

I wipe my cheeks and take the gift from him, giving it a shake. It sounds like there are thousands of tiny pieces inside or something broke.

'What is that?' I ask as Zack takes the seat next to me.

'Have a look.' He encourages me with a smile.

I quickly tear the wrapping paper and reveal a Lego box. On it, there's a picture of a beautiful bouquet of white flowers.

'They last forever.' Zack says softly, watching me for my reaction with a gentle smile. He got me flowers that will last forever. They will never die, this is so romantic! 'Like us.' He whispers the last part in my ear, and I know it's a promise he's making to me about our relationship. We are going to last forever.

'Oh, Zack… this is so thoughtful and romantic. I love it. Thank you.' I say, cupping his face and giving him a loving kiss.

We smile, gazing into each other's eyes until Meg reminds us that we're not alone in the room.

'So, who's gonna put it together?' She asks, breaking the moment.

'Let's do it together!' I exclaim, shaking the box in the air, making Zack laugh.

We sit down on the floor, and I carefully open the box, removing all the elements. We all glance at the instructions while sipping our mojitos.

Meg and I give up after about fifteen or twenty minutes, while Zack and Jack work eagerly on it like a perfect team. Honestly, Meg and I were a bit messy with it, mixing all the parts and making it harder for the boys. I thought it was a good idea to open all the bags at the same time. Well, turns out it was not.

In the meantime, our pizza arrives, and we all have a slice before the boys return to working on the Lego. I feed Zack from time to time as he works diligently on the bouquet. Meg draws a heart with her fingers in the air at Zack and me, and I can't help but giggle.

I turn my head to watch Zack. He's my everything. My whole world revolves around this man, sitting on the carpet, making me a forever-lasting bouquet of Lego pieces. The love of my life. My one and only.

Zack hands me the finished bouquet a few minutes later and kisses me on the lips. I take it from him and admire the gift.

'It's so pretty.' I smile, examining it from every angle. 'I already know where I'll put it. Next to my bed, on the bedside table, so I can see it before I go to sleep and when I wake up. Then, it will have a special place in our home, next to our bed.' I say, beaming.

'Our home.' Zack echoes, his smile mirroring mine. I can tell he's just as excited as I am. I'll be living with my boyfriend! Very, very soon.

Meg pours us another round of mojitos, and we all toast to me.

Again and again with another round. With each toast, they start to take turns making speeches.

'I want to toast to my best friend. My beloved friend that I can't imagine my life without. Someone who understands me like nobody else.' Meg says, a little tipsy. 'I hope you feel very special today, and any other day. You deserve it, Maddie. Because you are such a lovely person, always thinking about others, always caring about others. You have such a good heart. You know you deserve the world, right?' She takes a deep breath, getting emotional. 'You deserve every single good thing in this world. And Zack.' She points at him. 'Yes, you. You are very lucky to have her. Take care of her, alright? I trust you. Make her happy every day. And I know you are the perfect match for her. She loves you so much. A lot. I know it. We talked about it.' Meg jokes, and Zack kisses my arm. 'Anyway, Maddie. You are the best. To Maddie!' She raises her glass, and we all do the same, taking a sip.

'Okay, my turn.' Jack chimes in when we finish another one. 'Maddie, we've been friends for a few years now. And as Meg said, you deserve the world. You are such a wonderful, loving, and caring person. I wish you all the best in life, a wonderful future with Zack, and many more good times with us. We all love you. I'm happy that you are my friend too. Happy birthday!'

'Thank you.' I smile.

Zack clears his throat.

'I guess the last round is on me.' He says, looking into my eyes, and I maintain eye contact. 'Maddie, I feel incredibly grateful that you've become a part of my life. And I don't even remember how I could live before, without you next to me. You changed my life. For the better. You always make everything better by simply just being next to me. You know I love you so much. As your friends said, you deserve the world, and I can promise that I'll do my best to give you everything this world has to offer. I promise to keep this beautiful smile on your face, to make your heart skip a beat, and always make you happy. Happy birthday, darling.'

'Aw Zack.' I stick out my bottom lip before grabbing his face and kissing him.

I got a little emotional after all the kind words from my loved ones. Honestly, I could not be happier than I am now. We are good, we are happy, we are together, and that's all that matters.

Chapter Twenty-Seven

Meg and I officially graduated from university. It's finally done, it's over. The results are out, and while I nearly got the first, I'm still happy with what I've achieved. Meg got first, of course, and I couldn't be prouder of her.

Do I spend more time in bed? Of course I do! I deserve to finally relax after all the hard work. Do I give all my free time to Zack, Meg and Jack? Absolutely! I spend as much time with them as I can. Even Edward, my manager, asked if I wanted to start working full-time, but I declined. I prefer to keep working part-time over the summer, especially because I will be moving to Zack's place soon. I'll take a few more extra hours, but I'm not ready for a full-time job just yet. I need time to apply for jobs, attend interviews, and simply have some personal time. Right now, my focus isn't on working at the hotel.

My priority is to spend quality time with my friend before she leaves, ensuring my move goes smoothly, dedicating more time to Zack, and securing a job in my field of study. Meg and I are taking our time to pack our belongings, deciding what to keep, what to donate, and what goes into the trash. We have time, but we don't want to leave anything until the last minute.

Zack has been visiting more often, while I spend less time at his place. So far, it's working well, allowing me to balance my time between Zack and Meg. Tonight, Zack isn't coming as he'll finish work very late. I wouldn't mind, but that's fine.

Zack is still busy with searching for a new job, but all the openings on the job market seem to not work for him. He's still stuck at his current job, slowly sapping away all his energy. I wish

I could help him, but I don't know how. I don't like to see him like that. I can see the weariness on his face, he's clearly fed up with his current situation. I sincerely hope he finds something soon. All I can offer him is my love and support, which I give to him whenever he needs it.

My gaze lands on the Lego bouquet resting next to my bed, and thoughts of Zack instantly bring a smile to my face. I'm definitely the luckiest girl in the world. Searching under my pillow for my phone, I retrieve it with a grin. On the screen, a picture of Zack and I from my birthday catches my eye. We were pretty drunk at this point, and Meg took this picture of us.

We were laughing at the *What Do You Meme?* game, Zack had his arm wrapped around my neck, my head nestled against his chest as I pulled a funny card on him, and we couldn't stop laughing. My hand covers my mouth, Zack has his eyes closed, and both of us are laughing uncontrollably. Maybe the card wasn't that funny, and we were just intoxicated enough that everything made us laugh.

Though the picture is slightly blurry, it looks cool. It's candid. It's cute, capturing a genuine moment between us. I love it and I couldn't resist setting it as my wallpaper, it never fails to make me smile whenever I glance at it. With a warm feeling in my heart, I open my messages with Zack and quickly type him a morning greeting.

Good morning, handsome. How's everything?

I imagine he's still asleep. He worked late last night too and has to do the same today. My heart aches for him, knowing how exhausted he must be.

Out of curiosity, I decide to check my email, where I find a message from SparkArc. What the hell... My eyebrows furrow in confusion as I open it, and suddenly, my heart starts racing as I absorb the contents.

Dear Madison Martin... We are pleased to offer you an internship starting in July... in Sydney...

My mind races as I re-read the email, stopping on the same words as before. *Offer. Sydney.* Like Sydney in Australia. They're offering me an internship in Australia! I'm so stunned that my hand trembles, causing me to drop my phone onto the bed. How is this even possible? Wasn't I an unsuccessful candidate? And now I am accepted?

With shaking hands, I quickly pick up the phone and read it once again. I feel like my breath is stuck in my throat. How is that possible? Maybe someone declined the offer, or perhaps there's been some mistake. Clearly. Or I don't know. But my head feels dizzy. I can't wrap my head around it right now. I need some fresh air. I'm going to pass out.

I rise from my bed and make my way to the window, opening it and inhaling a large amount of fresh air into my lungs. With my eyes closed, I focus on slowing my breathing, attempting to calm my body. Why Sydney and not London? I mean, it's a once-in-a-lifetime opportunity. This is the best company in the world. I never expected to be accepted anywhere with them. Like, it always seemed impossible to work for the best company in the world.

With Meg, it was obvious, she's a perfect candidate. But me? Maybe they've sent it by accident? Probably. I should ignore it. It's a mistake. For sure.

My phone pings with a new message, and I walk back to my bed and pick it up. It's from Zack.

> Morning love. All good. I am just exhausted but fine. How are you? Any plans for today?

I stare at the message. Plans? What plans? My thoughts whirl, unable to focus. Could they have really sent me an acceptance letter by accident? Is that even possible? Or do they genuinely want me? But Sydney, it's on the other side of the world. Thousands of miles away from my family, from Zack. I glance at my wallpaper. What about him? What would he say?

Zack! You won't believe…

Guess what! I…

I begin typing, then delete each message. No, maybe I shouldn't text him yet. Should I call?

Well, I have some news! Call me when you…
Babe I have a surprise!

No, this doesn't feel right either. I delete everything again. I'll talk to him when I see him. It's better in person. But what do I want to say? Do I want to go? Should I even consider it? Should I decline?

I groan and cover my face with my hands. What do I want? What do I want? What do I... Meg! I need to speak to Meg. She'll help me to sort out my thoughts that are going absolutely crazy at the moment. Out of my control.

No plans at the moment, maybe I will just chill with Meg and see how the day goes.

I quickly send Zack a message back. With trembling legs, I rush to my friend's room and knock. Her soft voice invites me in. I push open the door to see Meg still in bed, removing her eye-mask.

'Hi.' I say with a husky voice, moving closer to her bed as she sits up.

'Hi Maddie.' She yawns. Jack is at work, so I can talk to her. 'What's up?'

'Nothing.' I start, settling down beside her and pulling her quilt over my legs.

'You sure?' Meg raises an eyebrow in suspicion.

'Okay, so…'

'I knew it!' Meg chuckles. 'Go on.'

'Is it possible to get rejected from something and then suddenly get an offer?' I blurt out.

'What do you mean?' She asks, her curiosity piqued.

'You know, I got an email from SparkArc, and it turns out they offered me the internship.'

'No way! Shut up!' Meg's reaction is immediate, her excitement palpable. 'That's so great Maddie! You can–'

'Yes, but there is a thing.'

'What?'

'They offered me the internship in Sydney.'

'Shut up!' Meg screams and covers her mouth with her hands right away. 'Oh my God, Maddie! You really got it? In Sydney? The same place as me?' Meg grabs my hands in excitement.

I nod slowly and show her my phone. Meg reads the email carefully, her eyes widening as she takes in every word.

'Maddie! This is great! This is... Can you imagine we can do this together? This is even more exciting now.'

'I know but there's one thing.'

'What?' Meg's voice softens, her concern evident.

'Zack? Zack and I? I'm moving in with him, we're planning our future together and–'

'Oh, right...' Meg's tone is sympathetic as she reaches out to squeeze my hand. 'So, what do you want to do?' Meg hands me back my phone.

'I don't know.' I sigh, feeling overwhelmed. 'I mean... I... It's just...'

'Hey, it's okay.' Meg places a comforting hand on my arm, giving it a gentle rub. 'Do what feels right for you. If you wanna go, go. Zack will wait. If you want to stay, then stay and be happy with the man you love. He's important to you, and I know it would be difficult for you to leave him for a year. You might get different opportunities in life. But, I think you just need to choose what's best for you. Not for others. For you, Maddie. Think about yourself, okay?' She looks at me, smiling politely.

'The thing is, I don't know what I want to do now. I want the life I discussed with Zack, but this job is my dream. It's my only chance to work for this company, right? If I reject them, they would never offer me a job again. They will have it in their system that I rejected the offer I applied for myself. Why didn't they offer me London?'

'I don't know. Maybe they got a free spot in Sydney and you were next in the line, so they contacted you. You put Sydney too, right?'

'I did. But I was just curious. It's not like I seriously considered going there. Obviously, I wanted London.'

'I know. But you still mentioned it, so they probably thought you were open to it and sent you this offer.'

'I fucked up.' I groan, covering my face with my hands.

'No you didn't. Just don't pressure yourself to make the decision right now. I don't know how long you can take to reply, you probably will want to respond as soon as possible, but just give yourself a day or two to think about it. Talk to Zack. See what he thinks about it and–'

'Oh God!' My eyes widen as an idea strikes me.

'What?'

'I should talk to Zack. I should tell him about the offer and suggest he comes with me, with us. I mean, he wants to change his job anyway. He's so unhappy. This job affects him too much, you know? He can take a break, go to Sydney, find something in a different place, try a different life. Something new. Then we all can come back here, with new experiences, ready to start the life of our dreams.'

'Maddie, that would be great! But do you think Zack will like the idea though?'

'I don't know. But why not? We are young, we should try things, right?'

'I mean, talk to him. See his point of view. If he agrees, that's great. But if not, then what?' Meg stares at me, and I try to find an answer.

What if he doesn't agree? Do I really want to move to Australia for a year? Is this internship worth leaving someone I love for a year? Will it strengthen our relationship or tear us apart? Is it worth the risk? But what if he's up for it? Would the three, or four, of us move to Sydney? Will Zack find himself a job he likes? Maybe he'd discover a new passion, find a new path in life, find this one thing he wants to do.

'Earth to Maddie.' Meg's voice brings me back to reality.

'Yes?'

'Don't rush it. Maybe make a list of pros and cons. And of

course, talk to Zack about it. Then, make up your mind. If you're still unsure what to do, of course. Because if you already know the answer in your heart, follow it. I'll be here for you no matter what.'

'I know.' I hug her tightly.

For a moment, I close my eyes, attempting to quiet my racing thoughts. She's right. I need to consider what's best for me. I need to discuss it with Zack too. His opinion matters. He's my boyfriend. We're planning our future together, and my decision might, or might not, affect it.

'Okay, let me get up and let's do something. No boys, girls only today. It's our day.'

'Love that. I'll go and get dressed.' I announce before leaving her room.

We're likely staying in all day, so I decide to wear black leggings and an oversized T-shirt. When I head downstairs, Meg is already there, making some smoothies. I grab a glass and take a sip of the refreshing drink.

Meg is trying to make healthier habits before moving to Australia, so she's started preparing smoothies, omelettes, toast with avocado, and other healthy breakfast options, and Jack and I are here to test them all.

And then it hits me, she's leaving Jack here in London, waiting for her. Would Zack wait for me too? Or would he take the risk and come with me?

'Meg, how do you feel about leaving Jack in London?' I ask warily.

'Honestly, Maddie? We just got back together, and it terrifies me.' She looks at me with sad eyes, and I instantly regret asking. 'He says he'll wait, that I'm the one he truly loves and can't imagine his future without. I know he loves me, but Sydney is so far, and I'll be gone for a year. What if he meets someone? I mean, we said we'd be okay, but... I don't know. A lot of things can happen, right?'

'Meg, I'll be here, I can keep an eye on him.' I joke, hoping to lighten the mood. 'Well, I think Jack got a taste of life without you and won't risk anything. He truly loves you. I know it, and you know it too. You two will survive this. This man is already planning a trip to Sydney to see you.' I chuckle. 'Of course, you'll be fine. There's no one else for him in this world.'

'And me.' Meg adds, scrunching up her nose. 'It's just scary, you know? But yeah, I think we'll be okay.'

'You will be.' I assure her with my warm smile.

For the rest of the day, we try to avoid discussing our relationship fears. Instead, we go out for a walk and treat ourselves to some ice cream. The sun is shining, the streets are buzzing with conversations, laughter, and music. I love spring. Everything feels so positive. It lifts my spirits.

When we return home, I assist Meg in preparing a chicken satay salad, and we enjoy it while watching TV. Everything feels simple now, but good. Later that evening, we have karaoke night. We play different songs on Youtube and sing to the TV remote as if it was a microphone. I burst into laughter as we attempt to recreate some dance moves to a song.

The thing about Meg is that she's up for anything. Costume party? She's in. Random cruise on the River Thames? Count her in. Wine tasting day? She'll do it. Last-minute concert tickets? She'll go. I could suggest a weekend in Italy, and she'd fly with me, if we had enough money, of course. She makes everything more fun. There are so many reasons to love Meg, and I feel incredibly grateful that she's my best friend.

Chapter Twenty-Eight

Over the past few days, I couldn't stop thinking about this offer. It was haunting me in my dreams, it was in my head throughout the day, and I kept opening the email and reading it over and over again. Every time I wanted to talk to Zack about it, something in me would stop me from doing that. I still don't know if I want to do it, so I'm not even sure if it's worth mentioning. Meg suggested making a list to help me sort out my thoughts, but it only seemed to add to the chaos in my head.

Staring at that blank page, my mind was racing with a thousand thoughts a minute. Frustrated, I simply gave up. Instead, I've been trying to listen to my heart, to learn what truly feels right for me. I understand now why Meg was so distracted when she found this. She must have been fighting her own thoughts, like I am right now. It's a tough decision to make.

If I go, I'll have to leave the place and the people I love behind. I mean, if I decide to go. Unless, Zack would want to go too. If he'd go with me, it would make it so much easier for me to decide. So, tonight, I want to talk to him about it. See what he thinks about it.

But, deep down, I feel like I know what I want to do. There's a quiet voice telling me to do it. This opportunity is a chance to shape my future, to secure a career I've long aspired to, one that promises financial stability and fulfilment. But there's one very important thing, and it's Zack. What will he think about it? What will he say?

As I lie in my bed, my gaze keeps returning to that email, as it has every night since I've received it. Almost unconsciously, my fingers navigate to that familiar blue square icon with a white envelope. With each reading, my desire to accept grows stronger.

But I need to talk to Zack and my family first. I need to see what they think about it and if they support my decision, if I decide to go. I know Meg would be very happy if I went with her, so I don't even need to ask her. She would be thrilled. It's the people I will have to leave for a year that I am worried about.

Would I be even able to live without Zack next to me for a year? Without his arms around me? Without his lovely kisses? Without hearing his voice in the morning when I wake up? Without the warmth of his smile or the sound of his laughter that never fails to brighten my day? Unless, of course, he decides to join me.

I rise from bed, slipping into cuffed shorts and a black sweetheart neck top with puffy sleeves. A few spritzes of perfume and a quick brush through my hair complete the look before I head downstairs, where Meg and Jack are already enjoying their breakfast.

'Morning, Maddie. Are you hungry? Meg made some avocado on toast.' Jack gestures towards the plate.

'It's better than the last one. I promise. Give it a try!' Meg encourages, her eyes sparkling with anticipation.

'Alright.' I clear my throat, feeling their curious gazes on me. Slowly, I take a bite, pleasantly surprised by the improved taste. 'You're getting better.' I smile at my friend.

'Are you off to see Zack?' Meg inquires.

'Yup. I'll be back tomorrow. And I am going to talk to him about Sydney.' I confess with a hint of uncertainty.

'Yay! I'll keep my fingers crossed!' Meg raises her hands to show me that she, in fact, has her fingers crossed.

'I'll be jealous if the three of you go without me.' Jack interjects.

'I mean, you can come, babe.' Meg suggests.

'I wish, but you know. I'd lose my job for sure. But I'll visit you as much as I can.' Jack reassures Meg, planting a gentle kiss on her cheek. 'And I'll be here, waiting to pick you up from the airport when you're finally back.'

'Okay guys, the house is yours.' I smile at them before leaving them alone.

On my way to the tube, I send Zack a quick message letting him know I'm on my way. Today, the journey seems shorter, perhaps because I'm filled with excitement and positivity. I have a good feeling about today.

We'll discuss my job offer and how it might affect our future together. I mean, I was supposed to move in with him soon, but we'll always have time for that, right? And who knows, maybe we can start living together in Sydney.

The lift brings me up to Zack's flat, and I let myself in with the key. As the door clicks shut behind me, I'm greeted by the sound of Zack's soft voice in the kitchen and the aroma of cheesy toast.

'Hello, darling.' Zack greets me with a smile.

'Hi.' I smile, heading to the kitchen and dropping my bag along the way. Zack is there, in his pyjama bottoms, preparing the toast.

'Late breakfast?' I tease.

'I just got up.' He replies, shooting me a glance over his shoulder. 'Do you fancy something a bit less healthy than Meg's kitchen?'

'Sure.' I chuckle, moving closer to steal a kiss. Oh, the taste of his sweet lips. I don't know if I can live without that.

'Have some.' Zack offers, passing me a plate with two cheese toasts.

I watch him, leaning against the countertop as he makes another one. This man gets more and more handsome every day, and I just can't stop staring at his strong jawline and slightly longer beard, which he'll probably shave tonight. Before I know it, my fingers are running through it.

'I need to shave.' Zack chuckles, his eyes sparkling with amusement.

'I actually like it.' I admit as Zack turns to face me, and we share a smile.

'Do you? But I'll scratch you.' He warns.

'I don't mind.' I shrug. It looks sexy on him, and I don't mind a little scratching.

'You look cute.' Zack says, his eyes roving over me, appreciating every detail of my body. 'I like that top.'

'Thanks.' I scrunch up my nose in response.

Zack finishes his toast and joins me by the countertop, both of us gazing out into the living room.

'I was thinking about rearranging the space before you move in. Maybe if I move the table closer to the kitchen and sofa closer to the door, I can fit an extra storage here. For our things. I think we might need more space for you in here.' Zack muses.

'I mean, I like it this way. Do you think we need extra space?' I inquire.

'We can see how you fit with all your things, and if we need more space, then I'll think about moving things. But I'm sure we will need more.' Zack replies with a soft chuckle.

'Alright.'

I'll talk to him later about the offer. I have to. I turn to face him as Zack circles his arm around me, his tender lips pressing against the top of my head.

'How do you feel about it?' Zack asks.

'Great!' I reply, upbeat.

Shit. If I accept the job offer, it means delaying moving in with him, something he's so excited about. I am too. I mean, I was, I am. Or I don't know what I mean. It all depends on my decision. It can change everything.

'Well, I can't wait to have you here.' Zack says, cupping my face as I meet his gaze.

He kisses me softly, and in that moment, I can't imagine my life without him by my side. I hope he'll be open to the idea of moving together to Sydney.

'What if you get tired of me?' I tease lightly.

'Never.' Zack chuckles, kissing me again.

Following Zack to the bedroom, I leave my bag on his bed while he gets dressed. I watch him patiently as he pulls on a T-shirt, catching a glimpse of my name tattooed on his chest, which makes me grin.

'So, I tried to rearrange my wardrobe.' Zack says, moving to the side to reveal some empty space. 'But I'm sure that's not enough for you.'

'I might need a little bit more.' I titter, stepping closer to him.

'Maybe I can get this massive wardrobe that will fit on the whole wall, then we should have enough space.' Zack suggests, pulling me closer.

'That's actually a good idea, and it shouldn't look too bad.' I clear my throat, feeling the guilt growing in my chest.

Zack is thinking about our life together, while I'm contemplating moving to Australia for a year. I feel the blood drain from my face as I swallow hard.

'Are you okay?' Zack gives me a concerned look.

'Yes, I'm fine.' I muster up the strength to give him my most convincing smile. I have to talk to him. It's tearing me apart. I just don't know how. But I have to do it.

Later, as we stroll around Canary Wharf hand in hand, my body is present but my mind is elsewhere. I watch the sunlight gleaming off the tall buildings, the clear sky above, the green trees, and the birds singing. Suddenly, Zack stops and studies my face with his deep brown eyes.

'Something is clearly bothering you, Maddie. Is it Meg?' Zack places his hand on my cheek, gently caressing my warm skin with his thumb. 'You won't be lonely, I'll be next to you, you know that, right? I'll make sure you always feel happy.'

'I know.' I sigh, feeling the weight of my indecision.

'And I know you'll miss your best friend when she's away, but I'll do my best to make sure you're alright. Everything will be fine. I promise.' Zack reassures me.

'I love you.' I say before he kisses me.

Everything will be alright. It will be. I trust him.

On our way back to his place, we stop for some groceries for dinner. Zack wants to prepare lemon honey-glazed salmon, and I can't wait to try it. All I typically do with salmon is wrap it in foil with asparagus and bake it with some herbs and lemon. His dish sounds more exciting than mine. I'm good at cooking, but Zack is much better. I used to go for easy and quick recipes because I didn't have much time as a student, but things will change now. I can make better food.

As we stand together in the kitchen, slowly preparing the food, there are plenty of "accidental" touches and kisses. At this moment, I wonder if it's worth risking it all for an internship offer. He makes me happy. I could easily find another job. I'll be alright because I will come back home to see him every day. But, maybe he'll want to try life in Sydney, and I can have both, my dream job and my dream boyfriend. Zack definitely needs a new job and a break to relax. I just need to talk to him. Just one conversation.

As we sit at the table enjoying our dinner and wine, I feel a bubble of anxiety growing inside me. I try to hide it and engage in conversation with Zack. Where is the positivity I felt this morning? Why am I suddenly scared and anxious?

I take a big swig of wine. It's time for the talk. I have to do it now. He'll calm me down and help to find a reasonable solution. He's smart. He's reasonable. He knows the answers. He knows what is good for us. We'll be alright. Everything will be alright.

'Zack?' I finally muster up the courage to speak up.

'Yes, darling?' He looks at me with concern in his eyes.

'Do you remember the internship I applied for with Meg?'

'Of course I do. I still can't believe they didn't take you. You're great. Is that what's been bothering you so much?'

'Well…' I clear my throat, feeling the weight of the moment.

'Are you still upset about it? Sweetheart, I'm sure you'll find something.' Zack reassures, placing his hand on mine.

'The thing is, I got it.' I choke out, looking up at his face.

'What? How? Are you serious?' I can see the excitement sparkling in his eyes. 'That's great, baby. I'm so proud of you. We need to celebrate, we need to–'

'Yes, but there's an issue.' I interject, my heart pounding in my chest. Why is it so hot in here? Is it the wine in my blood?

'What's wrong? I am sure there's a solution.' Zack says, frowning, confused.

'They want me to go to Sydney.' I announce slowly and warily.

Zack stares at me without a word, putting his glass down.

'Sydney?'

'Mhm.' I nod.

'Sydney, Australia.' Zack repeats, more to himself than me. 'It's ridiculous, you applied for London.'

'But, Sydney was an option too, and I added it. As well as New

York. I just didn't expect to get an offer there.'

'I thought you only applied for London. You never mentioned other cities. Anyway, I guess you said no.' Zack says firmly.

There's a silence between us, and Zack stares at me agog, awaiting an answer. But I don't know what to say. I can see the spark slowly leaving his eyes, his emotions shifting.

'I…' I stutter. 'I haven't replied yet. I don't know…'

'Why is that?' Zack frowns, his concern evident.

'I was just thinking about it.' I reply vaguely.

'About what, Maddie? What are you thinking about? You're not seriously considering going, right?' Zack's face falls.

There's another short silence and I sense a hint of panic in his voice. Is that disappointment I see in his eyes?

'Oh God.' He mutters before I can respond. 'Maddie, please, tell me you're not thinking about going.' Zack pleads, staring at me with a mixture of desperation and fear.

'I mean, I–' I falter, unsure of how to respond.

'When did you get this offer?' Zack interrupts, his voice turning cold.

'A few days ago.' I mumble.

'And why are you telling me this today? Why not a few days ago when you got this offer?' His jawline clenches, and I can see the realisation dawning on his face. 'Wait, actually don't answer. I know why. You're telling me because you've made up your mind.' Zack snorts sarcastically.

'No, I haven't. I just… I don't know what to do or say.' I stammer, feeling the weight of his disappointment.

'Oh, didn't you? Why do I feel like you did? Cut the bullshit, Maddie. Tell me the truth. I don't want to hear any lies. Because while I'm here, thinking about you, about our life together, about you moving in here, trying to make changes here for you, you're making a decision about leaving the country!' His voice rises, anger flashes in his eyes, and I feel a surge of anxiety spreading through me. He's furious.

'I thought about it, Zack–' I begin, but he cuts me off.

'About what? Please tell me because I'm curious.' Zack says sharply, pushing his chair back and standing up. I watch his movements, scared to say anything that could worsen the situation.

'I was thinking about what I should do. I thought about you, about us, and all the plans we made.' I continue, my voice trembling. 'How this would affect us if I went, how would it affect my future career if I declined. Whether I should chase my dream job or let it go and find something else. I was thinking what you'd say when I told you. I was thinking if you would go with me.' I blurt out.

'What? You considered having me move to Australia? Without even asking me?' Zack points angrily at himself. 'Did you plan everything already and expect me to follow your plan? I have a life here, my family, and friends. I was planning my future with someone I love. Here in London! And I have a job here.'

'But you hate it! You're unhappy. You wanted a change, so I thought you might like the idea of having a break from all of the things that bother you here. That you could try things there, that you would find something you like there.'

'I can have a change here, not on the other side of the fucking world. And I'm sorry that this is not what you planned, but I'm not going to risk everything just to go to Australia, to try something temporary that's not going to bring anything good to my life.'

'How can you know that?' I get out of my chair too. 'What if it would be amazing, Zack? You can find your path there.'

'I can find my path here. I can find everything I need here. I don't need to search for my happiness on another continent. You were making me happy, you were giving me the hope that things would be better. You were all I was thinking about all this time. Nothing bothered me when I thought you'd be living with me soon.

Even when I hate my job, all of it wouldn't matter when I got back home and you'd be there. I was happy that you were in my life. But, to my surprise, my girlfriend changed her plans and didn't even bother to mention anything until today. Until the day you made up your mind and created your own plan. You were basically lying to my face when we were talking about living together because in your mind, you were planning your little trip to Australia! Even a few hours ago when I told you what I want to change here for you and you fucking pretended like you still wanted to do it when you knew you would be leaving me!' Zack growls. 'I know what I want in life, and it's my future with you, but clearly, you don't want the same.'

'No! It's not like that! That's not true!' I try to reach for his hand, but he pulls away.

'So tell me, how did you imagine that? I guess you were hoping that I'd drop everything and run after you? That I'd leave my life I've built here, everything I have, and just go like that?' He picks up the plates and walks to the kitchen.

'No.' I watch him from a distance, dropping the plates in the sink and I swear something broke, a cracking noise coming from the sink.

'Did you consider what would happen if I said no? Or did you assume I would say yes?'

'It's just a year, I thought we could call each other, FaceTime, visit, do anything we could. We would survive that.'

'No, we wouldn't, Maddie!' Zack turns around, pain evident in his eyes. 'Do you realise how far Australia is? We would never have a chance to last! You can't fly there every week, or every month. It's like a once-in-a-year visit! How could I go from having you here a few times a week to not have you at all? I thought we were going to see each other every day, and now you're telling me that the only time I'd see you would be over a video call? Did you even realise that? I thought we were happy. I thought I was making you happy. That I was enough for you.' Zack says with pain in his voice. 'I thought we were on the same page about our future. Did it even mean anything to you or you were just agreeing to everything I said? Did you lie to me that you were excited to move in with me? That–'

'Of course not! I was happy about it too, Zack!' I immediately interrupt him. 'I wanted to live with you. I mean, I want to. I…Everything I said was true. I want my life with you. And of course, you're enough for me.' I feel like someone is stabbing me right through my heart. 'It's just a year Zack. I love you, and I know we can get through it.' My voice trembles, fear of losing him growing with each passing moment.

'I guess it's not enough.'

'That's not true!' I protest desperately. I love him so much, and I'm sure we can survive a year apart because our love is strong enough to go through it. 'I know you love me as much as I love you. We both know it.'

'I can't not have you here for a year, Maddie. This would never have a chance to last!' Zack rubs his face, his voice calming down.

'Yes, it would! Look, Jack is ready to wait for Meg and–'

'I'm not Jack!' Zack shouts, and I flinch at the intensity of his anger and hurt. 'Is this offer really more important to you than us? Does it mean more to you than our future together?'

'Zack, please…'

'Answer the question!' His demand hangs heavy in the air, the tension between us almost suffocating.

This is not going well. I want to run into his arms, but I fear he'll push me away. The look in his eyes tells me that if I don't give him the answer he wants to hear, he won't want me to come any closer. And it hurts.

I swallow the lump in my throat, but before I can say anything, Zack speaks again, his voice calmer this time.

'Are you doing this because of Meg? Are you going because she's going? You really can't survive a year without your friend?'

'No, I don't want to do it because of Meg!'

'Don't lie to me, Maddie! Just once, tell me the truth. Did any of it ever mean anything to you, or was it just a fucking game to you all this time?' Zack's voice is rough.

'I'm not lying!' I protest frantically. 'Of course, it did! It still does mean everything to me, but this is my opportunity to get the job I want, to do something I really like.'

'There are thousands of jobs here. You just need to look, but you only think about Sydney!'

'But maybe I want to go to Sydney!' I shout in frustration, unable to contain my emotions.

'Then fucking go!' Zack's chest heaves with each word he utters as he shouts back at me. 'I'm not going to stop you from pursuing your dream if this is everything you want! But don't come here and lie to my face that you were truly thinking about our future together while behind my back, you already planned to do something else. Don't come and lie to my face about how much you love me and about how happy you are with me when clearly, this job means more to you than us. Don't lie that you want to move in with me. What was all of that for? And don't lie to me because I'm not going to believe you this time. I'm not. Do you understand?' Zack mumbles as he walks to the table, passing me without even casting a glance in my direction, collecting the glasses and returning to the kitchen.

Complete silence envelops the room as I try to fight back tears, my bottom lip trembling with emotion. Zack stands with his hands resting on the countertop, his head down, his back facing me.

'I think you should go, Maddie.' Zack finally speaks, and I feel like someone has just twisted the knife they were stabbing in my heart.

'What? Zack...'

'You should leave.' His voice is feeble, shaky.

I stand there, staring at his back, hot tears streaming down my face. I want to say something, but the massive lump in my throat doesn't let me.

We stand there in complete silence, not saying anything until I manage to summon the courage to ask him the question that has been weighing on my mind the entire time. The question I'm terrified to ask, terrified to hear the answer to. But I do. I take a deep breath and ask.

'Are we... is it over?' My hands begin to shake. I feel like I'm going to be sick with all the anxiety.

I hope he'll turn around, wrap his strong arms around me, and tell me it's not over. That it's never over. That we'll be okay. That he loves me. But he says exactly what I feared, the opposite of what I wanted to hear from him.

'Yes, it is.' Zack's words pierce through the heavy silence, shattering my heart into a million pieces.

I stand frozen, unable to move or speak, tears streaming down my cheeks. Zack doesn't move or speak either.

After what feels like an eternity, I summon the strength to walk to his bedroom and retrieve my bag. I hold back the sobs threatening to escape, but with every passing moment, it becomes harder for me to breathe.

As I stand by his door, ready to leave, I steal a glance at Zack, still standing in the same position in the kitchen, not looking at me at all. With a heavy heart, I dart towards the lift, pressing the button repeatedly as if it would help bring up the lift faster. I can't hold it anymore. I feel like I'm choking on my own tears.

The lift arrives with a beep, and I can hear the door opening behind me, but my face is turned towards the hall. I don't move. I don't enter the lift. I stand there, hoping for Zack to rush out, to stop me, to tell me it's not over. When I hear the door open, my heart begins to race with a hope that he's coming. That he's not ready to let me go like that. That he'll stop and kiss me, and we'll be okay. Because we can't be over just like that. It can't end like this.

But it's not him. It's one of his neighbours, startled by my tear-stained face. Frantically, I press the lift button again and when the door opens, I step in, leaning against the wall. The neighbour decides not to join me, and when the door finally closes, I let out an agonising cry. The pain in my heart is unbearable and I feel like I might pass out, but I can't. I have to go home.

I force myself to leave the building, avoiding the curious gaze of the security guard. With trembling hands, I rush towards the tube station, oblivious to the stares of passersby. But I don't care about anything at this moment. Everything fell apart. Nothing went well. My relationship is over. I've lost someone who means the world to me. One moment has shattered something beautiful, something that brought me so much happiness.

As I finally walk home, I try to calm down, because I'm not ready to face Meg, or Jack. I want to slip into my room unnoticed, without them knowing I'm back, and cry in my bed.

Standing before our front door, with my remaining strength, I stop sobbing and wipe my face. I attempt to enter the house discreetly, but Meg spots me, holding a bowl of popcorn as she heads to the living room.

'Oh, hi Maddie. What are you doing here?' Her smile fades when our eyes meet.

Unable to contain my emotions any longer, I break down into tears. Meg rushes to my side, enveloping me in a comforting embrace, like I'm about to fall apart. Well, I am sort of. And I feel like it. I sob uncontrollably, and she holds me close, caressing my back, not saying anything.

That night, she stays by my side, listening to my broken sobs, reassuring me that things will eventually be okay. She stays with me trying to comfort me, give me some warmth. But I feel cold. I feel cold without Zack next to me, without his warm arms around me. Without him.

Chapter Twenty-Nine

It's been two weeks since Zack and I broke up. Two weeks since I saw him for the last time. Two weeks since I heard his beautiful voice. Two weeks since I was in his arms for the last time. Two weeks since I fucked everything up and destroyed our relationship. Two weeks since I accepted the offer.

The night we ended things, I was so hurt, sad and angry that we didn't solve it differently, that I grabbed my laptop, and I found myself impulsively accepting the offer with Meg asleep beside me. My family will be here, waiting for me. I already spoke to them, and they're thrilled that I'm taking this opportunity and will support me through it. They'll wait for me. But he won't.

He won't be here for me anymore. He's no longer a part of my life, and it's a bitter pill to swallow. He's gone, just like that. But the pain in my chest is the same whenever I think about how I've lost him. As he said, we're over. This is over, and even though my heart hurts and cries for him every day, I took it as a sign to go. To grab this opportunity before it's gone too. With Zack gone, I feel like I have nothing to lose because I've lost him already.

Since that day, I haven't reached out to Zack, not even to collect my belongings. I don't have the courage. Anyway, my things at his place are the last thing I have to worry about. The thought of hearing his voice or seeing his beautiful face fills me with dread. I still find myself in tears when his name comes up in conversation. But he hasn't reached out to me either.

I spend my days packing and preparing for the move, because we found people who want to move in, which is great for us. I'll spend my last ten days in London with my family, and Meg and

Jack will stay with their families. It's good, because we won't see our loved ones for a long time, so we should spend as much time as we can with them.

Next month, I'll be on a plane to Sydney. It all seems surreal and crazy. All the documents and necessary paperwork are done, with a lot of Meg's help. And I'm going. I'm going to chase my dream job because what else can I do? I was supposed to be moving in with Zack next month, but I'll be on the plane to the other side of the world.

Maybe it'll be easier to heal my broken heart there. I'll take this time to focus on myself, on my own future, trying to forget him, to heal after him. Maybe, as my mom says, if Zack and I are meant to be, we'll find our way back to each other. For now, I must focus on myself and my own future.

Maybe she's right. But I would be lying to everyone if I said that I don't care about him anymore. Because I do. I love him so much. I wake up each morning with thoughts of Zack in my mind, and that I should do something, but then I stop myself.

He didn't run after me. He didn't stop me. He let me go. And for now, that's how it has to be. But I don't feel happy anymore. I find myself feeling numb. I do things, I go to work, visit family, watch movies with Meg and Jack, but I feel nothing. The only feelings I feel sometimes are hurt and sadness.

I cry every time I look at the stupid Lego bouquet. It reminds me of my birthday, when Zack gave it to me because it *lasts forever.* But turns out, we don't. There's no *us* anymore. Everyone around me says we'll find our way back to each other, but I'm not so sure. They say that they've never seen anyone so in love, and that we're meant to be together. I wonder, how do they even know? I'm leaving the country, and he's staying. We don't even speak to each other. Oh well, because we're over.

Sitting on my bed in my cozy stay-at-home attire, I clutch the Lego flowers in my hands, lost in thought, when I hear a gentle knock at the door. Moments later, Meg appears in my room, her presence pulling me back to reality. I quickly blink away the tears that have welled up, uninvited.

'Hi, how are you feeling?' Meg's soft voice breaks the silence.

'Fine. No. I don't know.' I admit with a shrug, setting the flowers aside. Meg's gaze follows them, and she clears her throat.

'We've made some lunch. Come join us.' She offers with a warm smile.

'Alright.' I reply softly.

I follow Meg to the kitchen, where Jack has prepared three plates, each with a tortilla wrap neatly placed on it. They prepared some chicken, peppers, onion, lettuce, cheese, and fresh orange juice.

As we take our seats at the table, I can sense their concern for me. They're worried, and I understand why. Deep down, I hope I'll be okay. But when I look at them, I can't help but wonder why Zack and I couldn't make things work. Why he couldn't wait for me? Why did we have to end it?

But then I try to put myself in his position, and think what would I do? Of course, I'd be scared and wouldn't like the idea of not seeing him for a year, but I'd wait. I would wait for him to come back. I'd rather let him go, do something he really wants rather than lose him over it. I would wait. But that's me. He doesn't think like me.

I fold my tortilla tightly, pressing all the stuff inside in a safe wrap, and take a bite.

'So girls, I was thinking, when you go to Australia, I should come after you visit for Christmas. Maybe March or April?' Jack suggests, breaking the silence.

'That's a great idea.' Meg responds, her excitement palpable. I nod absently in agreement, my mind elsewhere. 'Or you could come with us and spend New Year's Eve there!' Meg suggests, her eyes shining with enthusiasm.

'Yeah, maybe I can do that.' Jack replies, smiling at Meg.

Their love for each other is evident in every glance they share. They'll be alright. Their love will survive the distance.

Meg and I have already decided that no matter what, no matter how expensive it might be, we'll be back for Christmas. I want to be with my family, I want to be back in London for this time of the year. We already checked the prices, and it can give you a heart attack, but it doesn't matter. I'm going to set myself a budget and keep it, so I have enough money to come home.

As Meg and Jack continue to discuss their plans, my thoughts drift back to Zack. Why couldn't he just wait for me? I would be back for Christmas, we would see each other. Then, maybe he would be able to visit, and later I would be back already. It would all pass by quickly. I would have been back before he knew it.

Then, we could move in together, I would have a good job and we could get a bigger place, go on a vacation together, do whatever we would want to. We could have built a life together. But he made his choice. For him, it was either stay or go.

It feels like I chose a job over him, but I didn't. He's more important to me than anything else. I still love him, and I always will. I just wanted his support, I wanted him to reassure me that everything will be alright, and that he'll wait for me, but he broke up with me instead. It was him who said it's over.

I didn't expect him to like the idea of me going, but at least I was hoping we would stay together. I believe we could get through it, but I don't know why he didn't. Why didn't he believe we were strong enough to survive a year apart?

'Maddie?' Meg's voice breaks through my thoughts, her concern evident in her eyes.

'Yes?' I reply, trying to compose myself.

'Are you okay?' She asks gently.

'Yeah, I'm fine.' I respond quickly, wiping away the tears. I didn't even realise I was crying.

'Alright then.' Meg says, clearing her throat. 'Do you want to talk?'

'No, I'm fine, Meg. I was just thinking.'

'I know. But you know, I'm here. So is he.' She nudges Jack's arm, and he nods in agreement.

'Sure, yes. I'm here too.' Jack adds, giving me a comforting smile.

'Thank you.' I manage a weak smile and finish the wrap that I'd barely touched.

Now I understand what a real breakup feels like. When you lose someone you truly love. Someone who was your everything. Someone who stole your heart. Sometimes I find myself placing my hand over my chest, just to feel my heartbeat and remind myself that I'm still alive. That all of this is real. Sometimes it feels like I don't even have a heart anymore, like it stayed behind at Zack's place that day.

Later, Meg and Jack want to watch *How I Met Your Mother*, so I join them in the living room. Wrapping myself in our favourite blanket, I sink into the chair, unable to move my eyes away from my phone, my home screen exactly. It's the picture of us on my birthday, and I just can't bring myself to change it for anything else. It gives me a false hope that things might work out in the end. That maybe something will change. That maybe, somehow we'll find our way back to each other.

A knock at the door breaks the silence, and we all exchange puzzled glances. I'm not expecting anyone, of course. But maybe they are and forgot to mention it.

'I'll get it.' Jack offers, rising from his seat.

I look at Meg, but she shrugs. But then, a familiar voice fills the air, and my heart stops. It's him. Zack. He's here. He came. Oh my God!

I leap out of the chair and bolt towards the hall, dropping the blanket on the floor behind me, nearly tripping over it. Did I hear correctly? Is it really him, or is it my mind playing tricks on me? Jack steps aside, and there he is, standing on our front steps. Zack. He came, he actually came here. Is he here to apologise? Is he going to tell me how much he loves me, that he'll wait for me?

'Oh, Maddie, Zack's here to see you.' Jack announces, pointing towards the door before retreating to Meg's side.

Okay, I need to calm down because my hands started to shake already. Taking a deep breath, I approach the door, my heart racing at the sight of the man I love. But he doesn't look well. His handsome face is tired, worn, and sad. He looks disheveled, and his eyes lack their usual sparkle. It breaks my heart to see him like this.

'Hi.' I say quietly, my heart swelling with hope at the thought of him coming here to fight for us, for me. I resist the urge to throw myself into his arms.

'Hi.' Zack replies, and there's a silence between us.

He just looks at me, and I wait for him to hug me, to kiss me, or show me some kind of affection that I miss. I need him close to me.

I step aside to let him in, but he doesn't move. It's already a sign that something isn't right. I swallow hard, searching for any indication that he's here for me, for us. Any sign that we might have a chance to get back together. He didn't bring my stuff, so there's a flicker of hope. But we can't stand here in silence forever, just staring at each other without a world.

'What brings you here?' I manage to ask, my hand tightening on the doorknob. I'm anxious. I want him to say, *you, I came to see you. I miss you, and I love you. I want to apologise. I want you to know that I'll be here, waiting for you. No matter what.*

'Did you change your mind?' Zack asks, and for a brief moment, I catch a glimmer of hope in his eyes.

Traitorous tears threaten to spill from my eyes, so I force myself to look away, shaking my head. Don't cry. Don't cry. Don't cry.

'Well, I guess… goodbye then.'

'Zack, wait.' I plead, looking up at him as a single tear escapes down my cheek. He can't leave. I need him.

'No, Maddie. You made your decision.' Zack says, turning to face me and shakes his head, heartbroken. 'It's… I… I can't. Goodbye.' He turns his back to me, walking to his car.

My cheeks are wet with tears as I watch him walk away from me, leaving me shattered into pieces, stealing the last glimmer of hope I had for us. I want to run after him, to stop him, but my legs don't work. I am unable to move, my legs trembling beneath me. I can't even muster up the strength to shout after him, my voice stifled by a lump in my throat as I open my mouth.

He only came here to see if I'd decided to stay. To see if I'd changed my mind. I need his hug so much. Why didn't he hug me goodbye? Just one hug. One, last hug. One last moment in his arms. But he doesn't even look back as he drives away, leaving me standing there.

As I close the door and lean against it, biting my fist to stifle a scream, Meg slowly approaches from the living room. I shake my head at her, unable to find the words to express my pain.

'Come here.' Meg says softly, enveloping me in her arms, and I collapse against her, sobbing into her shoulder.

We stand there for a long moment as I let my sobs fade away with time. My head hurts. But it's nothing compared to the pain in my heart, a constant reminder that I still have it. But I might not even want it anymore. It belongs to Zack, and if he's gone, I don't need my heart anymore.

I wipe my nose with the back of my hand and look up at my friend.

'I want to lie down.' I mumble, my voice husky from crying.

'I'll bring you some tea.' Meg offers, giving my arm a comforting squeeze before leaving.

A long, hot shower is all I need, so I make my way to the bathroom and let the water wash over me, allowing myself to cry. I know Zack came here just in case I changed my mind. He could have just texted me instead of coming all this way, saving me from this pain. But I know that he prefers to do things in person, face to face. He came because if I had changed my mind, he would have held me in his arms, kissed me with love and passion as he always does. But my answer was different, not what he had hoped for.

I know he wanted to see me, I know he still cares about me. Even though his eyes were full of pain, I could still see the love for me in them. But we're both hurting in this situation, and seeing him today broke me all over again. I miss him desperately. I love him so much. It's tearing me apart. I can't even find joy in the internship opportunity anymore. I don't feel happy. It's all gone. With him.

I slowly return to my room where Meg is waiting with two mugs of hot tea. We sit in silence, sipping our drinks, Meg patiently waiting for me to speak while I struggle to find the words without breaking down into tears.

My head is a mess again. What if Zack had come here and asked me to stay instead of just checking if I had changed my mind? Would I have stayed? Would I do it or would I still go? He never asked me to stay, but if he had, I probably would have changed my mind, and stayed with him. Simply because I love him, and would leave everything for him, only if he asked me to. But he never did.

'I miss him.' I finally admit, my voice trembling as tears blur my vision.

'Maddie, do you really want to do it? Do you want to go to Sydney? Because if you want to stay, it's okay. No one will be upset with you. If being here with Zack makes you happier, then I think you should stay. There will be other opportunities in life, you know? And seeing you like this, I don't know if it's a good idea for you to go. I know you love Zack more than this opportunity.' Meg says gently.

'But I really want this. It's my dream.'

'But your dream was also to find real love. To find the one. To find the person who truly loves you.' Meg counters, and we lock eyes for a moment.

'Why doesn't he want to try, Meg? Why? At least give us a chance and see.'

'I don't know.' She sighs, pulling me closer.

'I was so sure I wanted to go, but when he came today…'

'Listen, you still have time to change your mind. You can always do it. It's okay. I hate seeing you like this.' Meg says, wrapping her arm around me. 'I promise, nobody will be mad at you. Not me. Not your family. We'll understand, okay?'

'I love him so much.' I whisper, the weight of my love for Zack heavy on my heart.

'I know. Give yourself some time to decide what's best for you, okay?' Meg's words wash over me, and I nod, trying to think of what's the best for me. I can't keep fighting with my own thoughts and heart. I wish someone could just tell me what to do.

'It actually makes me so sad that he didn't support me. We could have handled things differently, but his first reaction was to break up with me.' I continue, my voice breaking. 'Why didn't he want to try? Why did we have to argue? We could have just talked it out. But the way he reacted, it showed me that maybe I should go. It made me angry, you know? And he didn't fight for me. I know I hurt him, but he didn't try to stop me. And he hurt me with his words. He gave up on us, just like that.' I ramble, taking a shaky breath. 'I would wait for him if it was him going. It would be killing me, but I would let him go and wait.'

'Would you?' Meg asks, raising her eyebrows.

'I love him so much that I think yes, I would. I would at least give us a chance because he's so important to me. It would be hard, of course, but then he would be back with me, and we could continue our life together. Maybe it would make us even stronger than before. It would strengthen our love.' I confess, my voice barely above a whisper.

'But he doesn't think like you, Maddie. You know, everyone is different.' Meg reminds me gently.

'I know.' I sniff. 'I know.'

'Maybe this will make you feel better. You know there's a saying that if you let someone you love go and if they come back, they're yours forever. Maybe when you're back, Zack will come back into your life. He's letting you go for now, but I know the future belongs to you two.'

'Maybe.' I sigh, resting my head on my friend's arm, her comforting words echoing in my mind. *If you let someone you love go and they come back, they're yours forever. The future belongs to you two.*

Chapter Thirty

Today the day we've been anticipating, has finally, or not finally, arrived. Meg and I are officially leaving for Australia, taking the opportunity of our dreams, hoping it will give us the future we've wished for. Leaving everyone we love behind, but knowing they'll be here for us, rooting for our success from thousands of miles away. They'll be waiting for our return.

My family is driving me to the airport, where I'll meet up with Meg. It's where we'll say our goodbyes and set off to start our new, albeit temporary, life in a foreign land. A new country, new faces, new adventures, and new beginnings await us. I'm grateful that we're going to do this together, because we will be able to lean on each other, and understand each other's struggles as we go through the same thing, side by side.

I haven't heard from Zack since the day he came to ask about my decision. My heart remains shattered, longing for him all the time. I miss everything about him, his smile, the sparkle in his eyes when he looked at me, his laughter, his scent, the warmth of his touch against my skin. I miss the comfort he gave me, the happiness I felt around him, the peace in my heart when he was by my side. I miss him every second of my life.

As we draw closer to the airport, my anxiety mounts because this is it, there's no turning back now. Also because I sent Zack a message last night. I couldn't suppress the overwhelming urge any longer. My head is still a big mess, my mind locked in battle with my heart. So now, I leave the decision in his hands. The choice is his to make.

My flight is leaving tomorrow at 6:45pm, from Heathrow, terminal 4.

Just this. No, "I still love you." No, "I miss you." No, "If you come to stop me, I will stay because I can't imagine my life without you."

Just this. If he shows up, I'm pretty sure I'll be ready to drop everything and stay. I'm actually sure of that. If he comes and says he wants me to stay, I will. Because the truth is I love him, and I'm ready to leave this opportunity for him. I'll figure something out.

But all I need from him is to show up, fight for me, and stop me. To show me that he still loves me too, which I believe he does. I need to see him fighting for me, not giving up on us that easily.

I watch the view outside the window, trying to save as many details as I can into my memory. I want to capture everything that will remind me of home when I close my eyes at night, drifting off to sleep. Because I'll miss this place. I'll miss the views. I'll even miss the rush hour in the tube, or the weird people on the streets. I'll miss the mix of different street foods. I'll miss my life here. I'll miss it here, because this is my home. This is where I belong, where I'm from, and where my heart will stay.

Every day, I've wondered if my decision was right, if I should chase my dream job or stay for love. Of course, I love Zack, but this opportunity is something I want to do for myself. I want to pursue it. But I'm scared. Is it going to be worth it in the end, leaving everything behind? Leaving him behind? My mind changes every five minutes. That's why I sent the message. And I know he opened it because I've been obsessively checking my phone since then.

Zack opened it around three in the morning, so I assume he read it after work. He didn't reply, but that's okay. Because if he'll do it his way, he'll show up at the airport. He'll do it in person, not over the phone. So the fact that he read it gives me hope for us. I didn't tell Meg that I did it. I didn't tell anyone. I'm keeping it to myself.

Do I have hope in my heart that he'll show up? Of course. I've been dreaming about it before I even sent the message, and the more I thought about it, the more courage I gathered to send it. In my mind, I saw him coming to the airport with a bouquet of roses, or without, running towards me, taking me in his arms. Us in the middle of the airport, holding each other. Me trying to hold back happy tears because he actually came, and I knew we would be okay.

I saw him telling me how much he loves me and me telling him how much I love him. Then, I saw us holding each other like there's no one else around us, kissing like no one is watching. Every time I think about it, this warm feeling in my heart returns. I should stop myself before I get disappointed. But... something in me tells me that this might happen.

Meg messages me, letting me know she's almost at the airport, and I reply that I have about twenty minutes left. Of course, we go there much earlier to ensure everything goes smoothly, that we have enough time to say our goodbyes, check in our luggages, and make our way to the gate.

I wonder how Meg and Jack feel about the fact that in just a few hours, Meg will take off, and they'll be thousands of miles apart from each other. They must be sitting in the backseat, holding hands, reassuring each other of their love. I admire and respect them both for facing this challenge together. It can't be easy for them. And I wish Zack and I could have done the same, but life had other plans for us, I suppose. Unless... No, I won't allow myself to create false hopes.

As I gaze up at the sky, I spot a plane ascending higher and higher, disappearing into the clouds. We're near the airport already. My heart quickens as we pass the welcome sign. Here we go. It's time.

Dad parks the car in an available spot, and he and my brother assist me with my luggage. Tears threaten to escape my eyes, but I push them back. I know I'll cry later, when it's time to say goodbye, but not yet. For now, I want to stay strong. Or at least pretend to be.

As we make our way towards the entrance of the airport, I steal a glance at my mom and notice she's struggling to hold back tears as well. She's never been good at hiding her emotions, and it hurts me to see her like this. I link arms with her as we step through the airport. I'm about to say something to my mom, but as soon as we enter the hall, I hear Meg's voice.

'Maddie! You're here!' She exclaims, rushing towards me and enveloping me in a tight hug. With a short glance at her face, I can see she's been crying a lot. 'I'm so happy you came.'

'I'm going with you, remember?' I say, though my attempt at humour sounds more like the beginning of a sob.

'Yeah, I know. But I was wondering if you changed your mind or something.' Meg replies, sniffing as she pulls away.

'I'm going.' I declare, trying to keep my voice steady.

Meg's family and Jack join us, and it's evident that nobody is in a happy mood. When I look around, I can see traces of worry, sadness, and uncertainty on each face present here.

Jack looks devastated, though he's trying his best to put on a brave face, but I bet his heart is breaking right now. Meg's parents cling to each other, mirroring my own parents. *We're not dying*, I want to joke, but, well… I'm not in the mood to joke myself. The truth is, nobody here is happy. We're saying goodbye, unsure of when we'll see each other again. But we'll meet again, definitely in a better mood in a year's time. Exactly the same spot, just everyone will be happier.

'Hi Jack.' I manage a feeble smile as I hug him. 'I'll take care of her. Don't worry.' My voice begins to tremble.

'Please.' He whispers into my ear. 'Take care of yourself too, alright?' His words tug at my heartstrings, and I nod in response.

'Okay, let's drop your stuff. I want to make sure you leave.' My brother jokes, attempting to lighten the mood.

I playfully roll my eyes at him, feeling a surge of gratitude for his attempt to lift our spirits. He nudges my arm with a smile, and maybe I can see a hint of worry in his eyes. I mean, we're siblings in the end. He may not show it, but I know he'll miss me too.

As we join the line, I can't help but scan the crowd, searching for one face that's missing here, Zack's. But he's nowhere to be found.

We very slowly approach the counter, and my heart skips a beat every time I see someone similar to Zack. Perhaps, it's just my mind playing games with me. Because every tall guy with black hair can't be him. I feel nervous. Is he coming? My eyes flit around nervously, my attention torn between my passport and the bustling airport hall. I look around every time I hear male voice, hoping it's him.

I pass my passport to the woman checking my luggage, all while scanning the crowd for Zack. But he's not there. Again. I can't find his beautiful eyes searching for mine.

'Ma'am?'

I feel a nudge on my arm from my brother. Startled, I look up to see the woman at the check-in counter gesturing towards the luggage scale.

'Yes?'

'You can put your luggage on the scale.' She points with her head, annoyed at me.

Luckily, it's within the weight limit, though I have no idea how I managed to pack everything. I mean, I had to be very strict with what to bring and what to leave behind. It wasn't easy and I needed my mom's advice. I glance over to my left and see Meg paying extra for a few more kilograms of luggage. She always prefers to pay extra rather than risk being without something she might need later, even though she rarely ends up using the extra items she insists on bringing.

We gather in front of the information board, engaging in small talk to avoid confronting the reality of our upcoming departure. The reality that Meg and I will be on a plane to Australia in less than two hours. My eyes look at the screen with all the flights listed there, and I stare at ours.

I swallow hard, knowing we're running out of time. Zack is still not here, and when my eyes dart around the bustling airport terminal, searching for his familiar face, I meet Meg's gaze. She notices that I keep looking around and frowns, but Jack, oblivious to her concern, distracts her with a kiss.

I lean my head on my mom's shoulder, seeking comfort, while my dad rubs my back reassuringly. They try to lighten the mood with their jokes and smiles, so I give them my warm smile. But I don't know if I can hold it anymore. My eyes are getting wet as I watch minutes pass by, the clock reminding me that I don't have much time left with my family. That I'll have to say goodbye any minute now.

'I'm scared.' I whisper.

'It'll be alright, darling. You're going to a new place where you don't know anyone or anything. It's normal to be afraid of such a big change.' My mom replies, offering me a warm smile. 'But look, at least you're not going alone. Meghan will be there with you, and that's a comfort to all of us, because I know you two will take care of each other.'

'You'll be great, and we'll be waiting here for you. We're very proud of you.' Dad adds, planting a kiss on the top of my head.

'I don't care.' My brother chimes in, nudging my arm playfully. I sniff, shaking my head with a soft chuckle.

There's no point in holding my tears anymore. Soon, we'll have to go. Soon, Meg and I will have to pass through security, leaving behind our families and stepping into the unknown. I try to postpone the farewell as much as I can because... well it hurts.

It hurts me even more that Zack didn't show up. That he didn't answer the message. That he didn't try. His silence speaks volumes, confirming my fears that he's given up on us. This is my sign from him. We're over, and there's no chance for us.

As we inch closer to the security check line, a wave of panic washes over me. Do I really want to do this? Do I want to board that plane and leave everything behind? Is it worth it? I feel sick to my stomach. My heart pounds in my chest and I seek comfort in the embrace of my parents, burying my face in their arms. Meg clings to Jack, tears streaming down her cheeks. This is so much worse than I thought it would be. I don't know if my heart can handle any more pain in such a short time. It's exhausted from everything I put it through. Why do we do it if it hurts so much to leave?

When I look at Meg's parents, they're as devastated as Jack, and my family. She's their only daughter, and she's leaving them for a year. She was here all the time, visiting them regularly, and now what? They'll see her only over FaceTime or when we'll be back for Christmas.

'You'll be great. You can do this Maddie. Me, your dad, and

your brother believe in you.' My mom reassures me, her hand gently stroking my back.

'We do, sweetheart.' My dad adds, offering me a comforting smile.

'Thank you.' I murmur, returning their embrace and wiping away my tears with the back of my hand.

'Maddie, should we go?' Meg asks, and I hesitate.

'I...' I look at my family, but then my eyes move away from them, desperately trying to find him in the crowd. They keep looking for Zack, hoping he's here.

I just need more time. Just a little bit more time. Just in case he's running late. Just in case he's actually coming. Maybe he's stuck in the traffic, or trying to find us at this massive airport.

'Can we wait a little bit longer, please?' I say, my voice trembling.

'Alright.' Meg nods understandingly, snuggling closer to Jack as we continue to linger near the security check.

I hug my parents tightly, silently praying for more time. Through the corner of my eye, I keep checking every person who passes by, hoping to spot the beautiful brown eyes I love, hoping to hear the voice that makes my heart skip a beat, to see the face of the person I love so much. I'm aware of time passing by, definitely too fast, but I don't want to go. Not yet.

'Honey, you'll miss your flight.' Mom's voice breaks through my thoughts.

'I'll be fine.' I mumble, glancing at Meg, wiping tears off her face.

'We should go, Maddie. We'll be boarding soon, and we still haven't gone through the security check. Look.' She points at the long line.

'Alright.' I say, but it's more like a whisper, before breaking into tears. We have to say goodbye now. There's no more time to wait. No point in waiting for Zack. He's not going to show up, and I have to accept that. I have to let it go.

I feel like my heart is falling apart as I hug everyone present here. I can't do this. I just can't leave. I want to stay with my family. My crying gets heavier and louder, and my body starts to tremble. I feel overwhelmed with all the emotions, and my parents wrap their arms around me, trying to give me the comfort I need.

When I finally calm down slightly, I approach Meg's parents, who wish me luck, and I promise them that Meg and I will take care of each other. Now it's two of us, facing our families, not able to move. It's too hard. But we have to go.

As we slowly move forward in the line, we keep turning around to wave to our loved ones, crying as much as us. I take my time to look around, hoping Zack will run towards the line any second, calling my name to stop me and kiss me goodbye. But it doesn't happen. Which makes me feel even worse.

I start crying again once we pass the security check and I can't see my family anymore. Meg grabs my hand and gives it a gentle squeeze.

'We'll be okay.' She smiles through the tears as we walk to our gate.

The flight is on the screen. It's here, waiting for us. It's happening, and I don't know why I keep turning around, like Zack is about to appear next to me. Why do I have a feeling in my heart that something might still happen? Like some kind of miracle, something I don't expect at all.

'Are you ready?' I ask Meg, my voice thick with emotion.

'I don't know anymore. If not for you, I probably would've never crossed the security check.' She chuckles feebly, wiping her nose.

'Same.'

'I can't believe I won't see Jack for so long. I don't know how we'll go through this. I love him so much, and I'll miss him like crazy. And my family.' Her voice breaks.

'You'll be okay. I know it's hard.' I reassure Meg, placing my hands on her shoulders. 'He was devastated when he had to let you go. But you'll be alright, you know why? Because you two are made for each other. You two belong to each other.'

I close my eyes for a short moment, memories of Jack holding Meg flood my mind. He didn't want to let her go. I swear, I saw tears in his eyes as he was whispering something into her ear. I bet he was telling her how much he loves her, that nothing will change between them, that he'll wait for her. That's how I imagined Zack and me, but it didn't happen.

We approach the gate and claim two empty seats. I find myself staring blankly at the airport, a sudden numbness washing over me. All of my emotions are gone, and I feel... nothing. This doesn't seem real anymore.

'You were looking for him, weren't you?' Meg's voice breaks the silence. I turn towards her, meeting her scrutinising gaze.

'What?' I frown.

'You were searching for Zack at the check-in. Who else would you be looking for if everyone was with us? I saw you looking around all the time. You had so much hope and desperation written all over your face.' Meg observes, her eyes fixed on me.

'I was. I was hoping that he'd come to say goodbye.' I admit softly, my voice barely a whisper. Swallowing hard, I try to get rid of the lump forming in my throat.

'How would he know where you were, Maddie?' Meg's tone carries a hint of suspicion. She knows I did something, and she just wants me to confess.

'I sent him a message.' I confess, showing her my phone.

'Maddie... do you really want to go? It's not too late yet. You don't have to board that plane. You can stay and–'

'And what? Go and beg him to come back to me?' I chuckle through my tears, shaking my head. 'He didn't show up. It was the sign I needed. He didn't fight for me when I told him... And I still love him. But...' I trail off, staring at the floor. Meg wraps her arms around me.

'I know. So, if you want to stay and *you* want to fight for him, it's fine. I can go alone.'

'No, you can't.' I interrupt, shaking my head. 'We're going together.' I declare, placing my hand on hers. 'We're in this together, we're going to do this together, we'll make everything work because we have each other.' I raise my pinky promise, and Meg entwines hers with mine, smiling.

'We are in this together.'

'We are.'

And as we board the plane, we hold each other's hands, offering the support we both need, the strength to do what we have to do. Maybe it hurts like hell now, but they say time heals, right? And with time, we'll get used to the change, we'll get used to the new place, new people, new life, new reality. And in the end, it's just temporary. Soon, we'll be on another plane, heading back home. We'll sit with our families, sharing our memories, and chuckling at the memory of us crying at the airport a year before.

Everything will be alright, because no matter what, we'll be there for each other, supporting each other in tough times. We'd never let the other person fall and give up.

As I settle into the window seat with Meg beside me, I try to sort out my thoughts of everything that happened, thinking about everything that led me here, led us here, to this exact moment. Because everything happens for a reason, and everything that happens to you teaches you a lesson. I might not understand it now, but someday, I will.

As the plane takes off, leaving the London ground behind, slowly disappearing in the clouds, I try to give myself some hope for this new life. A new adventure awaits for my friend and I. And when I turn my head to look at my friend, she's already smiling at me, her eyes full of hope, and I know we will be okay.

About the author

    Marta Westlake was born and raised in a small village in Poland, and later moved to London to follow her dreams. After earning her degree in art, she embarked on a writing journey, drawing inspiration from her life experiences, the people she's met, and her unique perspective on love.

    Her debut novel delves into the complexity of relationships, shaped by her thoughtful observations and personal reflections. As a devoted reader of romance literature, Marta is inspired by the works of authors she admires, channeling that passion into creating heartfelt stories that resonate deeply with her readers.

You can follow Marta on her Instagram: @martasromancebooks

Acknowledgments

Thank you to everyone who read the book, supported me throughout the entire process, encouraged my writing, or contributed to the publishing process—from creating the book cover to proofreading and editing. I am deeply grateful for your lovely reviews and kind words. I could never have published this without you all.

I would like to thank my friend Anna specifically for reading the story with so much enthusiasm and providing me with helpful advice. Your support as my number one fan and your belief in this story means the world to me. I truly appreciated your messages after each chapter, updating me on how much you enjoyed it. You truly made me believe that I could achieve something with this story.

Printed in Great Britain
by Amazon